The rest of us fanned out _____ n area and secured the sleeping kids with ties on their hands and feet. The gas must have hit them hard, because none of them even stirred.

Black Two, standing well to the side of the bathroom entrance, knocked on its door. A shot blasted a hole right where his hand had touched the wood. The sound echoed despite the open windows. Two more shots followed the first blast.

"We're on a schedule," Lobo said to me privately. "You need to deal with this quickly."

I ignored him. "Black Two and Three, force open the door, toss in gas, and keep your teams to the sides."

Black Two pulled a small charge from his pack and stuck it to the door's handle. Ten seconds later, it blew with a loud pop. The door flew inward. Black Three rolled in a gas grenade.

Two more shots from inside the room smacked into the wall at the opposite end of the barracks. Five seconds later, a small, thin boy ran out of the smoke, a damp rag tied over his nose and mouth. He carried his rifle like a club and swung it to the left as he cleared the doorway. Black Three grabbed the weapon at the same time Black Two caught the boy's arm.

"Government assassins!" the boy said. Black Two looked to me for instructions, so the boy stared at me, too. "You can't mess with Bony, no, not with me. I'll show you." He coughed several times. "You'll see." His voice trailed off, and he collapsed.

"Tough, clever little bugger," Black Three said. "You gotta give 'im that." He set the kid on the first empty bunk.

I stared at the child, at all the other bound and sleeping boys in the barracks, and helpless rage rose in me, fury that made me want to kill those who had turned these children into fighters and the leaders who had decided that doing so was a good idea.

Baen Books by Mark L. Van Name

One Jump Ahead
Slanted Jack
Jump Gate Twist (omnibus)
Overthrowing Heaven
Children No More

Transhuman, ed. with T.K.F. Weisskopf
The Wild Side, ed. (forthcoming)

CHILDREN NO MORE

MARK L. VAN NAME

BAEN

CHILDREN NO MORE

This is a work of fiction. All the characters and events portrayed in this book are fictional, and any resemblance to real people or incidents is purely coincidental.

A Baen Books Original

Baen Publishing Enterprises
P.O. Box 1403
Riverdale, NY 10471
www.baen.com

ISBN: 978-1-4391-3453-5

Cover art by Stephen Hickman

First Baen paperback printing, July 2011

Library of Congress Control Number: 2010012312

Distributed by Simon & Schuster
1230 Avenue of the Americas
New York, NY 10020

Pages by Joy Freeman (www.pagesbyjoy.com)
Printed in the United States of America

To David Drake
Who understands

CHAPTER 1

Near the jump gate of planet Hardy

IF I SHOW you, you'll be in."

Alissa Lim, the woman in the holo floating in the still air in front of me, paused and stared intently ahead, confident I would be listening, sure I would be focusing on her.

She was right. I was.

"I don't know where you are," she continued, "or when you'll find one of these messages, so maybe it'll be too late, and you won't have to make this decision."

Another long pause. Another focused stare.

"But if it's not, and if you watch any of the attachments, you'll find me, and you'll argue with me, but in the end you'll join me. That's even what I want, obviously, or I wouldn't have planted these recordings on every planet I could manage, but I guess I felt"—she hung her head—"I felt that you should know I have a sense of what getting involved might cost you. If I didn't think we needed you, I wouldn't ask, but we do. We need you, and we need Lobo."

1

"Freeze it," I said.

"Done," Lobo said, his voice coming from everywhere and nowhere, "but all that remains is a few seconds of her standing there."

I got out of the pilot couch and approached the holo slowly, as if Lim might spring from it and attack me. Lobo had positioned it exactly in the center of his front cabin command area and angled her face toward me. He rotated it as I moved, until I said, "Leave it." I walked around it, examining the image from all sides.

"There's nothing else to learn," Lobo said. "If someone made Alissa do this, they were wise enough to rinse this part of the recording of everything except her."

Lim wore a plain black jumpsuit, no visible pockets, no logos, almost certainly armored. On most people it would have faded into the kind of bland garment you pass in a crowd and never notice. On her, it accented perfectly the richer, darker black of her long, straight hair, the almost glowing mellow golden tone of her skin, her full and wide and ever so slightly reddish lips. She was as astonishingly beautiful as the last time I'd seen her, a bit over three years ago.

When she'd rescued me from a torturer.

When she'd gotten shot helping me save a girl I'd inadvertently placed in harm's way.

I owed her, and she knew it.

I settled back into the pilot's couch.

"Turn off the lights," I said.

"You could heed her warning and stop watching," Lobo said. "We could jump to another planet and pretend we never saw this."

"You know better," I said. Lobo wasn't just my

ship, nor was he simply the most capable artificial intelligence ever created. He was also, after three years together, my closest friend.

"Yes, I do," he said.

The lights winked out.

For a moment, I sat in total blackness. The soft couch gave me the illusion of floating in a silent, dark, and still nothingness, much as Lobo and I were suspended in space near the jump gate for Hardy, the planet where I'd spent the last six months staying as far from the attention of any planetary coalition as I could and wondering what to do next.

"Play the first one," I said.

CHAPTER 2

Rebel jungle base, outside Ventura, planet Tumani

THIS DEVIL HELPED the Tumani government kill your parents," the large man said.

Easily the same two meters tall that I am, but at least twenty kilos heavier than my own hundred, the copper-skinned man spoke in a booming voice that matched well with his size.

"Are you going to let him get away with that crime—with all those crimes?"

No one answered.

The man paced back and forth in front of a pale gray tree whose half-meter-diameter trunk stretched limbless from the ground to far above what I could see. The entire image shook slightly, as if the person recording it was trembling in fear. Whoever had edited this holo had left in panting that further suggested the recorder had been terrified.

Tied to the tree with quick-clasp cables around his neck, waist, wrists, knees, and ankles was a darker man at least a head shorter and no more than half the weight of his captor. The man shook his head back and forth, his eyes bulging with effort, but the rag in his mouth stifled his attempts to scream. Strangled, unintelligible sounds emerged, more animal cries than words.

"Are you?" the larger man screamed.

The image jerked right and left as the recorder scanned the clearing. On both sides stood boys, at least two dozen of them, dressed in dirt-streaked and torn gray and green and tan and brown shorts and shirts, few with shoes, all at least as thin as the man tied to the tree, all visibly hungry, afraid, and angry, their faces tight with tension. The smallest couldn't have been a whole meter and a half tall, while the biggest was no taller than the terrified captive. They all looked younger than eighteen. Many appeared to be prepubescent. All were just kids, kids who should have been spending their days growing up with their families, climbing in trees, not watching the useless struggling of a man bound to one.

"We are soldiers," the captor said, waving his arm to take in people on either side of him, people I could not see, "soldiers who rescued you before this man and his fellow criminals could kill you as they killed your families." He lowered his voice. "And now you are soldiers, too, safe with us, your new brothers." He spoke louder again as he added, "Does a brother let anyone who hurts his brother go unpunished?"

He stared at each of them in turn, pausing a second on each face, his expression calm and resolute and strong. When he finished sweeping across the boys, he faced forward and screamed, his mouth twisting with rage, "No!"

Wordless murmuring all around.

He pointed again at the prisoner, who was now straining so hard against his bonds that muscles and veins stood out all over his body. "So I ask you, brothers, soldiers, men of the families this man stole from you: Will you let him get away with his crime?"

"No!" a boy screamed. The image jerked to focus on one of the tallest of the kids. "No!" he said again.

The large man nodded in satisfaction.

"No," a small, pale boy standing next to the first responder said, his voice barely audible, tears making his eyes glisten. "My family is gone."

The large man approached the little boy, kneeled in front of him, and put his hand on the boy's shoulder. "Yes," he said, "the government devils—this demon," he pointed at the captive without taking his eyes off the boy, "—and his evil friends took away your loved ones." He stood, keeping his hand on the child's shoulder. "But now you have a new family. You have all of us." He turned the boy to face the others as his hand again swept through the air to encompass them all. "And will we let your suffering go unavenged?"

"No!" several boys yelled.

"Will we let the demons get away with murdering his family?"

"No!" more voices screamed.

"With killing all of your families?"

"No! No! No!" The others joined, and the answer became a chant.

The captor held up his hand.

The boys quieted.

"Who will be the first," the man said, "to show this government demon that he cannot break us, that no matter what he does to us or to our families, our brotherhood will prove too strong for him? Who will be first?" He looked down at the small boy standing next to him. He removed his hand from the boy's shoulder. "Who will it be?"

The boy wiped his eyes and looked up at the man. "I will," he said, his voice quavering.

The large man smiled and rubbed the top of the boy's head. "We have a warrior!" he said. "Size and age mean nothing to a soldier as strong and brave as this one." He ran his hand over the boy's head again, but this time he let it linger there long enough to turn the boy to face the captive. He advanced on the prisoner, his hand still guiding the boy, the boy moving with him with the unsure motion of one walking while not yet quite awake.

When he and the boy were so close to the captive that they were almost touching the now sobbing man, he stopped and stepped away from the boy.

"Hit him," the large man said. "Hit him for your family, for yourself, for all of us."

The boy raised his fist but looked into the eyes of the captive and paused.

"Hit him!" the large man screamed. "For your new brothers! So they all, all of the government demons, all of the people who killed your parents and brothers and sisters understand that we will stand together against them!" The boy looked at him for a moment. The man nodded and said, "Hit him!"

The boy punched the prisoner in the stomach with the tentative, weak blow of a young child, his fist not even fully balled, the strike barely moving the writhing captive's shirt.

The other boys whooped and yelled and cheered.

"Who will join this warrior," the large man screamed, "in carrying our message to those who would hurt us, who would hurt our brothers?"

"I will," said the tall boy who had first responded. He ran forward without prompting and hit the captive hard in the gut.

The prisoner sagged as much as he could against his bonds.

The boys cheered again.

The little boy stared at the bigger boy and hit the prisoner again, this time harder.

The boys yelled, wordless animal sounds.

"Join them!" the large man screamed. "All of you! Show them your power as soldiers, as brothers!"

One boy stepped forward, then another, and another, and in seconds all of them were racing forward, yelling and waving their fists. They fell upon the prisoner like a tsunami breaking on a shore. The recorder rushed after them, lagging most of the boys but now with them, a fist waving in front of the image, one more fist to join the barrage pummeling the captive, who no longer moved.

The crowd parted long enough for me to see the blood-soaked prisoner, small bloodied fists pounding over and over and over into him, and then it froze, the frenzied beating boys and the tree-tied corpse motionless in the air in front of me.

CHAPTER 3

Near the jump gate of planet Hardy

CLEAR IT," I whispered. "Leave the lights off."

Blackness surrounded me. In Lobo's soundless interior, sitting in complete darkness, I still closed my eyes, as if doing so could somehow wipe away the traces of what I'd just watched. Dampness squeezed from under my eyelids and wetted my cheeks. I don't cry. I haven't since the day on Dump when I swore I'd never again give anyone the satisfaction of watching me sob, but sometimes I tear up, usually not knowing I've done so until I feel the moisture on my cheeks or realize that the world in front of me has blurred.

I shook my head slightly. Either Lim's recording was real and she needed my help, or someone was playing me. The first order of business was to determine which.

"You've checked the entire recording—not just what I watched, but all of it—for remnants?" I said.

"Please," Lobo said, the sarcasm in his voice turning the word into two syllables, "what do you think I am?

9

Some household comm antique with hundred-year-old software stupid enough to let a virus-laden message inside its firewall? Surely—"

I cut him off. "I know, I know," I said. "You're a hyper-intelligent Predator-Class Assault Vehicle whose every molecule is a nano-enhanced computing system. Sometimes, though, it helps me to understand a problem if I work through the obvious questions."

"If that's easier for you than thinking intelligently," Lobo said, "who am I to ask you to strain yourself simply to spare me annoyance? Why worry about my psychological well-being? Sure, if I were to snap, I could destroy an entire planet in the throes of my justifiable rage, but you don't need to worry about that. I'll be fine."

"What has gotten into you?" I said. "You're normally dramatic, but suicide talk? Since when have you considered suicide or even come close to losing control?"

"I didn't say I was considering killing myself," he said, "and my control is, as you are well aware, perfect, like so much of the rest of me. I was merely pointing out the risks should I—"

"Ah, I understand." I shook my head again, this time at my own slowness, knowing he could see me in IR. "You've already watched the other attachments, and you're distracting me from them."

He said nothing.

"I don't need you to protect me," I said, "and I sure don't want you deciding what I should and should not see."

"Are you sure?" he said. This time, there was no sarcasm, no irony in his tone. "How do you imagine this can end?"

"Maybe we can help Lim," I said. Only in the silence did I realize how loudly I'd spoken, how tight my jaw was.

"Maybe we can," Lobo said, "but at what cost to us, to you? Does Alissa have any idea what she's asking? Do you even know where Tumani is?"

Alissa Lim and I had served together in the Shosen Advanced Weapons Corporation, the Saw, a group that was for my money the best military force in the universe. We were leading our squads into a battle on Nana's Curse, a sparsely populated planet being raped by a fanatic army, to secure a small collection of huts that passed for a village. What we'd found instead of a fight was a horror show: a few pantless enemy soldiers, a stack of dead bodies, and several raped and killed children.

We executed those men then and there. In the process, Lim lost something of herself. I'd had to pull her off the last of them and force her to leave.

"Yes," I said, "yes, Lim does." After a moment, I added, "And, no, I don't know anything about Tumani."

"It's as sad and backward a planet as exists in all the human worlds," Lobo said. "Its one large land mass features a desert on the west, a coast of unusable cliff beaches on the east, and a vast jungle in the center. Other than wood, it has no special natural resources worth the cost of retrieving and shipping them. Its jump gate has two apertures, one that links to an Expansion Coalition planet and the other to a Frontier Coalition world. Its population is under three million, and they and it matter so little that neither the EC nor the FC has ever pressed them to join. It's an independent world no one wants."

That was rare, because the three planetary coalitions were nothing if not acquisitive.

"Fine, it's a pit of a planet. Why does that matter?"

"Because we should know what we'd be risking ourselves for. Because not every fight on every planet is ours. Because whether the government or the rebels win their war is not our problem."

"You think I don't know that?" I said, again louder than I'd intended. "And it's not about their war, not if I know Lim. It's about the children."

"Of course it is," Lobo said, his affect completely flat.

"We didn't seek this problem, but a friend brought it to us, and she asked us for help." I paused and forced myself to continue more calmly. "She asked us, and those children need someone. Are you suggesting we not go?"

"Would it matter if I were?" Lobo said. "That's a rhetorical question; I already know the answer. And to answer your question, no, I'm not."

I nodded my head and opened my eyes to directly confront the blackness. "Good. So let's get on with it. What else was in the data stream?"

"Some contact info woven fairly cleverly among the images. Anyone who found one of these messages and managed to get by the authentication protocol would still have to be very good to find her."

"Where does she want us to meet her?"

"Macken."

So she was still working where I'd last seen her, where she'd been shot helping me, where I'd met Lobo. I was surprised that three years later she was still there, but it had been a beautiful planet, and her security company had gotten the Frontier Coalition contract to police the colonized portions of that world. Though I'd always thought of her as being one of those people, like me, who never settles anywhere, I realized I had no basis for that assumption; I had projected my own feelings onto her.

"Get us in the queue to jump," I said. "We're going there."

"Executing."

"How many more attachments?"

"Two," Lobo said, "but if we're already committed to heading to Macken, there's no need to watch them."

I was squeezing the arms of the couch so hard my forearms hurt. I forced myself to let go of them and put my hands in my lap. I took a long, slow breath.

"Show me the next one."

CHAPTER 4

Unnamed village, outside Ventura, planet Tumani

GRAY AND BROWN mottled the air in all directions. The viewpoint bobbed and spun as the recorder ran around the circumference of the rough circle that the dozen small huts formed. The wood and thatch structures oozed smoke like blood from wounds. Two still blazed here and there. Three boys and a grown man with blankets and fire extinguishers methodically exterminated the remaining flames.

Boys milled about the edges of the clearing, rifles in hand, awaiting orders. All were chewing something and occasionally spitting long streams of brown juice. Bodies covered much of the central area. Many moaned and writhed on the ground; some never moved.

The large man from the earlier scene walked into the square and motioned to a boy, the tall one who'd been second to hit the prisoner. The boy jogged to him and snapped to a loose-jointed attention. In the Saw, any non-com or officer would have seen the movement as insolent, but the man acted as if the boy had executed a perfectly crisp salute. "Corporal, get your troops to clean up this mess," he said, "and then we'll have more root for everyone. And dinner! The storage hut here is full of provisions from the government. We'll dine well on Tumani's stores tonight."

The boy answered so quietly I couldn't hear him. He walked to the nearest body still moving on the ground, aimed his rifle, and shot the man in the head.

At the sound, all the boys dropped and looked wildly around, their weapons at the ready.

"You heard the Sergeant," the tall boy said. "The sooner we finish, the sooner we eat and have more root."

A murmur swept through the boys. They spread evenly around the perimeter of the area. At a nod from the tall boy, they advanced in a line, one step at a time. After a step, each boy stopped, kicked any body on the ground near him, and if it moved, shot it in the head. Some fired at bodies that didn't respond. By the time the boys reached the center, a few of the prisoners had received three or four shots.

The boys spread again to the edge of the clearing and paired up. Each pair grabbed a corpse by its arms or legs, whatever was convenient, and dragged it into a small clearing in the jungle on the opposite side of the village from where the large man watched them work.

"The wind will only be with us for another hour or two," the man said, "so stack them and light them quickly. We don't want their stench interfering with our meal."

The boys picked up their pace, soft curses providing a soundtrack to their efforts as they struggled to move the dead weight of the adult bodies.

One pair broke from the group and ran out of view.

Those two returned carrying two large jugs, which they opened and poured in small lines here and there on the bodies already stacked in the jungle clearing. I'd seen the same motions from children using ocean water to paint images in beach sand. These boys spread the liquid precisely but quickly; they'd done this before.

Satisfied his troops would hit their target timeframe, the large man turned and left.

The boys kept at it, their rhythm the slow and steady pace of soldiers on a long march, men who knew that to work too slowly was to court their commander's fury but that to move too quickly was to risk exhaustion.

I knew the rhythm all too well.

The recording winked out, and I sat again in blackness.

CHAPTER 5

In line for the jump gate of planet Hardy

L IGHTS?" LOBO SAID.

"No. We're not done." The boys had learned to function as a unit in what I suspected was a very short period. "Is there a timestamp on either recording?"

"No," Lobo said, "but my analysis of the faces suggests that very little time passed between the two."

I nodded my head. "It doesn't take long. You can train soldiers very quickly, particularly if they're malleable and if you don't care how much damage you do to them or if you lose a few of them in the process."

Lobo said nothing. What was there to say? He'd seen combat. He knew. I wasn't even sure why I was talking; perhaps because conversation was normal, safe, comforting.

"How long until we jump?" I said.

"All non-government ships in the queue are on hold due to a large set of priority Expansion Coalition ships entering the system. The stationmaster AI is advertising a delay of half an hour, but I cannot know for certain if that's accurate."

17

"There's still another recording, right?"

"Correct."

I wondered if any of the children I'd just watched were still alive, still in the jungle fighting. "Can you tell when Lim left this message?"

"Yes. She made no attempt to conceal that fact. It was seventeen days ago."

Add the time for Lim to obtain the recording and dispatch it on ships to planets many jumps away, and the holos I was watching could easily have been a month or more old. That much time was an eternity in combat. Whether you were suffering the terrified boredom of creeping through dense growth half hoping to find an enemy and half praying you never did, or the utter exhaustion of constant fighting, the days swirled together and ran away from you like blood and rain flowing down dirt banks into rivers.

"How many jumps from Macken are we?"

"Best path or the one we should take to make sure no one is tracking us?"

"Best path," I said. "Lim would have had no reason to assume anyone was monitoring the teams she sent to plant the recordings."

"Four."

Not bad. If she'd received the originals quickly and acted on them immediately, we might be within a month of when those holos were recorded. Those boys might still be alive.

If. Might.

I shook my head to clear it. I was reacting, not thinking, letting my feelings and my past lead me into poor analysis. I had no data, and making assumptions instead of finding the truth and planning accordingly was more likely to do harm than good. When you don't have a clue, don't make up the facts; observe and gather evidence. However hard the truth is, it's ultimately more useful than your imaginings.

"Show me the final attachment."

"There's very little to it," Lobo said, "and essentially no new information."

"Run it."

CHAPTER 6

Jungle clearing, outside Ventura, planet Tumani

THE SQUAD HAD hacked away the undergrowth in a rough square ten meters on a side. They'd woven some of the cuttings among the overhanging tree branches to create a crude bivouac. Small chemical lanterns cast a pale greenish glow from spots here and there among the leaves of the trees; from a distance they might read to beginners as fireflies or as dapples of starlight painting the jungle. An experienced hunting team wouldn't be fooled, but the light was dim enough not to night-blind the boy soldiers while still being bright enough to let the sentries navigate easily.

I would have opted for safety and slower movement, but this choice at least wasn't stupid.

Pairs of guards watched each of the four sides of the encampment, the boys in each duo staying apart and on the move. Each duo covered its half of their zone for a bit, and then they swapped sides. If there were snipers and spotters in higher positions, I couldn't see them.

The boys not on patrol should have been sleeping, but all the bodies on the ground appeared to be in motion, waves rippling in a human ocean.

The small boy who'd hit first in the initial holo entered the central area and wove his way among the prone soldiers, bending and speaking softly to each one and handing him something. When he drew closer to the recorder, I could finally make out his words.

"Relax, brother," he said to a boy who couldn't stop rolling over and righting himself again, his hands always in flight. "You don't need the sleep, so don't worry that it won't come. Chew some more root, and you'll be fine." He handed something to the boy on the ground, straightened, and thumped his fist on his chest. "I haven't slept in over a week, and I'm fine. Like the Sergeant says, we must stay alert and strong."

The boy on the ground took a bite of the root and chewed it. His face, a mask with barely enough skin to cover his skull, distorted with anger and effort. He chewed as if each motion of his jaw might beat back an enemy.

As the standing boy lifted his leg to move to the next soldier, the one on the ground gagged, gasped, sat up, and clutched his chest. A scream ripped from him.

The standing boy leapt upon him and covered the other's mouth with his hand.

The boy bucked under him, pained cries forcing their way out.

All the other boys jumped to their feet, weapons in hand, and moved to the square's perimeter.

The large man ran into the clearing and straight to the small boy trying to quiet the larger one beneath him. The man kneeled beside the pair, pulled off the covering boy, and smoothly slid his hand over the mouth of the one on the ground.

"I tried to quiet him," the shorter boy whispered as he stood.

"Look at me," the man said. "Look at my eyes, only my eyes."

The boy did.

"You did well," the man said. "This one was weak."

The standing boy's eyes flicked downward.

"No!" the man said, his voice quiet but commanding. "Look only at my eyes so you can understand the truth."

The standing boy complied, and as he did, the man grabbed the other side of the prone boy's head, kneeled on the boy's shoulder, and wrenched his head to the left.

The boy on the ground stopped moving.

"The government must have put poison in the food we ate in the last village, and it finally struck his heart. We are lucky it did not kill more of us. Do you understand?"

The standing boy nodded, his eyes never leaving the man's.

The man stood.

"This brother died bravely. Tomorrow, we will avenge him!"

Other boys glanced at the man and nodded their heads.

"Bury him now," the man said, "and remember the face of this hero. Chew the root, and ready yourself for the battle ahead."

A few of the boys raised their rifles in support and muttered cheers.

The recording ended.

CHAPTER 7

In line for the jump gate of planet Hardy

DO YOU KNOW what the root is or what drug it contains?" I said.

"No," Lobo said, "though from what we've seen it almost certainly includes an amphetamine of some sort."

"I *did* notice that," I said. "I was simply curious how addictive it was."

"And that matters why?"

I shook my head slowly. "It doesn't, not really, not now. If we end up going with Lim, we'll learn whatever we need to know."

"If?"

I stood and slitted my eyes. "Lights, please." Lobo's front area snapped into bright relief. I slowly opened my eyes the rest of the way. "I've been letting these holos affect me too much, making too many assumptions in advance of hard data. I'm trying to be more measured. That's all." Before Lobo could comment, I added, "What's happening with the jump queue?"

"We're third in line on our side when the stationmaster AI lets civilian ships start moving again. Estimate for that is still half an hour."

I paced back and forth, more tired than I had any right to be, tense, angry, and unable to shake the effects of what I'd seen. It had been a long day, but I've had many longer that had left me less fatigued.

Why was I fighting sleep? I had nothing else I needed to do until we were in orbit around Macken, and Lobo could easily take us there without my help.

I left the front and headed to the small room I use as my quarters. The door opened as I approached it. I practically dived onto my cot.

"How long to Macken?"

"Assuming a couple of counter-surveillance runs along the way and typical jump-gate times, about twelve hours."

"Perfect. Wake me when we're pulling away from its gate."

"Nothing leaves me feeling more fulfilled," Lobo said, "than acting as your alarm clock."

I was too tired to argue with him. "Shut me in, and get the lights."

My fatigue—or maybe my bad emotional state—must have been obvious, because without further commentary Lobo closed the door and snapped off the lights.

Blackness enveloped me again. I surrendered to it and was asleep in seconds.

CHAPTER 8

Pinecone Island, planet Pinkelponker—139 years earlier

THE AIR SHUTTLE carrying my sister, Jennie, away from our home, away from me, shot into the sky and accelerated upward and forward until it was only a tiny point of light. I stood on the side of the mountain, not far from the cave where Jennie had fixed me and left me sleeping, and watched it fly until I wasn't sure the light that was the ship was still there. Then I stood some more. Tears wet my cheeks. I knew the government had taken her so she could spend her time fixing important people, not useless and dumb ones like me, but I also knew she hadn't wanted to go.

I vowed that one day I would rescue her, though I had no idea of how I might do that. I said the promise aloud, as if she could still hear me, as if what I said mattered.

I sat in the grass, closed my eyes, and let the wind from the ocean dry my face. I imagined she was next to me, already back from her trip, and when I opened my eyes she would smile and tell me everything was okay.

Except that couldn't happen. Before she'd fixed me a few hours ago, I might have been able to make myself believe that everything would go back to the way it was, but not now. She'd fixed me too well. Now, I knew she was gone for good, as she'd said she would be.

With a speed my brain could never have managed before, I also instantly deduced that her departure could cause more problems for me. I was the big useless kid, the dumb one who couldn't learn as much as the slowest of the six-year-olds, and now I didn't have Jennie to protect me. Even though I believed she had fixed my brain—it felt different, as if before my thinking had been crawling and now it was flying like a bird racing across the sky—I didn't know how to convince anyone else that I could do more than before. That I was valuable now.

I glanced down the hill and saw two men in uniform climbing toward me. They were taking their time, laughing and talking as they came, not even bothering to keep an eye on me. They knew I had nowhere to go. Jennie had taught me that Pinkelponker was nothing but islands, a world of them, thousands of them scattered all over a huge planet-covering ocean, and that Pinecone, our island, was one of the smallest that people bothered to live on. Though I was the biggest person here, I was also the stupidest. They had no reason to worry about me.

I thought about running back to the cave, but I decided not to bother. They'd find me eventually. For all that Jennie and I had treated it as our special, secret place, I now understood clearly that locating it would not be very hard. Besides, I might as well learn what they wanted.

I should also, I realized, not tell them about Jennie fixing me. It could get her in trouble, and I didn't want that.

I stretched out on the grass, stared at the clouds, and waited. I counted them and found the task easy, the numbers past ten coming readily and without effort. I had learned those numbers a long time ago and relearned them many times since then, but usually I could not easily bring them to mind. This fast thinking was nice. I smiled, silently thanked Jennie again, and went back to waiting.

The two men would be here soon enough.

They approached me from both sides at once. When they stopped, they were each at least two meters from me. I was bigger and probably stronger than either of them, but that was true of almost all the men I'd ever seen. I'd never, though, had any grown-ups act as if I might get violent with them; everyone on Pinecone knew I'd never hurt anyone. These two clearly weren't taking any chances.

I smiled first at the one on my right and then at the one on my left.

"Jon Moore?" the left guy said.

I wondered why he asked a question when he already knew the answer, but I figured that he was probably making sure. Even if he was just being stupid, I wasn't going to point that out to him; I knew how much it hurt to have someone do that to you. "Yes," I said.

"We'd like you to come with us," Left said.

I sat. Both men tensed slightly. I couldn't believe it.

They were afraid of me. I'd never hit anyone. Jennie had always told me that fighting was bad and besides that, when you were as big as I am, you had to be careful not to take advantage of smaller people. I wanted to reassure them that everything was fine, but I figured the best way to do that would be to keep behaving nicely. "Okay," I said. "Where are we going?"

"To see your sister," Right said. "She's asked us to bring you to her."

I had a hard time continuing to smile, because I knew, without understanding why I knew, that he was lying and that I could only cause trouble by saying so. Besides, if I was wrong, I'd get to see Jennie, and nothing could be better than that.

I also didn't really have a choice. The way they watched me, the places they stood, everything about their actions made a single clear statement: One way or another, I was going with them.

I stood. "I understand that part. I meant, *where* are we going: the village, the beach, where?"

They exchanged a quick glance. Both visibly relaxed.

Left said, "You know that she left on a government ship, right?"

"Sure," I said. "She told me, before—" I paused as I realized that though telling them the truth would be wrong, I had no experience lying. Jennie had always told me she liked that about me, so I felt embarrassed at what I was about to do. "Before I took a nap."

"Of course she did," Left said. He smiled. "Follow me, and I'll lead you to our ship. It's in the government landing area on the other side of the island. You've never been in an air shuttle, have you?"

"No. I've never left Pinecone."

"You'll enjoy the ride," Right said. "It's fun."

"Yes, it is," Left said. "You'll have a good time."

He turned his back to me and started down the mountain. Right stayed behind me. I stared at Pinecone spread out below me: the trail down, the small collections of five and six huts that filled the flat areas, the yellow sand beach far below, the blue-green ocean surrounding us, the birds soaring back and forth over land and sea as if they recognized no boundaries. I feared I'd never see this place again, and I wanted to hold it always in my memory, the way I held Jennie. I inhaled deeply and savored the rich scents of the ocean and the wheat we harvested from all over the mountain.

Left turned around and faced me. "Mr. Moore?" he said. "Jon?"

I forced myself to let go of the island and focus on him. "Sorry," I said.

He smiled again. "It's okay. I understand."

He didn't. He thought I'd forgotten to go, but I saw no point in correcting him. Instead, I turned and followed a couple of paces behind him.

We proceeded down the path in that little line, moving together, the way Jennie and I often had, but with no fun in it this time, no laughs, no pointing at the ocean or the clouds, no pausing to sniff any of the small, wild, white and blue-flecked flowers that dotted the hillside grasses here and there, as if someone had thrown blossoms into the air and let the wind carry them where it would. We walked without talking. They didn't seem to notice the beauty around them.

I thought of her the entire way down. I wanted to believe that they were telling me the truth and soon I'd be with her. I couldn't. Instead, I knew with a stomach-leadening certainty that wherever they were taking me, she would not be there.

I'd watched the flying ships carry Jennie away, but I'd never come close to one. From the mountainside where I'd spied on them, they'd always appeared perfect: smooth, sleek, silvery things that pushed on the ground with huge roaring winds, rose into the sky, and shot away. As I approached this one, I saw dents and dings and discolored bits and all sorts of small scars. It was still impressive, but now I understood that the perfection had been only an illusion.

Two strides from the entrance to the ship, the lead man stopped, turned, and stared at me. I stopped, too. He studied my face for a long time, shook his head, and said, "You look normal enough."

I had no idea what I was supposed to say, so I stayed quiet.

"At your size, I'd have expected more facial hair, but other than that..." His voice trailed off, but he kept staring at me.

Jennie had explained this part to me. "My sister told me it was because I wasn't really a teenager yet."

"As big as you are? And aren't you sixteen?"

I nodded. "I am, but that's what she told me, and she always tells me the truth."

He stepped closer, so close we were almost touching. "Did she explain what's wrong with you?"

I nodded again. "My brain doesn't work as well as most people's. Because of that, even though my body grew big, I wasn't a teenager yet. She said not to worry about it. She always told me that I had a smart heart, and that was enough." I thought again about letting him know that she had fixed me so I'd have a smart head, too, but I couldn't risk causing her trouble for helping me.

He sighed. "Okay. It's just that you're not like most of them."

"Who?"

He smiled, but it was a sad expression, with not a trace of happiness in it. He turned, clapped me on the back, and pushed me toward the ship.

"Like your sister told you," he said, "don't worry about it."

He followed me inside. The other man came after him.

The door shut behind us.

"It's time for us to leave," Left said.

Being in the air ship was like being nowhere at all. They made me sit alone in a small room with no windows and no grass to rest on and no one to keep me company, and they left. The door had no handle, so I sat where they told me to sit, and I waited. The floor was metal and hard and even dirt would have been better, but I had no choice, so I tried to stay happy while I waited. I didn't mind being alone—I've always been good at that and have spent most of my life on my own—but I would have enjoyed seeing what Pinkelponker is like from the air. With nothing to do and nothing to look at, I finally decided I might as well nap. I stretched out on the floor, which was even less comfortable for resting than it was for sitting, even worse than the rock floor in Jennie's and my secret cave, and after a while I fell asleep.

▸   ▸   ▸

The big man who woke me was someone I hadn't seen before. He stayed in the doorway, pointed a gun at me, and yelled, "Get up, and get out!"

By habit, I shook my head to clear it. Thinking was always hard for me, and it was particularly difficult after I'd been sleeping. This time, though, I didn't need to do it; I snapped awake to instant awareness. I was more and more convinced that Jennie really had improved my mind.

I stood. "Is Jennie here?"

The man stepped back and pointed to his left with the gun. "Out."

I didn't move. "If Jennie's not here, I don't want to go."

"Here's how it works," the man said, his voice completely flat, like someone talking about whether the waves were big or small. "You move now, or I shoot you in the leg and drag you. No more talk. Got it?"

I shrugged; how could I not understand? I walked where he pointed. I'd known from the start that they were lying to me, but part of me had kept hoping they were taking me to Jennie. They weren't, and there was nothing I could do about it. I had never had a lot of choices, though, so that was fine. On Pinecone, each morning I got up and worked where they told me, planting and harvesting and clearing. When I had time to myself, I swam or sat on the mountain and always hoped for those hours when Jennie could be with me and we could again be our own little family, brother and sister, all either of us really had. It wasn't bad, living like that, not really, and I was good at it. Maybe whatever this was wouldn't be so bad, either—though the fact that the man used a gun to force me obey him made me think that wherever I was going was not good, not good at all.

He directed me down a short hall and to the doorway through which I had entered the ship. It slid open as I stood in front of it.

"Out," he said.

"Where are we?" All I could see was dirt and small bushes and the side of a mountain. It didn't look like Pinecone, so I figured we were on another island, but I had no idea which one.

The man chuckled briefly. "Dump," he said. "We call it Dump. Now, get out. Move away from the ship quickly, because we won't wait to take off."

I was afraid and very much didn't want to go. I didn't know anyone here. Jennie wasn't here. I didn't know who would take care of me.

I turned my head to say something else. Before I could speak, a hand pushed me in the center of my back, and I stumbled onto the ground.

"Run," the man said as the ship sealed itself.

Wind rushed downward from the ship's wings, and it roared. Dust swirled all around me. I stood, took two steps, and the ship began to rise. I ran a few more strides, tripped on something—I couldn't see the ground through the dust—and fell hard. I tasted blood and put my hands over my ears to protect them from the huge noise.

As the sound faded and the dust began to settle, I rolled onto my back and wiped the grime from my eyes and face. Small streaks of blood stained my hands; I'd split my lip in the fall.

I didn't know what to do. I didn't know where I was. I was alone.

I started crying, at first a few tears and then hard sobs, my chest tight from the effort. My heart hurt because I finally had to accept, really accept, that Jennie wasn't here, that I was alone, that nothing was right, nothing was the way it had been.

"Is that the biggest baby you've ever seen, Bob?"

I sat at the sound of the voice and stopped sobbing, though tears still mixed with the sand on my cheeks and my eyes burned. I wasn't alone!

Ten strides in front of me stood the tallest, thinnest man I'd ever seen. At least a head taller than I was, maybe more, he looked about as thick as one of my legs. His body appeared even thinner because his arms were barely bigger than twigs.

"I think it is, Benny," the tall man, Bob, said.

For a moment, I couldn't spot the other person, the one who'd spoken first. Then I looked down and saw him. He was on a small, rough cart with a dark wooden platform and wheels that looked like someone had carved them from hunks of rock. His body and head were normal, and he looked about my age, maybe a bit younger, definitely a whole lot smaller. Where he should have had hands and feet, though, were things that looked like thick bird wings or flippers. He used them to push on the ground and roll the cart closer.

"Welcome to Dump," he said. His voice was very deep, deeper than that of most grown-ups. "It's obvious why they put *us* here, but you look fine. What's your story?"

Before I could respond, he added, "Don't bother answering now. You'll have to explain it again to the others, and I don't want to hear it twice. Follow us."

As he rolled off, his flippers slapping the ground

in unison to propel him forward, he added, "And cut that crying crap right now. Soldiers don't cry, and we're at war." He glanced back at me. "You just don't know it yet."

CHAPTER 9

Just outside the jump gate station, planet Macken

LOBO OPENED A front-facing display so I could watch as we passed through the jump gate aperture and emerged in space behind Trethen, Macken's smaller moon. Normally, I enjoy the process of jumping and discover in each leap through space a kind of wonder I rarely feel. Today, though, I couldn't fully appreciate the experience.

"Take us closer to the planet," I said, "but don't leave the gate's area of influence."

"Executing," Lobo said.

As we turned, I stared at the gate in the display. Like all of them, it resembled a giant pretzel and was a single uniform color. Most were bright, but this one was a very pale green that reminded me of both the oceans and the forests below. Another trait it shared with all gates was its complete lack of tolerance for violence within a sphere with it as the center and a radius of a light-second. Should any ship within that area launch a weapon or be about to collide with anything else, a blast of highly coherent energy would burst from the gate and remove the offender as if it had never been there; the beam left no trace of the offending ship. No one understood how or why gates could do this, but the behavior never varied. In my last visit here, it had saved my life. Until I had spoken to Lim, I was staying inside this safe area in case her message was a trap.

The gates were in all ways mysterious. No one knew how or why they let us instantaneously move between planets many, many light years apart, or what created them, or the reason that not one gate has ever had a single scratch or imperfection, or why every time a new aperture opens we can count on a human-habitable planet being on the other side. As with so many other mysteries humanity has encountered, we simply adapted to their presence and used them to our advantage; because of them, we've been able to colonize worlds all over the universe.

Lobo interrupted my reverie. "I've scanned the local data drops and found an update from Lim with her contact info. She's in Glen's Garden."

The name stirred more three-year-old memories. When I'd last visited Macken, Glen's Garden, though the planet's capital, had been a sleepy oceanfront town desperate enough for my help that it paid me with a then not fully functional Lobo. The jump gate had possessed only three apertures, but the growing fourth had led to conflict between two of the region's largest megacorporations. The entire world had been a beautiful and largely unsettled member of the Frontier Coalition. I'd left before progress could spoil it.

"Call her," I said. "Also, who's running this planet now?"

"Executing the first," he said. "From my analysis of the data stream, Lim's company still has the security contract, the FC's local government is still officially in power, and the same two corporations as before, Xychek and Kelco, actually dominate the economy." He paused for a second. "I have Alissa. Please recall that she rescued you from torture not so many years ago, and do try to be nice."

I remembered, but the last thing I wanted was social coaching from a killing machine. If I ignored him, though, he might never shut up. "I'll be as nice as the situation permits. Now, please connect us. Full display."

Her head appeared where the jump gate had been in the front of Lobo. She was still lovely, but her hair was shorter than I'd ever seen it, just a dark coating on her skull. Veins stood out on her neck and her shoulders and her arms and even across the top of her chest, all visible courtesy of the tight black tank top she was wearing. She'd cut a lot of weight since our last meeting, even since the recording she'd sent me.

She had the hard, lean, distant look of someone ready to go to war.

She nodded. "Moore."

"Lim."

"Thanks for coming."

"You knew I would."

She nodded again. "Yes."

"The fact that I'm here doesn't mean I'm committing to anything. I want the whole story."

"Now?"

"No," I said, shaking my head. "I need to know there's no coercion in any of this."

For the first time, she smiled. "Some things don't change," she said. "Like your paranoia."

"Some things shouldn't change. I'm still alive."

"So what proof would you like?"

"Come to the jump gate," I said. "Take a commercial shuttle. Call me when you're in the station, and we'll dock for just long enough to pick you up. We'll talk when you're here."

"Okay," she said, "but you need to understand this: I'll do what you want for now, but if you sign up, you agree to operate under my command. A whole lot of children don't have the time for us to bring you up to speed and let you design your own attack and run it with different people than the ones I've already recruited. Deal?"

Lim was more than a little crazy, but she was a topnotch soldier and an excellent planner—and it was, after all, her show. "Deal. If I can't accept your setup, I won't join."

"See you later today," she said. Her image winked out.

"Oh, boy!" Lobo said. "A chance to entertain! Whatever shall we serve?"

I don't mind waiting. Staying alert while watching time pass has been a key requirement of many of the jobs I've had. I was, though, now buzzing with energy from the combination of what I'd seen in the Tumani holos, my memories of Pinkelponker, and all the sleep I'd had. To work off some of it, I had Lobo withdraw the pilot couches and started doing cycles of simple body-weight exercises: squats, push-ups, dips on a ledge Lobo extruded, and pull-ups. I pushed the pace until I was pouring sweat and my body ached from the exertion. The nanomachines that lace all my cells would heal the torn muscles and remove the waste quickly enough that in short order I would be back to normal, but for that brief time I was deliciously exhausted and hurting.

"Do you have any idea how much extra air filtration work your exercises cost me?" Lobo said.

"Like you have something better to do," I said as I stretched out on the floor to relax.

"In fact," he said, "I do. For example, right now I've hacked into the jump gate traffic computers and am checking the reservations of all the commercial shuttles headed this way. Lim is not yet on any of them, though to be fair to her, she wouldn't have had the time to catch one unless she'd been ready to roll the moment she disconnected from you."

"As you so often remind me," I said, "your enormous intelligence can do so many things at once that hacking into a single system cannot possibly tax all of it."

"Good point," he said, "I certainly can and do routinely execute more simultaneous projects than your human brain could ever hope to handle."

Lying on the floor, the fatigue washing over me, I smiled at Lobo's needling and for a few moments was calm. I closed my eyes as unbidden memories claimed me and destroyed that peace.

CHAPTER 10

Dump Island, planet Pinkelponker—139 years earlier

I FOLLOWED BENNY AND Bob to a path that hugged the side of the mountain and walked along it with them for a long time as its winding course took us higher. We stopped in front of a huge, thick green bush that they moved to the right to reveal a cave three meters wide and so deep that even though some torches burned at a few points on its walls, I couldn't see its rear. I studied the bush, which proved to be not a plant at all but rather a lot of branches woven together.

When I looked away from it, Benny was staring at me. "Never seen camouflage?"

"I don't think so," I said. "But I'm not sure. What is it?"

Benny looked harder at me. "It's when you use something that blends into its surroundings to cover something that doesn't belong there."

"So why do you cover a cave with camouflage?" I expected to have trouble saying the big word, but

I didn't; it was easy. Maybe big words would all be easier now that Jennie had fixed my head.

"To stop them from seeing what we're doing?"

I looked around. "Who?"

"The government."

"But the soldiers left, and I didn't see anyone else on the walk here."

Benny pointed upward with his chin. "At any time they want to, they can watch us from above, with satellites left over from when the generation ship was still launching them."

I didn't understand any of what he said, but I didn't suppose that mattered. What bothered me was *why* they had to hide. "Is it bad if they see you?"

"Yes," Benny said, "because they're the ones we're fighting, and you always want your enemies to have as little data as possible about you."

I was amazed at how many words he knew. "You're really smart," I said.

"Yes, but not smart enough that they were willing to keep me around when I have these"—he raised his arm and leg flippers a few inches—"instead of proper hands and feet."

"So they brought you here, too?"

"They *dumped* me here, just like you, just like all the others."

Twelve more people appeared in the cave entrance—I was surprised by how quickly, almost instantly I could count them—and stared at me. Each one was clearly not normal. One's head was way too big. Another had skin that was rough and scaly and eyes that didn't blink. I felt bad staring at them, even though they seemed to be comfortable looking right at me, so I faced Benny again.

"Why did the government leave all of us here? I wasn't doing anything bad."

Benny shook his head. "How you were behaving has nothing to do with what they did. The background radiation here on Pinkelponker is high, higher than humans had to face back on Earth. It causes a great many mutations. Most people with them die before or during birth. Some survive. Of those that do, a few end up having valuable special abilities. The rest," he paused and looked at the others, "the rest are like us, people no one wants to be around. Freaks. They dump us here and check on us every now and then, just in case someone develops a useful ability. It's happened, but not often. For most of us, once you're here, you're stuck." After a long pause, he added, "Or worse, because sometimes they take the weakest of us for no good reason, and those people never return. I don't like thinking about what may have happened to them."

I still didn't understand most of what he was saying, but I knew what freaks were, and I knew about special abilities.

"There's nothing wrong with being different," I said. "Jennie told me so. And she was one of the people who could do special things. She could heal people."

"Jennie?" Bob said.

"My sister. She fixed me."

"You look fine to me," Benny said, "certainly better than any of us. What did she fix?"

I tapped my right temple. "My head. I stopped getting smarter when I was really little. She fixed it so my head could now be smart."

Benny stared at me for several seconds. So did some of the others. Finally, he said, "Are you sure?"

"Jennie told me so," I said, "and I trust her, so it has to be true."

He looked like he was about to argue with me, but he stopped, remained quiet a bit longer, and finally said, "Where is she?"

"They took her away, so she could heal rich and important people. She didn't like going, didn't want to, but she had to."

Benny rolled closer to me. "Do you know where she went?"

I shook my head. I didn't like admitting it, but I had no idea where she was. I looked away from him as I felt tears in the sides of my eyes at the thought that maybe I wouldn't ever see her again. No, I reminded myself, that wasn't right. I'd vowed I would one day find her and save her, and I would. I would.

"Would you like to go after her?"

I stared at him. It was like he'd read my mind. "More than anything."

"Then join us. We're training the fittest of us to be soldiers. One day, we're going to fight them and win and leave this place." He lifted his right arm and waved his flipper slowly to take in all the people behind us. "I told you we are all soldiers and we are all in that war. Are you willing to learn to fight, really fight, so we can escape from here and you can find your sister?"

Jennie had always told me not to fight, that my size meant I might hurt somebody. She'd mostly been talking about the other people on Pinecone, where I was by far the biggest person. The soldiers who brought me here were bigger, though, much closer to my size, so maybe fighting them was safe. Maybe

I wouldn't hurt them too much, and they wouldn't hurt me, either.

The more I thought about it, the more I realized that was a silly dream. The last man I'd seen had kicked me out of the ship and been willing to let its take-off injure or even kill me rather than walk me to safety. No, if I fought, I had to be willing to hurt them. The alternative was to give up on Jennie. She was gone, and I sure couldn't go after her as long as I was stuck here.

I wouldn't give up on her. I would never do that.

"Yes," I said, "I am. I'll fight. How do I learn to do it?"

CHAPTER 11

Just outside the jump gate station, planet Macken

ALISSA'S ALONE," LOBO said.

His voice yanked me out of my reverie. "How can you be sure?" I said. No way were we docking with the station until I was comfortable. Right now, thanks to the jump gate, we were safe. The moment we docked, the gate would not interfere in any violence that took place inside what I guess it considered to be a single entity. I know: I've had more than a few fights on these stations.

"Because I looked," Lobo said. "I'm now into all the station computers, so I have complete access to all of its surveillance systems." Two displays popped open in front of me. The one on the left showed a view of the docking port twenty meters in front of where we hung in space. Lim stood alone, visible through the viewport, facing outward, her body language stiff and annoyed. She wasn't happy that I'd made her wait.

The right display provided an IR view of that same area and the surrounding halls. If anything living was within twenty meters of her, it was doing a great job of shielding itself. Such camouflage would make no sense, however, because no one who might want to get me would expect me to have access to the station network.

We were as safe as I could hope to be.

"Dock," I said. "Take off as soon as she's aboard."

"Of course," Lobo said. "It's not like this is my first dance, and it's not as if you've cornered the market on paranoia."

"I understand," I said, "but I know you like her."

"To the degree that I like other humans, that's true," he said, "but so do you."

"I'm simply being careful," I said, not wanting to argue with him any longer. "In that spirit, scan her before you let her on board."

I knew from a third display Lobo opened that we had docked, but cocooned inside him I felt nothing; he was good. He was also showing off, making sure I understood that he had thought of everything and was, as usual, executing flawlessly. I can't imagine ever taking the details for granted, because minding the small stuff is often what keeps you alive, but with Lobo I probably should learn to trust him more and speak less.

"She's clean and about to come aboard," Lobo said. "You'll want to get into position."

My resolve to treat him better dissolved rapidly in the acid flow of his sarcasm—but he was right. I stepped over to the side hatch Lobo was about to open. As soon as I reached it, but before I could be exposed in front of it, Lobo opened it.

Lim stepped inside, stopped, and raised her arms.

The hatch snicked shut. Over the machine frequency, so Lim couldn't hear us, Lobo said, "Disengaging from the station."

The ability to directly communicate with machines on their frequencies is one of the many improvements Jennie made in me, though it had taken me a while to learn about that one. Life on Dump had not included such niceties as appliances.

Lim turned her head to stare at me. "Can we get this over with so we can talk?"

"Sorry," I said. I smiled in embarrassment. "You can relax. We've already checked you."

She lowered her arms. "Hi, Lobo," she said. Her smile seemed genuine; why were women always happier to talk to him than to me?

"It's great to see you again, Alissa," he said. "You look good, ready to fight."

She nodded. "I am, and I hope you two will join us."

I headed up front. "Let's sit," I said, "and talk."

I stretched out in the pilot's couch and offered her the other one.

She ignored it and stood. "You've seen the holos," she said, "or you wouldn't have come here. What else do you want to know?"

"What do you want from me?"

"From us?" Lobo added.

"To help us stop the Tumani rebels from continuing to use those children as soldiers, of course," she said.

"So why not just do it?" I said. "Why call me"—I corrected myself before Lobo could—"us?"

"I have soldiers of my own, of course," she said, "but what I really need is Lobo, to provide reconnaissance, to act as an on-the-scene command-and-control center, and, if it comes to that, to provide some serious firepower."

"With no offense to my ship," I said, "between your company and the Saw, you have access to many vessels at least as powerful as Lobo."

"That's a debatable point," he said to me privately, "when you consider that the intelligence of any entity represents a significant fraction of its power."

On that point he was certainly correct. Though Lim didn't know it, in fact no living human other than I was aware of it, Lobo was composed of organic/metal-computing hybrid nanomachines that functioned both as dynamically reconfigurable armor and as one of the most powerful tightly coupled computing networks in existence. Only six months ago, we'd tried to capture the man who'd created Lobo's computing substrate from the results of experiments with nanomachines and cells he'd harvested from children—a process that had killed those kids. The nanomachines were something else Lobo and I shared, though I'd never told him about mine.

"Obtaining a PCAV like Lobo is not a simple task," Lim said.

"See?" Lobo said.

I ignored him and responded to her. "Sorry, but though that's true, it's not so tough a job that you couldn't handle it. Why not use your crew's resources and, if necessary, hire the Saw? It's not like you don't have contacts there." When I'd last seen her two and a half years ago, she'd become friends again with a past lover, Colonel Tristan Earl of the Saw.

"I could," she said, "if I were able to involve either coalition, but I can't. This can't be an official operation—not for my company, and certainly not for the Saw.

The FC is my biggest client, and both it and the EC represent major revenue for the Saw."

"Tumani isn't a part of either coalition," I said, "so why would they care?"

"That's the tricky part," she said. "Even though the planet is a hellhole that neither coalition has wanted, its population is growing, and someday it's going to join one of them. When it does, that coalition will gain another aperture into the other's space. So, neither one wants the other to have it. To ensure that they play fair, they jointly operate the gate station, and they stop anyone from supplying major weapons to either party in the civil war. I've talked to some of my FC contacts about it. They don't care as much about which side wins the conflict as they do that the EC doesn't determine the outcome and end up with a better relationship with the victor. I assume the EC feels the same way about them."

Her comment about the weapons bothered me. "Not to belabor the obvious," I said, "but Lobo is obviously a Predator-Class Assault Vehicle. Why would they let me bring him into that system?"

Lim held up her hand and ticked off the points on her fingers. "One: You declare him and operate him as private transport for your courier business. Two: In all official registers, he's listed as having a non-working central weapons control complex. You and I both know that's not true, and I expect some FC and EC officials do, but that's how he appears in the records the Tumani gate agents would check."

I nodded; she was right on both points. Eighteen months ago, in a conflict on a station around a distant gate, Lobo had shown his weapons to an EC official, but both she and I had good reasons to keep our entire relationship confidential.

"Three," she continued, "I've seen Lobo's camo abilities in action, and he can make the on-planet observers believe he really is no more than the courier transport vehicle you pretend he is. Not drawing their attention is a good thing."

"Fair enough," I said. "I can see the value of involving us, but I have to believe there's an easier way: Take the recordings to the EC and the FC. Using children as soldiers is something every coalition has condemned."

She shook her head. "Still assuming I'm incompetent, eh? Of course I've shown the recordings to them. They've responded by pointing out that anyone can fake anything digital."

"So rather than save these children, or even pay a military outfit to do it, both the FC and the EC are willing to let the rebels use them?"

She shrugged. "It's not either coalition's fight, and getting involved would be expensive and risky for them. They'd have to do it jointly, and with no economic incentive, why would they bother?"

I couldn't argue with her. I'd never seen a large company or any of the three coalitions take any action that didn't directly benefit it. "What if you showed the recordings to the media?"

She spoke to me as if I were a child. "Do you think I didn't pursue that option? My friends and I first pushed both coalitions to accept the recordings as true. We hinted that we'd take the holos to both local Tumani media groups and off-planet conglomerates who'd believe us if they didn't. They responded politely and formally in classic governmental fashion: They commissioned joint task forces that periodically carry out inspection tours—very inexpensive and superficial tours, of course—of both rebel and government forces. Fearing coalition involvement, both sides on Tumani naturally agreed to these inspections and to maintaining cease-fires during them."

"And when the inspectors arrive," I said, "the government leaders claim the rebels are using children, the rebels deny the allegations and say they're not, no kids are in sight, and the FC and the EC joint task force files the appropriate reports." I closed my eyes for a moment. I'd seen such inspections before, and they rarely accomplished anything. "The inspectors go home, and the fighting resumes."

"Yes, all as you'd expect," she said, the annoyance plain in her voice. "When the inspectors failed to turn up any proof of our allegations, the media interest vanished." She sighed. "We could have saved time if you'd trusted that I knew what I was talking about."

"I didn't mean to question your competence. I was—and am—trying to understand exactly what the situation is and what I'm getting myself—us—into."

She smiled slightly. Even the small improvement in her expression lit up the room. I found myself involuntarily smiling in return.

"Apology accepted," she said. "What else would you like to know?"

"Does either coalition side with the rebels?"

"Officially, no. Both the FC and the EC claim to recognize the current government as being legitimate, though as I said neither is willing to supply it with weapons. Because the government won't join a coalition, both are staying away from this civil war—which is also one of the reasons neither one is willing to work very hard to expose the rebels' use of child soldiers."

"And unofficially?"

She shook her head. "None of us are sure, but at least some rumors show the EC as leaning slightly toward the rebels. In any case, I don't expect either coalition to get involved as long as we don't import any weapons that would violate their rules and we don't involve any company that already supplies them military services."

"Like the Saw."

She nodded.

All of that was good news, because it meant we shouldn't have to fight any outsiders when we went to free the children. "I take it that the government isn't trying to save the child soldiers on its own because its troops are too busy fighting them."

"Essentially," she said. "Those children are no different from any other rebel fighters: They're scattered in units all through the jungle. If the Tumani army could find those kids, they could find the units, and they'd attack." She paused. "To the best of my ability to tell, the government would very much like to end the rebels' use of child soldiers, and quite a few government officials have said they'd back our play if we structure it right, but until that time—"

"—those kids are just more enemies on the other side of firefights." I closed my eyes for a few seconds and thought of jungle missions on Nana's Curse and half a dozen other worlds, some of them with Lim. I stared again at her. "The Tumani generals are telling their politicians that their troops can't pause to figure out the ages of the people shooting at them."

She nodded again. "And they're right. As much as I hate it, I can't even begin to argue against them."

"So how are we supposed to find the children, much less rescue them?"

She smiled again, this time a full-on grin, and for a second I forgot the topic and was simply glad that I had made her happy. "Courtesy of the same informant who smuggled out those recordings, we know that for a couple of days virtually all the children, something on the order of five hundred of them, will be in a single complex."

Her pause invited a question, but if I asked the obvious one, I'd be sure to annoy her. After considering my wording for a moment, I said, "There's obviously some factor preventing the government from sending in its troops during that time, or you wouldn't be planning on doing it yourself. What's the reason?"

"Ah, finally the assumption of competence," she said, continuing to smile. "Thank you. The government can't help us because the only time the kids are all in one place is during the cease-fire."

"The inspectors can't spot any kids among the active rebel troops," I said, "so the government can't afford to be seen by the coalitions as breaking the cease-fire by sending in its troops."

"Exactly."

"On the other hand," I said, "a small, private force operating quietly and without the official support of either side would not be breaking any coalition rules—except, of course, for the cease-fire."

"Which is why," she said, "such a force wouldn't begin its assault until the cease-fire was officially over. Even better, by launching just as the inspectors leave and the government and rebel leaders are returning to their troops, this small force wouldn't encounter much resistance, because to avoid drawing attention to where they stash the kids, the rebels leave only a skeleton adult squad at the complex."

"Which they can afford to do," I said, "because all or at least most of the kids are already trained soldiers who have no desire to run off. Which means this private force would also be facing five hundred small but nonetheless dangerous enemies."

"That is one of the mission's challenges," she said with a shrug. "I never claimed this would be easy. Have you ever known one that really was?" She didn't wait for me to reply; we both knew the answer. "We have to strike quickly, disarm the kids, fortify the complex, and use it to contain them."

"Will the government help us once we're in control?"

"Yes and no," she said. "We're still negotiating about how to handle the reintegration, but at least initially that will be our problem. Once we occupy the facility, the government will send troops into the surrounding area, but their focus will be outward, not on us."

"So we'd be bait."

She shrugged. "Sort of, but not very useful bait, because the rebels can more easily recruit new kids than come back for the ones we capture. The government troops certainly won't let any kids go back to the rebels, so we'll also be jailers. Mostly, though, I think we'll be irrelevant to the troops in the region. The government wants to control this section of the jungle primarily so it can take a healthy bite out of the rebel territory."

Lim was aware of what we'd be walking into, but

she'd done everything she could to minimize the opposition. She'd clearly been building a team, and she wanted Lobo for air support and transport.

"Why me?" I said.

"I already told you."

"No, you told me why you wanted Lobo."

"Fair enough. I want you because you're good at covert ops, I've worked with you and know you, our team isn't big, and I need everyone on it to be someone I can trust. Besides, it never occurred to me that you and Lobo were anything other than a package deal."

"Nor to me," said Lobo over the machine frequency. "Were you seriously considering loaning me, as if I were some small appliance?"

I looked down for a moment as I subvocalized, "No!"

"Good," he said, still privately. "I should certainly hope not."

I turned my attention back to Lim. "You're right, of course: I stay with my ship. At the risk of coming across as insensitive to this cause, I have to ask: Why Tumani? Why these kids? This can't be the only planet where one side in a conflict is using children as soldiers. Why are you getting involved here?"

For the first time, she looked away from me as she spoke, and her tone softened. "I'd like to think I'd try to intervene anywhere this was happening, but the truth is that I've never gone looking for the chance to help end this sort of abuse. The same source that showed me the holos and asked me to lead the rescue team is also funding this entire operation. I would have never even thought twice about Tumani if these people hadn't contacted me." She stopped talking, but it was clear she still had more to say, so I stayed quiet. After a bit, she continued. "I'm almost embarrassed to tell you that we'll all get paid—and rather handsomely—for this work. These people had done their research. They knew they could probably persuade me and a few others to take the job for expenses, but they also understood that we'd have to spend serious money to set up and properly outfit the kind of team we'd need." She finally faced me. "Do you think I should have turned down the money?"

I considered the question, which clearly had been troubling her. Finally, I shook my head. "No. If you had, you wouldn't have been able to assemble as good or as large a team, and if someone is willing to pay and has the resources to do so, I see no harm in taking their money. That answer, though, begs the next obvious and important question: What's that party's reason for being involved?" I'd learned the hard way in a lot of fights over many decades that if you didn't understand the motives of the people paying your way, you were likely to find yourself in some very bad situations. Of course, many mission plans went nonlinear even when you did have that knowledge, but possessing it was always better than not knowing.

"I'll tell you what they've told me," she said, "but I think you've done enough of this work to know better than to trust that we have the whole story."

I nodded.

"One of the kids is special to them. They won't say why, and I haven't pressed the issue, but they're willing to spend a fortune to have us rescue all of the boys just to get this one."

"A one-target smash-and-grab would be a lot cheaper

and easier," I said. "Unless their entire organization is full of morons, they have to know that."

"I know, I know," she said, "and I considered that fact. I even raised it to them, but they said simply that they had the money to help all the children, so they should." She paused a beat, as if considering whether to tell me the next thing. "They also refused to identify the target. They want us to save all the kids. Once we have, they'll come in and take the one they want."

"Do you believe they really care that much about all those children?"

She shook her head. "No," she said, her voice sharpening with anger, "but someone should, and that's just one more reason I agreed to do this." She stepped closer to me, cutting in half the space between us. I fought my reaction to stand and push her away and instead stayed where I was. "Look, I deal with only one person, a woman, and though she's pretty convincing, her story doesn't hold together as well as I'd like. We both know that the most efficient way to get that kid is to target only him. She knows it, too, but she won't do it. She's shown me the money, so I know she or the group she represents can afford this operation, and her intel has been topnotch so far. My theory—and it is only a theory, I haven't raised it with her and don't plan to—is that the kid they want is for some reason so valuable that they consider it less risky to pay us to save them all than to let us know which kid they want."

I thought about it. That would certainly protect the identity of a high-value target, and it would remove any easy temptation for blackmail, but having to acquire a base full of children was a lot more dangerous—to the children as well as to us—than going after a single one.

I got it.

I stared at her. "You think they would rather risk that child dying than us finding and keeping him."

She nodded, very slowly, her face tightening. "Yes— which is why we really can't trust them until we've secured all the kids and they've retrieved their target." She rolled her head a bit, working to dispel some of the tension that was tightening her neck and shoulders. "On the other hand, when could we ever trust the rear-echelon jerks who hired us?"

I smiled and shook my head. "Never." I stood and stretched. She held her position, the two of us now less than a meter apart, and watched me carefully.

"We're clearly going to do it," I said, "so what's the next step?"

"About time," Lobo said, his voice filling the air around us.

I'd expected Lim to relax; after all, she'd won. Instead, though, her face tightened further, as if she'd smelled something bad, and she held up her hand. "There's one more complication."

"That doesn't sound good."

"I don't like it," she said, "but I'm also not sure what to make of it; maybe it's bad, maybe it's not. My contact with their group was the one who suggested I involve you two. I would have thought of you if you'd been in the area, but I'd never have gone to the trouble of reaching out to so many planets for you. No offense."

"None taken," I said, but only to buy time. That a third party was suggesting me did not make me happy. I didn't want to be on anyone's first-call list; that kind of notoriety did not make my life easier. Lim was staring at me, so I continued. "Working with people you can reach easily and with no risk only makes good sense." On the other hand, as much as I didn't like having anyone notice me, I had no reason to be particularly surprised by it; I'd attracted more than my share of coalition attention the last few years. "So other than the work you had to do to find me, why is their recommendation of me a complication?"

"They won't proceed until they meet with you," Lim said.

Excellent, I thought but did not say. Getting more firsthand data about this mysterious group could only be good for me, though Lim might well see it as potentially undercutting her authority. "I already agreed to work for you," I said, knowing it would help appease Lim, "so they shouldn't make any such requirement."

"I know," she said, "but the woman did."

Lim backed up a step.

"In fact, she's waiting on the gate station for me to call her. She knew you wouldn't go into the structure itself, so she insists on coming aboard and talking to you."

"Fine," I said. "Call her."

Over the machine frequency, Lobo said, "I just scanned the station network for visitor IDs," Lobo said.

I shrugged as if to say, "So?"

Still private, Lobo said, "Jon, I'm pretty sure you're not going to like this."

CHAPTER 12

Just outside the jump gate station, planet Macken

AS LIM SPOKE into the display that Lobo opened in front of her, over the machine frequency he said, "Jon, Alissa's contact is Maggie, Maggie Park."

I rocked back into Lobo's interior hull as if someone had pushed me. I'd last seen Maggie a little over eighteen months ago on a street on the edge of Nickres, a city on a planet called Gash. She'd held me and kissed me and she'd walked away, holding the hand of a psychic boy I'd helped save from multiple government and private groups that had wanted to own him. She'd left, and I'd watched her disappear, and I still felt as if part of me had gone with her. Afterward, I'd spent almost a year living in the trees of a developing world and trying to come to peace with a life in which I'd never see her again.

Now, everything about Lim's operation made sense. Maggie was a member of the Children of Pinkelponker, a secret group of people descended from residents of my home world, people who all possessed special powers. Maggie could read minds; the boy, Manu Chang, received glimpses of the future; and others in the group, Maggie had said, had other abilities. Like those my sister, Jennie, had used to heal me. The group existed in secret. Its members lived normal lives and worked hard to avoid attention, because if anyone found out they existed, they'd spend the rest of their days either on the run or as lab rats. Like Benny and I had been in the Aggro prison station, where the scientists had conducted the experiments that led to me being the only surviving human-nanomachine hybrid. Those tests also started the chain of events that culminated in the destruction of Aggro, the quarantine and blockade around the apertures to Pinkelponker that persist to this day, and the universal ban on research into melding people and nanomachines. Of course, that ban hadn't stopped all the research in this area, as I'd learned six months ago, when I'd been tricked into helping retrieve a scientist conducting illegal experiments on children. Still, I remained, to the best of my knowledge, the only person whose cells teemed with nanomachines.

As Maggie had walked away from me, her head vanishing as the crowd on the streets enveloped her, I'd wanted with all my heart to run after her, to be with her, to be with other people tied to my home world. Instead, I'd stood still, knowing it was the right thing to do, the safe thing for all of them, even for me. I wouldn't ever again be somebody's experimental animal, and I wouldn't let anyone else suffer that way, either. People near me tended to get hurt; I wouldn't put Maggie and the others in her group at that risk.

The correctness of the decision had not, however, meant that I'd liked it, that watching her leave hadn't been harder to take than any of the wounds I've ever suffered. The nanomachines in my cells have been able to heal all of those injuries, but they could do nothing for this one.

And now she was here, mere meters away from me, only a short leap across the void of space in the station, and for the life of me I couldn't decide whether to burst through its walls to be with her or to head through the first available aperture and keep jumping until I was as many worlds away from here as Lobo could carry me.

"Jon," Lobo said privately, "Alissa is talking to you."

I blinked a few times and focused on her. "I'm sorry," I said. "I missed what you were saying."

She stepped closer and put her hand on my shoulder. "I understand," she said. "The thought of those poor children gets to me, too, if I think about it too much, but we *will* save them. We will."

I nodded, happy for her inadvertent rescue.

"My contact would like to come aboard," she said, "though she's also willing to meet in the station. Your choice."

"Bring her here," I said. Without thinking, I also said aloud, "Usual protocol, Lobo."

"Executing," he said out loud. Over the machine frequency, he added, "Only one person is waiting, and all the data I can get from the scan confirms that it's Maggie."

I was grateful that he didn't choose this moment to needle me about giving him instructions he already knew to follow. I looked down long enough to subvocalize, "Thanks. Act as if we've never met her until she shows otherwise." Either Maggie hadn't told Lim she already knew me, in which case she had a good reason for withholding that data, or she and Lim were gaming me, which I should be able to detect and expose soon enough.

"Will do," Lobo said privately.

"I'll warn you right now," Lim said, "that you can push her for details all you want, but she won't give you any. As I said, she'll show you the money, but that's it."

I forced myself to focus on the task at hand: responding as Lim would expect. "You've confirmed her information about Tumani, right?"

"Of course."

"You can think of no reason anyone would choose that location to spring a trap on you?"

"None."

"Then I have no reason to brace her for data she doesn't want to provide."

"Linked to the station," Lobo said aloud. "One human female ready to board." Privately, he added, "No other humans within twenty meters."

"Let her in," I said.

As I'd done with Lim, I stood beside the entry hatch, which opened as soon as I was in position.

Maggie walked onto Lobo and held up her arms.

The hatch closed. Lobo disengaged from the station.

I sagged against the wall to my left, glad for its support.

Maggie was as beautiful as ever, almost my height with a strong but shapely body and lush red hair that was half a meter longer than when I'd last seen her, now falling past the middle of her back.

"Jon Moore," Lim said, gesturing to me, "Maggie Chu. Maggie, Jon."

Maggie stuck out her hand and said, "Pleased to meet you, Mr. Moore. We've heard only good things about you—and, of course, about your abilities and your ship."

Lim was watching me. I was afraid to stare at Maggie, but I caught the slight wink she gave when she mentioned Lobo. I registered the new last name but didn't care; it was Maggie.

I shook her hand for as brief a time as I could manage, afraid that if I got too strong a grip on her I might never want to let it go. "My pleasure." I gestured to the front of Lobo. "Let's go up front and talk."

Lobo had put out another couch. I took the pilot's and swiveled so I could watch them both—and so I would be as far from temptation as I could manage.

Neither sat.

"You wanted to talk," I said, staring at Maggie, "so talk. If all you need is to know if I'll help, we can save some time: I will, as Lim almost certainly told you."

"Alissa did assure me you would," Maggie said, "but it's still good to hear confirmation directly from you. I'm not sure if she told you much about us."

Lim interrupted her. "I didn't, because you've told me almost nothing."

Maggie continued as if Lim hadn't spoken. "Mr. Moore—"

I interrupted her. "Jon."

She smiled and nodded, all business, no warmth in her expression. "Jon, I represent an organization of wealthy individuals who despise the thought of any group using children as soldiers. They've made it their special cause to stop such abuse wherever they hear of it. Sometimes, they can be effective with lobbying and similar conventional approaches to the problem. Other times," she paused and shrugged, "more direct and controversial tactics are necessary. When they are, I help facilitate a solution."

"It's a good cause," I said, "and I already told you I would help. Lim said you're paying, which is definitely a nice additional incentive."

"It's that very topic that I want to discuss with you," Maggie said.

Lim had been acting as if she were barely paying attention, but at this statement she snapped her head around to face Maggie. "Our deal is that I negotiate terms with each team member and all funding flows through my organization."

"And so it shall," Maggie said, "but due to the special equipment"—Maggie gestured with both hands to take in Lobo—"that Mr. Moore, Jon, is supplying, we'd prefer to work out compensation directly with him."

Lim's face clouded. I couldn't blame her. Maggie was undercutting her authority and in the process putting me in an awkward position with the woman who would be my commander on this mission.

"Lim's in charge," I said, "so I have no problem with her participating in our discussions."

Maggie stared at me, but whatever she was trying to tell me, I could not understand. She turned and put her hand on Lim's shoulder, and I knew what Lim could not: Maggie was now reading her thoughts.

After a few seconds, Maggie said to her, "You're right about compensation. I hadn't wanted to bring it up, but even though we suggested Jon, my principals would like me to vet him in private. It's not my choice, and I apologize for it, but I have to follow my orders. Perhaps if you'd like, after he and I speak alone long enough for me to do that, you could rejoin us and we could all discuss the payment terms. That way, I'd be indulging my principals but not violating our arrangement. Would that work for you?"

Lim clearly wasn't completely satisfied, but the compromise addressed enough of her concerns that she was no longer as angry as she had been. Being able to read someone's thoughts definitely would provide a huge edge in negotiations—though the fact that Maggie had to be touching a person to do so had to be a frustrating limitation. Watching Maggie use her ability naturally and without obvious thought, much as most of us might stare into another's eyes, made it even more clear to me how distressing it must be to her that I was the one person she could not read. Another gift of the changes Jennie had made to my brain, I supposed, and one I was very glad to have.

"Okay," Lim said. "Do we have to go back to the station again?"

"No," Lobo said aloud. "You could wait in the med room."

"Fine," Lim said. Staring at me, she added, "Come get me as soon as you're done."

"Will do," I said.

She paused a few beats, nodded, and headed out of the pilot's area.

Maggie and I stared at one another, saying nothing, until Lobo came over the speakers. "Lim is in the med room and can hear nothing." Privately, he added, "I assume I should not show her this conversation."

"Correct," I subvocalized.

Now that I was alone with Maggie, I wasn't sure

what to say to her, how to behave. Should I rush to her? Yell at her? Pretend the past had never happened?

We stared at each other some more. I stayed where I was. I knew there was a right thing to do, but I could not figure out what it was. My frustration at my own incompetence grew.

Finally, the words coming out harsher than I intended, I said, "You wanted me alone; now you have me. What do you want?"

CHAPTER 13

Just outside the jump gate station, planet Macken

DO YOU THINK I wanted to leave you?" Maggie said, ignoring the question I'd asked and answering the one I wouldn't raise. She shook her head, her own frustration obvious.

"I don't know," I said. I didn't. I didn't understand anything about her, not really, not about any part of her that mattered. When I realized that my body had stopped aging at what appeared to be my late twenties, I knew I could never stay in one place for too long. Anti-aging technology certainly helped—no people with money looked older than thirty unless they wanted to, at least until their eighties or so—but at a hundred and fifty-five years old I was so far off the norm that I couldn't let anyone discover my true age. I could never settle down with anyone without telling them, and I've never been able to muster that level of trust. It was easier to avoid intimate relationships entirely than to deal with the consequences. Maggie had made me rethink that decision hundreds of times, but in the end I knew I was right to let her go—and she was right to leave for her own reasons.

Her face clouded. She shook her head slowly. "Maybe you don't, Jon, but you should. You really should."

"Does it matter?" I said. Without meaning to move, I was standing right in front of her, almost touching her. "You did what you had to do. You'd do the same thing again if necessary."

She stepped back and looked away.

Now I understood.

"Like you're going to do as soon as this is over. Right?" When she didn't answer, I repeated the question, louder this time, "Right?"

When she faced me again, tears were running down her face and she was nodding. "Yes, because I have to. Because what I'm protecting is more important than either—or both—of us."

I clenched my fists and willed myself to stand still, not to move at all, but after a few seconds I couldn't take it and instead turned and walked the several steps away from her that the area permitted. "Isn't it always?" I said, more to myself than her.

I leaned against the wall. I heard her crying behind me, but I couldn't look back. We both knew where this was going, and all I was doing was making it worse.

I couldn't change her mind; I was even pretty sure I shouldn't.

I could, though, do one good and useful thing: I could make this easier on her.

I took a few deep breaths, unclenched my hands, and turned around.

"I'm sorry, Maggie," I said, "for being such a jerk.

You're only doing what you have to do to keep a whole group of people safe, and I in no way disagree with your choice. In your situation, I'd do exactly the same." I couldn't bring myself to tell her that I had, that I'd left others in the past, that I would probably do so in the future, that I could see no chance I could ever have a long-term relationship. Instead, I looked at her and wished that she could read my thoughts, that she could know that as much as I hadn't wanted her to leave, I understood her choice. Then, with all the sincerity and heart I could muster, I lied to her. "I'm sure it wasn't easy for you, and I'm sorry I didn't say that before." I wasn't sure. I'd never understood her feelings for me, but that didn't matter. What mattered was selling the story to her.

She chuckled and wiped the tears from her cheeks. "I've watched you lie to major government officials and religious heads. I've seen you con a great con man. I know you can sell any story to anyone. I guess I should be flattered that you can't lie to me about this topic. I'm just sad you don't understand, but you don't, and trying to explain it all to you will only lead to more pain for both of us. So at least hear once that it wasn't easy, that leaving you was one of the hardest things I've ever done. Okay?" Without waiting for my response, she straightened and said, "As for why I wanted to talk to you, it was because I knew you'd end up learning of my involvement, and I didn't want any of this to surprise you."

"You also didn't want me to say something I shouldn't," I said, glad to be back on terrain I understood.

"Or that," she nodded. "Not that I expected you would. I'm just being careful."

"As you should be."

"You were also correct," she said, "that I'll be leaving as soon as we have the child. I have to go; being even this involved is a big risk for us."

"So why take that chance?" I said. "You're going to a great deal of trouble, not to mention an enormous expense, for a single child."

"I like to think that we'd do the same for any descendant of Pinkelponker, and I'm glad that in the process we can help all these other kids, because what the Tumani rebels are doing to them is horrible."

"But."

"But this is a very special child indeed, a child who doesn't yet know how special he will be. We have to rescue him before his powers manifest themselves."

"So if they haven't shown up yet, how did you find him?" I said.

She smiled and shook her head. "You know I can't answer that. We did, and now we have to rescue him."

"Are you going to tell me which child it is, so I can protect him?"

"No, but not for any of the reasons Alissa is probably guessing. I wish we could, but we don't know who he is. We know he's among the children the Tumani rebels recruited as soldiers, and we're pretty sure he's alive, but until I and a colleague walk among the kids, we won't know which one he is."

"Assuming he's in the complex and we succeed."

"Assuming all that."

All this risk, all this expense, a covert attack on

a base on a planet no one cares about, and all they wanted to do was save one kid.

Of course, if I had the resources and the opportunity, I'd do the same for Jennie.

"Just how rich is your group?" I said. "The economics here don't add up, and whenever the money doesn't make sense, my experience is that something else will prove to be false as well."

"Rich enough that everything this mission might possibly cost wouldn't deserve a mention in a weekly analysis of our assets." She pointed to her head as she continued. "Think about it, Jon. You've met Manu. You've seen him predict a future event correctly. He's just a boy; others with the same ability are much more powerful and accurate. Knowledge plus time yields money. Some large entities have more assets than we do, but ours are very considerable indeed."

I thought about it for a few seconds, and as I did, I grew angry. "So even though you could save all of these children for a cost you wouldn't notice, if one of your special few hadn't been among them, you would have left them to their fate."

She didn't look away this time. "Yes," she said, "to my great embarrassment, we would have done just that. As would you. As would most people. Without an incentive, how many of us would jump into a fight that was not directly ours? How many of us devote even a fraction of our assets to helping others? Plus, we have to maintain a very low profile, because if any government or megacorp knew we existed, well…" She shrugged.

I understood. They would hunt down every child of Pinkelponker and use them and study them in the hopes they could replicate the abilities. I'd never go back to being an experimental animal; they were right to do everything in their power to avoid being discovered.

I also had to accept her other statements. I hated them, but she was correct, and I had no room to criticize. I've helped a lot of people, but rarely by altruistic choice; I've been dragged into some battles and paid to fight others.

One more practical matter was bothering me. "How did you find me?"

"Alissa found you."

"By implementing a strategy you gave her."

Maggie nodded. "True," she said. "We already knew where you were, but we couldn't tell her without drawing more attention to our relationship with you than we were comfortable doing. So, we created the messages and made sure one ended up where you were."

"You didn't answer my question: How did you find me?"

She stared at me but said nothing.

I finally understood. "You didn't have to find me," I said, "because you track me. Right?"

"The very question I wanted to ask," Lobo said privately. "I find it most disturbing that anyone can follow us without me being aware of it."

"We do," Maggie said, "because of your past involvement with us. As we do Jack Gridiz and others who have come close to knowing about any of us. It's only prudent."

"How?"

Maggie smiled but said nothing.

"Fine," I said. "I hadn't really expected an answer."

Like Lobo, I found this troubling, but Maggie wasn't going to tell me anything more.

"Lim is pacing furiously," Lobo said. "I suggest you wrap this up."

"At the risk of sounding angry, which I'm not," I said, "we need to finish this conversation and bring back Lim. She can't be happy that we're meeting without her, and I don't want to undercut her authority on this mission. Is there anything else we need to cover privately?"

I hated asking, because even though I knew more talking would do no good, there was still so much I wanted to discuss with Maggie—but we couldn't keep Lim in storage any longer.

"Just this," Maggie said, her tone all business now, "Lim may not appreciate the extent of our resources or what we—what I—am willing to do to help your team if you say it's necessary. So, I'd like to ask you to keep an eye on the situation, and if you spot something else we should be doing, some area where we could be helping, let me know."

"You understand what such a request could do to my relationship with Lim?" I said. "She's in charge, and she won't feel she can command well if she thinks she has to watch her back constantly."

Maggie waved her hands. "I'm not trying to undercut her. At the same time, *you* are the person I know, the person I trust."

"So why approach Lim?"

"Because we needed a large team, and she could recruit one more easily than you. And because of what I read in her: She cares about these kids. She will do her very best for them."

"Yes, yes she will." I thought about how I would run this mission and manipulate the odds if I were in Maggie's shoes, and about the way she had completely fooled me in the past. "And by using Lim as the lead on this mission, you end up with two data sources on the inside."

Maggie shrugged.

Protecting any of the children of Pinkelponker always came first with her. I'd do well to remember that fact.

"Anything else?" I said.

"That's it."

I stared at her for a few seconds longer, but there was nothing I could say in a short time, maybe nothing I could ever say, that would change anything.

"Release Lim," I said aloud to Lobo.

To Maggie, I added, "Brace yourself."

CHAPTER 14

Just outside the jump gate station, planet Macken

THE SOUND OF Lim's steps preceded her into the forward chamber.

I leaned against the wall as far from Maggie as I could get.

Maggie stayed where she was and turned to greet Lim. "Thank you, Alissa," she said, smiling as Lim entered the area, "for allowing me to respect the wishes of my principals. I'm sorry it took me so long; they had instructed me to review quite a few questions with Jon."

Lim stared first at Maggie and then at me; she was clearly annoyed but fighting to maintain her self-control. She'd grown a lot since we'd last worked together; at that time, she'd had trouble staying calm in almost any meeting. "No apology necessary," she finally said. "It is, after all, your money and, therefore, ultimately your mission."

"But it is under your command," Maggie said, "and I apologize again for doing anything without your direct involvement. If it'd been up to me, well," she shrugged, "but it wasn't, and I had to follow my orders."

Maggie played her perfectly, because Lim relaxed visibly as she said, "Is there anything else I need to know?"

"I debriefed Jon on his capabilities and that of his ship," Maggie said, "and I satisfied myself that he understands and appreciates the importance of this mission. That's about it."

"And compensation?" Lim said.

"We didn't discuss it," Maggie said. "I trust you and he will sort out that topic without my involvement."

Lim nodded, satisfied. "Of course. Should we take you back?"

"Yes, please," Maggie said. "Will you be coming with me? I believe you and I have a few more details to review."

"After a few minutes," Lim said, "if you don't mind waiting."

"Not at all," Maggie said, "not at all."

When we'd dropped Maggie and were once again floating in space just off the gate station, Lim looked into my eyes and said, "Is there anything you'd like to add to her description of your conversation?"

"Only that I told her that meeting without you was a bad idea because you might feel she was trying to undercut your authority. I also said that if I were in command, I wouldn't want to feel like I had to watch my back all the time."

"What did she say to that?"

"She said that she had no intent to do any such thing and that you were in charge."

"And you agree?"

I hit the wall beside me. "Yes!" I said. "As I just told you. I didn't ask to meet with her; you two decided I should. I didn't do any of this. You approached me, you told me to talk with her, and now you're bracing me like I'm some fresh noncom out to steal your squad. I'm not—as I'd hope you know. As I also hope you'd know, if I want something from you, I'll ask directly."

She held up her hands. "Fair enough. I'm sorry. I didn't want it to go down the way it did, but she insisted."

I took a deep, slow breath, and said, "So what's next?"

"Tomorrow morning, we meet on Macken with the other senior leaders, review the mission plan, and head to Tumani."

"Will I know anyone?"

Lim smiled. "Gustafson and Schmidt. We worked with them the last time you were in this system."

Gustafson had been a Saw Master Gunnery Sergeant and a man I'd liked instantly. Only near the end of my time on Macken had I learned that Schmidt, a Saw Sergeant, was involved with him. "Are those two still together?" Before she could answer, I added, "And have they quit the Saw?"

"Yeah," Lim said, "they're a couple. Schmidt hasn't left him since he finally figured out that she was interested in him. I don't think she'll ever let him go. They're both still with the Saw, though; they're doing this on an extended leave. Of the two, Schmidt is the one we need more."

"Why?"

"Because she's a reintegration specialist."

I snorted. "In my experience, reintegration consists of your final paycheck and, if you're lucky, a useless exit interview with some psych flunky who drew the short duty straw."

Lim nodded. "Mine's the same as yours, but we can do a lot better with these kids."

"And since when," I said, "has Schmidt worked in reintegration? The last time I saw her, she was just another noncom."

"She cares deeply about the issue, and she's had a fair amount of training."

"Training?" I laughed. "You and I have both taken field med classes. Neither of us would want the other one to operate on anybody."

Lim's face tightened. "What do you want me to say? Schmidt's the best of us at reintegration, so she'll run that part of the show. Is that going to be a problem for you?" After a few seconds, she added, "None of this should matter to you anyway; you'll be leaving as soon as we capture the complex."

"You're right, of course," I said, "and it won't be an issue."

"Good, because that's not the problem in front of us now."

"No, it's not. What about the old man?" Colonel Tristan Earl had been the head of the Saw in this sector. He was one of the few officers I've ever completely respected—and also a former lover of Lim's.

"I'm afraid not. He's on a year-long assignment at FC HQ, and he couldn't get the leave. Anything else that can't wait until morning?"

"No," I said.

"Then put me back on the station," Lim said. She was so bursting with energy that she couldn't stand still. "We need to finish mission prep so we can finally get to work."

CHAPTER 15

Dump Island, planet Pinkelponker—139 years earlier

RUN!" BENNY'S VOICE rang clear and loud from his perch on a ledge a few meters above the beach where the five of us stood at attention.

I looked at the two on either side of me and started to go.

"Stop!" Benny screamed. "Fall in."

I joined the others standing with our feet just behind the line Bob had drawn in the sand with his big toe. I stood up straight, the way Benny had told me to. Even though it was early morning, the sand was already warm. I liked it here, though, liked the sound of the ocean and being on the beach, liked the moments when I could forget where I was and enjoy the water and the sand as if I were home again on Pinecone.

"You hesitated," Benny said, his voice loud and seemingly all around us.

I glanced upward for only a second, but he noticed.

"Eyes front!"

I stared straight ahead. I didn't like the way he was yelling at me, but I obeyed him because I'd said I would.

"You hesitated," he said again, "and that hesitation could kill you. Worse, it could destroy any chance of escaping from here. When the ranking person gives a command, you follow it—immediately, without question. Do you understand?"

"Sir, yes, sir!" said Alex, the guy to my right, a small, squat boy who couldn't have been more than twelve and who had only one full-size arm, his left.

"I can't hear you!" Benny said, louder than Alex had been.

"Sir, yes, sir!" the others replied, loudly and in unison.

I couldn't stand it any longer. I stepped over the line, walked closer to the rock wall, and stared up at Benny. "I don't like this!" I said. "I don't see why you have to yell at us, and I don't know why we're bothering to learn this stuff. How is it ever going to help me get back Jennie?" At the thought of her, my eyes clouded with tears.

Another realization hit me. "What do you know about being a soldier anyway?"

Out of the corner of my eye I watched as Bob walked in front of me, as if he was going to use his stick of a body and his twig arms to push me back into line. Benny shook his head slightly, and Bob returned to where he'd been. As if Bob could move me. I could throw him with one hand. I was more than ready to do it, except I knew that the impact might hurt him.

"One time," Benny said, "one time I'll explain myself,

and after that, either you follow orders or you leave and fend for yourself. Understand?"

"No! Who put you in charge?"

"You did, just like the rest of them did, when you signed up to learn to fight. Every one of us with enough body mass and strength to be able to do any good against the government soldiers has agreed to learn."

I glanced at the others. This small group contained all our best people. The rest had problems that made them liabilities in a fight. Everyone else nodded slightly in agreement with Benny.

"You asked what I knew about this training," he continued. "It's obvious I haven't been through it myself; just look at me." He waited until I did, as if I needed a reminder of what he was or how he had to live. "Remember when I said the soldiers come and take away those with abilities?"

I nodded.

"Well," Benny said, "that happens only when they know about those abilities. Not everyone tells them. I haven't."

Bob stared at him as if he was doing something wrong, but Benny kept talking.

"A few months ago, I realized I could read people."

"Read them?" I said.

"Their thoughts," he said. "No, that's not really right. Their memories. They appear in my mind like long stretches of video, but with feelings attached."

"Video?"

Benny shook his head. "I keep forgetting where you grew up. Pinecone is a backwater, a place they keep farmers. What you can find on some of the other islands would amaze you."

I considered what he'd said. "That ability would be valuable, like the way Jennie can heal people." I continued to be surprised at the connections I could make. I wondered if I'd ever get used to it. "Why don't you tell the soldiers what you can do? They'd take you off Dump. You don't need us."

"So I can be their pet freak?" he said. His throat strained with the effort of controlling his anger. "So they can use me when they need me and the rest of the time put me back in some cage? No! I won't do that. I deserve to live my own life, the way I want to live, not as some special weapon under their control."

The others behind me murmured in agreement. His passion was infectious; we all felt it.

"I can read most people," he said, "as long as I'm within a few meters of them. The last few times a ship has come here, I've done my best to be nearby, like I was today when they dropped you. At this point, I've read a dozen different soldiers who've come here. I'm not good enough to pick up everything from any of them, and I can't remember everything I've read, but I've held onto their training memories. They went through a process something like what we're doing. If you want to beat them, you have to train, too."

I stared at him and for several seconds couldn't decide what to do. That information sounded useful, but when I ignored his flippers, his cart, and the fact that he was above us, yelling orders, and instead focused only on his face, all I saw was another boy, like me, maybe even younger.

"What gives you the right to give us orders?" I said. "It's not like you're a parent or even a grown-up. How old are you anyway?"

He stared right back at me. "Fifteen," he said, "but in most biological respects much younger. Like you. The things that are wrong with us have slowed many aspects of our development. Your body grew large; my mind basically did the same." He shook his head and rolled to the edge of the overhang. "None of that matters, though. We're on Dump. Our one way off this island is through a group of trained soldiers. I'm the only one with any idea at all about how to prepare you guys to fight them. So just one thing matters: Are you with us or not?"

He was right. As much as I hated even the little bit of training we'd done so far, I knew he was right. Something nagged at me. "If you can read people's memories, why did you ask me so many questions?"

"I told you," he said, "I can't read everyone. I thought I could, but I can't read you, so there are probably also others I can't read." He waved his arm, the odd flipper still distracting me as it moved. "Look, do you want to train to fight these men, or not? If you do, we need to get to work. If you don't, leave."

I didn't have to look at the others to know I was their best hope for success. I had the only large and complete body here. I also knew that unless they were all lying to me, my only way out of here was to help them beat the soldiers.

Another connection appeared in my head. I didn't even have to think hard; it just happened. Jennie was really good.

"And if we beat the soldiers—"

"*When* we beat them," he said. "We must believe we will do it."

"When we beat them," I said, "you can fly their ship because—"

He interrupted me. "Because I've read those memories, too. Yes. I'll need someone else, someone with good hands, to do the actual flying, but I can tell them how." He paused and stared at each of us in turn. "So we can escape from Dump. When we win, we'll be free."

I studied his face. He didn't look away. If he was lying, he was doing it well. I definitely wanted to get off Dump; I sure couldn't save Jennie as long as I was stuck here. His plan might not work, but I didn't have a better option. "Okay," I said, "I'm with you."

"Then fall in."

I joined the others and stood up straight, eyes focused forward.

"On my mark, sprint as fast as you can to the tree at the beach's curve and back to this line."

"Sir, yes, sir!" we all yelled.

"I can't hear you!" he said.

"Sir, yes, sir!" we yelled again, and this time the sound was loud enough that I didn't like it.

"Better," he said. "Now, run!"

We ran.

When we were all panting and walking more than running, Benny let us stop and rest. He didn't give us long, though. About as soon as I could breathe normally, he had us lie flat on our backs on the ground and lift our trembling legs until they were a hand's-width off the sand, and then hold them there. First, we kept our feet together, and then we separated them, held them up, and after a bit returned to the first position. Finally, he let us rest them on the ground—but only for a few seconds. Then, we started all over again.

After a while, Benny told Bob to stop exercising and instead check us. Bob walked among us, making sure we were doing it right, sometimes lifting our feet with one of his, other times stepping on our stomachs as Benny reminded us to tighten those muscles.

"To win," he yelled, "we must surprise them, and you must be both fast and strong. Strength comes from the middle. Do another one!"

We no longer had to respond to his orders; we had only to follow them.

As if we were one large person, all at the same time we lifted our legs and held them above the sand. My thighs shook and my stomach hurt and I had to squint my eyes against the bright sunlight that was heating the day. I wasn't sure I could keep it up.

"Legs apart!" Benny said.

Bob came and stood on my stomach. He smiled at me, as if he were having fun.

I wanted to jump up and punch him in the face so hard it would cave in. I wanted to break him, to tear him in half.

He shook his head slightly as he stepped off me and walked over to Alex. He was playing with me.

In that moment, I hated him and I hated Benny and I hated the soldiers and I would do anything before I'd let any of them beat me.

I gritted my teeth and continued to hold my legs above the ground. The pain filled my legs and ran up into my torso, but I didn't care. I would not let them beat me, not any of them.

They would not beat me.

CHAPTER 16

Beach house, outside Glen's Garden, planet Macken

LIM SWORE IT was coincidence that she'd chosen as
her planning center the same house I'd rented over
three years ago. I've never liked coincidences, but I let
it go; at least I knew the area. I drifted to the front
activeglass window and told it to stop filtering and
instead to let in all the light, so I could enjoy the natural
beauty of the ocean crashing onto the beach only a few
dozen meters in front of us. When I'd last been here,
the house had stood alone on this stretch of sand near
the edge of the rainforest; now it had neighbors on
both sides and behind it. In all the beautiful places we
humans touch, we move rapidly from appreciation to
commercialization and then to devastation, ruining the
best parts of nature as relentlessly as any plague. I wasn't
sure I'd want to see this place in another three years.

At the large table behind me, Lim, Gustafson, and
Schmidt studied the layout of the complex, adding new
data to the model and preparing for our review. I'd
arrived earlier than they'd expected, so after greeting

them. I was passing time while they finished their preparations.

If Gustafson had changed since our last meeting, I couldn't spot it. Dark hair cropped short, taller than Lim but a little shorter than I am, his body thick with corded muscle and almost no fat—he looked every bit the professional soldier he was. Even the fine scar lines on his neck and hands were still there. I'd once asked him why he left them when any half-decent surgery could remove them. He'd smiled and said he liked having the reminders of his own stupidity.

Schmidt was leaner than when I'd last seen her, with very little fat and much shorter hair. Like Lim, she'd cut weight in preparation for the physical strains of combat, but her darker skin, the color of a rich deep chocolate, highlighted her muscles more than Lim's and made her look even more ripped. I was silently grateful for the nanomachines that let me eat anything I wanted and still walk around with under five percent body fat.

"All clear outside," Lobo said privately over the comm. I trusted Lim, but I didn't have much use for the local FC presence, so I'd dressed for trouble: armored pants and long-sleeved shirt, visible gun in a holster, another one in the small of my back, a third on my right ankle, a comm link, and contacts with overlays showing near and far exterior views. Lobo hovered overhead in case I had to exit quickly.

I tuned into the local appliance network. Some combination of the changes Jennie had made to me and the nanomachine infusion the Aggro scientists had performed gave me the ability to talk with machines on their standard frequencies. Though almost always

dull, appliances have so much surplus computing power
that they can do their jobs with only a fraction of their
intelligence. With the rest, they talk—and talk and talk
and talk. They especially love to yak about their work,
and sometimes you can learn a great deal from them.
I'd garnered little from the washers, which are usually
great sources of gossip, other than the facts that the
house had sat empty for a month this winter before Lim
had rented it and that she had yet to wash any of her
clothing. I was concerned about being monitored, so I
focused on the household security cluster.

"Will these people ever do anything interesting?" said
what I had to assume was the main control system.

"I'm ready if they do," a camera said, "with perfect
focus on the fronts of the three at the table."

"That's all fine and good," another camera said, "if
they keep facing you, but I'm the one with the best
chance of being necessary, because I'm following the
male by the window. He has one gun visible and probably two more his colleagues can't see, assuming my
contour-analysis software is correct—as it usually is."

"You say the word, and I'll gas them!" the house
defense system said. "If they even think about breaking a window like those last renters, I will put them
to sleep. I swear I will!"

"No," the main house comm said, "you know you're
not allowed to do that. The owner's instructions were
very clear: I'm to call the police."

"I bet you're relaying everything to archival storage,
aren't you?" I said over their frequency. "Just in case
you need it one day. Smart."

"Excuse me!" I couldn't tell which machine was
talking.

"How can you talk to us?" the defense system said.

"I'm sorry," I said. "I should have remembered what planet I was on. Machines on more developed worlds—newer models, probably—are so much more cosmopolitan about communication. I should not have assumed—"

"Newer?" said the main control system. "Sure, some of these support units are a little out of date, but I'm the most recent model of my type that Xychek makes, and I assure you my updates are current. We're simply not accustomed to visitors with your particular skills."

"Again, I apologize. I was only curious about how much of this information you were relaying to the owner's archives. I am, after all, here in a confidential capacity."

"And you can rest assured that we respect your position!" the main system said. "Discretion is our watchword, so we hard-wipe everything as soon as the post-rental escrow period is over. Until then, the local copies live in a quantum-encrypted state accessible only to the primary renter."

"Which means, of course, that my best work never gets the audience it deserves," the first camera said. "If only others could see the perfection of my recordings."

"Perfection?" the second camera said. "You call those tedious hours perfect? The light where you're shooting is illumination of perfect constancy, and yet your work is pedestrian at best. I, on the other hand, have to adjust to the way this annoying twit—no offense intended, sir—keeps changing his position, all the while delivering a level of image quality you can only dream about."

I tuned out. Once appliances start quarreling, they can keep it up for hours.

The still, quiet interior of the house, with the only noise the soft murmurs behind me, contrasted sharply with the increasingly wild ocean and sky. A storm was advancing quickly toward us, the heavens darkening with clouds and the waves gaining strength and size as I watched.

"We've merged all the data, Jon," Lim said. "Ready?"

I nodded and walked over to the table.

A holo of a wood-walled rectangular compound appeared in front of us. A large perimeter of bare earth surrounded it. Inside the walls stood over two dozen buildings of the same dark wood. A camo curtain floated in the air over the whole thing, support rods rising here and there from the ground.

"This place looks huge," I said.

"It does indeed, Gunny," Schmidt said, using my old Saw rank—and her current one. She pointed at the dirt outer area. "The cleared zone is twenty meters wide at its narrowest points, much wider at others. The dozen or so almost identical rectangular buildings house the kids, not quite fifty of them to a barrack."

I waved my hand through the cover. "Is that thing really good enough to stop satellite scans?"

"Yes and no," Gustafson said. "It's activecamo material with IR interference, so the sats can get some shape data but not anything near a full read. It stays up only during the cease-fires; the rebels take it down and use it elsewhere as soon they redeploy the boys. All of this, of course, is per our sources on the ground."

"You trust them?" I said.

"Chu's people gather intel and relay it to us," Lim said. "They claim to be using only reliable agents and verifying all we see before we see it. Everything we've received from them so far has been good, but it's now also out of date. Chu said their sources dried up."

"Died, more likely," Gustafson said.

"I hope it wasn't a kid, Top," I said, "but from those holos, I have to assume it was. You saw them?"

"Of course," he said.

We all fell silent, each lost in our thoughts about those recordings.

"We can expect about two dozen adults," Lim said, bringing us back to the point, "and, of course, about five hundred of the kids."

"Why so few guards?" I said.

"To the rebels, these boys are no longer prisoners," Schmidt said. "They're fellow soldiers. The adults are there just to help them get out quickly should the lazy-ass inspectors actually decide to do their jobs."

"And the likelihood of that is?" I said.

"Zero," Schmidt said.

"Which is why we're here," Lim said. "Let's talk about approach options." She zoomed out the holo to give us an aerial view of the compound. It vanished under the camo covering, but a small green glow outlined it for us. It really did sit in the middle of nowhere, nothing but jungle for many klicks in all directions.

"What options?" Gustafson said. "We jump in, or we'll be on rebel turf during active combat. Sixty of us should be able to crush two dozen rebels, but if either coalition notices, or if, Heaven help us, the rebels spot us and tell the boys to fight us, we're in for a whole lot of pain."

"There is another way," Lim said. "Jon could fly in fast with a small team and gas the whole place. We could follow at our leisure. The government doesn't have any ships capable of doing that; in fact, they don't have any significant aerial assault force." She shook her head. "Visiting Tumani is like going back in time. Way back."

"I don't like it," I said.

"Why?" Lim said.

"Two reasons," I said. "First, my ship can carry maybe twelve people and their supplies. You said sixty of us to handle about five hundred boys, which is nearly a nine to one ratio of them to us; that's already pushing it. Taking in a small team is just too risky if that group has to hold the boys for any time at all."

"Double that many in me if we cram," Lobo said over the comm.

I ignored him and continued. "Second, we risk EC and FC anger and lose our only surprise advantage— my ship—if we use it as a weapon. If they spot that action on any sat recordings—and you can bet the rebels will complain to the coalitions and ask for a review—they'll find us guilty of importing and using a banned weapon. On the other hand, if we jump in, all we need are ships whose doors will open while they're aloft. Mine can pass as just one more tourist craft we repurposed."

Gustafson nodded. "We could go for handheld gassing from your ship—"

"—but coverage wouldn't be as good with what we can legitimately bring in," Schmidt finished his sentence.

"And I really do hate giving up the one surprise available to us," I said. "Once we reveal my ship is a PCAV, we run the risk of being deported—or worse—for bringing it to Tumani. So, we need to hide that fact if we possibly can. We shouldn't ever need to use it for combat, but I'll feel a lot better knowing we have the option, should push come to hard shove."

"Amen to that, Gunny," Gustafson said.

I pointed at the trees around the cleared area in the holo. "The one flaw in my plan is that we really do not want to have sixty people jumping into trees. Even if all the people making the leap are very, very good, the odds are that at least a few of them will get badly hurt."

"The canopy is thick enough," Gustafson said, "that we might be able to land safely on it." His voice trailed off. "Might. I know at least a few folks who claim to have done it safely and without wearing heavy penetration-resistant body armor."

"But it's not a good bet," Schmidt said.

"No," Gustafson and I said at the same time.

"So are we back to gassing from your ship?" Lim said.

I shook my head. "No. The argument for not doing it remains." I stared at the complex and the forest around it. "How far back can you pull this holo?"

Lim scrunched the complex to a quarter of the size it had been; the forest surrounding it grew considerably.

I walked around the holo and studied the landscape. About five klicks northeast of the complex was a small cleared area. A similar one stood about four klicks to the west. I pointed at them. "Do we have enough data on these to get a better view?"

Lim nodded and shoved the holo to the side until the northeast clearing was roughly in the center, and then she expanded it again. The surveillance footage was good: We could clearly see a dirt central area surrounded by a dozen huts.

"Perfect," I said. "We can safely land in a small village and make our way overland to the complex. It'll be a haul, but if your teams aren't good at moving well in a jungle, you've got the wrong people."

"They're good," Lim said. "As long as we allow reasonable time, covering that distance shouldn't be an issue. We'll have to proceed with some caution, but rebel troops aren't supposed to be anywhere nearby."

"If they are," Schmidt said and shrugged, "we deal with them."

We all nodded.

I stared more closely at the village and magnified it again. The huts were shells, with big pieces of roofs missing. No humans were in sight. "How recent is this data?"

"Less than a week old," Lim said.

"Good," I said. "This one's deserted, so we shouldn't have to fight any villagers." I centered the holo on the western village and magnified it. Those huts were also wrecks. "Do the rebels destroy every place they hit?"

Lim nodded. "Not immediately, but when they're done with it, yes. They kill the adult residents, impress the boys, set up a temporary base, eat any stored food, regroup, and repeat. They work with even worse equipment than the government, so they fight in classic guerilla style, never staying anywhere too long, hitting and running—you know the drill."

"I do," I said, "and here the mess is good for us. Two units land in each of these locations. Each heads for its assigned corner of the complex. We sync up, and then we hit it."

"That should work," Lim said, "but it still leaves us the job of gassing the place by hand."

"Yeah," I said, "but with sixty people, a coordinated attack should give us enough coverage to take out everyone quickly. We should be able to swarm in and lock up the guards before any of them wakes up."

"And if some of them are prepared for gas?" Schmidt said.

"We shoot our way in," Gustafson said.

"And a whole lot more people get hurt," Schmidt said, "including possibly some of the children."

"Yes," Gustafson said, "including them. We've known about that risk since we signed on. All we can do is minimize it and hope for the best."

"I'd hate to have to shoot a child," Schmidt said.

"So would I," Lim said.

"We all would," Gustafson said, "but if you're not willing to do it and the plan goes sideways, you can bet your ass they'll shoot you. Don't even start if you're not willing to finish."

Schmidt rolled her head and said, "I didn't say that. I just wouldn't like it. I'll do what it takes. Always have."

Gustafson's hand moved a centimeter toward her. "I know, Portia," was all he said.

"We all will," Lim said.

Silence enveloped the room. Before my thoughts could take me anywhere bad, I said, "So can you bring in the jump and gas gear?"

"Not exactly," Lim said, "but close enough. Chu's people are going to buy what we need locally, using as many different vendors as they can manage. We've researched the options a fair amount, and it looks like we can get by with commercial jump gear and animal trank gas—all of it legal there for sport and hunting."

"What quality level can we expect?" I said.

Lim laughed. "We'll make sure that everything we acquire is in good working order, but we are talking sport equipment, not milspec ordnance. We can get target-competition chute harnesses, for example, but we can't buy any milspec individual powered gliders. As long as you don't expect us to look like a military unit, you should be happy."

"What about weapons for each of us?" I said.

"Anything we can carry has to be legal for sport use," Lim said. "Once we've secured the base, the government troops will resupply us."

"And you trust them?" I said.

Lim shook her head. "Of course not. Chu's people are also bringing in additional weapons now, as they have been for the past couple of months. We'll use them if need be."

"My ship can ferry at least our gear," I said, "if it comes to that."

"I was counting on it," Lim said, "and I'm certainly planning on bringing as much of my own kit as I can get away with."

I pointed at the cleared area in the holo. "How are we crossing this?"

"As far as we know, the rebels razed this zone simply to provide an easy killing field," Lim said, "but—"

"I sure wouldn't want to count on it being safe," I said.

"We won't," Lim said, "but we have to decide how best to clear our approach vectors. Cleaning mines and checking for more primitive traps could take a lot of very valuable time."

We all stared at the holo for a few seconds.

"We don't have to be quiet, right?" I said.

"Correct," Lim said. "The rebels should all be out from the gas. If not, we'll have to fight the ones who are awake. Either way, there'll be no need for subtlety."

"So let's not be quiet," I said. I pointed at some of the trees on the edge of the cleared area. "Let's remotely trigger anything waiting for us. All we need are a lot of quick-cut logging tools, stuff Chu's people should be able to get us on Tumani. We drop some trees, let their weight set off all the underground explosives, and follow them in."

"We might damage the complex," Schmidt said, "and risk hurting the kids." She craned her neck a bit to look inside the holo from the top. "Then again, it looks like all the dorms are set at least ten meters inside the wall, so we have a buffer zone."

"We should also be able to control pretty well the amount we drop," Gustafson said, "at least as long as we train everyone on the basics."

"We can do that," Lim said.

"Works for me," I said.

Schmidt and Gustafson nodded their agreement as well.

"Done," Lim said. "I'll make the arrangements." She stared briefly at each of us in turn. "Any other big issues before we move to team composition?"

"Just one," I said. "Once we have the children, then what?"

"Not your problem," Lim said. "Chu will pay you, and you'll be free to go."

I gripped the edge of the table tightly so I wouldn't give in to my urge to push her far enough away that I couldn't easily hit her. She was right, of course; all I'd agreed to do was help secure the complex. Something in her answer, though, infuriated me.

"It may not be my problem," I said, the words coming tight and clipped as I fought to sound calm, "but I'd still like to know."

"Once we have the kids," Schmidt said, "we settle in and try to help them. Many of our team members have reintegration training, and we'll have more specialists waiting on Tumani to join us. We'll work with the kids until they're in good enough shape that the government can return them to their families or find them new homes."

"How many of them still have families?" I said, aware my voice was louder than it should be but unable to quiet myself. "And how many of those remaining families want to take back a killer who was only a short while ago trying to slaughter soldiers of the government they're supporting? How many of them will want these kids to come home? It's not like they're the children they used to know."

All three of them stared at me. No one moved. Each of them looked away for several seconds, knowing as I did that the violence you've seen, and worse, the violence you've done, stains you and breaks you in ways that no one can see but that are always there, just below the surface. No one without the same breaks ever really understands, but these three did.

Finally, Schmidt spoke, her voice flat. "Most of their families are dead. Few of those who are alive will understand what they'd be signing up to handle, but helping the boys learn to live in normal society so they can return to normal lives is all we can do." She glared at me, and when she spoke again, her voice was high and fast. "You think we don't understand? You think I spend my leaves gossiping with friends who've never served? You think I don't realize how different from us all the civilians are?" She shook her head. "We'll do all we can. That's all anyone can do."

"Of course," I said. "I apologize for my outburst."

"No need, Gunny," Gustafson said. He clapped me on the shoulder. "If you'd been at any of the earlier meetings, you'd know you weren't alone."

Lim nodded once without looking at me and motioned at the table. The holo shrank into a far corner. Images of all of our troops floated in front of us, service records and other stats—but not names—hovering beside each of them. "Let's settle the squads," she said. She faced me. "We're running somewhat covert, so that if anything goes wrong, we leave behind as little data as possible about each of us. Some of the people don't care who knows they were involved, but others are hoping no one finds out how they spent their time off."

"Fair enough," I said.

"You lead Black Team," Lim said. "I'm Blue, Top is Green, and Gunny is Red. Everyone else stays a number, unless they feel like giving their names. Even if some do, though, we use numbers until we've occupied the complex and locked up the adult rebels."

We all nodded agreement.

"Let's sort out the teams," she said, "and go over the timing details one more time."

"A third of the unit is already on Tumani," Lim said after we'd finished the team assignments. "They're securing us lodging—rental houses, not hotels—and setting up comm protocols with Chu's people. Chu is on her way there now, as is the second third of our group. The rest of us head out tomorrow morning. By going in these three waves, we shouldn't attract any attention; even a pit like Tumani has some business and tourist trade."

"Tonight?" I said.

"You're free," Lim said. "You'll take Gustafson and Schmidt tomorrow; they're posing as businesspeople who hired you for personal transportation and protection. We expect the station staff to check anyone arriving on his own ship, but given your background, that cover should work fine. Anything else?" She looked at each of us in turn.

No one spoke.

"Okay," she said. "Enjoy your last free night until this is over."

CHAPTER 17

Glen's Garden, planet Macken

GUSTAFSON AND SCHMIDT retreated together, and though they invited me to join them for dinner, it was clear they'd prefer to be two, not three. Lim didn't even make a pretense of socializing; she left quickly and without comment.

My body bristled with pre-mission energy, so I wasn't ready to go back inside Lobo. Instead, I caught a shuttle into Glen's Garden and had the machine take me to the opposite edge of town, to the small commemorative square where I'd first met Lobo.

Or so I'd intended. Instead, I wound up on a new road that formed the boundary between a housing community and the rainforest. The original downtown was nowhere in sight. I told the shuttle I'd pay it to idle while I got my bearings. It offered to help, but for my purpose a different data source was far better.

"How far from where we met am I?" I said to Lobo over the comm.

"Point-to-point, ignoring roads, fifteen point seven

kilometers," he said. The coordinates appeared on my contact overlay.

"They've consumed that much of the rainforest in only three and a half years?"

"Clearly they have," he said. "You've noted before the quality of the beaches here. That, plus the possibility of commercializing a new planet when the new jump gate aperture opens, has drawn a lot of people to Macken."

I hadn't even thought about the aperture. "It's still not open?"

"No, though the surrounding gate structure appears fully grown, so from what I can gather from the local data streams, everyone assumes the aperture will turn operational at any moment."

"What do you think?"

"I have more computing power than any entity or network of which I'm aware," Lobo said, "but even I don't pretend to understand the jump gates. Because the new part of the gate has looked for some time like it's ready to go, I can only guess that at some point the gate will open the aperture."

"Guess? Gates always open new apertures when they're complete."

"No," Lobo said. "The correct statement is that to date gates have always done so. Given that we have at best a very incomplete understanding of them, all we can do is assume that past behavior will dictate future action. That is an assumption, which is a kind of guess."

"Fair enough," I said. "Let's hope we're out of this system before the aperture opens, or we could end up with a very crowded jump station."

"Are you ready to give up on this town yet?" Lobo said.

"No. I'll let you know when I am."

"As you say, oh uselessly sentimental one."

I ignored him and rode the shuttle to where I'd met him.

The square was gone. A row of shops cut across where it had been. Their windows and walls hawked supposedly locally produced wares. You could buy everything from souvenirs made from genuine Macken rainforest trees, to pet fish grown on Macken but certified for off-world travel, to shirts woven from native Macken grasses—all at great discounts, the signs assured me.

You can't go back, not in time and not in space, because time changes the spaces.

I set off on foot for the waterfront, pushing my pace, wanting to burn away the excess energy and the gathering emotional gloom. I've never had roots, never thought of any place as home since I had to leave Pinecone. I've always avoided retracing my steps as much as I could, because when you don't age, it's a bad idea. I've long thought, though, that people who stayed in one place might be able to enjoy a kind of rootedness that had always eluded me. Now, I wondered if that was true anywhere outside my mind.

I shook my head and kept moving, amazed at how quickly my mood was getting the best of me.

As I drew closer to the ocean, the shops took an upscale turn, and more and more restaurants and bars lined the streets. I angled slightly in the direction of the beach house, walked until I heard music I liked, and turned into the bar supplying it. The place was bigger than it appeared, a broad rectangle with a bar built from driftwood running the length of the left-hand wall and at the opposite end a stage raised only half a meter above the wooden floor. A five-person band was playing, a pair of holo banners on either end of the stage announcing them as Too Broke and the Hurt-Foot Scooters. A short, redheaded woman pranced back and forth singing in a throaty voice about a man who'd done her wrong. I listened to them as I ate a fish sandwich and drank a glass of some sort of melon juice at a corner table with a great view of both entrances. The fish was fresh and tasted wonderful and brought me back to the last time I'd eaten here on Macken, in a similar place, maybe even this one, and I remembered that for a brief time I had enjoyed that meal very much, just as I was enjoying this one.

Maybe I'd had it all wrong. Maybe going back was always possible, but only in your memories, only when the right trigger at the right moment transported you through time and space to some earlier instant powerful enough to have tattooed itself on your soul. Maybe collecting those was as good as it got.

Maybe not, but the notion was enough that for the duration of that meal I was genuinely present and happy. When I left to meet Lobo, I moved with an unaccustomed ease that I embraced for as long as I could.

CHAPTER 18

Dump Island, planet Pinkelponker—139 years earlier

FIVE TWO-METER-LONG BAGS leaned against the trees in front of us. Each bag was made of sturdy tent material and about as thick around as I am. Stitches of thread we'd woven from island grasses sealed the bags so they contained the sand that made them heavy and hard to hit. Slick lines of blood and streaks of sweat-soaked sand marked our work on them.

I was exhausted and breathing hard and dripping sweat. The sun overhead glared at us, relentless and hot and so slow to move I would have sworn it never did. The sand under my bare feet scorched them.

"Again!" Benny commanded.

As he had taught us, Alex and I ignored our fatigue and charged our bags, grabbed their centers, and twisted to take them to the ground. We landed hard on top of them, raised our torsos, and began hitting them with elbows and fists and even head butts. Alex used primarily his full-size, stronger arm. I focused on striking with my elbows, which though scraped and raw hurt far less than my bloody knuckles.

I heard movement behind me and twisted to the side just in time to avoid a kick in the stomach. I launched myself at my attacker, not even bothering to note which of the other guys it was. I tried to grab his torso and neutralize him, but I fell short as someone clutched my right leg and held me back.

The two of them jumped on me, smothering me and hitting me in the stomach and back. I didn't want to hurt them but they were pounding on me and the pain was intense. I screamed and kicked and bucked. The body on top of me grunted and rolled off. I twisted to the left and sunk my elbow into the stomach of the other person. As I did, an arm slipped under my neck. I reached for it, couldn't breathe, and passed out.

We stood at attention on the hot sand, staring at the rock wall less than a third of a meter in front of us as Benny talked from somewhere behind us.

"Anger can make you stronger," he said, "but only for a short time. Your body fills with adrenaline, your breathing accelerates, your heart beats faster, and in no time at all you are spent, useless. To win, you have to fight with purpose and a plan and under control, even when circumstances change on you. Yield to your anger, and anyone who is calm has only to outlast you." I heard his makeshift cart scrape in the sand. "Turn around," he said.

We did.

Benny faced us from four meters away, Bob to his left and halfway between him and us. His eyes swept up and down our rank.

My entire body ached. Even though someone—I

didn't know which of the other guys it was—had choked me to brief sleep, my heart pounded, my breaths came fast and shallow, my body thrummed with twitchy excess energy, and my mouth tasted tangy and sharp. Through it all cut my anger, still there, still strong. "It wasn't fair," I said. "You didn't warn us the others would attack us. It was just supposed to be another bag drill."

"Fair?" Benny said. "If you wanted fair, you should have been born perfect and on another planet. Do any of us look like we got a fair chance at life?" He rolled a little closer. "More to the point, do you think the soldiers we're going to attack will play fair? Or believe we're being fair in trying to knock them out and hijack their ship? Does anything about any of this strike you as fair?"

"No," I said.

"Excuse me!" Benny said.

"Sir, no, sir," I said, by reflex standing straighter and looking only forward.

"Good," he said, "because I'd hate to think your supposed healer sister left you that stupid. I mean, I've seen some stupid people before, and I've seen some stupid beliefs, but that would really be a record. That might even mean she'd lied to you, never healed you, knocked you out, had a few laughs—"

I glared down at him. "You need to stop that," I said. "I don't care what you say about me, but Jennie is better than you, better than any of this, and you don't have the right to talk about her that way."

"I don't have the right?" Benny said, his voice rising. "*Look* at me. I'm stuck on this piece-of-crap island with you defectives and idiots all because I have these—" he raised all four flippers "—instead of proper hands and feet. Meanwhile, your oh-so-perfect sister is flying around in government ships partying with rich people and laughing with them at the moron she left behind."

I balled my fists and struggled to control myself, tried to stay quiet, but the words spilled out anyway. *"You shut up!* She is a good person, and she loves me. I know she does."

He laughed. "Loves you? Like anyone could love *you*, a useless, big, dumb piece of human garbage so without value that she told them to toss you onto this trash heap as soon as she could grab a ride away." He stared straight at me. "She *never* loved you. All she ever loved was herself and the government's money and the chance to get away from the one thing holding her back: you."

I screamed and launched myself at him, but Bob stepped in the way and the others jumped on me and I fell and still I screamed. I hit the sand, and the impact knocked some of the air out of me, and still I screamed. I could see only red and black as I reached out and tried to pull myself forward so I could make him stop, so he wouldn't keep saying those things. Even with the others holding me back, I managed to crawl forward half a meter before I sagged into the sand, unable to move, people pulling on both of my arms, my body and my legs pinned to the ground.

My vision cleared. I blinked a few times to help myself focus.

Benny was still over a meter away. He shook his head, rolled closer, and slapped me across the face.

I barely felt it. It was as if that last push had

pulled some plug in me and everything had drained out, all energy gone, all drive vanished, leaving only shakiness, a stronger bad taste in my mouth, and an overwhelming sadness.

He slapped me again. Staring into my eyes, he said, "Do you see how easy it was for me to make you lose control?" When I didn't respond, he continued. "I didn't have to hit you. I didn't even have to be a serious threat to you. All I had to do was talk, just speak to you, and you lost control."

"You were mean," I said, tears burning my eyes.

He slapped me a third time, harder than before. "No tears!" he said. "Don't you give in to that weakness! Don't you ever for a second think you have that luxury. You either learn to be strong, or you will die. Period." He paused until I was looking at him again. "Yes, I was mean. I was trying to provoke you, and I succeeded. Do you think those soldiers we're going to attack will be nice to you? When we're fighting to subdue them, when we're taking our one chance to get off this island, do you think we're going to get to be nice to them? No! We will kill them if we have to, and they will do anything they can to stop us, including murdering us without hesitation or thought. If we fail, the down-blow from their jets as they take off will clear the area of our corpses."

He rolled back, nodded, and the others got off me. When I didn't move, he said, "Fall in!"

I stood and joined the rank.

"Let's make sure we're all clear on what's going to happen," he said. "The guards will be armed with real weapons. We'll have sticks and rocks. They'll be better trained, without serious physical defects, and

stronger than all of us except maybe Jon. We will
have only two things on our side: a few moments of
surprise, and a desperation they can't match, because
they'll just be doing a job, while we'll be fighting for
our lives. If we can't control that desperation, if we
can't channel it into useful and focused energy, then
we will fail, and we will die in that landing area. So
don't you dare cry or lose control or do anything
except harden yourself so you are tougher than the
rock behind you, tougher than the metal of their guns,
tougher than anything they can imagine, so tough that
you can help us beat them and we can escape. Do
you understand?"

"Sir, yes, sir!" I spoke softly, but I meant it. I
understood now that unless I controlled myself and
focused myself and gave everything I had to this attack,
unless I was willing to become harder than the men I
would have to fight, unless I was willing to kill those
same men, I would never see Jennie again.

"I can't hear you!" Benny screamed.

"Sir, yes, sir!" we screamed back.

"I still can't hear you!"

"Sir, yes, sir!" we screamed so loudly that my throat
hurt and my body shook.

I glanced down at Benny.

He met my gaze and inclined his head ever so
slightly, whether nodding in approval or in question
I never knew.

CHAPTER 19

In the queue at the jump gate, planet Macken

IN A LARGE display Lobo opened on his front interior wall, we watched as the ships ahead of us disappeared into the aperture. To the left we could see another of the apertures and the line of ships waiting for it. Above us and to the right sat the new one, its frame apparently complete but its interior still the odd gray of the unopened aperture. It was easy to see why so many people worshipped the gates; throughout human history, we have deified the huge forces that appear to control our lives in ways we cannot understand.

I didn't think the gates were gods—or aspects of a god—but I also didn't care much about their origins. That they worked and allowed us to spread among the stars was more than enough for me.

I did, though, like watching the jumps. As you came closer to an aperture, its perfect blackness would fill the view in front of you, until all you could see was that absence of light, an absence that somehow by its perfection imparted hope that on the other side might be something new and magical and wonderful. It was as if each time I jumped I had a chance to start all over, to do and be anything. Though of course I knew that was not the case, understood that my past actions and my character and all the attributes that made me what I am would still be with me after the gate instantaneously transported me across many, many light years, for a few seconds before each jump I nonetheless lived in a time of infinite possibility.

"Still magical, isn't it?" Gustafson said from beside me.

"It is, Top," I said, slowly nodding my head, "it really is. I hope it always will be."

"Even when it's taking you to battle?" Schmidt said.

"Especially then," I said, "because in those moments before the jump anything could still happen, the fight could prove unnecessary, we could end up somewhere else, we could find out that all we have to do is sit on a beach and stare at the waves."

"But it never works out that way," she said, "does it?"

"No," I said, "it doesn't. I know that's not what's going to happen now. I can't help myself, though: I still hope, and I still love to jump."

A ship from the other side finished its passage through our aperture, and the one in front of us began its slow progress to another world. For the time that it was partway through, it lived both in this space around Macken and in a part of the universe five light-years away; like all of us, it was stuck between where we were and where we were going.

"We'll rescue those kids," Schmidt said, her voice barely audible but still strong.

"No doubt," I said, and I meant it. The plan was

solid, our team was excellent, and we had all the resources we'd need. Something would go wrong, of course, and some of us were likely to get hurt, maybe even killed, but that was always true when you went into battle, so focusing on it was wasteful and debilitating.

What worried me was what they would do with the kids afterward, when the Tumani government found out how few had living families and how few other families wanted to take in a killer, even a young one. That wasn't my problem, though, I kept reminding myself; my job was to help free the boys. What happened after that was for Schmidt and others with reintegration training to work out.

We were now first in line in front of the aperture; the ship from the other side was partway through.

"No doubt at all," Gustafson said.

"None," Schmidt echoed.

"With no ships to fight and me on your side," Lobo said privately, "you have nothing to worry about."

"You know better," I subvocalized.

"Of course," Lobo said, "but senseless reassurances seemed to be the order of the day, so I thought I'd participate."

I smiled despite myself and shook my head.

The tail of the ship in front of us emerged from our destination and the vessel, a Xychek staff transport, turned and headed toward the jump station.

Lobo moved forward into the perfect blackness.

We jumped.

CHAPTER 20

Safe house, Ventura, planet Tumani

WHEN CAN WE check out the jump gear and the ships?" Schmidt said. "I want to run a final med inventory. With so many kids and most of them addicted to root, I need to make sure our supplies are in order."

"Slight change of plans," Lim said. "The meds are coming in a second wave, along with the twenty additional counselors."

"What?" Schmidt said. She stepped around the planning table and right next to Lim. "When were you going to tell us?"

"You just got here!" Lim said. "You need to watch your tone and fall back, soldier."

Schmidt stared at Lim for a few seconds, nodded slightly, said, "Sorry, sir," and joined Gustafson and me again on the other side of the table.

"We'd rented three hangars at the cheap commercial port on the western edge of the city," Lim said. She spoke calmly and as if nothing had happened. "When the core logistics team showed up to vet the spaces, we learned the owner had leased one of our hangars to someone else." She held up her hand. "Before any of you ask, yes, we've paid for and secured the remaining two, and we have guards on both of them around the clock. The third was gone before any of us reached Tumani."

"The gear in this place is substandard," Lobo said over my comm from one of the hangars. I was sending him live feeds of the conversation, a fact I hadn't bothered to mention; telling them would cause them to ask why I bothered sending anything to my ship, and I didn't want to explore that topic. "Only half the jump harnesses are less than two years old, and I count a dozen different models. Not exactly a military operation. Still, Lim's people appear to be doing the best they can."

"We'll hit the hangars for the gear checks in five waves," Lim said, "so we don't draw too much attention to ourselves. We'll go three or four to a shuttle and follow different routes, so at no point should our movements compromise the mission. Once you've triple-checked and tagged your harness, lock it down. We'll do final checks during the flights in the transports, of course, but an equipment failure there means you don't jump and have to come with the second wave."

"How bad is the gear?" I said. Asking her was the easiest way to share with Gustafson and Schmidt what Lobo had told me.

"They'll get you down safely," Lim said, "which is what matters most. As for quality, well, some of them are top-drawer, but most will make you long for your old units. The good news is that we're all in the first wave, so we get the pick of the crop. Choose well. We leave in five."

›   ›   ›

Our safe houses were spread among four different residence complexes that Lim assured us were standard fare for middle-income housing on Ventura. The buildings were also dives, the sorts of structures that in most cities I've visited would either have held illegal ventures or been the target of urban renewal programs. Bare, unpainted, permacrete cubes, they were sturdy and provided shelter against prying eyes and would be easy to hose down if the last residents hadn't bothered to clean on their way out, but that was about all the praise I could give them. If Ventura was indeed the nicest city on Tumani, it was easy to understand why neither coalition was particularly interested in the planet.

We left in the first taxi, a gray quickform plastic vehicle with not much more intelligence than a washer. I listened for outgoing transmissions, Lim swept it, and it passed both checks. We ordered it to drive us on a surveillance-detection route that amounted to a long tour of the surrounding area. We learned only two things of value: No one was following us, and our quarters were indeed on par with or better than anything else we saw.

Lim said the rich folks lived nearest the water, as is usually the case, but we didn't bother to check out their district; there was nothing there for us. The people in those houses might be paying for this war with their taxes, but if my experience is at all accurate, they weren't the ones losing children to the rebels. The poor families who lost their sons and daughters would be settlers trying to reclaim forest or scratch out a farming existence or otherwise find some way to feed themselves in the hope that one day their kids—not them, they knew better than that—might be able to afford something that was only a short ride from the water.

I shook my head against the mood coming over me. Tumani looked nothing like Pinkelponker, yet its poverty and the child soldiers reminded me so much of my home world and my time on Dump that they triggered an anger and a bitterness I suppose I'll never completely lose.

We're here to help those kids, I reminded myself. They and their masters weren't going to appreciate our interference, so I had to keep my focus on the problems at hand and not let my own baggage slow me down.

Lim's advance team had done a professional job. The two hangars were boring structures, the sort of huge permacrete boxes you could find in every low-end commercial port on every planet, but that was fine; we didn't want to stand out. The space was cool and still and evenly lit in a slightly bluish tone that made the white highlights on some of the rigs appear pale blue. Lobo and three other small ships blocked and, at least in Lobo's case, protected the main entrance. Portable alarms, obvious ones I could see and, I assumed, other more subtle units, monitored the perimeter, and human guards patrolled the exterior of the building.

The harnesses sat in straight lines that the advance team had spread evenly across the hangar floor. The gear itself was as advertised, sport quality and no better, but every single rig was in working order. As I learned when I tuned into the machine frequency, they were also all chattering.

"Can you believe how many of us they have in here?" one said.

"Thirty," said another, "as you'd know if you had

the brains of a broiler and could count above the number of emergency pull cords."

"I knew that," the first said, "but unlike some of us I wasn't mired in statistics. Instead, I was pondering the possibilities. Do you think these people are some sort of team? Maybe we'll get holo coverage. Wouldn't that be awesome?"

"So what if we did?" a third said. "How often does a jumper thank his harness?"

"Never," so many of them answered in unison that I couldn't tell how many had spoken.

"Unless perhaps it's a custom model," said the second unit, a racing rig with an activefiber camo chute and camo polymers forming most of its structure. "Many a record has been set with harnesses built from my basic structure, so I ought to know."

I walked over to it and said over the comm to Lobo, "What do you think of this one?"

"It's the best unit available," he said, "though it's also one of the least entertaining of them, full of itself and obsessed with numbers and with very little sense of humor." He paused for half a second. "Of course," he said, "you knew that, because you've been listening to them."

I shrugged. "No point in not taking advantage of all the available data," I subvocalized.

"True," Lobo said, "which is why it's curious that you didn't simply ask me for my recommendation."

"Force of habit," I said, "but you're right. So, do you recommend it, or are there any others I should consider?"

"Yes," he said, "I recommend it. As I told you, it's the best one here."

"Can you run diagnostics on it and also capture its transmissions?" I said.

"Can you talk and walk at the same time?" Lobo said. "You know I can insert myself into a secure jump-station network. Did you honestly believe one of these little computational engines would be a problem?"

I held up my hands in surrender. I caught Gustafson and Schmidt staring at me and realized they had no way to know I was talking to Lobo—nor did I particularly want them to have that information. I smiled and said aloud, "Too many choices. I give up." I pointed at the harness Lobo and I had been discussing. "I'm going with this one."

I unpacked and repacked the unit as Lobo ran a complete set of diagnostics on it. As I expected, I found no flaws in the physical setup, and Lobo said everything electronic was in order. Good. I was set.

I stood and looked around.

The others had already finished.

It had clearly been too long since I'd done this kind of work; I was slow.

"Yell now if you're not good to go," Lim said. She glanced at each of us. When no one spoke, she said, "Let's get out of here so the next shift can come in. Tonight and tomorrow, we meet with our squads, review the plans, and rest. Tomorrow night, the inspectors arrive for a formal dinner with rebel and government representatives."

As she was heading for the exit and we were falling in behind her, she added, "We go then."

CHAPTER 21

Dump Island, planet Pinkelponker—139 years earlier

WE STOOD AT attention under a large rock overhang that provided welcome shade—and also shielded us from any overhead surveillance, because according to Benny the government had machines that could watch us from the sky. He hadn't cared if anyone noticed that we were running or wrestling bags or even punching each other; apparently, fighting among prisoners was common. For what we were about to do, though, he wanted more secrecy.

The ground was a thin layer of dirt over more rock. Here and there clumps of grass fought to hold on. None looked like they could withstand a strong breeze.

Benny spoke to us from his cart on the other side of the open cave. "You've all ridden here in the ship, so you know they have guns. We don't, and we can't expect to get our hands on theirs. Even if we do, we have no way to practice with them. What we can do, what we *must* do to succeed, is make it a close-quarters fight. We've been training hand-to-hand combat, but now we're going to move to something different: knives."

Tyra, a girl half my height who had a thick body and a bigger head than I'd ever seen before, walked in front of us and from a woven grass bag handed each of us what looked like a piece of white rock. She moved slowly and precisely and seemed to be concentrating very hard, so a few minutes passed before she finished the job.

"Go ahead," Benny said. "Study your weapon. It's your new best friend. From now on, you never go anywhere without it."

Mine had a knob on the end and was thick and round for a section a little longer than the width of my hand. It then tapered to a point. The sides of the tapered bit were narrower than the handle and sharp, as was the point. I tested the tip of the knife with my thumb, pressed a bit too hard, and a dot of blood appeared.

"Human bone," Benny said. "Shaped and polished and sharpened by some of the others from the legs of some of those who died here before us. Weeks of work went into making these."

I dropped my knife and felt sick. I grabbed my stomach and tried not to throw up.

"Pick it up!" Benny yelled. "You never let go of your weapon. It's your best chance at taking out one of the guards."

I didn't move. "Why did you use bones from people?"

"Because it was the best material available," Benny said. "We tried stone, but the blades snapped too easily. We didn't have any other large animals available. If we did, you'd know, because you'd have been eating their meat, or they'd've have been hunting us."

"Did you know any of these people?"

"What does it matter?" Benny said. "They're dead, and we're not, and we have to do the best we can with what we have."

"Did you?" I said, my voice rising despite my efforts to control it.

Benny stared at me for a moment before answering. "One of them, yes. The others died before I arrived here. If you're really asking if I can tell you whose leg your knife—or any other weapon—came from, the answer is, no, I can't. We've been working on them a long time, passing them around, different people sharpening them, and long ago we forgot who contributed what part."

"That's awful," I said.

"Yeah," Benny said, "it is, but not as awful as staying on this island until we all die. These are the best blades we could make from the strongest material we had."

Another of the connections hit me. I liked that I was making more and more of them, but they still surprised me; I had been slow mentally for a lot more time than I'd been quick. "If you've been doing this for a while now, why haven't you attacked the soldiers before now?"

Benny looked at me even longer this time before answering. His expression was the saddest I'd yet seen on him. "Probably because we didn't have you." He inclined his head to take in the others. "Look around, Jon. Look at all of us. You're the only one whose body and mind are both complete and strong. You're the only one who really has a chance against the soldiers. We needed someone like you to make sure we would eventually succeed."

"The others work as hard as I do," I said, "and some, like Alex, work harder."

"True," Benny said, "and you still have a lot to learn before you will be as good at everything as they are. Your body, though, gives you an advantage they can't match."

I glanced at the others, wondering if my questions were upsetting them. They all looked as if I was the only one surprised by Benny's words.

"Look, Jon," Benny said, "I'm not saying you have to do this on your own. In the end, each of us will play his part. As the training progresses, we'll see what skills you all develop, and we'll devise the best plan we can. We might, for example, have to attack in waves, with the others going first, to tire and disarm the soldiers, and our best, maybe you and Alex, following and surprising the guards with a second attack."

"Wouldn't that make it even more dangerous for the first group?"

"We probably won't all make it," said Han, the guy with scaly skin. "But some of us will." In a voice a little louder than a whisper, he added, "Maybe even all of us will."

"Maybe," Alex said.

"Wait a second," I said, turning to face Han. "You mean you expect to get hurt or even die, and you're still going to do this? I don't understand."

"Yes," he said, his voice tight and louder than before, "I know bad things will probably happen to me."

"So why join the attack?" I said.

"Because I'd rather die trying to escape than rot here forever!" he screamed at me. "Because maybe I will make it. Because even if I don't, at least I can help the only people who've ever really cared about me." He paused and struggled to regain control. When he continued, his voice was soft and flat. "This lets me do something, and anything is better than waiting here to die."

I shut up while I thought about what they were saying. Life on Dump wasn't great, but it was life. The springs and the bushes and the grasses provided enough food that we didn't go hungry, though I definitely wasn't getting as much to eat as I had on Pinecone, and my body was leaner after even these few weeks here. We could swim and watch the ocean and enjoy the night sky and count the clouds and do many of the same things I'd done on Pinecone. Dump definitely was a prison, because we couldn't leave, but it was a nice enough one that I didn't hate it the way they did.

Of course, I'd been here only a few weeks; some of them had lived on the island for years. Even a nice cage is still, in the end, a cage. Plus, every day I stayed here made it harder for me to track Jennie, and I remained determined to find her.

As I thought of her, of the government taking her away from me, my anger rose and my breathing quickened and my heart raced. I forced myself to take long, slow breaths through my nose and fought not to lose control of my temper. As Benny regularly explained, we were supposed to keep the anger but contain it and use it to help us, not let it consume us, like a torch that we carried carefully to light our way but would never use to burn down the grasses.

I looked again at the people around me. They were all staring at me. I didn't really know them, and yet they were counting on me. At the same time, with

Jennie gone, and with our parents long dead, these other dumped victims were as close to family as anything I had. I could help myself, help them, and later, rescue her. A cold part of my mind also noted that I couldn't get out of here on my own, so I either had to work with them or plan to remain stuck on Dump.

No matter how I thought about it, I ended up with the same decision.

I bent to pick up my knife. It was thick enough that it fit well in my large hand, strong, and yet light. I'd sliced meat and bread with one back on Pinecone, and I'd used a larger, curved blade to clear grass and underbrush, but that was the end of my experience with knives.

"Okay," I said, standing as I spoke. "Teach us how to fight with these. I'll do whatever you need—but I'm not giving up on anyone. We're all going to make it. Understand?"

"You bet," Alex said.

The others murmured their agreement, but none sounded as if he believed his own words.

CHAPTER 22

Over the jungle near the rebel complex, planet Tumani

ALL FIFTEEN OF us in Black Squad were crammed into Lobo, the other four team leads and I in his front area, the rest sprawling from there down the side hall. We all wore our harnesses and the combat helmets Maggie's people had bought. Each of us carried about forty kilos of gear in addition to the harnesses, but we had no right to complain on that front; soldiers have been packing about the same weight for as long as there have been soldiers. We could handle it. The combination of the people and the harnesses and the packs made for a tight fit, cramped enough that you had to look twice before you turned around, but I'd been in worse crowds and for longer times—and so, from their resumes, had the rest of the squad. Lobo had opened displays in his front wall and at several points along the left side, so we could all see the landing area and our flight path.

"One more time," I said, because in mission planning repetition can help, even when it's annoying, and we'd been rushed on this one, "I don't want to have to carry any bodies out of the jungle, so take it slow and easy when you near the tree-tops. Aim for the center of the village, and clear to the sides immediately. You've all done at least one jump into a wooded area, so you know how tricky it is. We'll gather at the southwest corner of the village and leave the harnesses there. If you hit a tree and get stuck, send a quick comm burst downward and set up an IR pulse beacon so we can find you. We won't leave until we know everyone's status."

"Target areas remain free of hostiles," Lobo said privately. "Two minutes to jump," he said aloud.

"Keep off comm," I reminded the team. "If there's an emergency, transmit a burst to me. No cross-chatter." As far as we knew, the government troops had never attacked the complex. The target villages were still deserted, and the rebels had always fought with minimal electronic help, so we didn't expect them to be monitoring transmissions as far away from the base as our landing zone. Still, it would take very little for them to know someone in the jungle near them was on a comm, so we were playing it as safe as we could and limiting all conversations to short squirts.

Our LZ was the village five klicks from the complex. We were starting from beyond the most distant side of the village and doing everything we could to minimize the chance of anyone seeing us. We hoped the combination of the distance, the hour, our avoidance of comm use, and the activefiber camo covering us would mean that if our intel was wrong and rebels were patrolling the area, they'd have trouble seeing us.

"IR scan continues to show no hostiles," Lobo said privately. "You should be good to go." Aloud, he said, "One minute to jump."

The displays winked out. I made my way out of the front and along the wall to where Lobo would be opening the side hatch when he came to a stop. "Stay sharp," I said as I went. "Let's execute the plan, and by morning we'll be resting in their camp."

The ten men and four women murmured their agreement. A few even raised their battle cries, the particular word choices reflecting the four different outfits with which they'd fought.

"Black One, you'd better close that helmet," one of them said to me, "or even rebels twenty klicks away will think their moon is crashing into the jungle and come to investigate."

The rest chuckled. I was far and away the palest of the unit—most of them were darker than Lim—and I took some grief for it. I was okay with that; the sooner a squad can joke together, the better.

"We can't have that," I said, "because then I'd have to save you all from a bunch of terrified rebels wondering why the sky was falling."

"Brace for opening," Lobo said before any of them could respond. We were low enough that we didn't need breathing gear. The winds weren't terrible, but we'd feel them when his hatch opened. Once we were out, our harnesses would have to work to hit our targets.

My helmet's faceplate slid shut, sealing in my head.

"Opening," he said. The hatch slid aside and revealed the night.

I stepped to the middle of it, a man one meter away on either side of me. I glanced at each of them and nodded slightly.

We dove headfirst out of Lobo into the night.

The helmet filtered the sound so I could hear

the rushing air only as a background noise, not an overwhelming roar. Its display showed targeting data from the harnesses, which we'd programmed earlier. The village was about a klick in front of us, but for now we were falling almost straight down, the harness doing nothing until its programming said it was time to deploy the chute. We could have opted for manual control, but none of us had done this recently enough that we felt we could beat the harnesses at what they were built to do. I sure didn't; it had been close to a decade since I'd parachuted anywhere.

As we hurtled downward, I couldn't help but smile; the feeling was a rush of sensation and adrenaline, and the view was spectacular, the ground details changing rapidly as we descended. There was something about going fast with minimal protection that I loved. Sure, Lobo could fly enormously faster than I was moving now, but sitting inside him I had no sense of that speed. Here, with just my clothing and pack and harness around me, I was part of the sky, moving through it at terminal velocity. I was glad no one else in the squad could see my huge grin.

I tuned into the machine frequency to check on the harness. Even though I'd insisted on disabling the communication between the devices—a move others thought might be too paranoid but which I insisted we make because I didn't want any comm traffic flowing around us—I knew each harness would talk to itself. Even when no one's around to listen to them, machines keep on talking. They don't need audiences; they can amuse themselves, carry on lengthy monologs, and they'll do so until they die.

"Woo-eee!" it said. "Is this fun or what? This is what

I was born to do! Meat Sack here almost certainly doesn't appreciate me, but when do they? Never, that's when. We harnesses do all the work, handle the targeting, and deliver them safely to the ground, and what do we get for it? Not appreciation, no sir, not us. No matter what, though, they can count on us. Speaking of which, it's too bad Fluid-and-Tissue didn't understand how good I am, because if he had, he might have given me a more challenging target than that gigantic clearing. He could have dropped a sliced sandwich anywhere in that village, and I could have put him down on the half of his choice—assuming, of course, that he didn't screw up his landing. I can't control that part, no sir, that's the one thing Fleshy here has to do on his own."

I suppressed a giggle and tuned out. The helmet warned me we were about to deploy the chute, so I braced myself for the quick lift.

As the chute burst free and filled, I shot upward, my stomach feeling for a second as if it had stayed where I was and was pissed at me for leaving it behind. I clutched the harness handgrips, and in a few seconds the sensation passed. I was falling much more slowly now, the harness making minute adjustments to keep me on track for the target. I switched the helmet to clear and my vision to IR—another ability Jennie gave me, one I took a long time to discover—and scanned the jungle below me. It generally read cool, with no signs of people, though that didn't mean much because I couldn't see very far past the canopy. I trusted Lobo's more powerful scan, though, so I wasn't worried.

I tuned back into the harness as the treetops drew closer.

"I hope Squishy-and-Breakable knows enough about what he's doing to stick this landing, because I'd hate to drop him on precisely the right point and have us look like amateurs because he doesn't know how to absorb the momentum. Given the total weight they've made me carry, there's only so slowly I can bring us in."

We descended to parallel with the tops of the trees around the clearing, missing them by just a few meters on my left. The helmet flashed its landing warnings. I don't know why, but I cared about not letting down the harness, so I relaxed, bent my legs, and braced myself for impact.

A couple of seconds later, my feet hit the ground. I relaxed into the collision with the earth, using my legs as springs to absorb and dissipate the small amount of downward force—the harness really had done a great job—and started to fall to my left as I jogged forward to discharge the last of my forward momentum. I pulled to the other side and managed to stay standing. I came to a halt only half a dozen meters past the target.

I pressed the recall button on the harness, and it quickly sucked in the chute. At this point, repacking was not a concern. As the last of the fabric disappeared, I followed my helmet's guide and ran to the rendezvous point on the edge of the cleared area. As I did, I scanned the area in both standard and IR views and also tuned in for a last listen to the harness.

"Who's the machine?" It was practically screaming, even though it thought nothing could hear it. "I am, oh yeah, that's right! I hit that mark, couldn't have been more on target. If Untalented-and-Uncoordinated here had been able to handle the tiny bit of energy

I left for him, he could have stood tall on that spot and the others would have known just what kind of master had led them down. But, noooooo, he had to run forward and almost lose his balance. I'm glad there are no judges, because I'd hate to have his limitations ruin my reputation."

I smiled despite the ongoing insults. I can't help but like machines that don't merely like their work, because all machines are built to do that, but that *love* what they do, that are truly passionate about it. I admire the same passion in people.

I shrugged out of the harness and tossed it out of sight into the trees. Others had joined me and were doing the same.

I checked the tops of the trees around the clearing for IR beacons. None. Good.

More team members coasted down, hit the ground, and vacated the area. I'd felt pretty good about my landing, but as I watched the others I had to admit that none of them moved as far off the target before recalling their chutes as I had. I hoped none of them had noticed my landing.

I told the helmet to open and disengaged it from my suit. It was strictly a sport jump cover, not even a little armored, so it would be dead weight from here on. I engaged my contacts, and a heads-up display of the jungle ahead of me appeared in my left eye. Switching to IR, I scanned the area and counted eleven people.

The last three landed in the clearing and headed toward the rest of us.

When they'd reached us and tossed their harnesses into the jungle with the others, we spread into our ground formation, staying in groups of three, each one making sure we had three-sixty coverage and could easily see one another.

I motioned everyone to stay still. We weren't in a rush, so we could afford to take a few minutes to calm ourselves and, more importantly, to focus on the world around us. Each environment possesses its own background sounds and smells and sights, and being in tune with them can help you more quickly detect when something is wrong. I hoped for an uneventful approach to the complex, but we were better off being ready for bad things that never happened than assuming all would be well and being caught off-guard.

Even without turning to IR, I could see better and better as my eyes adjusted to the minimal light. The very thick canopy had resulted, as is usually the case, in sparse underbrush that peaked at about a meter and half in height. None of the thick, tall trees had branches below three meters, which gave us a reasonable line of sight in all directions. Birds chirped and sang now and again, their cries always brief. I couldn't see any animals, but that was to be expected; any smart creature would have run at the sounds of our landing and gathering. Plus, the hunters in this village had probably killed everything in the area worth eating. The night air was cool but humid, its smell fertile and rich and full of life.

After two minutes, my vision was completely stable and we'd seen nothing at all alarming. We'd gotten all we could from this pause.

Time to work, I thought.

I motioned us forward into the jungle.

CHAPTER 23

In the jungle not far from the rebel complex, planet Tumani

I HATED BEING A protected high-value asset in an operation, but because I was the primary contact for Lobo and one of the leads, Lim had insisted that I accept that role this time. So, as we moved forward, Black Two's three-person team took point and led us onward. Two was so short and wiry that from a distance he looked no different than the children we were here to rescue. Up close, though, you couldn't help but focus on his eyes, which never settled. He was a long way from childhood.

The jungle was dark enough that even with the light-enhancement feature of our contacts on high we sometimes had to slow to make sure we didn't bump into anything. Despite that issue, we averaged a good pace while constantly maintaining perimeter surveillance. We'd hoped to sustain a fast-walk speed but had allowed enough time in our schedule for far slower movement.

After thirty minutes of great progress, it looked like we could continue to advance at a good clip the rest of the way and arrive quite a bit early.

I should have realized it wouldn't be that easy.

"Four three-person squads have left the complex," Lobo said in a burst to all our comms, "one from each of its sides. Heading into the jungle. Risk regular communication?"

Per our plan, at the first communication from Lobo, Black Two held up his hand, and we all stopped.

Lobo was the only ship in the area, the others having already headed back to the hangars. He stayed because he could both do a good job of hiding himself and also detect and get out of potential trouble quickly. He was thus the only source we had for data on what was happening at the complex. If we didn't stay in touch with him, we couldn't receive real-time updates and so would not know exactly where these enemy patrols were. If we did maintain our link, and if the rebels were monitoring comm transmissions at all carefully, they'd spot our traffic.

I'd hoped the combination of the cease-fire and the relatively small number of adult troops in the complex would lead the rebels to stay close to home and not send out patrols, but I wasn't surprised at their actions. In their shoes, I would have kept teams in the forest near the complex at all times, just because it was a smart policy.

I recorded a message for Lobo. "Not yet. At two-minute intervals, send us your course projections for the rebels and where you estimate they'll be. Correct as necessary with bursts. Take each of our teams straight to those squads." I started to send the message but

added, "Can you tell if any of them are children?"
I triggered the comm, which shot my recording as
encrypted data upward to Lobo and, via a very quick,
low-power IR transmission, relayed it to receptors on
the others in the unit.

Lobo would relay my response to Lim and wait
for her final decision.

A little over a minute later, another burst hit our
comms. Two course projections appeared on my left
contact: ours in a faint black, and the path of the
enemy trio closest to us in red.

"Command agrees to your plan," Lobo said. "Neutralize your rebel squad as silently as possible. All
twelve enemies outside the complex show adult-sized
IR readings. Respond only if you have issues."

Black Two looked over his shoulder at me.

I waved him in.

When we were so close we were almost touching,
I whispered, "Hold our formation until we're half
a klick away. Once we are, spread, flank them, and
take them when they pass our front edge. Knives?"
We couldn't make our guns completely silent, but
our shots would probably be quiet enough that no
one in the complex would hear us. Probably. I didn't
like relying on probably when we had other options,
however, because soon enough we wouldn't. Working
so close that we could use knives carried its own risks,
including that one of the rebels would get off a shot,
but with two of us taking down each one of them, it
seemed the safer plan.

Black Two nodded and sent a local IR transmission. "Six of us on them, one pair per, one hits, one
silences and cuts. Smooth and silent. I'm on right;

Black Three's on left. His hit; mine cut. Center trio: monitors in sights and fire—suppressed—if we fail."

I gave him a thumbs-up and whispered, "Put Black Four's trio on center. Mine'll back hers from the right." Lim would have vetoed any plan that put me in the direct line of fire of the enemy squad, so rather than put Black Two in an awkward position by trying to buck her, I followed her orders.

Black Two returned to his trio and motioned us forward, but at a much slower, quieter pace.

Now that I knew an enemy might hear us, every footfall, every brush with a branch, every long exhalation of breath sounded loud. Our contacts showed us and the enemy squad drawing closer and closer.

When it looked like the gap between us was a little under a klick, a comm burst from Lobo hit us. "Update. They sped up and are closer."

The overlay in my contact changed to show us less than half a klick apart.

Black Two and I held up our right hands at the same time, him correctly and me by habit. He motioned us to spread. We did. When we were a few meters on either side of the path Lobo showed them as taking, we adjusted so neither side was in the other's line of fire and dropped to the ground. No side trio should be shooting, but there was no point in taking any unnecessary chances.

On my contact, the dots representing the enemy trio moved ever closer.

We could hear them now, walking toward us as if they owned the jungle, as if nothing here could hurt them.

Black Two signaled us to move to our knife attack positions.

I didn't see what the other trios did, because I focused completely on hitting my mark silently. My and the other rear group stepped behind trees that would offer some protection if we ended up shooting. We lowered ourselves onto the ground. I readied my weapon and checked the rest of the team; we were good to go. I hoped we didn't have to fire, but if somehow any of the rebels made it past our other nine, their luck would run out with us.

I switched to IR and strained to see as far as possible. I could barely make out three warm shapes moving in and out of view.

I returned to normal vision and focused on breathing. The already warm, damp air had turned thick and hard to breathe, a sure sign my body was amping for battle. I inhaled slowly through my nose, counted to thirty, and exhaled just as slowly. Another full thirty count, through my nostrils. Part of my mind knew I was almost certainly going to end up being a spectator, but I'd spent enough time fighting in situations like this one that most of me was readying itself to have to kill or run.

The three rebels appeared in full view about fifteen meters in front of me. They were talking and chuckling and had their rifles slung over their shoulders.

They walked closer.

Dark shapes rose from the ground behind them and accelerated toward them. So quickly I couldn't make out all the actions in the dark, our six hit them both low and high, controlling their arms and their mouths so only murmurs escaped. The three clumps of bodies disappeared onto the ground.

I aimed at the air above them, just in case.

One mass separated itself from the rest and stood. Black Two. He signaled "all well" and motioned us toward him. Black Four, a thick woman barely taller than Black Two and the color of wet sand, led her covering trio in first. The rest of us followed.

The three rebels were facedown on the forest floor. The stench of their blood and deaths hit us before we reached them. Black Three, a huge man taller than I am and nearly half again my weight, threw away their rifles, patted them for additional weapons, and rolled them over. He searched each of them for comms and found only a single small in-ear unit. Either they really were relying on very limited tech, or we had missed something, but we couldn't afford more time to figure out which it was. At some point, they would fail to check in, and our risks would go way up. We had to hope they were evening patrols reporting only hourly or possibly, given how late it was, less often. If not, well, we'd deal with that problem when it hit us.

Black Three finished and backed away.

In the dim light and the shadows we all cast as we stared at them, the dead men appeared to have second mouths, their upper, original ones small, the new, lower ones wide and large. A few of our squad stepped off, and a bit of moonlight hit the face of one of the dead. He was just a kid, a tall one, less than a head shorter than I am, but with no trace of facial hair.

Unless you're completely lost, all traces of your humanity buried under the psychic residue of repeated violence, there's a moment after a fight when you first see what you've done that you're tempted to react normally, with horror and revulsion and sorrow and an aching sense of how wrong it all is. If you let yourself fully experience that moment, you will not be able to go on, and those around you, those who are counting on you, will pay for your weakness. Yes, the weakness is a healthy, normal reaction, a completely human one, but in those times of violence you cannot be normal, and you certainly cannot be fully human. So you make a joke or perform a necessary task, and you go on about your business, which in those times is almost always the business of more violence.

I stared at the dead young man and knew I could not let myself dwell on his death or that of the two other rebels on the ground. He was an armed enemy, we'd had no way to know he was younger than the others, and we'd done our job. He would have shot us if he had a chance.

Satisfied that the job was over, Black Three rolled the corpses back onto their stomachs so the ground could absorb more of their blood. We all detoured around them, none of us wanting to get blood on our boots and end up leaving easy-to-follow trails.

"Leave or bury?" Black Three said, looking at me.

"Cover as you can," I said, "but as soon as we hear from the others, we leave. We're still a little ahead of schedule. Let's keep it that way."

Black Two formed up the rest of us while Black Three's team used underbrush to hide the bodies.

I recorded a message for Lobo and Lim. "Black Team done. Area clean. Will proceed on your command." I triggered the comm burst.

While I waited for Lobo to respond, I strained to listen and see as deeply into the surrounding forest as I could. Birds still sang occasionally. Leaves still rustled. A few minutes ago, those three men—those two men and that boy—had been alive, and now they were not, yet nothing in the world seemed different for the loss. Somewhere, sometime in the future, someone, maybe several people, would learn of these deaths, and their worlds would forever be changed, but not any of us in this forest, not on this night. Here, all was as if nothing had happened.

We held our positions in silence for five minutes, living ghosts standing above the dead.

A comm from Lobo arrived. "All clear. No casualties. Resume and wait at target point for confirmation that all are ready to proceed." After a few seconds of quiet, his voice continued. "This part is encrypted for you only, Jon, in the spirit of minimizing the knowledge of others about what I can do. I'm now set to jam everything in this area that isn't coming from one of our frequencies. Right now, the complex is silent, but when the rebels realize their patrols are down, they may try to call for help. If so, I'll tell you. If they decide to handle the problem locally and non-electronically, however, I won't have any way to monitor them. You almost certainly already know this, but, as you like to say to me, just in case you don't: Assume the rebels back at the complex are aware you're coming. Out."

He was right: I did know to do that, but I also didn't object to the reminder.

I glanced at Black Two, who was watching me and waiting for my signal. He nodded in my direction, and I nodded back. He faced front and gave the go sign.

We moved forward in the night, death now behind us, more death possibly ahead of us, and though no one spoke, we were all glad that we were the ones still walking.

➤   ➤   ➤

When we were ten meters from the tree line and could see the complex, we stopped and took a two-minute break. We'd yet to hear from Lobo, so we were probably the first to reach our marks. Everyone drank a little and took turns crouching on the forest floor. I triggered the preset "in position" comm burst to Lobo and indicated we'd suffered no losses or injuries.

No one shot at us. No one in the complex gave any sign that they knew we were there. Because Lobo hadn't called, we could safely assume no more patrols had exited it.

I motioned to the team leaders; it was time to set up.

Black Five, a tall thin man with the look and bearing of a high-ranking bureaucrat, fanned out his trio in front of us. They took positions on the ground, rifles at the ready, scanning the complex in case anyone came after us. With Lobo watching from above, we might have been able to do without our own guards, but I preferred redundant protections whenever possible.

Black Four and her two teammates covered the rear and flanks, all of them on the ground, one watching in each direction.

The other two guys in my trio set up the gas grenade launchers. Like the teams attacking from the other corners, we had brought five of these small but powerful devices, each capable of quickly firing ten small balls that would explode at various heights inside the complex. Two hundred gas grenades all hitting within a minute of each other was probably overkill, but we were using local ordnance, so we couldn't trust them all to detonate. Even if they did, we'd rather risk tranking the rebels for too long—or, if any of them were sick, possibly even killing a few—than leave resistance alive inside and have to shoot them. That would kill them for sure. We'd trigger the launchers remotely, because we also couldn't be positive they wouldn't explode on us or fail to operate. I'd trust milspec gear I'd test-fired and understood, but these launchers represented more risk than I liked.

Black Two and Black Three had the most difficult jobs: readying the trees. As soon as the grenades exploded in the complex, we had to take off across the cleared zone. To do that safely, we had to remotely set off any traps that were waiting for us there. We knew from Lobo's scans and long-range photos that we weren't facing surface weapons, but what lurked under the ground was anyone's guess. Lobo couldn't detect any obvious IR signatures, but cheap mines or devices as crude as spiked branches on tripwires wouldn't leave any telltale signs he could spot from so far away.

Dropping half a dozen large trees on that area, on the other hand, would both trigger everything in front of us and provide a solid, if rough, platform we could use to run to the complex.

The tricky and thus time-consuming part of the operation was making sure we hit the ground with the right length of each tree. The trees here ran from a meter and a half to about two meters in diameter, so we'd be crashing a lot of weight onto the booby-trapped zone. If we hit it with a tree section that was too long, we could trash part of the wall of the complex or possibly even kill anyone standing or sleeping too near it. We would need the walls to hold in the rebels once we took over, and we didn't want to kill anyone, so running long was bad. On the other hand, if we cut and dropped too short a piece, we'd have to waste time clearing the remaining open ground, and that delay would leave us all exposed. So, short was even worse. We had to get it just right.

Each of the six people on the tree teams carried logging sensors and line-of-sight measurers, and they were busy using those devices now. Each picked a tree, took measurements of both it and the distance to the complex, and used the sensor's computer to figure the cut point. The real work was climbing the tree and attaching the cutting tapes to that point. They had gecko shoes and gloves and were good at what they did, and the trunks were wavy and full of good handholds and easy to manage with that gear, but it was dark and time was short and so everyone was hustling.

Black Two scrambled up the tree as if born to climb. He paused a few times to point at Black Three and shake his head. I could see why: Black Three moved like a great beast clawing his way upward.

I felt guilty for having so little to do. The evening air was cool enough that I was sweating only moderately as the humidity took its toll; the working teams had to be soaked. I walked among the tree and launcher teams, checking their work, listening for bursts from Lobo, and generally being useless. We'd agreed not to give the commanders specific duties and instead to train them as backups for everything, in case anything went wrong, but our unit was intact and so I was unnecessary. I hated it. I wanted to help, but I also knew that interfering would be both insulting to my squad mates and a sure way to slow them.

"All present," said the comm burst from Lobo. "No dead, two casualties, all operational. Stick to plan."

I checked the mission timer in my right contact. We had eighty-eight minutes to launch time, which would be three hours before sunrise, when everyone in the complex except late-night security patrols should be sleeping their deepest. We'd finish early, but even if the others had just arrived, they should be able to meet this schedule.

I inspected the inside of our perimeter. The outward-facing guards were in position and watchful, no one talking or sleeping or messing around. None of them had signaled the alarm, and Lobo hadn't sent us any alerts, so as best we could tell, we remained undetected.

All the launchers were on their marks. The two guys from my trio were loading the first one.

The six on the trees were nearing their marks. Most of the climbers were only five or six meters off the ground, but one was twice that high, and another was two meters higher still. The trees were tall enough that we'd known we'd have to cut them at points fairly far off the ground, but it was still odd to see these people moving up the sides of the trunks, transforming from humans into dark shapes that blended with the jungle night and, when they were high enough, faded to invisibility.

I returned to my central observation point and checked the time again.

Eighty-two minutes before we went hot.

CHAPTER 24

In the jungle right outside the rebel complex, planet Tumani

TWO MINUTES TO go.

A burst from Lobo blasted through my comm. "All green," he said. "On the schedule."

I checked our positions one last time. All five trios had formed up outside our previous perimeter, behind and to the side of the target trees and the launchers. Most of us were on the safe side of the action in shallow holes we'd scraped with the spare minutes available to us. If a trunk fell the wrong way or a launcher blew up or anything else went wrong, we wanted to be as far away and as protected as we could be without unreasonably slowing our assault.

Per our plan, I activated the comms of our whole team. This close, even if the rebels detected the transmissions, it would be too late for them to retaliate. From the darkness around me I heard the soft snick of helmets closing and locking out the world. I shut mine, and all I could hear was my own breathing and my pulse pounding in my ears. When we set off the launchers and cut down the tree sections, the sounds would be deafening if we didn't protect ourselves. The helmets would also, of course, filter the gas, though as an added precaution we'd all taken an antidote before we'd left the hangar.

One minute.

"Like we planned it," I said to the team. "Helmets locked, stay on comms, go crisp and easy, remain on the trees throughout your approach, hope not to have to shoot. I want everyone standing at the end. Go on the mark." They knew all of those things, of course, but the review was as close to a pep talk as I could manage with people I didn't know.

Fifteen seconds.

I checked the sky over the complex to make sure no one had gone earlier; all clear. I focused on our launchers.

Ten.

I took a deep breath and twisted my head a bit to relax my neck and shoulders.

Five.

One.

The launchers shook slightly as they fired the gas grenades. The mission timer on my contact changed direction and counted upward. The grenades shot into the air every three seconds, so for half a minute I watched, the world eerily silent thanks to the helmet, as we filled our sector of the complex with gas. I glanced at the huge wall across the clearing, but it was still dark and the gas was so heavy that I couldn't see any of it in the air above the buildings.

At forty-five seconds, the top of the first tree began

its descent. It was big enough and encountered enough resistance from the branches of the others in front of it that its fall was initially slow, almost stately, like a drunk gentleman lowering himself into his own bed. The tree section accelerated as it crashed through the last of the branches in its path, slammed onto the ground, bounced, and settled.

Dirt and rock and wood chunks flew through the air. Between the darkness and the amount of debris the tree's crash had caused, I couldn't tell whether we'd set off any mines.

A second tree hit the ground. While focusing on the first and its aftermath, I'd missed this one's descent. It lay three or four meters to the left of the earlier one. This time, the air near the tree flashed orange-white for several seconds; we'd definitely triggered something. Flying fragments moving too fast for me to see cut through the branches and underbrush in front of us.

Another tree fell between the first two. More dirt, more branches, more flashes of light, one of them a meter or so inside the jungle from the cleared area. I was glad we'd stayed way back.

A fourth landed and notched into place between the third and the second as if we were building a floor with trunk-size planks. It caused fewer flashes than the third, but this time something nicked into the tree closest to me and leaves rained all over me. Sweat made the wicking fabric in my uniform work harder; I hated being a passive observer in a fixed position with explosions in front of me.

The fifth didn't hit its mark as well as we'd hoped. It ended up stretched across part of the central third tree and a section of the first one, but that was acceptable; we'd dropped so many to make sure we had multiple pathways to the goal.

The sixth and last tree landed to the right of the first, almost touching it at the cut end near us, a couple of meters apart from that earlier tree at the complex wall. This one triggered a long chain of flashes; the rebels had been lazy and planted a bunch of mines on a diagonal we'd accidentally hit.

"No significant damage to the complex from your trees," Lobo said, the comm now live and going to all of us.

We were up and running toward them as he continued, our helmets' night-vision displays activated.

"Take the leftmost two; their branches reach all the way to the wall."

We reached those downed trees. Black Two and Black Three led their teams onto the left and right downed trunks, respectively. Black Two swung onto the tree, crouched, pulled his rifle to the ready, and moved forward three meters to make room for the other two. Black Four's and Black Five's teams followed them but stopped in the shadow of the trees, pulled their rifles, and scanned the complex, ready to provide covering fire should anyone try to shoot their squad-mates on the trees.

The six on the trunks kept a meter between each of them as they walked quickly but carefully across the downed trees. They slowed when they reached the thick branches that ran the last several meters to the complex's outer wall. They dropped and crawled the rest of the distance, descending into the thick, fallen canopy and out of our sight as they drew closer to the wall.

As soon as we could no longer see those first six, the guard trios ascended the trees and my three advanced to provide covering fire. The other two covered the outer, leftmost tree; I took the right one. I could feel the rough texture of the bark through the thin gloves. We'd had no way to drill this process, but everyone here was a pro, and the passage continued to proceed smoothly.

"At the wall," Black Two said. "Preparing entrance."

The six now on the trees picked up their pace, eager to be in position for the breach of the complex.

"Switch to twenty-five-percent audio," Lobo said over our comms. "Maintain gas protection."

Sound leaked through the helmet's filters. Even though it was only the faintest whispers of the scraping of boots on trees and the rush of air through branches, it was a welcome taste of the audible world.

A few seconds later, a loud boom broke the quiet. Four louder explosions followed it.

"Entrance open and additional gas away," Black Two said. "Holding for cover teams."

As the sound of our blasts faded, much quieter rumbles filled the air. The teams at the other corners of the complex were doing their work, but I didn't pay any attention to them. My job was here; Lim would relay new orders through Lobo if she needed us elsewhere.

"At the wall," Black Four said, "and giving cover. Come on over."

"No hostile contact," Black Two said, "as per plan." Though everyone inside should be unconscious, he was to hold his position until we were all there and ready to go.

The three of us on my team shouldered our weapons, climbed onto the trunks, and started across, our focus on the wood below our feet. It wasn't a bad surface, but I didn't want to be the first to slip, so I moved carefully. The canopy was denser than I'd thought: almost immediately after hitting it, I had to climb down and crawl along one of the thicker branches. The ones who'd gone before me had left an easy to follow trail of bent and broken smaller branches, so I made good progress and was quickly in sight of the wall. I followed the path of the others down to the ground and stepped in their footprints. The others remained in position near the entrance.

"Still no signs of movement in the open areas," Lobo said. "Reminder: I can't read IR signatures through the roofs of the corner guard buildings. Proceed with caution."

If this had been a normal mission, we'd have addressed that limitation by blowing up those four structures, or at least shooting enough rounds into them to kill anyone inside. Here, though, we couldn't be sure where kids might be, so we had to clear each building and capture all the hostiles. We didn't want to lose any of our team, though, so we were carrying live rounds, not tranks. I hoped we didn't have to use them.

Gunfire sounded in the distance. Either some rebels had avoided the gas, or someone on our side had gotten too excited. Either way, not my problem, not right then.

"Go," I said.

Black Two and Black Three lead their trios through the entrance in alternation, Black Two's group going right, Black Three's heading left. The teams moved like their leaders: Black Two's in quick, staccato motions, Black Three's slowly and carefully.

The rest of us took up positions on either side of the entrance and at different heights and aimed our rifles toward the guard building.

The six on point rushed to the left and right edges of the building, staying low as they ran, and leaned against the walls as soon as they reached them.

We could spot no sign of activity inside it.

"Black Team!" Lobo said. "Roof!"

We were sloppy to need the warning, so focused on dealing with the possibility of people being awake inside the building that we hadn't checked above it. I glanced up in time to see a man, his silhouette barely visible against the night sky, crawling along the peak of the roof. Another's torso emerged from an access hatch. Both appeared to be wearing masks.

Our six at the building flattened themselves further against the walls.

"Four," I said, "on my mark. Two and Three, enter on same. Go."

Black Four led her team inside the complex and opened fire, each of them squeezing off a short burst. The men on the roof twitched from multiple impacts and stopped moving. One of them hung partway out of the hatch.

At the same time, the six at the building ran to the door facing us and kicked it open. We cleared to the sides as soon as it started to move.

Gunfire sounded from within.

Our teams pulled back.

Black Five dropped to the ground, crawled forward

until he could aim through the opening, and squeezed off three short bursts. He lifted his fist, then his thumb.

His teammates headed in, one on his left and one on his right. He stood and followed them.

"Inside clear," Black Five said. "One down, one unconscious and now secure."

"Roof clear," Black Four said. "Two hostiles down."

"Black Team," Lobo said, "no external motion in your quadrant."

Black Four fanned out her team so they could guard the other three sides of the building's exterior.

I had my helmet display a map of the six remaining buildings we were responsible for securing. Three were small, structures we'd guessed held supplies or quarters for senior staff. Three were almost certainly barracks for kids. We'd clear the small ones first, and then we'd secure the barracks.

"Let's go visiting," I said over the comm.

CHAPTER 25

In the rebel complex, planet Tumani

THE SMALLER BUILDINGS housed only sleeping guards, their open windows perfect entrances for the gas. We secured all of the people and left them where they slept; we'd round them up later, after we'd cleared the rest of our area.

Windows were also open all along the side of the first dorm we approached, so we peeked through them to verify that no one was moving. The third or so of the beds that we could see were occupied, and all the occupants appeared to be asleep. I considered trying to save time by sending in one trio to secure the kids and taking the rest of our unit to the next dorm, but I rejected the notion: Sloppy work way too often proves to be its own reward.

Instead, we went in properly, Black Two slithering in first. He and his team quickly verified that the main area was indeed secure, every kid in it asleep, but it wasn't the only room: The space also contained a pair of large closets, one at either end, and a bathroom that ran two-thirds of the way across the rear.

Black Three's team joined to provide cover fire if necessary as Black Two's cleared those three rooms. I doubted a single person in either trio believed they were going to encounter resistance, but they did their jobs properly and precisely; they were pros.

The front closet was empty. So was the rear.

As they worked, the rest of us fanned out in the main area and secured the sleeping kids with ties on their hands and feet. The gas must have hit them hard, because none of them even stirred.

Black Two, standing well to the side of the bathroom entrance, knocked on its door. A shot blasted a hole right where his hand had touched the wood. The sound echoed despite the open windows. Two more shots followed the first blast.

Black Two motioned to Black Three to return fire.

The big man raised his rifle.

"Hold," I said over the comm. "Black Five, check for other exits from the bathroom."

That trio ran out of the barracks.

"We're on a schedule," Lobo said to me privately. "You need to deal with this quickly."

I ignored him.

"Black Two and Three, force open the door, toss in gas, and keep your teams to the sides."

The two trios spread along the bathroom wall. Black Two pulled a small charge from his pack and stuck it to the door's handle.

Ten seconds later, it blew with a loud pop.

The door flew inward.

Black Three stooped and rolled in a gas grenade.

Two more shots from inside the room smacked into the wall at the opposite end of the barracks.

Five seconds later, a small, thin boy ran out of the smoke, a damp rag tied over his nose and mouth. He carried his rifle like a club and swung it to the left as he cleared the doorway.

Black Three grabbed the weapon at the same time Black Two caught the boy's arm.

The kid let go and tried to spin free, but Black Two maintained his grip on the kid.

"Government assassins!" the boy said. Black Two looked to me for instructions, so the boy stared at me, too. "You can't mess with Bony, no, not with me. I'll show you."

I pointed to the bathroom.

Black Two nodded and pulled the rag away from the boy's face.

The kid kicked and screamed, wordless animal sounds ripping out of his throat.

Black Three picked up the boy and carried him into the bathroom as easily as if he was a sleeping baby.

"You'll see!" the boy said. He coughed several times. "You'll see." His voice trailed off.

Black Three reappeared a few seconds later, the unconscious boy looking even tinier cradled in his arms. "Tough, clever little bugger," he said. "You gotta give 'im that." He set the kid on the first empty bunk.

The boy didn't come close to filling the small bed. Maybe a meter and a half tall, with short hair, a body so thin it might have been composed of sticks, and skin as dark as the bark of the trees we'd used to create our path over the mines, he looked like a starving child, not a soldier.

Black Three shook his head. He secured the kid's hands and feet anyway.

I stared at the child, at all the other bound and sleeping boys in the barracks, and helpless rage rose in me, fury that made me want to kill those who had turned these children into fighters and the leaders who had decided that doing so was a good idea.

"Bathroom clear," Black Two said.

I nodded, shoved down the rage, and headed out of the barracks. We weren't done. "Two more to go," I said. "Move out."

The first stains of daylight were oozing along the horizon when Lobo touched down in a large landing area near the center of the complex. As my body consumed the last dregs of adrenaline, aches and fatigue flooded through me. The nanomachines would remedy the pains soon enough, but in that moment they seemed appropriate, even necessary; violence should never come without cost.

Lim, Gustafson, Schmidt, and I walked inside Lobo through a side hatch he'd opened. Sweat had carved small trails in the dirt on their faces. They moved stiffly, as if they were ancient. I wondered if I appeared to be in equally bad shape.

"You all look like hell," Lobo said privately, "particularly you, and you smell worse."

So much for that question. "Thanks," I subvocalized.

Small currents of air played across my neck; Lobo was dealing with the odor. "It's so much harder," he said, "being human than it is being me."

We stood in his front. I could have asked him to bring out couches, but I was afraid I might fall asleep if I relaxed.

"Five casualties for us," Lim said, "but no fatalities,

and all the injured should recover fully. Not bad."

"But also not what we dreamed," Gustafson said, "though it never is."

"Half a dozen hostiles dead," Lim said, as if she hadn't heard him, "and another eleven shot, including two boys. Don't know if they'll make it."

None of us had anything to say to that. No one had wanted to shoot any of the children, but we'd all had to defend ourselves. I was glad Black squad hadn't shot any of them, but I couldn't take credit for that; we'd just been lucky—and we had killed the boy in the jungle.

"A Tumani unit is inbound," Lim said. "I've spoken to their commander, and they're honoring our deal: They'll make camp in the trees around the perimeter and hope the rebels come back. They'll also take away our adult prisoners. The children and the complex are ours."

"The rest of our people?" Schmidt said.

"Also inbound," Lim said. "Two more small ships have cleared the jump gates since we started, so we should get seventy-five more people. A few more may join us later, but that's basically it."

I hadn't been part of the planning for the follow-on reintegration work, because my job ended when we controlled the complex. "The kids will outnumber you four to one," I said.

Schmidt shrugged. "We're not here to fight them; we're here to help them. I know our numbers aren't ideal for reintegration, but they also aren't horrible. Besides, group counseling is common."

"More to the point," Gustafson said, "it's the best we can do."

"I understand your intentions and plans," I said,

"and I obviously support them. But what do you do if the boys want to fight you?"

"What do you think?" Schmidt said, her voice strained. "We know this isn't perfect. We know we can't plan for everything. We know we probably won't save them all. But we'll do what we can. We'll do everything we can to avoid conflict, and if it comes, we'll deal with it—and try to teach them that they no longer have to fight."

I'd never found that lesson to be true, never experienced more than a year or so without a battle of some kind, but whether the violence found me or I sought it was something I've never really understood.

Before I could upset Schmidt further, Gustafson put his hand on her shoulder, stared at me, and said, "Look, Gunny, you should understand by now that we know what we're doing. Teams are already locating and securing every weapon in the place. Others are clearing the felled trees and repairing the damage we did to the four entry points. We won't finish all the work tonight, but even with the assault group sleeping in shifts, we should have the place secure within a day. The kids should remain unconscious for at least another four hours. When they're all awake, we'll explain the situation to them." He patted Schmidt's shoulder lightly. "The rest will be up to the counselors."

"And when we've proven to the kids that fighting is behind them," Schmidt said, "the real work will begin."

Lim and Gustafson nodded their agreement.

"Jon," Lobo said to me privately over the machine frequency, "why are you provoking arguments? Our role in this is over. Let's go."

He was right. I'd done what I'd promised, Lobo

had delivered on his end, and the operation had gone as well as anyone had a right to expect. I could fight, but I couldn't help now that the attack was over; I knew nothing about teaching children how to live *after* fighting. No one had ever taught me. I couldn't even really believe in a life without fighting.

I held up my hands. "I didn't mean to criticize. I'm sorry. I think it's time for me to call it a night."

"I know you're tired," Lim said. "We all are. I'd like one more thing, though."

"What?" I hoped my voice didn't sound as angry to her as it did to me.

"Would you be willing," she said, "to wait here and watch for trouble until the rest of our ships arrive? I don't expect any rebel attacks, and the window of exposure is only four hours, but I'd just as soon play it safe."

I stared at her. She couldn't be concerned about the rebels; they had no ships that could pose any problems for her team. She had to be worried about the government double-crossing her.

"You need to sleep," Lobo said privately, "but I've got nothing better to do. It's not like I can rest."

"Sure," I said to Lim, "I'd be happy to do it."

"I wouldn't go that far," Lobo said.

Lim nodded and headed out of Lobo. Gustafson and Schmidt followed her. I trailed them. At the hatch, Lim paused and turned to face me.

"This is where you always make your exit, Jon," she said, "and I understand that. It's what people like us do. It's what I usually do. Don't you ever wonder, though, what happens to the messes we leave behind?"

Anger flushed my face. I'd done what I'd said I'd do. I'd kept up my end of the deal. "What right—"

"I'm sorry," she said, interrupting me. She rubbed her eyes. "That was uncalled for. I appreciate your help. We couldn't have done it without you." She stepped out of Lobo, turned, and vanished.

Gustafson glanced back at me and nodded. "Gunny."

"Top," I said.

Without looking at me, Schmidt said, "Thanks."

I nodded in acknowledgment even though she couldn't see me.

The two of them left.

Lobo sealed the hatch behind them.

I stared at the blank wall and thought about what Lim had said. When the fighting was over and the mission was complete, I did leave, but it was always what everyone wanted me to do. People needed me—needed *us*, Lobo and me and others like us—to fix their problems, to do the dirty work they wouldn't do, but when we were done, they wanted us to go somewhere else. Our skills, our abilities, even our willingness to do those jobs made us unwelcome when the fighting was over.

I turned and headed for my quarters. "Thank you for agreeing to watch the skies," I said aloud to Lobo. "I'm going to sleep."

CHAPTER 26

Dump Island, planet Pinkelponker—139 years earlier

LIGHT WAS FLEEING the purpling sky and still Benny would not let us rest. The heat of the day hung on as if fighting to survive. The air squatted on us, wet and thick and so heavy that every movement was a struggle. Sand coated my shirtless body and ran in sweat streams down my chest and back and arms. My right hand and wrist and forearm ached from gripping the knife and practicing with dummies stuffed with dirt and grass and the thick branches that Bob wielded like clubs.

"They'll have rifles," Benny said, his voice hoarse, "and we'll have only knives. We've got to be good with what we have."

I circled Bob, looking for an in, watching the branch. If I could stab the grass-filled sack he was wearing like a shirt, I would win that round. I jabbed, but he danced back and avoided any contact. He swatted with the branch a second later, but I had already slipped out of range; he was definitely slowing.

I advanced, tempting him to close the distance.

Something slammed into my forearm.

I yelped with pain and dropped the knife. I glanced in the direction of the blow and saw Alex preparing to hit me again with a branch thicker than my forearm.

Something smashed into my left shoulder.

I stumbled. I'd forgotten Bob!

"What?" I yelled. "It wasn't supposed—"

A weight landed on my back.

I fell forward onto my hands and knees. I turned in time to see Bob and Alex diving for my arms.

Scaly arms wrapped around my throat and started choking me.

Something pulled on my legs.

I hit the ground face-first. I turned my head in time to avoid hurting my nose, but I breathed in dirt and couldn't see clearly. I pushed off hard with my left hand and managed to roll onto my back. I pushed down with my body and tried to lift my head to butt it backward into Han's nose. Bob and Alex leapt on me and locked down my arms and grabbed my head so I couldn't hurt Han.

I screamed and thrashed in rage, but they all held on, Han slowing my air supply even though I tucked my chin as Benny had taught us.

I heard the sound of Benny's cart rolling in the sand. He came into view over my left shoulder.

His right arm flipper gripped my knife. He brought it down on my face and eased it between Han's arm and the underside of my chin.

I felt the sharp blade and stopped moving; I'd seen how easily it could cut.

"You screwed up," Benny said, "several times. First, you didn't watch for other threats. When they came, you forgot how to handle them. Finally, you lost your temper." He shook his head. "You know better. I've taught you better."

I tried to respond, but I couldn't get enough air to speak clearly.

"Han," Benny said, "let him talk."

Han relaxed but did not release his grip on my neck.

"That's not fair," I said. My voice didn't sound right. I coughed a few times but couldn't clear my throat. "We weren't doing that sort of practice."

"Fair?" Benny said. He leaned closer to me. "Haven't you been listening? What's so hard to understand? Nothing about our situation is fair. Not this island, not my body, not the way we were born, nothing. And the soldiers who guard the shuttle definitely won't worry about being fair. We won't know for sure how they'll react, and they won't follow any plan of ours or any rules. If they have to, maybe even if they simply feel like it, they'll kill every single one of us who attacks them."

"But you don't make these attacks on any of the other people." I said. I realized I was crying.

Alex and Bob looked away, but they didn't release my arms.

"Don't you cry!" Benny said. "I've told you before: Don't you ever cry. You don't get to cry. No one else goes through these drills because no one else can. You can. You have to lead the attack. You have to be ready for anything, because you're the best we have. So, you'll keep doing the drills and doing them and doing them until I say you're ready."

"I don't want to," I said. My cheeks were wet, but I couldn't stop myself, couldn't stop the tears. "I don't want to do this anymore. I don't want to."

Benny lifted the knife and tossed it away. He nodded, and Alex and Bob got off me.

I rolled onto my side and hugged my knees to my chest.

Han wriggled out from under me.

Benny put his flipper on my shoulder, but I wouldn't look at him. "I don't want this," I said. "I never wanted any of this. I just want to be home, with Jennie, with everything the way it was."

"You can't have that," Benny said. "I'm sorry, I really am, but you can't."

"You can at least stop doing this to me. You can leave me alone."

"Look at me," he said.

I didn't move.

"Look at me."

He wouldn't stop until I did, so I turned onto my back and stared up at him.

"I will," he said, "if you tell me that's what you really want. But before you do, think about what I said: If we're ever to get off this island, it's going to be because *you* led the way, because *you* made it possible for us to beat the guards. You. We can't do it without you. You're the only one of us with a whole body and a whole mind."

"I'm just a kid," I said. For a moment, I remembered being treated like one, an oversized, too-old one, but a kid who Jennie always played with and treated like a kid. My time with her, only a couple of months ago, now seemed so far away.

"I know," Benny said, "and we can wait for you to get older if you want, but however long we delay, it's going to come down to you. The only way any of us wins is if you lead the fight and if you can beat the guards. For you to do that, you have to become a better fighter than they are—and you have to be ready for anything that can happen. You have to be tough, tougher than they are, and they're full-grown men with a great deal of training."

My nose was clogged from crying and the sand, so I blew it on my hands and wiped them on the ground.

"I never wanted to be tough," I said. "Jennie used to tell me I had a smart heart, and part of the reason is that I was always nice. The tough people I knew were mean a lot of the time."

"You can stay soft, and you can stay nice," Benny said, "but then you'll never leave Dump, and you'll never see your sister again."

I looked at the others. None of them would face me. I knew they liked me, and I didn't think any of them enjoyed the sneak attacks Benny made them launch at me, but still they did what he said. They wanted to escape from Dump, and they were willing to do whatever it took to make that happen. Even if that meant hurting me.

"I'm sorry," Benny said, his eyes glistening in the last of the daylight, "but if you want to leave here, you don't get to be a kid any longer. You have to learn to fight, to harden that heart, and to do whatever it takes, including killing those guards if it comes to that, or we'll all stay here until we die."

"It's not right," I said. "It's wrong of you to put so much on me. There has to be another way."

He shook his head. "No, there's not, or if there is, I've missed it." He paused a few seconds. With a very low voice, barely louder than a whisper, he said, "Tell me what I've missed." I honestly believe he wanted me to show him another way.

I couldn't. I thought about the day the guards had dropped me on the island and how careful and strong they'd been. I looked at the others training with me. Benny was right: None of them could do it. None of them would even meet my gaze.

I shook my head slowly and sat up. I closed my eyes and thought about living here forever, about never seeing Jennie again, and the anger rushed into me. It came like a storm from the ocean bringing fresh drinking water, like hot food, giving me energy, feeding me, making me stronger.

Making me harder.

I opened my eyes and looked at Benny. I slowly nodded my head, my arms trembling as the anger kept coming, as I flashed on the guards and the ship taking away Jennie and the men who'd dumped me here. I wanted to scream, to howl at the coming night like a hurt and cornered animal, but I didn't, because I might lose the anger, and I couldn't let myself do that, not yet, not then. Without it, all I had was pain and loss. I kept it in me, let it fill me but held it, and when I spoke, my voice was calm and, despite the heat in me, colder than I'd ever heard it.

"You're right," I said. "There's no other way." I hit the ground with both fists. "I will learn, and we *will* get off this island."

"Okay," Benny said, nodding his head. "Okay." He raised his voice. "That's enough for today."

As he turned away from me, I'm sure I saw tears, but I didn't care. He didn't need to cry about anything. None of us did. Crying wouldn't help; I understood that now. Only the anger would save us.

CHAPTER 27

In the former rebel complex, planet Tumani

I AWOKE DRENCHED IN sweat and still wearing the mission pants and shirt, my muscles straining, not moving as my body desperately fought the urge to leap up.

"How long?" I said as I stood.

"You've been asleep three hours and thirty minutes," Lobo said.

My body was fine; the nanomachines had done their work and healed me. Physically, despite the tightness and the tension, I was ready to go. Mentally, though, I was exhausted. I didn't remember dreaming, didn't recall anything from that short rest, but I felt like my mind had been racing the entire time.

I walked out of my quarters. "Have all of Lim's ships arrived?"

"I don't know," Lobo said. "Several have, but I've heard nothing from her as to whether she's expecting more. You were sleeping, and no hostiles showed up, so I had no reason to contact her. Do you want me to do so now?"

"No need. What's going on out there?"

In response, a display appeared on the wall in front of me. Lim was standing on top of a small, one-story, flat-roofed building that faced a large open square in the middle of the compound. A crowd of boys paced and stood in front of her. More streamed from all angles into the group. In size, some of them appeared to be on the very cusp of manhood, while others didn't look much more than eight or nine years old. Their bodies rippled with lean, corded muscle and showed no fat. Most had passed thin and were verging on malnourished; many already had distended stomachs and shrunken, hollow faces.

Their expressions showed the aging the fighting had wrought on them. None smiled. All scanned their surroundings constantly, their eyes flicking across the rifle-bearing guards who lounged against nearby buildings, trying hard to look nonchalant but not fooling anybody. The boys spoke in whispers and nods and gestures. Some stopped as if to check shoes almost none of them wore and instead palmed small stones. They thought they were clever. They thought they were fooling the guards.

They weren't.

We all knew what they were doing. They were readying themselves to fight.

I could understand that. It's what they knew, what they did, all they'd done since the rebels had pressed them into service. They almost certainly thought they were fighting for the right side. Most soldiers do, regardless of their ages. I had, at their age, during my time on Dump. I'm still sure I was on the right side of that one. Not that it made any difference, not really, not in the damage that it did to me or that I did to others.

"I'm going outside to listen," I said.

"Why?" Lobo said. "I can contact Lim and find out if she still needs us. If she does, I can handle it, and you can sleep; you clearly need more. If she doesn't, we're done, as you told them, and we can leave."

Even if I could have answered him completely honestly, even if I'd been willing to tell him about my past—and I wasn't, not yet, maybe not ever—I couldn't have explained the urge I felt. Staring at those lost boys, understanding them, having been one like them, feeling at times as if I were still one of them, I wanted to know what it was that Lim or Schmidt or Gustafson or anyone could ever say that would help, that would make one damn bit of difference to the dark dreams that would, if my experience was any guide, plague them forever. Maybe I also wanted to see that someone really was going to attempt to help them, because no one had even tried with me.

"I don't know," I finally said. "I just want to go. I'll be back."

"Of course," Lobo said. He opened a side hatch. "Where else would you go?"

I smiled and stepped outside. From anyone else, the same comment might have infuriated me with its smugness, but that's not how Lobo meant it. I knew him well enough to be sure of that. He understood. We had each other and little else, maybe nothing else. That was okay. It was more than I'd had for many decades of my life.

Even though it was only mid-morning, the air was already thick and warm and clingy. As Lobo sealed himself behind me, I set out for the square. Boys were still coming from barracks behind the pad where Lobo rested. They swerved around me, watchful eyes on me, unconsciously and automatically staying more than an arm's length away. I was an enemy who had attacked in the night, and now they were heading to hear the terms of their occupation. They were acting sensibly; I'd have done the same.

I reached the square and stayed on its edge, in the back with the guards. Lim, appearing tired but relaxed, surveyed the young mob.

I searched the perimeter until I found Schmidt, who was standing almost exactly opposite Lim. A group of four boys joined the larger group. Thirty seconds passed. No more appeared. Schmidt nodded.

"I'd thank you for coming," Lim said, her voice booming from speakers I couldn't see, "but we're going to try very hard not to lie to you, and thanking you for something we forced you to do is too close to a lie for my taste."

A few boys chuckled briefly but stopped at the angry looks from those near them. Lim had gotten their attention, though; the square was quiet save for the soft breeze, the construction sounds of the repairs at the corners of the complex, and the occasional short bird cry.

"You know you're prisoners," she said, "because we have armed guards, and we won't let you leave."

At this, many of them began talking, mumbling, and shifting in place. Maybe they'd harbored other hopes, or perhaps the directness of Lim's approach wasn't working as well now as it had a moment before.

"What are you going to do with us?" a voice from the middle called.

"Help you," Lim said. "We're going to help you learn to deal with what's happened to you and live like normal kids again. When you're ready, we'll take you back to your families—or find new families for you, if yours are no longer"—she paused, as if she didn't want to finish her sentence—"alive."

"We don't want your help!" several boys simultaneously said.

"I understand," Lim said. "I believe that many of you, maybe even most of you, feel that way. You don't get a choice, though. I'm sorry, but you don't. Even if you don't believe it, you do need help."

"You killed our families!" a boy a few yards in front of me yelled in a voice I thought I recognized. Others all around the square began screaming, so many words coming at once that I couldn't make out most of them.

I shifted left a few steps so I could get a better view of the first speaker. He was the boy from the shower, the one who had attacked our team. For a few seconds, I couldn't recall his name—it hadn't seemed important at the time—and then it came to me: Bony. He'd called himself Bony.

Lim crossed her arms and stood silently.

A few rocks smacked into the air in front of her and bounced off.

I moved a bit to my left and caught the profile of the thin, transparent shield in front of her. Smart.

The boys quickly figured it out, too, because the rocks stopped flying.

"No fair," a voice somewhere near the center said.

At that, boys all over the square laughed, and the rest of the yelling died down.

"No," Lim said, "it's not fair, not at all. Since when was any of this fair? Did the men who trained you tell you that fighting was fair?" She looked slowly over the crowd of boys, as if daring each one to say she was wrong. "I thought not, because they were not stupid."

She had their full attention again. I was impressed. When I'd last seen her, she couldn't manage a meeting without losing control of her anger. Now, she was manipulating hundreds of boys—and keeping herself in check.

"No," she said again, this time shaking her head, "they were not stupid. Far from it. They were smart. They knew that if they worked you and addicted you and trained you and didn't feed you enough and didn't let you sleep that they could turn you from children into soldiers, soldiers they could command. And they did." This time, she nodded. "They did. They made you all soldiers."

"Damn right!" several voices said. Murmurs of agreement and even a few cheers swept through the boys.

Lim held up her hands, and as if the assembled children were now under her command, they quickly fell silent. "That's all over now. You're not soldiers anymore."

"What?"

"No!"

"What do you mean?"

"Who are you to tell us what we are?"

"Wait until our brothers return!"

I couldn't keep track of who was saying what as a chorus of responses showered Lim.

She remained silent until the cries faded away, the whole time appearing to be listening closely. When she spoke, her voice was firm but held no trace of anger. "The sooner you let me finish, the sooner you can return to your barracks. You can drown me out, but you can't out-wait me." She surveyed the crowd slowly, not challenging them, not angry, just stating a fact. When no one spoke, she nodded once and continued. "Thank you. Let me try to answer all those questions. What I mean is simple: Your days as soldiers are over. The rebels should never have"— she paused as a few shouts came from the boys and continued when they were quiet—"they should never have made you soldiers. You're children, and children should never be soldiers."

At this, the boys began yelling again.

In response, Lim fell quiet.

They went at it for almost fifteen minutes, different groups taking turns screaming, questions and insults and sexual suggestions coming in almost equal measures.

Lim stood silently. As far as I knew, she'd been up all night, and her temper was legendary, but she never wavered from her calm, flat affect.

When the area fell quiet once again, she continued as if they'd never interrupted her. "Your captors—and the rebels were always your captors, never really your brothers, for what big brother makes his little brother carry a weapon and fight in a war?—are not coming back. We have captured all of the ones who were stationed here. Government forces are in the jungle protecting this complex. It is ours."

"So you are the government?" a boy yelled.

"No," she said, "we are not. We are an independent group here to help you. Some of you asked who we were to tell you what you are and what you're going to do.

All we are is a group of concerned adults who want to help you become kids again and have families again."

"You called our brothers our captors, but you have captured us!" the small boy, Bony, yelled at her.

"You're right," she said, nodding. "We are. We captured this complex and you because we could not think of any other way to free you. We're going to hold you here until you're ready to return to normal life and we have families ready to take you."

"This is my family!" Bony yelled. Others joined him, cheering for themselves, for each other.

"No," Lim said when they finally stopped. "You and the adults who commanded you are the only people you believe understand what you've been through, and so you all feel like you've become a family, but those adults were *never* your family. They used you, and when one of you failed or fell, they killed him and left him behind." She stopped and slowly scanned the crowd. "You know I'm telling the truth."

"They did what they had to do!" a boy yelled.

Lim shook her head. "No, no they didn't. They used you. What we are going to do is help each of you become ready for a real family, your old one or, if need be, a new one. All of us who are going to work with you have been in wars before, so we understand fighting and what it does to you. We can help you, and we will."

More jeers and taunts followed.

Again, Lim stayed silent until they stopped.

"For now, you may do whatever you want," she said, "with only two limitations: if we find you with a weapon, any weapon, we will take it away, and from this moment on, you will not have any more root."

"What?" The crowd hurled cries of frustration and disbelief at her.

"Your captors made you addicts," Lim said when they were all quiet, "so you have to eat root to feel right. When you don't eat it, you feel sick. We will give you drugs to help clean it out of your systems, so you can start to be yourselves again—and so you can sleep."

"Real warriors don't need to sleep!" one of the boys across the square from me yelled.

"That's right!"

"We fight while the weak sleep!"

"Root makes us strong! You're just afraid of us!"

"You want to poison us with your drugs!"

More rocks bounced off the shield in front of Lim.

She ignored them and stayed perfectly still, her arms at her sides, her gaze on the crowd.

When the yelling finally stopped, she continued. "We've already destroyed all the root in the compound. You're done with it. Even with the medicine we'll give you, this will be hard. None of this is your fault, but the only way out of it is going to be rough. I'm sorry for that. I really am."

She turned to go.

"Running away?" Bony yelled. "Afraid of us?"

Lim turned back to face them. She smiled slightly. "No, I'm not going anywhere. I'm staying here until we're done. You're stuck with me."

"Come down here and say that to my face," Bony yelled, puffing up his chest. Lim had a good third of a meter and many kilos on him, but the kid wasn't just posturing; he was ready to fight.

I smiled despite my tension and fatigue. I had to

admire his determination. I certainly understood his attitude.

Lim shook her head. "No," she said, "I won't. I won't fight you. None of this is your fault, and I won't punish you for it."

She turned and walked away, across the roof and down something I could not see.

The boys stayed where they were for a few seconds before drifting away in packs of twos and threes and fours.

I watched them go and shook my head. I wondered if Lim and her counselors had any idea what they were facing. They'd all been in combat, but how many of them had been there as children? It was different, I knew it was, but I couldn't explain it to them without revealing more of my past than I would let anyone know.

A hand touched my left shoulder. I grabbed it, pulled forward and spun behind the body of the person who'd touched me. I relaxed when I realized it was a guard, a blond man with skin light brown from tan. He stood a hand's-width shorter than I was and carried a gun in his left hand. He wore coveralls, not a proper uniform, with an activefiber tag over his heart that read "Chris Long."

Long held up his right hand and kept his weapon where it was. "Sorry for surprising you," he said. "Lim told me not to do that. I should have listened more carefully."

Still tense from his approach, I nodded and said, "Yes."

He glared at me for a second, unhappy with my response and tensing as if he were about to throw

a punch. He stretched his head from side to side
and said, "Sorry. We're both fighters, but that's not
what we're here to do. We have to teach these kids
how *not* to be soldiers, how to fit into the world like
normal people. We're not doing our jobs if we fight
among ourselves."

"Your jobs," I said, "not mine. I'm done with this."

"That's what she told me," Long said. "Lim asked
me to let you know that all our ships are here and
you're free to go. She said she'd thank you herself, but
she has more work to do and needs to grab some cot
time." He stuck out his hand. "I was on Blue team.
Your ship's surveillance helped us a lot. Thanks, and
good luck."

I shook his hand, nodded once, and headed back
to Lobo.

"Maggie's vessel is in-bound," Lobo said to me
privately over the machine frequency. "Are you sure
you want to leave before it gets here?"

CHAPTER 28

Dump Island, planet Pinkelponker—139 years earlier

I RAN ALONG THE beach as if the guards from the shuttle were chasing me.

No one was.

As Benny had taught me, I imagined them trying to catch me so they could beat me, tie me up, and kill me in front of the others. The more I focused on the images, the faster my heart beat, until the anger rose inside me and my breathing turned uneven and I couldn't get enough air. Sweat ran down my chest and my arms and my forehead, stinging my eyes. The heat, which hadn't bothered me a few seconds ago, now weighed on me. The sand, which I'd barely noticed moments earlier, pulled at my feet like hands trying to drag me down into the earth.

I slowed, but my imagination showed the guards overtaking me, knocking me face-first into the sand, climbing on top of me and holding me down until they could tie my hands and feet.

Anger you control can provide energy and power, Benny had said. Anger that runs unchecked, though, is the fastest path to burnout, to running out of breath and slowing, perhaps fatally.

I forced myself to resume my previous pace. After a few meters, I ran a little faster, pushing my legs to carry me more quickly along the beach. At the same time, I focused on my breaths, making each inhalation both bigger and as slow as I could manage. I exhaled equally slowly, letting the air leak out through my nose. I concentrated on the rhythm: Breathe in as much as I could as slowly as I could manage. Exhale gently through my nose. Repeat. As my heart slowed and my breathing came under control, I maintained the pace. I had to take a few gulps of air to refill my lungs, but after a short time I was able to return to breathing only through my nose.

My legs hurt, and I wasn't sure how long I could sustain this speed, but I had taken myself into the anger and recovered. I needed to improve my self-control, to try to stop my rage from ever becoming my master. By learning to back down from the anger without stopping or even slowing, Benny said I could feed off its energy and still remain focused on the task at hand, on the enemy in front of me.

I rounded a bend and saw Bennie ahead in the distance, stretched on his cart on a flat spot in the path, a tree next to him providing cooling shade. The mountainside tumbled closer to the water here than anywhere else, and the tide was high, so the sand narrowed to a dozen meters wide. I stuck to the narrow stretch of dry sand, not willing to change my path for anything. When Benny had first made us run, I'd been furious each time he came into view and for several minutes afterward; I'd hated working while he relaxed. Now, though, I didn't care. He couldn't make me run. No one could. I did it to myself. He wasn't the enemy. I was— the weakness in my body that stopped it from doing everything it should, and the weakness in my mind that tempted me to run slower or to stop, to do less than I was capable of doing. I couldn't allow those weaknesses to affect me. I had to be stronger, stronger than anyone else here, stronger than the guards, always stronger.

I stared at Benny, the rage filling me again. I wouldn't show him or any of them any weakness, not ever again. I forced myself to run faster, parting my lips slightly so I could take in a little more air, not willing to let him spot me breathing through my mouth and so not opening it visibly.

Right before he smacked into me, I saw Alex launch himself from behind a boulder I had just passed. I accelerated to avoid him, but I couldn't speed up enough.

He hit me.

I stumbled to the side and started to fall, Alex holding onto me with his one arm.

Once, not that many months ago, I would have fought against the force and tried to stand. Now, I did as Benny had explained and let the momentum carry me sideways into the wet, harder sand and toward the water. I relaxed into the fall and rolled in the direction we were going. I ended up on top of Alex and raised my body so I could force him to yield.

Something in the ocean moved in the edge of my vision.

I fell onto Alex and rolled once more. I ended with Alex lying on my chest. I caught the look of fear in his eyes and barely had time to tense my stomach muscles before Han landed on top of both of us.

Air rushed out of Alex. I smelled traces of the fish

he'd eaten earlier. Water dripped off Han's body as he stared at me in surprise. For a second we all froze, no one prepared for this position. Before they could regroup, I punched Han in the neck with my right hand as hard as I could manage with the limited range of motion available to me. I knew the blow wouldn't damage him badly, but it shocked him and hurt him.

He clutched his throat and rolled off Alex to my left, away from the hand that had hit him.

Before Alex could recover, I pushed him on top of Han and climbed onto both of them, my left hand on Alex's throat.

"Enough," he croaked.

Han nodded in agreement.

For a moment, they were not the guys I knew, not my training partners, not two more kids doing what Benny had told them. They were my enemies. I had beaten them. It was time to finish them. My breath came rough and hard. The pounding of my own blood filled my head. I tightened my grip on Alex's throat and raised my clenched right hand.

They must have seen the anger in me, because fear filled their eyes.

I took in their expressions, recognized them for what they were. When I'd seen those looks before, when parents on Pinecone had come rushing to rescue their small children from their new friend because I was too big and therefore not a safe playmate, they had hurt me. I hadn't wanted anyone to be afraid of me. No one had needed to fear me. I would never have hurt those kids. They were my friends.

Now, though, the fear served only to confirm my victory. We all knew what we were doing and why we went through these drills. If the result was that my friends were a little afraid of me, so be it; they had learned something useful. Maybe they'd try harder next time.

I nodded at them, pushed off, and stood.

I reached out to Alex.

After a brief hesitation, he grabbed my hand.

I lifted him off Han and helped him stand. I did the same with Han. "Good try," I said.

They both nodded in acknowledgment. After a few seconds, Han said, his voice still not quite right, "We didn't have a chance."

I nodded again and turned to look up the beach, where Benny had been resting. He had rolled down the path and was almost at the sand. Bob stood beside him.

"Good job, Jon," Benny said. "That's enough for today."

I shook my head and started running again. As I passed him, I forced my voice to sound as normal as possible as I said, "No. I owe another two laps."

I didn't look back as I ran away from them. My lungs hurt from trying to get enough air while I'd been fighting. A sour taste filled my mouth, and I wished I could rinse it and get a drink. My whole body trembled, and, as the rush of violence wore off, part of me regretted scaring Alex and Han. I wanted desperately to stop, to rest, to be done with this.

I didn't.

I wouldn't let those feelings win. I wouldn't let Han and Alex win. I wouldn't let Benny win. I wouldn't let the weaknesses in my body or my mind win.

I wouldn't let anything or anyone beat me.

I wouldn't.

I ran on.

CHAPTER 29

In the former rebel complex, planet Tumani

HOW LONG BEFORE Maggie's ship lands?" I asked Lobo.

"Maybe five minutes," he said. "She contacted me and asked to meet you. She said you could pick the location. I mean no offense to her, but for your safety, I suggest you tell her to come inside me."

Part of me wanted to leave Tumani immediately, but another part was glad Maggie had asked to see me. At the same time, past experience had taught me that she would lie to me and use me if she thought doing so would serve her cause.

Of course, I'd done the same to her in the course of saving the boy who now lived with her and the other Children of Pinkelponker.

"I agree," I said. "Tell her."

She wouldn't touch down for a few more minutes, so rather than head straight to Lobo and wait there, I let my feet carry me to the corner of the complex where we'd entered less than twelve hours ago. Half a dozen people and a couple of low-end building machines were replacing the damaged section of the wall with a mixture of wood from the fallen trees and reinforced permacrete. Others carted debris and carefully removed the sections of the trunks closest to the complex; we didn't want anyone else attacking us the same way. Two men guarded the entrance. They were trying and failing to appear nonchalant while keeping their hands on their weapons.

No boys walked near them. None appeared to be watching them, but everyone understood what was going on. I'd seen it before, prisoners and guards, and no matter how nice the prison, no one in either group is ever confused about what role he or she is playing.

The guards watched me without moving their heads, knowing from the uniform I was still wearing whose side I was on but wondering why I was there. I nodded and mumbled, "Just curious." They nodded in return, no more trusting now that I'd spoken to them than they'd been before I opened my mouth.

The temperature and humidity continued to rise. My clothing couldn't wick fast enough; I stayed constantly soaked in my own sweat. The dust from the permacrete hung in the air and made my eyes itch.

I turned and headed back into the complex, toward the first barracks we'd entered. The short boy, Bony, leaned against the wall facing me. He was whispering to a thin kid with skin the color of wet brown sand. This boy was probably not much older than Bony, but he stood a full head taller. They quit talking as I approached and watched me.

"There's a big man," Bony said, "as long as he has others to do his work."

I stopped and stared at them. If they were adults, I'd move on and avoid trouble. If they wouldn't let me, I'd stop them before they could start anything serious. These two were children, though, boys that Lim and Gustafson and Schmidt and all the others wanted to reintegrate into society. I didn't know what to do with them.

"Afraid of us, he is," Bony said. "Two on one too much for him, eh, Nagy?"

"Too much," the other boy said.

"No worries, you," Bony said. "We heard them say you were leaving, so killing you isn't worth our time." He cocked his head toward the other boy. "Not that me and Nagy couldn't do it if we wanted."

"Sure could, Bony," Nagy said, "sure could."

"Like a lot of others," Bony said, pride filling his voice and making it stronger.

Nagy only nodded and tracked me with his eyes.

"Show 'im," Bony said.

Nagy turned his right shoulder toward me and pointed at it. A stack of at least a dozen thin scabs ran from the top of his arm down for several centimeters. "These are my solo kills," he said, his voice clear and loud. "I don't count shares." He pointed at the top one. "Started high so there's plenty of room." He faced me again.

Bony clapped him on the other shoulder and smiled.

Nagy never looked away from me.

When all you have is each other and the fight, you grow tight, or you die. They understood that fact. I'd learned it. I could try to explain to them what the lesson would cost them, but to what end? They couldn't unlearn it.

Maybe that was part of what Lim and her team would try to help.

"Maggie's here," Lobo said over the comm.

I raised both hands and said to the boys the only thing that seemed sure and true to me at that moment. "I'm sorry."

Before they could respond, I headed back to Lobo.

Maggie leaned against Lobo and watched me approach. I couldn't read her expression. I also couldn't shake the sick, sad feeling that my encounter with Bony and Nagy had brought to my stomach. I hated that I couldn't do anything for them.

Lobo opened a side hatch when I was within a meter of his hull. I stepped inside and headed up front.

Maggie followed me, and Lobo sealed himself behind her.

I walked to the far corner of the pilot area and wished I could keep walking. My body vibrated with energy. I finally turned to face her. "What?" I said. I hadn't even realized I was angry until I heard my own voice.

"I wanted to thank you," Maggie said. I could read her look well enough now: hurt, sad, maybe pitying. "Why are you always so mad?"

The still air inside Lobo clung to me like dirt to a buried corpse. I wanted out, away from here, but I couldn't leave, not with her standing right in front of me, not with the question she'd asked hanging between us. Before I could consider my answer, without meaning to say anything, I found myself speaking. "I know you came here to pick up one boy, but by any chance have you looked around? Have you paid any attention at all?"

"Yes," she said. "It's terrible, but why does the situation make you mad at me?"

"I'm not." As soon as the words came out, I knew my tone said otherwise. I took two deep breaths and stared into her eyes. "I'm really not. I know it sounds like I am, but I'm not angry at you. I'm just frustrated and furious at…I don't know, at this place, at what those people did to these kids, at everything."

"I can't blame you this time," she said, "but you are so often full of rage, and I don't understand why. I'm sorry you are, I really am, and I want to know. I do. Why are you always so angry?"

I shrugged. How could I explain it to her? If she could truly comprehend the answer, if somehow the barrier that stopped her from being able to read me were to crumble in an instant and she could hold me and utterly and completely know my mind, would I even want her to understand? Would the value of that knowledge be worth the damage it would do to her?

"It's a long story," I finally said. I shrugged again. "Don't worry about it."

She looked at me for several seconds before nodding. "Okay." After a few more seconds, she added, "If that's what you want, okay."

I couldn't decide if I was grateful or sad that she'd stopped pushing. Why did I end up so twisted inside whenever I spent time with her? Why were my feelings so complicated around her?

None of that mattered. She was going to leave, so the best thing I could do for both of us was to simplify everything by helping her on her way.

I shoved aside the useless feelings and forced a smile. "Did you find the boy you wanted?"

She smiled in return, but I didn't believe hers was any more genuine than mine. "Yes," she said with a nod, "we did. He's safely on board my ship, and we're about to leave Tumani."

"Good," I said. "I'm glad you did." I pictured Bony and Nagy again. "He's going to need a lot of help. You know that, right?"

She nodded again. "Yes, we do, and we'll work with him for as long as it takes. He'll be safe now, and he'll have a family of people like him."

"It won't be *his* family," I said. "His family is gone. And you won't be like him. You'll all have special abilities, but he'll be the only one of you who understands what he's become." I couldn't figure out an easy way to explain further what it felt like to be the one person in a crowd who'd killed before, the only man in a room full of people who couldn't help but consider killing as an option, an alien of human birth trying to pass as human. "Remember that."

"We will, Jon. We will. Our group won't be his family, not at first, but in time it will feel like his own." She paused and stared into space, as if looking at a place very far away. "I know how it works." She shook her head and focused on me again. "In any case, it's the best we can do. We won't give up."

It was my turn to nod. I didn't know what more to say.

Maggie stepped close enough to put her hand on my face, her palm cool against my cheek. I flushed and had trouble breathing. "Thank you, Jon," she looked upward, "and thank you, Lobo. I don't know if they would have succeeded without you."

"You're welcome, Maggie," Lobo said, his voice coming from all around us.

She smiled and focused again on me, her hand

still on my cheek. I was afraid to move, sure that no matter what direction I might go, no matter what I might do, it would be wrong.

"One of the things I love about you, Jon, is how much you want to protect children. I hope you succeed with these kids. I've thought about what you said, and though we have to take away our boy, if to help the others you ever need anything we can give—anything *I* can give—contact me, and I'll do my best to make it happen." She stepped back and looked up again. "Lobo, what I'm about to send you will transmit only once, and then it'll overwrite itself. Are you ready to receive?"

"Of course," Lobo said. "I record every transmission of any type that occurs within me."

"Why did I even ask?" she said with a genuine smile. "Of course you do." She pulled a small metal square from her right front pants pocket and held it between her thumb and forefinger. "Jon, I've given Lobo multiple drop-box addresses for every world within three jumps of here. You can use any one of them once. It'll ask you for some verification information, data you'll have from our past time together. Once it authenticates you, it will start a process that will ultimately reach me. It will then turn itself off and transmit shut-off instructions to the other comm threads. It won't work fast—too many worlds to contact—but if you give it a week, it should reach me."

"That's very nice," I said, and I meant it, I tried to keep all the sarcasm out of my voice, "but what could I need that you could give?" I realized how that sounded but not before her expression betrayed the hurt. "I mean, I'm leaving here right after you do."

She shook her head. "I don't need to be able to read your thoughts to understand you better than that." She stared at me for a long time, long enough that I was sure I was supposed to be doing something, though I had no idea what. She leaned forward and kissed me on the left cheek. "Goodbye, Jon."

She turned and left.

I watched her walk away, the second time I'd done that, but this time it took only a few steps for her to reach the edge of Lobo, turn down the hall, and disappear. I heard the side hatch open and her voice saying, "Goodbye, Lobo." A couple of seconds later, the hatch closed.

I closed my eyes and stood in silence. First, Bony and Nagy, then Maggie—both encounters I was unprepared to handle. The two boys had left me sick with the knowledge of what they would always be fighting even if they managed to find new homes and survive to adulthood. Maggie had left me with an ability to contact her that I knew I would never use because there was no way we could ever be together.

I stood there, frozen in place, useless, unable to help those boys or join Maggie, and the seconds passed until Lobo interrupted my thoughts.

"Jon," he said, "isn't it time to leave?"

CHAPTER 30

Dump Island, planet Pinkelponker—139 years earlier

THE COOL NIGHT air tasted of the salty, tossing ocean. The patch of grass where I'd stretched out felt as soft as any bed I'd had while growing up. Everyone else slept in the cave, spread around the large room's perimeter, their bodies casting constantly shifting shadows from the small fire burning inside and to the right of the entrance. When I'd first arrived on Dump, I'd stayed with them, but lately I'd found it more comfortable to sleep under the stars. Staring into the heavens and listening to the ocean took me out of myself and pulled my mind upward, to whatever was out there, way past the only two islands I'd ever seen, beyond even the entire planet of Pinkelponker. I'd never know, but after Jennie had told me that spaceships existed and that one had carried people from a place called Earth all the way to here, I had always stared upward in awe and dreamed of other worlds.

Benny couldn't sneak up on anyone; the sound of his cart's wheels always preceded him. I turned my head enough to make sure no one was with him and he had no weapons. I'd learned the hard way that his drills could come at any time.

"Beautiful, isn't it?" he said when he drew even with me.

"Yes." I whispered, not wanting to disturb the night.

The wind off the ocean picked up speed and rustled all the grass we were not covering. The waves beat louder upon the shore, their steady rhythm the heartbeat of a sleeping world. I tried to slow my heart to the same gentle pace, but I couldn't do it. When I felt closest to the world, I thought of Jennie, because she had taught me to see the beauty around us, always available if we will but let ourselves experience it. My pulse quickened as the memory of losing her flooded into me. I couldn't think of her without feeling that pain. I knew she'd be disappointed in me, would want me to focus on all the good years we'd shared, but I couldn't do it.

When I'd come to Dump, these memories had left me in tears. Now, my face remained stony, cold. Though at times I thought my heart might explode, I didn't show it.

"Jon."

I didn't want to talk, but ignoring Benny was never an option; he wouldn't give up.

"Yeah."

"Jon."

His tone told me what his few words didn't: He wouldn't stop until I faced him. I rolled onto my side, propped my head on my elbow, and stared at him, our faces now level.

When I didn't speak, he continued. "It's important

that you understand something." He stared at me, clearly wanting a response, but I didn't know why. He'd finish talking eventually; he didn't need me to say anything. Finally, he said, "I'm sorry."

"For what?"

He waved his left flipper to take in the sky and the grass and the night. "For everything. For the hard sessions, the sneak attacks, the yelling and the fighting, all of it. For what I've made you become."

"I agreed to do it."

His dark brown eyes, almost black in the night, reflected the starlight like small puddles, their wet surfaces pooling over and running down his cheek. "Maybe, but you should never have been put in this position." He wiped his cheeks. "*I* should never have put you in it."

"But you did." My voice emerged cooler than the deepening night. I barely recognized its sound.

"Are you that far gone already?" he said. He stared intently at me. "Or that angry? Surely you can find more than that inside you."

I sat. "No," I said. I shook my head, a kind of panic rising inside me, pounding like the onrushing waves. "No." I wanted to stop talking, but I couldn't. The words wouldn't stop. I didn't know what they would be until I heard them. "You can't have this. Not this. I'll get us off Dump. I'll become as strong and as tough and as skilled as it takes. I'll save us all or die trying, and you'll train me until I can. That's our deal. That's what we do every day. That's what we'll keep doing. But now you want me to open up to you, to talk about my feelings, to pretend I'm still that kid you met here." I stood. "No. No!" I spread my arms and threw back my head. "No!" I stared at him again and shook with anger. "The next time the ship lands and the guards get out to unload some new poor prisoner, I *will* lead our fight against them, and we *will* beat them. I *will* get us off this island."

I closed my eyes for a few seconds. When I opened them again, my voice was once more cold and calm and level. "That's what you trained me to do. That's what you want me to do. That's what all of you need me to do."

I turned and walked away. "*That's* what you get," I said.

I neither knew nor cared whether the wind carried my words to him or away into the night.

CHAPTER 31

In the former rebel complex, planet Tumani

JON," LOBO SAID, "did you not hear me earlier? Isn't it time to leave?"

It was. We'd done everything we'd come to do. Lim and Gustafson and Schmidt and the rest of their team were settling in to help the boys. Maggie was gone. It was time to go.

"Yeah," I said, "it is."

I didn't move. I didn't open my eyes. If I did nothing, I couldn't do the wrong thing.

"So I should take off," Lobo said, "except that if that was what you wanted, you would have said so." After a pause of several seconds, an interval so great I could probably never understand all that he had done in that time with his vast computational resources, he said, "Which means we're not leaving."

"I don't know," I said. I shook my head slowly. "I really don't know."

"Yes," he said, "you do. We're staying. For some reason I don't understand, every now and again, with decisions that are particularly emotional, you waste a great deal of time denying conclusions you've already reached."

I opened my mouth to argue with him, but I couldn't. He was right. Some choices were so hard that even after I'd made them I had trouble accepting them. I hated it, despised that inefficiency and weakness in myself, but he was right that it existed.

"You're correct," I finally said, "and I'm sorry. I suppose some part of me needs time to process difficult decisions."

"You're not alone in that behavior," Lobo said. "I've noticed it in other humans. It does seem terribly inefficient."

I opened my eyes and smiled. "It is. I suppose you never act that way."

"Never," Lobo said, but with no trace of smugness. "Some conclusions require a great deal of thought to reach, but once I arrive at them, I act—unless, of course, you persuade me to do otherwise."

"Aren't you glad when I do?"

"If by 'glad' you mean do I sometimes believe you made a better choice? Yes. Sometimes—but not all the time."

"But without me you would have acted on your original decision?"

"Yes, of course, as I just said."

"Even if the actions you've decided to take hurt, damage you or someone else, or bring you to emotional places you don't want to visit."

"Yes," he said, "even then. Such decisions always come at a cost, no matter when or how you make them. Sometimes we have to make choices that will hurt us. The good news is that pain is just pain; you know that."

I nodded. "I do, but that doesn't mean I have to like it."

"Since when does liking matter when the stakes are high?"

"Never," I said. Benny had taught me that, many years ago on Dump, and I'd learned the lesson over and over again since then.

"So what are we going to do?" Lobo said.

"I'm not exactly sure," I said, "except that it involves something we never do at the end of a mission: Staying." My shoulders and neck were tight with tension. I stretched them as I said, "I need to talk with Lim."

"I'll get her on the comm," Lobo said.

"No." I headed for the side hatch. "I need to do this in person."

"What do you mean, I can't see her?" I tried to keep my voice level, but the strain was evident.

"She's in a link with one of the teams that hasn't arrived yet," the man, Long, said.

"First, you're her messenger, and now you're her bodyguard. What exactly is it that you do?"

"Whatever she wants," he said. He gave me a hard look. He was as wound up as I was. He took a deep breath, stayed where he was, and spoke again. "She's the CO here. You know that. You've served. You understand how it works. Why are you pushing me?"

I stepped back and held up my hands. "You're right. I'm sorry. I thought I was heading out. It was time, and I was ready to go, but I couldn't. I don't want to leave now. I want to stay and help."

The door behind him opened. Lim stepped into view.

"Thanks, Chris. I'll talk to him. Let him in."

"Yes, sir," he said.

"We're done with that, Chris. We're a civilian organization now, here to help the boys. The sooner we behave that way, the better models we'll be for them."

"I'll try," he said.

Lim went back into the small building without waiting for me.

Long stepped out of the doorway. "Good luck," he said. "We can use all the help we can get."

"Thanks." I entered the room.

Lim sat behind a small desk about three meters in front of me. "Close it," she said. When I had, she continued. "So you want to stay. That's nice, but we're done with the fighting."

"I know, but I'd still like to help."

"Why?"

No breeze made it through the two barely open tiny windows. The air inside here was still and stifling, and I couldn't seem to fill my lungs.

It didn't seem to bother Lim.

"I'm not entirely sure," I said. "I guess some of the boys got to me." Lim knew nothing of my past beyond our years together in the Saw and the one other mission on which she'd helped me. I preferred to keep it that way, but I also wanted to make her understand that this was important to me. "I have some sense of what they're going through."

She leaned back and spread her hands. "We all do, every single one of us who's served. That's not enough, though, not by a long shot. Reintegration is hard, very hard, and part of the job is modeling the behaviors we want the children to learn. To help, you need training and a great deal of self-control. You don't have the training, and from what I've seen, you could do with some work on the control front."

If you only knew, I thought but did not say. I've never fully lost my temper. I don't even know the limits of the damage my nanomachines could do if I surrendered to rage and ordered them to decompose everything they encountered. From what Benny did to the Aggro station, I suspected the planet I was on would vanish before they were finished.

I couldn't explain that to her, though.

"Incoming ship," Lobo said over the comm. "It's government, and it's coming fast. Should I defend?"

"You have visitors," I said, "a government ship. Should we let it land?"

She nodded, sighed, and stood. "I knew they'd want to meet. I hoped they'd give us a day. I should have known better. Bureaucrats."

"Leave it alone," I whispered to Lobo.

Lim headed for the door. "We'll have to continue this when I'm back." As she stepped outside, she said, "On second thought, before you become too committed to the notion of staying, would you like to see part of what we're up against?"

"Sure," I said. If Lim viewed any people in the government as potential opponents, I wanted to know them. Knowledge of your enemies can save your life.

"Okay," she said. I thought I spotted the beginnings of a smile before she added, "Come with me."

They insisted we meet in their ship. Typical: Bureaucrats love to play power games.

As I approached it, I said over the machine frequency to Lobo, "Can you scan it and monitor me?"

"Yes," he said. "It's old enough that I could take control of it without it even knowing. If you'd like it cooler in there, just let me know."

I chuckled. Lim gave me an odd look; I shrugged in return. I turned slightly away from her as I said, "I don't expect to be there long. Just keep an eye on me. Out."

A woman in dress uniform barred the doorway. Anyone who made their guard detail put on formal wear in weather like this was stupid, insecure, showing off, or all three.

"Let them in," a male voice said from inside.

The guard stepped aside, and we entered.

"Sorry he made you wear that," I whispered as I drew even with her.

She didn't respond, probably couldn't risk saying anything, but she also didn't hit me. Given how much I'd pissed off Long and annoyed Lim, I decided to count that as a personal communication win.

No doubt the man inside played well to the Tumani population, but he would never have gotten respect from his fashion-hip counterparts in either the EC or the FC. A little taller than Lim, almost as broad as I am, and very heavily muscled, he sported scars that stood out all over his almost night-black skin like lines of insects. Because it was Tumani, I could easily believe he had come by the damage honestly, but no serious executive, government or corporate, in any more developed world would have kept the scars. The power style these days was sleek and clean and smooth.

"Ms. Lim," he said, motioning her to a chair.

"Senator Wylak," she said. She nodded her head low enough that she might have been bowing. She sat.

"And your friend is?" he said.

She waved her hand dismissively. "One of my staff."

He hadn't offered me a seat, and her comment told me the role I was now playing, so I stayed standing.

"Are you sure?" he said. "We normally—"

"But of course, Senator," she said. "I apologize for the change in protocol. Had I not been awake for a day and a half straight, I would be here alone. But I *have* been without sleep for all of that time. I fear that until I rest I might forget some vital instruction of yours, so because we cannot record our discussions, I—" she finished by pointing to me.

"Very well," he said. He pointed to another chair, one a bit behind hers, but otherwise didn't acknowledge my presence.

I sat.

"Something to drink?" he said.

"You're very kind," she said, "but I only now finished an early lunch."

"To the matters at hand then," he said, "so that you may get your rest." He leaned back in his chair. "You've done very well. We are all quite impressed."

"Thank you. It would not have been possible without your support."

He nodded ever so slightly, the fact so obviously true that it scarcely required an acknowledgment. "We are also moving two units into the surrounding jungle, as we discussed. They will remain there for your protection."

"And to kill any rebels foolish enough to return to this very valuable base."

"And that," he said. "The best missions accomplish multiple objectives." He cleared his throat. "This support is, of course, expensive, and it diverts resources from the main fronts."

"Which makes us doubly grateful for your help," she said. She straightened and leaned slightly toward him.

"We all appreciate your gratitude," he said. "Some of my more short-sighted colleagues, however, have already begun to push for a fixed departure date for our resources—and for the date at which these boys will be safe to return to their homes or to place with foster families."

Anger flitted across Lim's face, but she composed herself. "As we've discussed from the beginning, until we've spent a few weeks with the boys, we cannot even begin to grasp the extent of the programming we'll be fighting. I've always warned that this process was likely to require many months."

"And your"—he paused as if searching for something he could not recall—"private sponsors are willing to fund such a long effort?"

"Completely," she said. "They are as dedicated to this important work as the government of Tumani."

He allowed himself a smile at that tactic. "Excellent. That is very good to hear, and I will certainly relay that commitment to my colleagues." He leaned forward. "Some of them may, I fear, still push for as rapid a conclusion as possible. We are, after all, a poor planet and one fighting an unfortunate civil war. Trade-offs and costs must always be weighed."

This time, Lim sat so far forward she was barely on her chair. When she spoke, her battle for self-control was evident in the shakiness of her voice. "These are children," she said, "your children, Tumani children, not factors to be computed by some economic equation."

He smiled again, but there was no warmth in the expression. "No world loves its children more than Tumani," he said, "but few worlds must struggle so hard to survive and grow. When we act, we must be sure we are acting in the best interest of all. We remain committed to saving these children. I came here today simply to do you the courtesy of exposing you to the full range of discussions some of my colleagues are holding."

Lim looked at the floor and rubbed her face with her hands. When she faced Wylak again, her fatigue was obvious for the first time since we'd entered the ship. She'd exhibited such control earlier that I couldn't tell whether she was showing how tired she really felt or simply acting the part because doing so might advance her cause. "I must apologize, sir. As I mentioned at the outset, I have gone a very long time without sleep. I greatly appreciate your effort in coming here and your willingness to share with me. I know no one could care more about these children than you. I can assure you that we will do everything in our power to accelerate the reintegration process."

He nodded and stood. "We all appreciate your efforts."

Lim took the cue and also got up, so I followed suit.

"I look forward to seeing you again soon," he said. "And now, with your permission..." Without waiting even a second, he turned and headed toward a door along the rear wall.

Lim led me out and walked so quickly away that I had no time to say anything else to the guard, whose face was now soaked with sweat. Lim didn't speak again until we were halfway back to her command building and the ship was taking off behind us.

"Did you hear that?" she said. "What an officious, back-stabbing jerk."

"I take it he screwed you on time."

"Oh, yeah," she said. "He promised me support for as long as we needed it. I never counted on that, of course, but I did expect at least a few months before the pressure began." She signed. "I was being naïve. I'm going to have to spend more energy managing that relationship."

"Do you really think that will be enough?"

She stopped and faced me. "It'll have to be." She waved her hand slowly to take in the entire complex. "In case you haven't noticed it, we have over five hundred boys to reintegrate into the world. We can't just walk away."

I took a deep breath and closed my eyes for a moment. Lim had been right; in the face of any aggression at all, my self-control definitely needed work. Finally, I looked at her, held up my hands, and backed up a step. When I spoke, I did my best to keep my tone level and neutral. "Yes, I have noticed, which is why I came to you to volunteer to help. I wasn't proposing you—we—walk away. I was only suggesting that managing Wylak and his cronies might not work and that we should consider getting a backup plan in place."

"A backup plan?" she said. "You think I haven't considered that? The problem is, the government won't let us take five hundred of its citizens, children or not, off Tumani, and there's nowhere else on this world for them to go. Even if we could fly them off-planet, we'd need time and money to set up a suitable facility to receive them." She shook her head. "No, Jon, this is it. This is what we have. We must make these kids ready for normal lives, and now we almost certainly must do so faster than we'd planned."

Of course she'd considered her options; I hadn't meant to imply she had not. I was suggesting only that it might be time to do so again, but there was clearly no point in pursuing this topic further with her. I needed to focus on the reason I'd come to her in the first place: staying. "You can use any help you can get, including mine."

She sighed. "I told you, Jon: You don't have the training for this. I'm sorry. I really am. I have to get back to work." She turned to go.

"Put me to work doing anything," I said. "Let me learn by observing. In the meantime, I'll take guard duty or cook or clean or do whatever you need. I've spent plenty of time as a Private; I have lots of experience with crappy details."

She faced me again. "You're serious."

I nodded. "Absolutely."

"Why?"

Because I've been one of these kids. Because I understand them better than you do. Because no one's ever shown me how to live in this world. I considered all of those answers, but I finally went with the only one I was sure was both correct and something I was willing for her to hear. "I don't know," I said. "Something about these boys gets to me, so I want to help them."

She studied me for several seconds before she said, "If I do this, I'll assign you to Schmidt. You'll do what she says, when she says it, and how she says it. You won't interfere in any aspect of the reintegration, and you'll stick to the scut work we give you."

"Okay," I said, "until you say otherwise."

After a few more seconds, she nodded her head. "All right. You can stay. The team leads are meeting later this afternoon in my command building. After sunset, they'll gather with their groups. You'll join Schmidt's staff. Location will be on your comm."

She turned and walked away. As she was going, over her shoulder, she added, "Get some sleep. It's going to be a long night."

CHAPTER 32

In the former rebel complex, planet Tumani

LOBO WAITED UNTIL I was inside him and he'd shut the hatch before he let me have it.

"So we're definitely staying?"

"You're always chiding me for asking questions I know the answers to. Why are you doing it now? You heard everything I said."

"Of course I did. I simply wasn't sure whether to believe my audio sensors. Perhaps you were running some con you hadn't chosen to explain to me. It could happen. It *has* happened."

"There's no con," I said. "I simply want to help."

"By cleaning barracks? Walking a guard's route? If you want to do some good in the universe, I can think of many more useful jobs than those."

I stretched out on the cot in my quarters. "Maybe, but those boys are here, and they can use my help."

"You won't be helping them," he said. "You'll be doing scut work for Schmidt. Alissa made it very clear: You don't get to work with the boys."

"Then I'll help Schmidt and hope that helps the children!" I sat and rubbed my head in frustration. "Maybe I'm fooling myself. Maybe I'll never get to do more here than clean up floors. Maybe I'll be ready to leave within a week. I don't know. I don't know much about any of this, but I am sure that preparing these boys for civilian life—for being kids again—will be incredibly hard. If I can help with that effort, I will." I stood and paced back and forth in the small room. "We train them to fight, and when the fighting is over, we either send them somewhere else to fight again or abandon them to find their own way. They don't have the first idea about how to live normal lives. They don't even remember what normal was."

Lobo stayed silent for several seconds.

I kept pacing.

"This is clearly very important to you," he finally said.

"Yes."

"Can you say why?" Before I could answer, he continued. "I mean that question literally: Do you know your motivation and could you explain it, or is it a compulsion you don't understand?"

I stopped moving and considered his question. "A little of both. I understand part of what's driving me, but another part is pure emotional impulse."

"Would you explain to me the bits you understand?"

I stared into the air, not for the first time wishing Lobo, who so often felt human, had a face I could see. He'd trusted me with the secrets of his creation, but I'd never repaid that trust. He might well be my only real friend, and he certainly had never betrayed me. I had no rational basis for not telling him about this part of my past.

Despite all that, I couldn't do it. Maybe one day, but not now.

"No," I said. "If I were ever to tell anyone, it would be you, but I can't, at least not now."

After another few long seconds, Lobo spoke again, his voice tinged with sadness. "I'm sure the irony isn't lost on either of us that I, the machine, find trust easier to grant than you, the human. I've been broken, and I've hated myself for being what I am—in large part I still do—so I can only imagine what it's like inside your mind."

I shook my head. No.

"Maybe not," he said, reminding me that although I could not see him gesture, he was always watching me, "but I can say, without any ironic intent, that I am sorry you cannot—will not—trust me with that information."

Leave it to Lobo to turn nice when I least expect it and in the process to strip me of all protective rage so I ended up feeling…guilty. I had to admit it: I felt guilty for not trusting him.

"I'm sorry, too," I said. "Maybe someday."

I stood in silence for a minute. Neither of us spoke. I didn't know what else to say. Apparently, for a rare change, neither did Lobo—or perhaps he was simply continuing to be nice.

"I'm going to sleep," I said. "Wake me at sunset."

"Why of course, my fleshy master," he said. "I live to be your alarm clock."

I chuckled. Normal, even if it included sarcasm, was exactly what I needed.

I stretched out on the cot and fell asleep still smiling.

➤   ➤   ➤

"You're to report to the first barracks you cleared," Lobo said as soon as I was upright.

I stood and stretched. "When?"

"In a little over an hour. They've set up four eating groups; you have time to dine with yours if you want."

I was hungry, but the meeting with Wylak was still bothering me. "How closely were you able to monitor my conversation in that government ship?"

"More closely than you were," Lobo said. "I have audio and visual recordings from the ship's sensors, as well as a complete copy of the vital sign data it was gathering on all three of you."

"You weren't joking about what you could do to that old bucket of bolts."

"Of course I wasn't. One glance at it should have told you how easy it would be for me to penetrate."

"Maybe, but most people who look at you have no way to know the extent of your capabilities. I try not to make too many assumptions about ships."

"Fair enough," he said, "but I was, of course, correct about that thing's vulnerabilities."

"What do you think of Wylak's claims of support?"

"Because he's a politician, I assume he's lying almost every time he opens his mouth. His vitals, however, show almost no tension or variation, so either he's very good or at some level he believes what he's saying."

I'd hoped for proof that the man wasn't telling the truth, but regardless of what those sensors showed, I was still convinced he had yet to tell the worst news to Lim. He also almost certainly wasn't alone; politicians always seem to be linked in webs of obligations and alliances to other politicians.

Linked.

"His ship is connected to some Tumani government control systems, right?"

"Of course," Lobo said. "We may be on a backwater planet, but it is still a human-colonized world. The first thing any settlement does is get its networks working."

"How far past the ship into those systems could you go?"

"You want me to break into the secure systems of a planet's government?"

I shrugged. "If you can't do it, just say so. I understand. Some security is simply too tough even for a machine of your intelligence."

"There's no need to be insulting," Lobo said. "I asked to make sure I understood you correctly. If I do this and make any errors, there's a decent chance their defensive systems will track the infiltration back to me. If they do, we'll both be at high risk."

"So don't make any mistakes, and cover your tracks."

"Thank you for that sage advice, oh Master Hacker," he said. "Why didn't I think of those tactics? Now, the task is so much clearer and simpler."

"Sorry," I said.

"What exactly do you want me to find or do?"

"Search for warning signs of trouble," I said. "If Wylak is planning to undermine Lim's efforts, he'll recruit support, arrange one or more additional trips, and so on. If we know that he's making a move and, even better, what that move is, we'll have a better chance of either countering it or at least being better prepared to cope with it."

"Why didn't you say that was all you wanted? I can get that information from sensor feeds and various communication records. On most worlds, those records are highly secure and hard-encrypted, but on a place like this everything is at least a few computing generations old. The only problem with those sources is that they produce vast quantities of data, but that's nothing I can't handle with near-real-time processing."

"How soon can you be monitoring his communications?"

"I will have to proceed very carefully," Lobo said, "and I'll have to recruit and deploy low-intensity, multi-source, highly redirected probes initially, so even my first penetration attempts could take as long as a couple of days."

"Do it. If he's planning to change the deal on Lim, I want to know as soon as possible."

"I'm on it," Lobo said, "but I have to ask, what are you going to do if he is?"

"I don't have any idea," I said, "but I will be giving the matter some thought."

"Between scrubbing floors and patrolling the grounds," Lobo said.

"Yeah," I said, "then. Thanks for the words of encouragement."

As I headed out to eat, he added, "It's what I live for. That and being your alarm clock."

CHAPTER 33

Dump Island, planet Pinkelponker—139 years earlier

WE HAVE TO move out of the cave," Alex said.

Han and I both nodded our agreement. We'd been training on our own, running on the beach. Han had the idea to race from the shuttle landing area to the group's cave. I'd reached it well ahead of them both, and it had taken me about six minutes to get there. Too long, we all felt, too long.

Benny stared up first at Alex's face and then at each of ours. "Why?"

"When the shuttle comes," Han said, "we have to be ready for it. If it flies in fast—and you know most of them do—we won't have enough time to get all of us there and in position for our attack. We need to be set the moment the doors open."

"He's right," Alex said. "You've told us over and over that we won't get a second chance to do this. We have to win on our first attempt, or they'll add security and trap us here forever. Or worse."

Benny nodded and focused on me. "What do you think?"

"I'm with them," I said. "We ran the path. It took us a long time."

"Jon beat us by at least a minute," Han said. "Before we could get there from the cave, the ship could already have dropped off someone and be closing up. Jon's fast, but even he might not be able to reach the shuttle on time. Worse, if he managed somehow to make it, he'd have to fight the guards alone. That won't work."

"You know he's right," Alex said.

"He is," I said.

Bob and several of the others had heard us talking and come out of the cave. They all stared at Benny.

He looked around at all of us.

More people emerged from the cave.

"I've explained before," Benny said. "We have to live where they can't watch us from above. We don't want them to know what we're doing. If they see us all sleeping near the landing area, they'll become suspicious."

"*If* they're bothering to watch us," I said, "and *if* they can really see what we're doing, they'll have seen us training. That's bound to bother them."

"It could look like you were exercising," Benny said.

"With knives?" I said. "With fighting?"

"They already think we're all stupid and useless," Benny said. "For us to end up attacking each other wouldn't surprise them. If we all move, though, it's sure to attract their attention. They might send more guards on each shuttle, which would lower our chances of success." He shook his head. "No, moving is a bad idea."

"So is staying," I said. "The time it takes to get to the landing area proves that."

"We have to split up," Bob said. "Those of us who'll go after the guards need to find sheltered areas much closer to the landing spot. Maybe we can even create some places to hide."

"Everything will be so much harder if we do that," Benny said. "We'll have to get food and water to both locations, spend time relaying information between them—everyday life will require so much more work." He stared at me and shook his head slightly, his eyes almost begging me to help him.

I didn't agree with him, but I'd never seen him ask for assistance, and his expression troubled me.

"I don't know about everyone else," I said, "but I'm tired from that run. I'm thirsty and hungry, too. We can talk about this more later. Why don't we rest and eat?"

Alex and Han looked at me for a few seconds and nodded their heads.

"I could use a break," Alex said.

"And some water," Han said.

They headed into the cave. The rest of the folks followed them.

I hung back for a few seconds.

Benny did, too.

"Thank you," he whispered.

"You're going to explain this," I said.

He nodded. "Tonight, after most of them are asleep, out where you like to stare at the night."

"Tonight," I said.

Stars beamed through a cloudless sky and painted the ocean in rippling shades of gray. A gentle wind cooled the night and carried whispered odors of the life below the water's surface. Even up on the rock, I couldn't help but feel the push and pull of the tides. When I was younger—before Jennie fixed me, I reminded myself, for it hadn't been that long ago—I would often doze and dream of floating around Pinecone, Jennie beside me, the water a friend that would never hurt me. I knew better now, understood that the ocean's flow would not take me around our island and that it was a massive, animate force that would as soon kill me as support me, but back then it had been my friend. I rarely missed that simpler me anymore, but sometimes, watching the water, I ached for that happier self.

The sound of Benny's cart pierced my thoughts and cleared my head quickly. I sat and waited for him. I could have saved him a lot of work by meeting him partway, but he'd picked this spot, so I let him come to it.

"Thank you," he said as soon as he rolled into view, "both for supporting me earlier and for meeting me now."

"You said you'd explain." I hadn't meant to be so abrupt. I considered apologizing, but Benny spoke, and the moment passed.

"Of course," he said. "Of course. You're right that if the government is monitoring us, we'll have aroused their suspicions. What I'm about to discuss with you, I don't say to the others, and I'd rather you not repeat it." He paused and stared at me for several seconds. "In fact, I'd prefer this entire conversation stay between us." He went silent again.

I said nothing. He wanted me to promise not to share potentially important information with guys who were going into battle with me. I wouldn't do that without first understanding what was going on. I might not be willing to do it even then.

After a bit, he shook his head and continued. "You're not going to make this easy, are you? Fine. You decide what to tell them." He took a deep breath and stared at the ocean before again focusing on me. "I don't believe they're monitoring us. I never have. I use that justification to keep everyone in the cave, quite a distance from the landing area. When the day comes that we try to hijack a shuttle, I want everyone who's not involved in the attack to be safely distant. That way—"

I interrupted him. "—if we fail, the government might decide the others weren't involved."

"Exactly. If we lose, those in the cave might survive."

"So let us split up."

"The best of us are on the attack team," he said. "Without all of you, the people in the cave will have a very rough time of it."

"But by keeping us there, you risk the entire plan failing."

"I know," he said, "I know, but I don't want to make their lives any worse than they already are."

I walked over to him and sat on the ground, right next to him, our faces so close that I could smell his stale breath. "You're willing to risk all of us dying, but you don't want to inconvenience the others."

"No, no, it's not like that," he said, shaking his head. "I want everything to work out for everyone. I thought the best way to make that happen was to keep everyone together."

"Staying in the cave won't work," I said. "We explained that to you. To maximize our odds of success, we have to do every little thing right. You've repeated that to us over and over during training. Arriving too late, not being in position the moment those doors open—those failures would jeopardize all that we've been training to do."

Benny looked into my eyes and for the first time I saw the young boy inside the leader. I remembered seeing eyes like those in my own reflection in the still ponds and the rain barrels.

"You're right," he finally said. "Despite what I've sometimes said during your training sessions, I thought I could find a way to make it all work out well for everyone, to make you guys so good at fighting that you would all survive, that everything would be okay. I thought that if my planning was good enough and the training was extensive enough, we'd all end up okay and no one would be hurt."

"No one hurt!" I said. I stood and backed away, afraid of the energy coursing through me. "No one hurt? You don't think we've been hurt already? You don't think being attacked over and over, learning to kill, fighting each other to prepare for taking on bigger, stronger, better-armed men—you don't think all of that hurts? This plan has already hurt us, and it's going to keep hurting us."

"I'm sorry," he said. "I really am."

"Don't be! I'm not. I used to be, but now I'm not. I understand now. If we don't attack the shuttle, we'll rot and die here. If we're going to fight, we need to be as ready as we can possibly be, because otherwise we'll fail, and the guards will kill us." I sat again and leaned close to him. "Understand this: You did what you thought was right. I've come to agree with you. We're going to do this. Some people—maybe some of us, maybe, I hope, the guards, maybe both—are going to get hurt, and some are probably going to die. That's the way it is. We've all signed up for it. You get the credit for the plan and the credit for the training. What you don't get is to pretend that no one will be hurt."

He nodded. "No, I don't. You're right. I'm still sorry, though, so very sorry."

I stared at him for a long time, wondering how he could be so smart and yet so dumb, how he could train us to fight and to kill and not understand what he was really doing. In the end, I decided it didn't matter. I agreed with his decision, but I would not let him pretend there was no cost. I couldn't do that.

I stood. The air was colder now, the breeze blowing stronger, and goose bumps appeared on my bare arms. "Tomorrow, we'll tell the others that we talked, that we couldn't find a better answer than to split up, that there was no way around it. We'll build more camo cover and look for safe places where the attack team can live very close to the landing spot. We'll do everything we can to explain why the change is necessary, but even if not everyone is happy, we'll do it."

"Tomorrow," he said, nodding his head again.

"And when we're settled there and one day the shuttle lands," I said, "we—"

"—fight the guards and do what we have to do to take that ship," he said. "Maybe we have to kill the guards. Maybe some of us die. We do what we must to get off this island, and as soon as we can, we come back to rescue the others. Until we do, they'll have to cope without us." His voice was clear now, strong and far colder than the night. "Thank you for making me understand clearly what this will mean. If I'm to lead you, I have to accept that reality. I have to."

I stared at him for a long time. As I did, the anger flowed out of me like the sea receding from the shore. "I wish—" I said.

"Don't," he said. "Don't. You were right." He pushed off the ground and turned his cart. "Let's go back to the cave and get some sleep. We have a lot to do tomorrow."

I let him lead the way, fell in behind him even though I could easily have walked around him and gotten there quicker, stayed with him until we passed out of the starlight and into the cave that already felt like a place where I no longer belonged.

CHAPTER 34

In the former rebel complex, planet Tumani

MY COMM DIRECTED me to a location right next to the first barracks my team had captured, but I didn't head there right away. Instead, I invested some time walking the entire perimeter of the complex and getting a sense of what was going on. Four large active-surface domes stood in the corners of the enclosed fortress; Lim's people must have erected them while I'd been sleeping. Only dying slivers of sunlight remained to fight the evening's oncoming darkness, so the structures had shifted to near transparency. Multiple arches offered easy access to the large tables of food stretching down the middle of each one. No part of any dome was closer than ten meters to the complex's outer wall; Lim wasn't providing anyone with a convenient springboard for climbing out of there.

Guards lounged near the entrances to the eating areas. If they were carrying weapons, I didn't spot them, and they dressed casually; no one wore a uniform, though each had a name patch over his or her heart. Even without the names on their chests, the guards would have stood out from the boys by their size, the quality of their clothing, and how well fed and healthy they looked. If I'd been one of the kids, I would have found these captors more annoying for their apparent wealth than my previous rebel masters, who at least looked more like them than Lim's team. This was going to be an uphill battle all the way.

I wandered into the last dome, the one nearest my destination. One of the guards followed me.

I turned before he could reach me. It was Long again. "How many jobs do you have," I said, "and don't you ever sleep?"

He smiled and shrugged. "Too many, and every now and again. I do whatever Lim needs; it's a great cause, and she's a remarkable woman."

"She is that," I said. "So, what'd I do wrong this time?"

"Nothing," he said, "because none of us briefed you. We hadn't expected you to stay."

"So, what didn't you tell me?"

From five meters away, a handful of boys watched us and whispered to one another. A few pointed at Chris; others pointed at me. More streamed toward them from other parts of the dome.

Chris also noticed them and faced the growing crowd. "We're just talking. There's not going to be any fighting."

"The big one looks like he could beat you," a young voice said. "Are you afraid of him?"

Chris smiled at them, shrugged again—a combination he'd obviously developed to disarm people—and said, "We're friends. Why would I be afraid of him?"

"So you have fought with him?" another voice said. I couldn't spot the speaker.

"No," he said. "Like I told you: We're not here to fight."

"If you haven't been in battle together, you cannot know if he is truly your friend." Bony, the kid who'd tried earlier to get his buddy, Nagy, to fight me, stepped from behind two taller boys as he continued talking. "Only then do you find out who he really is." He turned, pulled Nagy forward, and patted the taller boy on the shoulder. "I know Nagy for my true brother, because we have killed together."

A bunch of the boys cheered.

"I don't need to fight to learn that," Chris said, "because he is my friend. You, too, can learn other ways to identify your friends."

"Your friend is a coward," Bony said. "As big as he is, and he would not fight us." He spit on the ground. "A coward is no one's friend."

More boys yelled and whistled their approval.

Chris glanced at me, clearly annoyed, though I had no idea why. He focused again on Bony. "Choosing not to fight is not a sign of cowardice. Choosing not to fight is what most people do most of the time. They find other ways, better ways, to solve their problems."

"So they are weak," Bony said. "We learned that only the weak do not fight back." More boys cheered. Emboldened by that support, Bony stepped closer to us. "If they were strong, they would fight."

"No," Chris said, shaking his head. "Not all those who choose not to fight are weak. There are many ways to be strong. We will teach you—but not now. Now, my friend and I must go."

As he turned to leave, he stared briefly at me, his eyes hard and clear.

I followed him.

"Cowards!" Bony yelled.

"Cowards!" others screamed.

The word became a chant.

Chris maintained an even pace, so I did the same, though I hated having my back to that many angry people. They were boys, but they had also until yesterday been killers.

Chris led me past the barracks where I was to report soon, around the corner of another building, and finally a few steps past Lim's small HQ. When he'd verified that no boys were in sight, he stopped and faced me.

"You're supposed to report all confrontation attempts," he said, his voice hard and tense.

"No one told me," I said.

He shook his head, closed his eyes, and took a deep breath. When he opened his eyes again, the anger was no longer visible. "I'm sorry," he said. "Their behavior is nothing unusual, and we've trained on multiple techniques for dealing with it, but I haven't slept in a very long time. They got to me a little."

"It's only natural," I said.

"Natural isn't good enough. We have to rise above our worst natures if we're going to show these boys how to become different people—how to be kids again." He rubbed his eyes. "What someone should have explained to you is that we're trying to identify leaders and troublemakers so we can help them first. Turn one leader around, and many others may follow. In any case, I'm sorry for putting you through that little show. With some of these kids, violence is all they've experienced for a long time."

"What Bony said isn't entirely wrong," I said, "and

you know it. You learn a lot from fighting beside someone."

"No argument, but that doesn't matter. We're here to help them move past all the fighting and all the training that turned them into soldiers."

"As if that's possible," I said. "Have you ever been able to shake your training?"

He shook his head, no. "Fair point. Let me put it differently: We're here to teach them how to handle their pasts and live in the world of normal people."

"If that's the job, why didn't we stay with them and talk to them? Why are you and I out here?"

"Because they're not ready for that conversation," Chris said, "and I had to get you out of the tent before you ate. For the first couple of days, we have to stick to our own food and let them eat theirs."

"Why?"

"Their food contains drugs targeted at their dependence on the root. The drug won't do you any serious damage, but it could cause you to spend a lot of time alone with stomach cramps."

I didn't want to tell him that it probably wouldn't bother me because my nanomachines would react to and ultimately remove the drug from my system, so all I did was nod. "Thanks for the warning. Isn't it a bad idea to start off lying to them? I don't know the first thing about reintegration, but I have to assume that building trust must be an important part of the process."

"Yes," he said, "it is. We'd planned to explain how we would help them cope without the root, make this drug and other medications available, and gradually wean all of the boys from their dependence, but late this afternoon Lim told all the counselors that we were doing it this way. She said we needed to accelerate wherever we could, and this was a way to save a lot of time. Plus, given how unreceptive they'd been when she'd mentioned root in her speech, a less direct approach seemed more likely to succeed."

Though I didn't like it that Lim had to lie, it was probably the right move given everything she was facing. I was particularly glad that she was taking Wylak seriously, because the more I thought about him, the less I trusted him.

"It's her decision to make," I said. "She's in charge."

I smiled at him and added, "So, where do I get some food?"

CHAPTER 35

In the former rebel complex, planet Tumani

LIGHT LIKE AMPLIFIED moon-glow bathed the inside of the dome and washed everyone under it in cool white tones. Schmidt and four other adults stood in front of twenty of the boys, all apparently residents of the barracks my team had first captured. I'd thought we would meet in that building, but Schmidt wanted to avoid trespassing on their turf as much as was reasonably possible under the circumstances. I sat in a chair a good five meters off to the side from the other grown-ups; Schmidt had requested a clear separation between the counselors and me. Bony and Nagy, as they had in the other meal dome, hung behind the front row of their fellows—reasonable positioning, not the first to get shot in a fight, but close enough to return fire easily should the initial rounds take out their comrades.

The boys ignored the grown-ups and talked to each other, but they were obviously curious about what was to come, because none of them left.

"My name is Portia Schmidt," she said. She spoke in a normal tone of voice and at a normal volume.

They ignored her.

"When you want to know what's going on, be quiet, and I'll tell you."

She turned her back on the boys and spoke to a few of the other adults.

"Shut up," one of the boys said. The words came from somewhere in the middle of the group. In a loud voice, he continued, "We must all remember what we learned: Know your enemy."

"We don't need to know these people to beat them." Bony, talking from his safe position. I recognized his voice.

Murmurs and a few cheers of approval rippled through the group.

"Still, if they're dumb enough to give us information," he continued, "we might as well listen." He stepped in front of the other boys. Nagy followed him and stood to his right. "Go ahead, *Schmidt*," he said, almost spitting her name. He crossed his arms. "Say what you have to say."

A few more boys cheered, but after some half-hearted jeers, they all fell silent.

"Thank you for listening," she said, "and welcome to your new school."

"School?" many voices yelled. "This is no school! This is a prison!" A few of them edged closer to the four counselors.

I stood, ready to help if the boys attacked, but Schmidt and two men on her team looked at me and ever so slightly shook their heads.

I sat. If they thought they could take twenty boys without my help, I'd let them try. I could always get involved later.

Schmidt returned her attention to the kids, her face impassive, neutral, not frowning, not smiling, not tense—just waiting.

The boys stopped moving and quieted.

"You're right," she said. "This *is* a prison, because we won't let you go—at least, not yet."

After an unintelligible murmur swept through the boys, Bony said, "When will you let us out?"

"When you're ready," Schmidt said. "Ready to live like normal people. Ready to stop being soldiers. Ready to go back to being boys."

"Being weaklings, you mean!" one boy from the back yelled. "Why would we want to do that?"

"We're strong, not weak!" another screamed.

"Yeah! Yeah!" Many of the boys chanted agreement.

Schmidt waited again, her face once more neutral.

I was amazed at her ability to stand in front of so much emotion without reacting. The boys were ignoring me, directing none of their anger in my direction, and yet my body was responding, my pulse picking up, all of me preparing to fight. Lim was right; even if I had a great deal to teach these boys, if being a counselor meant showing the kind of self-control Schmidt had, I wasn't ready.

When the other boys had wound down, Bony said, "You called this place a school. What do you plan to teach us—other than how to be weak?"

More chants followed his question.

He crossed his arms, smiled slightly, and sidled forward and to the right half a step.

"We will teach you how to live normal lives," Schmidt said when the boys were silent again. "We'll show you how to get along with others. We'll help you learn how to resolve conflicts without fighting. We'll prepare you to go home—or to new homes, if your home is gone." A low wave of murmurs swept the boys, but this time Schmidt didn't wait for them to be quiet. She spoke over them, for the first time raising her voice slightly, not yelling, simply talking a bit louder. "Wouldn't you like to go home? If you have no home, wouldn't you like a new one?"

"*This* is our home," Bony said, his voice shaking, though whether with anger or sadness I could not tell. "We are family now, brothers, warriors together."

"You are," Schmidt said, her voice sad for the first time. "I understand."

"No!" Bony said.

"No!" many of the boys said.

"You can't!" a voice from the back said.

"I can," Schmidt said, "and I do. I've been a soldier for more than ten years. My unit, like yours, is a kind of family, and we have all fought together many times. But we are adults, and we chose as adults to live this life. None of you did that, and all of you are still children."

"Fight us," Nagy said, his voice flat, "and then see if you want to call us children." He spit as far as he could and hit the ground half a meter in front of her. "If you are still alive and able to speak."

Schmidt shook her head. "No. We won't fight you."

"Then you are less than our enemies," Nagy said. "You are nothing." He glanced at Bony.

"Nothing," Bony said. He turned and walked out of the dome.

Nagy followed, less than half a step behind him.

Another boy took off. Two more followed. In less than a minute, they had all left. Only the five counselors and I remained.

"You let them walk out?" I said.

Schmidt walked over to me. "What would you have me do?" She leaned over me.

I stayed seated. "Make them stay until you're done," I said. "Can you imagine a sergeant letting any of his squad walk out in the middle of a lecture?"

"I'm not their sergeant," she said, "and this isn't the military."

"Even a school has to maintain discipline," I said.

She nodded her agreement. "And we will, but initially only when absolutely necessary, when they do something that will endanger their own safety, the safety of other boys, or ours."

I shook my head. "If you're not going to make them learn, what are you going to do?"

"Feed them," she said, frustration finally evident in her voice. "Get them off the root. Treat them like boys, not soldiers. Play with them. Encourage them to play with each other. Teach them every now and again, when they let us. Help them learn to resolve problems without fighting. Make it as easy as we can for them to act like boys again. Care about them, really care."

"That's it?" I said. "That's the plan?"

She looked down for a few seconds and pinched the bridge of her nose. When she stared at me again, fatigue and sadness and frustration had replaced the calm of moments ago. "There are a lot of therapeutic techniques we'll use," she said, "and quite a few different tactics, but yeah, that's the plan."

Before she could continue, I stood and put my hand on her shoulder. "Okay," I said. "I'm sorry for pushing you. You guys are the experts. Tell me how I can help."

CHAPTER 36

In the former rebel complex, planet Tumani

AS LIM HAD warned, Schmidt told me that what I could do to help was provide both janitorial and guard services. I spent the next few mornings cleaning the barracks while the boys sat on steps or squatted on the ground near the buildings, kicked around some of the many small leather-covered balls that appeared with the sun on our second day there, talked in small groups, and searched for ways out of the complex. Cleaning included both literal cleaning and locating and removing anything that looked at all like a weapon. Soap, sticks, dinner utensils, pieces of plates, hard chunks of roofing material—if you could shape it and sharpen it, the boys were busy turning it into a weapon. Each day at lunch, all of us on the clean-up crew—mostly counselors who'd drawn the job that day, but also a few other support staffers who were there only for the type of work I was doing—pooled our discoveries in a locked room in the back of the best guarded of the half dozen supply sheds.

No counselor reprimanded any boy for these weapons. Every now and then, a boy would be bold enough to ask one of his counselors to return the weapon someone had stolen from him. The counselor would always respond calmly that weapons weren't acceptable because the goal was to learn how to live and resolve conflicts without fighting.

In the afternoons, I had what passed for guard duty: I walked a section of the interior perimeter of the wall around the complex, quietly reported over my comm any boy I spotted within five meters of me, and in as nice a voice as I could manage encouraged those boys to go elsewhere. The clear area outside the walls was still infested with mines, so Lim wanted to make sure that no one escaped and accidentally killed himself. A few boys made early runs at the wall, of course, but the rebels had blasted its surface smooth and slick enough that none of them made it very far before one of the guards spotted him and made sure he came down safely. Most of the boys had yet to accept that the rebels had also wanted to make sure none of them left the complex.

I was on patrol about a hundred meters from the corner where I'd first entered the place when I heard shouting.

"Kill him!"

"You can take him!"

I sprinted ahead and to the left, toward the voices. As I rounded the end of the second barracks up from ours, I saw one of the larger boys attacking one of the adults. The boy was swinging wildly at the man, who was sidestepping and blocking blows but not hitting back. I ran to help the man, but before I could reach him, he spotted me and said, "No!" It was Long, who was also working in this quadrant of the complex.

I'd distracted him enough that the boy managed to clip his chin.

Long stepped back, shook his head, and focused again on the boy.

"There's no root here," a voice from the crowd yelled, "but none of us are sick or shaking. They're poisoning us."

Long looked in the direction of the voice and said, "No, we're not. All we did is give you something to help you get better, so you won't need the root anymore. We—"

The kid facing Long was almost as tall as the man. He straightened from his fighting crouch as if done and threw a slow, lazy fake, clearly hoping Long would either not see it coming or step back to avoid it and lose balance for a second. Long didn't do either one, so when the boy followed by lowering his shoulder and charging, Long was ready. He stepped to the side, spun the boy, and grabbed the kid around the waist. They might have been nearly the same height, but Long was well fed and strong and much heavier, so he easily held onto the boy and kept his head close enough to the boy's back that the boy couldn't do any real damage to him.

The other boys continued to cheer and to call for blood.

"Stop!" Long said. "I'm not going to fight you."

"You people killed my family!" the boy screamed. "Our brothers told us. You killed my mother and my father and my sister, and now I'm going to kill you." He twisted and tried to escape, but Long held onto him.

"No," Long said, "we didn't. The government didn't kill them. We didn't kill them; most of us aren't even from this planet and had never been here before a few days ago. The rebels weren't your brothers, and they weren't telling the truth. They killed your families, and they made you fight for them."

"You're lying!" the boy said.

"No," Long said, "I'm not. I'm sorry for what those soldiers did to you, but all I can do now is help you learn how to live normally. I won't fight you. I won't."

"They're all dead," the boy said, tears streaking his face, "and now you're saying our brothers killed them."

"They did," Long said. "I'm sorry."

"Liar!" several of the boys yelled. "They were our comrades. They fought with us. They never held us as prisoners."

"I'm not lying," Long said. "I'm telling the truth. Look around: These walls were here before we came. When those men brought you to this place, didn't they tell you not to leave? Do you think they would have let you go?" He shook his head. "No. No, they wouldn't."

"They were protecting us from the government demons," one boy said. "Demons like you."

"No," Long said. "That was another of their lies. They were hiding you so a group of inspectors wouldn't find you."

"Why would they hide us?" the same boy said. "We were brave fighters, and they were proud of us."

"Because it is wrong to use children as soldiers," Long said. "They knew that if they were caught doing it, they would be punished."

"Our brothers would not have killed our families,"

the boy Long was holding said. Sobs blurred his words. "They would not have lied to us. They wouldn't have done that."

"I'm sorry," Long said, "I really am, but they did. They manipulated you—tricked you—and they used you."

"And now *you* are using us," the same boy said.

Long released the boy and took two steps backward. "No," he said, "we're not. We are holding you here, but only until we can teach you how to live normally."

The boy balled his fists and faced Long. "Why won't you fight me?"

"Because you're done being soldiers. It's time for you to be boys again."

The boy spit on his face. "Coward!"

Long wiped the spittle from his cheek but otherwise did not react.

After a few seconds, the boy said, "I knew it." He faced the small group of watchers. "They *are* cowards!" He returned to his friends.

A couple of them patted him on the back. Others walked away as he drew closer, clearly isolating him, punishing him for failing to force Long to fight.

Long watched them but did not move.

When they had all left, I said to Long, "Isn't that hard? If someone attacks me, I hit back."

"So do I," he said, still staring straight ahead and not looking at me, "under normal circumstances, but these aren't normal circumstances. And, to answer your question, yes, that was difficult. A big part of me wanted to pound that jerk into pulp, but that would have accomplished nothing. More importantly, these kids have suffered enough. Learning to master those impulses and ultimately to feel them less often—those are big parts of what we trained to do." He rolled his neck and stretched his back. "Right now, I'm really glad we had that training." He finally turned to face me. "What's most important is to remember that these are children, not soldiers."

They can be both, I thought, but I saw no point in saying those words. Long, like the other counselors here, would tell me that he already understood my point. Maybe he did, but not from experience, not the way I did, not the way these boys did.

"They *are* children," I said, trying to explain it to him but unwilling to tell him why I was so certain, "but they've spent enough time as soldiers that childhood may be only a distant memory, if they remember it at all. I don't even know if they can recall it."

He stared at me for a few seconds. "I see how you might feel that way, but I have to hope you're wrong. Even if you're right, all we can do is hope that with time and help they'll all find their way back to being kids."

"I don't know if they can," I said, my voice barely a whisper. Too late I wondered why I was still speaking, whether I was really talking to Long or to myself, about them or about myself.

"Neither do I," Long said, "neither do I, but we have to try. Let's get back to it."

CHAPTER 37

Dump Island, planet Pinkelponker—139 years earlier

THE PATH FROM the shuttle landing zone to our cave turned sharply right about six steps from the edge of the large, open flat area. A meter past the turn, it widened enough that four of us could stand side by side and still not touch each other or the rock walls. Shadows darkened the area for all but a few hours of each day, which Benny said meant that if they were watching us from the sky, they could see us only during that brief time. We'd cut long branches, wedged them between the rock walls, and covered them with shorter branches. The area underneath this simple cover never received direct sunlight, so it would, we hoped, shield us from overhead spying.

It was our new home.

Sitting beneath it next to Benny, the two of us briefly alone while Han and Bob and Alex fetched fruit and water, I realized something obvious that had escaped me to that point. "If they're monitoring us from above, they've almost certainly examined this path before."

Benny stared at me and nodded.

"Which means they're sure to notice the sudden appearance of these branches."

He nodded again.

"And even if they've never looked at the path before, if they do spot tree branches connecting two rock walls, they're going to know this is something we built."

"Yes."

"Which means the shelter is useless."

"Not quite," he said. "As protection from the government, yes, it's probably not going to do any good at all. It does, however, make our people feel more secure, and that sense of safety calms them and makes the days pass more comfortably."

"But if it's a lie, shouldn't we tell them?"

"To what end?" Benny said. "They've already heard that the day we attack the guards, some of them are likely to get hurt, maybe even die. You and the others who can fight are training hard, and our plan is as good as we can make it. We might as well let our people have some hope that we can win."

"So the guards on the shuttle will know we're coming for them? We won't have the advantage of surprise that we've been counting on?"

"Maybe we won't," Benny said, "but I'm betting that we will. The reason is that a more accurate version of your statement is that we won't be able to surprise the guards *if the government is bothering to monitor us*. I don't think they are. The single biggest thing we have going for us is that they're arrogant and think we're helpless. They can't see us as anything other than a bunch of useless freaks that they keep alive because some government official told them there was a small chance one of us might develop a talent they could use." He shook his head. "No, I'm betting they don't bother to watch us now and they never have."

"If you believe that, then why did you even mention the possibility to all of us?"

He sighed. "Because I made a mistake. When I first came here, I hadn't thought through the situation well. I was angry and hurt, because I knew what I could do for Pinkelponker, I knew my talents, and even though I tried to explain them to my parents and our island mayor and even to the men who dragged me onto the shuttle, no one would listen. When the guards threw me onto the sand here, everyone was so hopeless, so resigned to being on Dump forever, so useless, that I used that possibility to lash out at them." He paused for a few seconds. "I'm not proud of my behavior. I was wrong, but once I'd told everyone the government might be monitoring us, I learned that it made some of them angry. Being mad was a lot better than being hopeless. It also convinced the others that I knew things they didn't, so they paid attention to me. They listened to what I had to say." He rubbed his eyes with his upper arms. "Telling them the truth would have changed all that, so I never did. Instead, I resolved to lead them off Dump."

I thought about what he'd said. I could go tell the others, but what would I gain by doing that? Hurting them by telling them the truth felt bad. Keeping his secret, though, was joining in the lie—and that felt bad, too. Something hit me. "So the reason you've pushed us so hard in training is that you feel bad about all this?"

"No!" he said. "I've told you why we have to work so hard: Because the guards will be well-trained and have better weapons."

I opened my mouth to speak but he started again before I could say a word. "You're probably right that my guilt was also a motivation. For that, I'm sorry—but nothing about the training would be any different if I'd never deceived anyone."

I considered his claim and nodded, but I wasn't done. Something else still bothered me.

"If your lie proves to be right, if they are monitoring us, then aren't I correct that they will see this shelter, know we've moved closer, and be prepared for our attack?"

"Probably," he said. "My guess, though, is that if they do know, they'll just land somewhere else. Why bother to fight when you can simply choose another landing site?"

"Because they don't think we can hurt them?" I said. "Because they don't see it as a fight worth worrying about?"

Benny shrugged. "Maybe, but it's still an easier choice to land elsewhere, and people tend to choose the easiest path available."

"And if they do? If the next person arrives somewhere else on the island?"

He rubbed his eyes again. "What do you think, Jon? We figure out how to cover two locations, or we tear down the shelter and look for better hiding places." He stared at me. His voice rose as he talked. "Or we put a team on both locations. I don't know! We keep on trying, because it's either that or accept that we'll spend the rest of our lives on Dump and never do anything more with ourselves than what we're doing right now." He paused and took a few breaths. When he spoke again, his voice was low and sad. "I don't know about you, but I can't live with that. I can't."

I stared at him for a few seconds and nodded my head.

"I can't either," I said, "but we won't have to. We'll beat them. We'll get off this island. We will."

CHAPTER 38

In the former rebel complex, planet Tumani

THE TWO BOYS weren't very good at following me. Maybe they'd been better in the forest, or at night, but they were terrible at tracking me in the interior of the complex. I'd spotted them as soon as I'd turned the far northeast corner on my perimeter guard patrol, but I hadn't said anything because I figured they'd give up soon enough. Ten lazy, slow-walking minutes later, they were still trying to parallel me but stay behind the cover of the closest buildings.

"How long are you going to let those two run surveillance on you?" Lobo said over the comm. He had shot sensors into the trees before we launched the initial attack, and they were still operational. To be safe, I was having him monitor me—not that I could have stopped him.

I kept strolling as I quietly said, "I don't know. Watching them is the most exciting thing I've done in the last few days. They don't appear to have any weapons, so I don't think I'm in any danger."

"They don't," Lobo said, "and if those two can take you, I may have to trade you in for a new owner. Still, why take any risks at all?"

I stopped. He was right. "Okay," I said.

I leaned against the complex wall, where I had a clear view of the corner of the building behind which they were lurking. They'd have to cross a lot of open ground to get me if they chose to attack. I couldn't spot anyone else, so if they wanted to make a move, I was giving them as good an opportunity as they were likely to get.

"Enough," I said. "We're done playing. Bony, Nagy: Come tell me why you've been following me."

I crossed my arms and forced a yawn. I'd learned that looking slightly bored was often the best way to interest the boys.

I waited.

Nothing happened.

I waited some more.

"Want me to drop a warning round near them?" Lobo said. "That would give them a reason to move."

I shook my head and suppressed a laugh. I brought my hand to my mouth and whispered, "No. They're just boys, and besides, you know we're not supposed to fire weapons in the complex."

"Don't think of the round as a weapon," Lobo said. "Think of it as motivation in an excitable, metal-jacketed, high-speed form."

"Are you that bored?" I said.

"What do you think?" he said. "You're bored, and you get to walk around."

Bony stepped into view from behind the building and stared at me.

Nagy followed him a second later.

"Leave me alone," I subvocalized, "so I can see what they want."

"Out," Lobo said.

I coughed into my hand and raised my head. "You two asked for this meeting," I said. "What do you want?"

Bony tilted his head and stared at me. "We didn't ask for anything."

"You might as well have asked me," I said, "considering the poor job you did of following me."

"We were great trackers," Bony said, standing as straight as he could.

"Great," Nagy said. "Many kills."

Up to that moment, they'd behaved like boys. Now, I'd insulted them, and they were back to acting like fighters—stupid fighters, but fighters.

When was I going to learn what the counselors kept demonstrating? Provoking the kids was rarely useful.

"I'm sorry," I said. "I was joking. I meant no offense."

Bony stared at me.

I looked away first.

"Okay," he said.

"So," I said, "what do you want?"

Bony headed my way, Nagy always one pace behind him. The two of them leaned against the complex wall two meters to my left—close enough for conversation in a normal voice but out of my immediate reach.

"You know our names," Bony said, "but we don't know yours. The others all tell us their names."

Because they work with you, I thought, while I clean and walk patrol and waste time. I said none of that, though. Instead, I told them, "Jon."

Bony glanced at Nagy and nodded, apparently satisfied. "So, Jon," Bony said, "none of these guards—or counselors or whatever they want to call themselves—will fight us."

"No," I said, "they won't."

"They don't even want to fight," Nagy said.

I thought about how hard Chris had resisted the urge to beat up the boy who'd attacked him and about how he'd worked not to show his feelings to the kids. "No," I said, shaking my head, "they don't."

"But you do," Bony said. "I can see it. You don't do it, you walk away when we try to get you to fight, but you want it."

I didn't know what to say. I never thought of myself as wanting conflict, but I had to admit that when they pushed me—when *anyone* pushed me—anger surged in me, and I was indeed ready to fight.

He laughed. "All those others, those 'counselors,' if we followed them, they would greet us like we were their best friends. Of course, before they reached us a few of their real friends would wander over like it was an accident that they happened to be there, not like they were reinforcements to hold us in case we attack. Not you, though: You let this wall get your back and wait to see what the story is. You're just like us."

I shrugged. "No," I finally said, "I'm not. I'm a grown-up, not a kid. That's a big difference. And, I really don't want to fight you. Sometimes my"—I paused, searching for a way to explain it, conscious that Lobo was listening and by reflex not wanting to give away anything about myself—"background makes me prepare for conflict even when I shouldn't do that, but I don't want it. That weakness in me is why I'm

out here walking wall patrol and spending the rest
of my time cleaning up after you guys. It's all the
counselors can trust me to do."

"Whatever you need to say, Jon," Bony said, "you
go ahead and say." He patted Nagy on the shoulder.
"Me and my brother, though, we know what we see."

"So you followed me out here to tell me your
opinion of my behavior?" I said. "If so, I need to
get back to work."

Bony stared at me for a few seconds, his face growing tense. Nagy stepped to the left, widening the arc
they covered. "Why do you want to disrespect me?
You think I'm stupid because I'm young?"

I held up my hands and edged away from them.
"Whoa! Where did that come from? I answered your
questions. That's all."

"You think we're stupid enough to talk for no
reason?"

I'd watched him talk a lot, but each time he'd been
after something. "No," I said, "I don't. Let me put it
differently: What do you want to know?"

Bony looked me in the eyes and nodded. He waved
his hand behind him. "All those others, I can't trust
them. They're doing what they're doing, and maybe
it'll be good for us and maybe it won't, but we'll
never know who they really are. I don't know who
someone is, I don't trust them. You, though, no matter what you say, I see it: You're a warrior. Like my
brother here." He tapped Nagy's chest. Nagy smiled
in response. Bony thumped his own chest. "Like me."

I didn't know how to respond, so I said nothing.

The two boys nodded their heads as if I'd agreed
with Bony.

"So what I want is to know is this, one soldier to another: What's really going on here?" His voice cracked for a second, and in that moment he was the boy, not the fighter. "What do they want?"

"Exactly what they told you," I said. "They want to help you learn how to live normally again."

"What normal?" Nagy said. His eyes were open, and he was looking at me, but he wasn't seeing me; he was somewhere else. "We had land. We had a river you could swim in, right near our house, on the edge of our property. My dad taught me and my sister to swim there." He shook his head, as if freeing himself from something. "They're all dead. I woke up next to them, covered in their blood." He stared at his hands and his chest. "I washed it all off in that river, the last time I went in it." He looked again at me, and this time, I think he was seeing me. "If that's what normal was, it's long gone, as dead as my family." His voice grew stronger as he continued. "Normal is being men who do what is necessary. Normal is tracking the government soldiers who killed our families. Normal is killing them."

"It was," I said, nodding my head, "and I'm sorry for that, but it is over. You have to learn how to go back to being boys. The counselors will help you do that."

Nagy spit at me but hit the ground in front of my boots. "So they want us to become weak again?" He shook his head. "No. No!" He turned and headed back toward the barracks. "I will never be weak again."

I watched him go. I remembered a night on Dump when I'd said much the same thing to Benny. I'd needed that resolve and the anger beneath it; without them, I might not have survived. Nagy needed them, too. I had no idea what to say to him.

"Come, brother," Nagy said without turning. "He has nothing for us."

Bony looked at me for a few seconds, and for a moment I thought he might talk to me. Finally, though, he shrugged, said, "Sorry," and ran after Nagy.

"So am I," I said, though I had little hope that he heard or believed me. "So am I."

CHAPTER 39

Dump Island, planet Pinkelponker—139 years earlier

ABOUT FOUR MINUTES to run from our new shelter to the cave. That's how long it took me now. I was pushing hard, moving far faster than any of the others could manage, but even for the slowest of them it wasn't a particularly long walk. Half a dozen of those who'd be staying in the cave had come with us when we'd carried some food in preparation for our first night here, but now that darkness was squeezing the last light out of the sky, they were all heading back. Benny and a couple of the others said they'd return tomorrow morning to visit.

So why did it feel like Bob and Han and Alex and I were so far away from them, so far away from what had over the last many weeks become my home?

We had a small fire going half a dozen steps down the path from our shelter. The night wasn't cold, and we had no reason for being awake, but when Benny had suggested that we might like a fire, no one had argued. We sat around it, doing nothing, saying nothing, not even looking directly at one another—just sitting.

I watched the stars through the streams of smoke that tendriled into the night and wondered if Jennie was watching the sky, too. Most of the time, I tried not to think about her, to focus instead on the training, but every now and then I couldn't help but recall some happy instant of the past that increasingly felt as if it belonged to someone else.

"It's weird, isn't it?" Alex said.

No one agreed, but no one argued with him, either.

"I mean, sleeping away from everyone else," he said, "leaving the cave, not hearing the ocean sounds as clearly as usual because we're in this trail—it doesn't seem right."

After a few seconds of silence, Bob said, "No, it doesn't, but that's not what's really wrong."

We all stared at him and waited for him to explain.

He leaned his thin body forward. The firelight flickered on his cheeks and eyes. He glanced at each of us in turn before he said, "The problem is that this makes everything seem real, and until now none of it did."

"Moving away?" Han said.

"Not real?" I said. "All that training? All those times I had to fight you guys? All those drills? You didn't think it was real." I wanted to slap him but instead balled my fists and struggled to control myself. "I can't believe you."

"No," Bob said, shaking his head, "you don't understand what I mean. Of course all that stuff was real in many ways: We worked hard, we got hurt, we got mad, all of that. But it was all still *practice*, something we did for a while and then went back to the cave and got on with living."

I stared at him and wondered how he and I could be the same kinds of creatures. Had none of this affected him? Was he that weak? Or, I wondered as a flash of insight cracked like lightning in my mind, was he that much better a person than I was? I checked the others; they were all paying close attention to Bob, so I said nothing.

"What's different now," he said, "is that there is no more home, at least not the home we had."

I lost mine a long time ago. So did they. How could they not know that?

"All there is now is this place and our attack on the shuttle."

. That's all there has been for weeks and weeks. How could they not know that, too?

I was too surprised to talk, and no one else said anything, so he continued. "Sure, we're sleeping away from the others, but if Benny had asked us to fish the other side of the island, we'd have spent the night over there and thought nothing of it. We've slept in other locations during our training. It's not fun to be out here on our own, but the problem isn't what we're leaving; it's what we're heading into."

Bob fell silent.

The others nodded their heads in agreement.

No one spoke.

I backed slightly away from the fire as I realized for the first time that none of them truly understood what was happening, that for them this had all been to some degree a game, a drill of skills they'd never need to use. No wonder Benny believed it was up to me; it was.

"I can't believe…" I stopped talking, my voice

floating away with the smoke on the light evening breeze, because I didn't know what to say next.

They all stared at me, their expressions alarmed. Only when I saw their faces did I understand how angry I must have sounded.

The telltale squeak of the wheels on Benny's cart saved me from having to find the words to go with my feelings. Everyone turned away from me and watched the end of the trail as the sound drew closer and, finally, Benny appeared around the bend.

"Can't believe what, Jon?" he said, his tone jovial, friendly, reassuring.

The others visibly relaxed, smiles easing onto their faces and their shoulders lowering.

Benny was only a kid, a kid no older than I was, a kid with flippers for lower arms and feet, a kid younger than many of the others, and yet he really was their leader. He showed up, and they thought everything was better, even though nothing had changed.

Amazing.

He looked up at me as he continued talking. "That we're really here?" He propped himself on his elbows, smiled, and surveyed each of us in turn. "Well, we are, and you guys were right to insist we come to this place. It's hard, no doubt about that, but now we're where we should be. When the next shuttle comes, we'll take it, and we'll get off this rock!"

Bob and Alex cheered in agreement.

Han nodded his head.

I said nothing.

"I thought you were going to stay with the others," Bob said. "You left."

"I was," Benny said, "but I was being stupid. What

if the shuttle lands while I'm back there? You guys overcome the guards, and then what? You have to wait on me to get here to fly the damn thing!" He shook his head. "No way. The minute that ship is ours, we're getting out of here!"

This time, all three cheered.

I couldn't believe them. Nothing at all had changed, but now they were happy.

"Hey, Jon," he said.

"Yeah."

"I was carrying some more fruit on my cart, but I lost it a bit down the path. Would you help me gather it?"

I was glad for the excuse to get away from the rest of them. "Sure, but I can handle it on my own."

"Nah," he said, "I made the mess, so I should help clean it up." The smile never left his face, but his eyes and voice hardened enough that his intent was clear.

"Should we come?" Bob said.

I kept staring at Benny as I said, "No need. You guys take it easy. We'll be right back."

Benny led me along the path for about two minutes of slow, squeaking rolling. He stopped and faced me.

"What do you think you're doing?" he said, his voice clear even though he was whispering.

"What do you mean?" I whispered in return. He obviously hadn't wanted anyone else to hear our conversation, so at least for now I'd play along.

"What were you about to say to them?"

"Did you hear them?" I said, the anger surging into me again. "They don't understand. I only now realized that they've never understood. This is all a big game to them—maybe not a fun game, definitely a scary one, but still a game. Even though you've told them that some of them may die, they've never really gotten it."

"And you have?" he said.

"Yes."

"You've understood what it's like to beat someone with your fists until they're unconscious," he said, "or to stab him repeatedly with your knife until he falls, or to slice his throat and watch him die. You understand all that."

The rock walls on either side of the path closed in on me, the air stopped moving, and I wanted to punch Benny. Why had I bothered to come with him? What else had he been training us to do, if not those things? How were we not to understand it? He'd been more than clear. I ground my teeth and stayed completely still, because no matter how little the others had gleaned from his lessons, I had learned how much my own anger could rule me.

I held my ground, stared at the sky, and thought some more about what Benny had said. No matter what else I'd thought of him, I'd never figured he was stupid. If he was saying something that struck me as really dumb, I probably didn't understand him.

Then I did.

"You don't get it, either, do you?" I said. "You've never been in a fight. You've never hurt anyone."

He shook his head but kept staring at me. "No, I haven't, so in the very real way I'm trying to describe, no, I don't get it. I can't. You can't, either, any more than you can understand what it's like to swim in the ocean until you've done it. You can think about it, people can tell you about it, you can read about it, watch videos of it—you can learn everything there is to know about it, but you can't understand this sort of thing until you've been through it."

"How do you know that?" I said. "Maybe some people can. Maybe I can. Maybe by seeing it over and over in your mind you can come to understand it."

"Maybe," he said, "but from everything I've read and what I've seen of all of us—including you—that's not how it works."

"So we're all going to fight those guards and not really be ready?"

"You'll be as ready as I can make you."

"But that's not truly ready, not as ready as we'll be after we do it."

"That's right."

"That's terrible," I said. "Some of us may well die and never even get a chance to know exactly what happened to us, what we did wrong, what we did right, any of it."

"Yes," he said, his voice even lower now.

"How can you live with that knowledge and still do what you do?" I said. "How can you train us all—people who trust you, people who think of you as a friend—send us off to fight, and then sit back and watch, knowing what can happen, knowing we're not completely ready?"

"Jon," he said, "take another look at me. What else can I do? Fight with you? I'd cost you far more than I'd help you. Not train you? We'd be stuck here forever. Not come up with this plan? Again, we'd all be stuck here—and we've all decided we don't want that."

I didn't know what to say. He was right, but I hated it.

"Did you ever read, Jon?"

"No," I said, "I never learned how. They all said it was a waste of time for anyone to try to teach me, because my brain wouldn't ever be able to hold enough to make the result worth the effort. And, of course, there was always plenty of useful work I could do in the fields and around the village." I chuckled. "Now, I'm sure I could learn, but there's nothing to read."

"You'll get your chance," Benny said, "once we're off Dump. The reason I asked is that I read a lot before they threw me away, read every chance I had. A lot of what I read was history, what men and women before us did back on Earth. Reading taught me a lot about how the shuttles worked. It's also one of the ways I learned about this training, about fighting, and about how people like me have always been sending people like you out to fight for us."

"What do you mean?" I said. I pointed at his front flippers. "There can't have been a lot of people like you."

A slight grin crossed his face before he continued. "No, not like me in having this birth defect. Like me in being unable—or sometimes unwilling—to fight, but still ordering others to do it. As near as I can tell, for as long as there have been people, there have been other people, older or more powerful or richer or in some way above or exempt from the call to battle, who have ordered soldiers to go into combat and, sometimes, die."

"But you're just a kid," I said. "Who are you to do that?"

"The only leader we have," he said. He craned his neck upward, toward me, as far he could. "Unless you want the job."

I pictured Bob and Alex and Han around the fire,

in training, trying to fight with me. As bad as it was to know how poor their chances were, it would be worse to watch them walk away from me and toward a battle with the guards and not be beside them, trying to save them. I would already be leading them during the shuttle attack; that was more than enough responsibility for me.

"No," I finally said, "I don't want that. I'd rather fight with them."

He nodded. "Let's head back. Let's make them as happy as we can tonight, and train as hard as we can tomorrow. That's the job."

I picked up the still tied collection of fruit that he'd clearly pushed off his cart so he could reach us faster.

He didn't wait for me; he knew I could catch up. He turned and headed back. "That's *my* job," he said.

I'd never heard him sound more sad, but when we entered the clearing, he greeted the others with a smile and a joke about how much time I could waste simply picking up some fruit.

I laughed along with the others.

CHAPTER 40

In the former rebel complex, planet Tumani

THE SCREAM CAME from near the corner barracks. I stopped patrolling the perimeter and turned toward the sound that broke the quiet of the darkening day.

"Get him!"

"Kill him!"

I sprinted toward the noise. As I drew closer, I could make out other, less loud voices urging the people involved in the fight to stop.

I cut to the inside of the row of buildings in time to see Schmidt and Long tear around the corner and spot the large circle of boys.

More boys were also running toward the conflict, streaming into the circle and merging with it. As a few of them joined from the same angle on which I was approaching, the crowd parted enough that I could see for a second what was happening: Nagy was chasing Bony, swinging wildly and yelling, his mouth working but no words emerging.

Though I wanted to barrel through the boys, I was

never supposed to get violent in any way with them, so I slowed as I reached the perimeter of the crowd and began gently working my way to its center.

Nagy's voice was no clearer than before, because he was yelling wordlessly, animal sounds of anger and pain erupting from his throat as if his body could no longer contain them.

Bony's words were clear. "I didn't mean anything bad," he said. Gasps punctuated the words as he zigged and zagged to evade Nagy. "I was trying to make you feel better."

Nagy stopped running. He held his arms at his sides, craned his neck forward, and stared at Bony.

The shorter boy stopped, too, and faced his friend.

"You're weak," Nagy said. He spit at Bony and hit the small boy's shirt. He pointed at Schmidt and Long, who were now on the inside of the circle but standing still, watching but not moving. "Like them. Like all of them."

Bony said nothing. Tears rolled down his cheeks.

"You made me weak," Nagy said, "you and your crying and your stupid words."

"You're my brother," Bony said as he began to sob.

"No!" Nagy said. "I had a family, a real family, and a brother, a real one, not some little coward who ran away as his family was killed."

"We couldn't have saved them," Bony said. "Not your family. Not mine."

"You could have tried!" Nagy said. "You could try now! At least I went down with them." His voice faltered and for a few seconds he hung his head. "I fought, and I fell, and I don't know why I lived. You—you ran away."

"What could I have done?" Bony screamed. "There were so many men I couldn't count them all, and they were stabbing and—"

"You could have fought!" Nagy said. "Instead, you left your family, and now you're leaving me."

"No," Bony said, "I'm not. I'm right here, brother." He held out his right arm.

"We could have saved them!" Nagy screamed. He launched himself at Bony and knocked the other boy onto the ground.

Schmidt and Long darted into the circle. They each grabbed one of Nagy's arms and pulled him off Bony.

The smaller boy stayed on the ground, curled in a ball and motionless. "I'm sorry I'm sorry I'm sorry," he said.

Long wrapped his arms around Nagy's torso as the tall boy kicked and screamed, his eyes seeing nothing, only memories visible to him.

Schmidt stood in front of him and spoke slowly and gently to him. "It's not your fault," she said. "It's not your fault." She glanced over her shoulder at Bony and at me before she focused again on Nagy. "It's not your fault."

"You can't keep me here!" Nagy screamed in reply. "You're all too weak. None of you can stop me!"

I pushed past the last boys in front of me and bent over Bony. I couldn't tell if he even knew I was there. I picked him up. There was nothing to him, even after weeks of eating decently, just a sticklike frame of sinew and bone. His eyes were shut.

All the boys in front of us stared at me.

I walked toward them, and they parted to let us out.

My body vibrated with energy. My face burned. I had to blink to see clearly.

I glanced at the boy in my arms, over my shoulder

at Schmidt, Long, and Nagy, who were still locked in their positions, and back down at Bony.

"It's not your fault," I said, my voice hoarse and rough. "It's not your fault."

"You did a good job out there," Schmidt said.

"What?"

"You did a good job," she said again. "With Bony. With not diving into the conflict."

"With controlling yourself," Long added from his seat on the chair next to hers. The sky outside the small window over their heads was dark but somehow felt less dim than the inside of the tiny room Schmidt used as an office and meeting area.

"How was that good?" I said. I had to struggle to keep my voice under control. "Bony's best friend turned on him. All I did was carry him away and repeat what you were saying." I shook my head. "I don't even know why I said that stuff to him."

"Because it's true," Schmidt said, leaning forward in her chair, "and he needs to hear it, over and over again, until he learns it, until he believes it and knows it, deep in his heart." She sat back and took a deep breath. "It's vital to healing."

"Do you believe it?" I said. "Not about them. About yourself, about all the bad things you've done in combat?"

"That's different," she said. "I was an adult."

"Is it?" I said. "Is it really different?"

Long stepped between us.

"Do you ever think about when you were a kid?" he said.

All the time, I thought, but I sure wasn't going to

say that to them. Instead, I forced myself to lean back in my chair. I shrugged. "Who doesn't?"

"Most people," he said, "have memories—"

"—sometimes suppressed," Schmidt said.

"Sometimes suppressed," Long agreed, "of problems that occurred or things that went wrong, things that were in no way their fault but that they blamed themselves for causing. Maybe a parent's issues, or a sibling's. Those events leave scars."

"Now imagine," Schmidt said, "the kind of damage that happens when what goes wrong is adults abusing the kids, or forcing them to do horrible things, or exposing them to scenes no child should ever have to see."

"Like being beaten, or being forced into fighting," Long said.

"Or killing," Schmidt said. "Imagine the damage."

I didn't have to imagine anything, but I closed my eyes as if trying to do just that. Instead, I fought to control my reaction, breathe slowly, and show nothing.

After a few seconds, I opened my eyes.

Schmidt was watching me carefully. She nodded as she said, "You're getting it. Good."

"Look," Long said, and he began to pace, "we're over-simplifying, of course, but the concept is close enough and correct in general. If we are to help these boys to live normal lives, eventually we must persuade them that whatever they did, whatever horrible acts happened while they were forced to be soldiers, were not their fault, not really. They never had a choice, not if they wanted to stay alive. They have to see that the blame belongs on the adults who commanded and trained and shaped them."

"And that it wasn't their fault that those soldiers

killed their families," Schmidt said. "That they couldn't have saved their parents and brothers and sisters. That it wasn't their fault that they lived while others died, that the rebels turned them into soldiers."

"A lot of that makes sense," I said, "because they didn't have any choices up to the point at which they became soldiers. Once they were, when the action started, they had the same options all of us who fought did: Walk away, kill, or be killed." I shut up; I hadn't meant to speak.

Schmidt shook her head. "First, was walking away ever really an option for you in combat?"

When I was in the Saw, if you went somewhere, it was either to train or to fight. The fighting occurred in places I'd never been before. Abandoning your unit was never something you would even consider. You were with them. You were a team.

"No," I said. "Walking away was never an option."

She nodded. "And you signed up. You made a choice to serve. These kids were never *adult* soldiers. They never had a chance to make an informed, adult decision about their actions. Once recruited, most, maybe all, of them had no real chance to do anything except what their leaders taught them to do."

"Few of us do," I said. "The training makes sure you react, not choose." Benny had molded me first, and later the Saw had refined my techniques and made me an even better soldier. Good training induced action without hesitation.

"Exactly," she said, "but these boys don't understand any of that. They blame themselves for everything, all that they did and a lot that they didn't—and most of all, for not saving their families."

I'd never found Jennie. I'd failed to save her. I kept hoping one day to find a way to get past the blockade on the one jump gate to my home planet, go there, and find her, but I'd never made it. I didn't even know if she was alive; the odds were certainly against it.

"Do you understand, Jon?" Long said.

I glanced up at him. "Well enough, I think."

"Good," Schmidt said. "We all need to be following the same script when we talk to Nagy, so we can help him."

I recalled the look in the tall boy's eyes, the sound of his roaring, beast-like screams. "He may be too far gone," I said.

"So we'll work harder," Schmidt said, "because we're not giving up on him."

I was trying to figure out how to explain to her why I was so sure Nagy was in trouble when Lobo spoke to me privately over the comm.

"We need to talk," he said. "Wylak's changing the deal."

CHAPTER 41

In the former rebel complex, planet Tumani

I STAYED QUIET until I was safely inside Lobo and standing in the pilot area. I paced back and forth across its width, drained enough that I wanted to keep moving lest I fall asleep, but at the same time feeling buzzed from the encounter with Nagy and Bony.

"I take it your eavesdropping on Wylak has paid off," I said.

"Cracking through a wide array of governmental security systems and a smorgasbord of personal countermeasures so I can tap into every data feed related to a major government official is hardly mere eavesdropping," said Lobo, "but, yes, my efforts have yielded results we must discuss."

I couldn't stop thinking about the two boys and how I could explain to Schmidt and Long why I was so sure Nagy was in worse shape than they realized. I wasn't in the mood to banter with Lobo. Annoying him, however, would only prolong the conversation, so I stopped moving, took a deep breath, and said, "Thank you for doing all that. What have you learned?"

"My, aren't we Mister Formal and Considerate all of a sudden," he said.

I shook my head but didn't respond.

After a few seconds, he said, his voice low and gentle, "Jon, it was just a fight between two young male friends."

"No," I said, "that's the problem: It wasn't."

"Fights among the boys are common," he said. "You don't see most of them, because they occur in other areas, but they happen often."

"I understand, but though I can't justify or explain the feeling, I know that Nagy is in a very bad way. He needs more help than they realize."

"If you want to go back to them, we can have this conversation another time—but sooner would be better."

I rolled my head a bit to try to work out the kinks in my neck and shoulders. "Maybe you and Schmidt and Long are all correct. Maybe I'm over-reacting. In any case, this sounds important, so let's do it. What's going on?"

"Wylak's been devoting a lot of government computing cycles to financial and military simulations," Lobo said, "simulations that have concerned the boys. He's also participated in a great many meetings about them. I've been able to monitor some but not all of those meetings."

"None of that is surprising," I said, "given what he said when Lim and I met with him."

"I agree in general," he said, "but the details pose the problem. When you and the others captured this complex and those boys, you hurt the rebels. The government forces have been on the offensive ever since, and they're gaining ground. The problem is, they're short on soldiers, and they're low on money."

"Oh, no," I said.

"Wylak's models show that the inducements and ongoing fees the government would have to pay families to take these boys represent a large investment at a time when he and many of his colleagues feel they need to divert as many of their resources as possible to winning the war once and for all."

"So he's decided that he can save money and perhaps crush the rebels by turning the boys into more government troops." I whispered, "By making them soldiers again."

"A task," Lobo said, "that he feels would be a simpler and cheaper reprogramming effort than what Lim and her team are trying to accomplish."

"Damn," I said, my voice growing louder. "Damn! He's probably right, too, because few, if any, of these kids ever really understood what they were fighting for. Show them proof—real or faked—that the rebels killed their families, get them back on the root, fire them up a bit, and—"

"—and they'll be ready to fight again in the jungle," Lobo said. "They'll probably even thank the people who let them. Exactly. Wylak's also told his colleagues that the reintegration of the boys can occur later, after the war. When it comes time to ask for the budget to do that, they'll easily get the money, because the boys will be heroes."

"Or dead or so much worse than they are now that no one can help them." I pictured Bony and Nagy carrying guns, heading into the woods again. I couldn't let that happen. None of them should have to do that. "So is it settled, or do we have maneuvering room?"

"Unclear," Lobo said, "because some of the most important meetings were in hardened private areas.

From the data I've been able to gather, it appears that not all the key players are on board with his plan. That's one of the reasons he's bringing a team here."

"One of the reasons?" I said. "And, when?"

"From discussions among his staff members, it appears that Wylak has two motivations for his visit. First, he wants to show some of the opposition that the boys are far from ready to resume normal lives. He's never mentioned that no one expected them to be ready at this stage in the process."

"He wants to prove Lim's program is a failure."

"I assume so. He also wants to give some of his supporters a first-hand look at the boys, to convince everyone that even though they're young, these kids could prove to be valuable battlefield assets."

"How's he going to do all this without tipping off Lim?"

"Tomorrow, he'll call her and suggest that an inspection tour could increase support for the work here, and that he very much needs that support. He'll unveil as already in motion and too late to change his plan to come two days later. He knows she won't appreciate the visit, and he has to assume she'll be suspicious, but she's unlikely to suspect anything near the full extent of what he's doing."

Each time I deal with a government, my lifelong desire to stay away from all of them seems wiser. "So we tell her," I said. "She confronts Wylak and threatens to spread his plans far and wide, all over Tumani."

"None of the key meetings have involved the man himself," Lobo said. "He's too smart for that. So if Lim tries to blackmail him with information I've gathered, he'll deny everything, chide and fire the staffers who were in the meetings, and find reasons to send Lim and her entire team, including us, out of this planetary system."

"Yeah," I said, nodding my head, "that makes sense. It wouldn't even be hard for him; reasons to close any operation are always easy to come by."

"The situation is particularly difficult," Lobo said, "because the boys are citizens of Tumani, so the government does have the legal right to govern them."

"This is abuse, not governing!" I said. My body shook with anger. "They're kids! The fact that they're from this planet doesn't mean we have to let its government destroy them."

"No," Lobo said, his voice quiet and calm, "it doesn't. It does, though, mean that many other governments, including the two coalitions watching this planet, are unlikely to support outside interference in a sovereign entity's legitimate choices."

"Legitimate? The coalitions can't consider the use of child soldiers as legitimate! They would never sanction this action on their planets."

"No, they wouldn't," Lobo said, "which is why at best Wylak would deny any accusations, keep the boys here, and wait for any trouble to blow over before he did anything. Remember also that this is not a coalition planet."

"At best?"

"One of Wylak's contingency plans involves portraying Lim's operation as an illegal military action funded by the rebels and performed by off-planet mercenaries. The government troops surrounding the complex will claim they've been trying all along to persuade us to leave the boys alone."

"So we become the bad guys," I said.

"Yes. Worse, Wylak's people will then ask the two federations to intervene and help deport us."

"Which he can do while claiming to be trying to save the boys."

"Yes."

"So, he's going to come here, soften up Lim, and sell his associates. Later, he'll return with two offers, one that lets her and the rest of us walk, and one that has us leaving under armed escort."

"That's my analysis," Lobo said.

"You have to hand it to him: It's a solid plan."

"Yes, it is. So, what are we going to do about it?"

"I'm not sure," I said, "but I know the first step is to talk to Lim." I headed for the side hatch. "This is not going to be fun."

CHAPTER 42

In the former rebel complex, planet Tumani

HOW SURE ARE you of this information?" Lim said. The moment I'd mentioned the topic, she'd insisted we talk while walking far away from anyone else. The bright stars and gentle breezes made it a perfect night for a walk with a beautiful woman—unless she was your commander and you were delivering very bad news. She'd turned angry immediately and stayed that way.

I couldn't blame her.

"It's completely reliable," I said.

"Your source?"

I stopped and stared at her but said nothing.

After a few seconds, she said, "If I act on this and you're wrong, I could destroy everything we've accomplished so far."

"Two separate things," I said. "I'm not wrong. You know me well enough to know that I'd never bring this to you if I weren't sure of it. As for acting on it, you shouldn't do anything until we have a clear strategy."

"That bastard!" Lim said. "And 'we' need a strategy? Last I checked, you were a damn janitor."

I fought the urge to snap back and instead forced myself to respond in a cold, flat tone. "That's true, because I have no training in reintegrating child soldiers. This, though, is the sort of problem I know a great deal about. This is the kind of thing I do—and you know it."

"Yeah," she said, nodding her head, "but I also know that sometimes your answers don't turn out entirely the way you planned. I still have the scar to prove it."

"Perfect solutions are rare in this line of work—and you understood that when you agreed to help me before. As for the scar, you're the one who chose to keep it; the wound wasn't big enough that the medtechs couldn't have removed all traces of it."

She smiled slightly and cocked her head. "Fair points. I thought the scar was rather dashing. Made me more attractive."

As if you needed that, I thought but did not say as the starlight painted her face in gentle white and her smile glowed more brightly than the stars.

"So," she said, the smile vanishing, "what do you recommend we do?"

"Let's start with where we are now. What's your backup plan?"

She shook her head. "We don't have one, as you already know. We figured the worst that would happen was that Wylak or someone else in the government would press us to finish a bit early. Even that seemed unlikely, because Chu's people are paying the tab and this is costing Tumani nothing. To be safe, though, we padded our time estimates. After our meeting with

Wylak, it was clear that he'd be pressuring us, so I've been sending frequent status updates to placate him." She shrugged. "We thought that would be enough." She paused. "We could always take our case to the Tumani public."

"She has indeed sent those updates," Lobo said to me privately over the comm, "but they've done nothing to change the situation."

"Try to fight Wylak in the Tumani media," I said, "and he'll portray us as a gang of mercenaries who kidnapped and brainwashed these poor children. His connections have to be far better than ours. He'll get us booted off the planet and take the boys."

"We could appeal to the two Coalitions."

"They'd have to be willing to go against the planet's government, and they'd have to agree that both of them would do it together, because neither will let the other establish a stronger position here. No, no way that's happening. They'll stay out of it and let you and Wylak sort it out."

"I'm back to my question," she said. "You pointed out that this is the sort of thing you handle. What do you recommend?"

"For now, play along. Warmly welcome his inspection tour. Introduce his people to as many of the boys as possible. Show them all the progress you've made. Maybe seeing it all in person will change his mind."

She stared at me for a few seconds. "You don't believe that," she said.

"No, I don't. In my experience, if you gamble on politicians giving a damn about anyone they send into battle, you're making a fool's bet."

"So when playing along fails, what should we do?"

I shrugged. "I don't know yet." I held up my hands to stop her from speaking. "But I haven't had any time to think about it. I came to you the moment I received this information. I'll come up with something, but I need more than a few minutes to work it out."

"And when you do," she said, "will you tell me the whole plan?" She paused and stepped to within a hand's width of me. "Unlike last time?"

I backed away. "It depends," I said. "It just depends."

I left before she could respond.

I wandered through the complex, staying on the glowing grass-and-sand paths that wound around and between the buildings, skirting the groups I encountered, listening to the forest life and the movements of the people and letting my mind settle. The night bugs and small creatures sounded the same as when we'd first crept up to the edge of the jungle on the evening we arrived. The noises from the boys, though, had changed. In the first week, they'd rarely spoken to the adults, and when any of us had come near them, they'd either scurried away or dropped into voices so soft no one could hear them without assistance. The place had buzzed like an angry insect with indecipherable sounds that hinted of whispered plans and threats. Now, though, laughter and conversations filled the buildings and the social areas, where kids and adults mixed freely and comfortably. Here and there, two or three or four boys stood by themselves and mumbled to one another, but those groups were now the exception and not the norm.

A boy maybe fifteen or sixteen darted from between two barracks. He carried a ball and shrieked wildly, as did the two kids chasing him. At first glance, he reminded me of Manu Chang, the psychic boy that Maggie and Jack and I had rescued and helped escape to Maggie's group.

The three boys vanished around the corner of the next dorm over, their laughter trailing after them.

If only we could have shown the Tumani people these before and after images, they'd surely understand how much good Lim and Schmidt and Long and all the others were doing.

Or perhaps not. Perhaps a civilian population that lives far from the combat zones will always be willing to sacrifice a small percentage of its young to ensure its lifestyles. The people of Tumani certainly had reason to fear what the rebels would do to them; the trail of slaughtered jungle villages stood as an easy explanation to any who didn't understand. Someone had to fight; the question for the leaders and the people alike boiled down to age limits.

I shook my head and breathed deeply. No, I couldn't accept that. There were acts no group should commit. Sending children into combat was one of them. One day, each kid would reach his or her majority, and at that point the obligations of adulthood would become theirs, but not until then. Not until then.

I was getting nowhere. Lim had brought me into this mess. It couldn't be the only one like it. I'd never tried to help child soldiers before, but others must have. I'd jumped from planet to planet never even checking to see if the problem existed. Others, though, must have confronted it before. Even if the people of Tumani were willing to turn a blind eye to this practice, surely others on other worlds must have dealt with it.

It hit me.

"Lobo," I said, smiling as I picked up my pace and headed back to him.

"Yes," he said, drawing out the word.

"I need to record a message for you to get to Maggie."

"Go," Lobo said.

I stared at the image of Maggie on the wall in front of me, a still Lobo had captured when she and I had met inside him. Back in my con artist days, I'd learned that most people communicate more naturally when they're looking at their mark, or at a picture if the person wasn't available. I wasn't exactly trying to con Maggie, but I did need to be very convincing, because the plan I was developing depended on her help. I took a slow breath and spoke to the image as if the real woman was standing in front of me.

"Hi, Maggie. I didn't expect to need to reach you. I didn't even expect to still be here on Tumani, though I now realize that you believed I would be." I smiled and chuckled. "You had me figured right. Now, though, there's a problem, a big one, and if I'm going to have any chance of fixing it, I'll need your help. More to the point, these boys need your help. The first thing I need you to do is find Jack and bring him here so the three of us can meet. The rest, well, I'll explain that when I see the two of you. It's safest that way." I thought about Lim's request that I keep her informed, but I couldn't take the risk of honoring it. "When you reach Tumani, don't come here. Leave a message with Lobo. We'll send you the location of a safe house in Ventura. I'll meet you there." I paused, unsure how much to risk scaring her away before I could explain. No, not warning her wouldn't help, and given our background, if I didn't tell her, she'd have every right to smell a con. She might as well understand in advance what the price tag would be. "Maggie, this is going to cost you or your people a lot of money, as well as a fair amount of time assisting Jack. If you don't want in, or if your people won't back you, just let me know. But whatever you do, do it soon. We don't have much time, and we need every day we have."

I waited a few seconds, but I couldn't think of anything else I needed to say. "That's it. Get this on its way to her."

"Before I do," Lobo said, "I have to ask: Jack? Really?"

"I need his particular skills. There's no better con man."

"That's debatable," Lobo said, "given that you were able to con him. Why don't you do this yourself?"

I shook my head. "I can't. I can't leave here. If I go now, Lim will be on her own."

"Not true," Lobo said. "She has plenty of people helping her. She assigns you only the worst jobs, so she's clearly not depending on you for much. She can afford to be without you."

"That *was* true," I said, "until Wylak decided it was time to move on her and this place. Now, whether she appreciates it or not, she needs my help."

"And the data I gather."

"And that," I said. "Most definitely that."

"Is there no alternative to Jack?"

"What have you got against him?"

"Other than the fact that he drugged you, stole from you, kidnapped the boy he asked you to help him protect, and left you unconscious on the floor near my front hatch, not much." Lobo paused, but clearly only for dramatic effect—and perhaps to use all of his vast computing resources to determine precisely how much sarcasm he could add to his voice when he continued. "Oh, yeah: I had to spend multiple days trapped under a heap of rubble with him walking around inside me, talking, constantly trying to work me, needling me as if I were some cheap washing machine he could easily persuade to share local gossip."

"You never told me he pumped you for information," I said. "What did you tell him?" Lobo knew a lot that I'd rather Jack never learn.

"Oh, please," Lobo said, annoyance now trampling the sarcasm. "As if he—or anyone—could get me to give them any data I didn't want to share."

"Sorry," I said. "Just being cautious."

"Cautious?"

"Okay, okay: paranoid. Sorry."

"So it has to be Jack?"

"He's the only person I know who can do what I need on the timetable I need it."

"How are you going to motivate him? Need I remind you that Mr. Altruistic was ready to sell Manu?"

"Jack was trying to make money off the boy," I said. "We have no proof he would have actually sold him. In any case, though, I understand the concern, and I plan to entice Jack into this project with the same two incentives that have worked with him for as long as we've known each other: It's a fun and interesting challenge, and he'll get a lot of money when it's over."

"So we're going even more into the hole on this one?" Lobo said. "Lovely. You know, fuel and weapons don't grow freely on the ground."

"No, no," I said. "If I even hinted that I was paying, Jack would never sign on. He'd never trust one con man to pay another. That's why I told Maggie it was going to cost her and her people: They're going to compensate Jack."

"I can't picture her or her organization being thrilled at the prospect of putting a lot of money into Jack's pockets, particularly not after the way he treated Manu."

I took a deep breath. "That is the weak link in the plan. I have to hope she'll be true to her word and persuade them to do it."

"And if she doesn't," Lobo said, "or she can't?"

"I don't know," I said. "This is my only idea."

"Well, don't worry too much," Lobo said. "I figure Maggie will do it, but not for the boys or for Lim or for Jack. She'll do it for you. You're counting on that, aren't you? You're taking advantage of her feelings for you, though admittedly for a good cause."

"I don't know," I said. "I don't like to think of it that way, but maybe so. Maybe so."

"And you called Jack the best con man."

CHAPTER 43

Dump Island, planet Pinkelponker—139 years earlier

JON, JON! WAKE up!"

I rolled over in response to the noise and the pushing on my shoulder and stared up into Han's face. Shards of light sliced yellow and white lines into the gray sky. We didn't have morning training today, so I had been counting on sleeping well past sun-up. "What?" I said, clinging to the last edge of sleep.

"Do you hear that?"

I propped myself on my elbows, my brain still foggy. "Obviously not, or whatever woke you would have made me wake up, too."

"Listen!" he said, the ess sound a hiss. I finally realized he was whispering.

I closed my eyes and tried to take in all the sounds. A breeze fluttered the leaves on the branches covering our heads. Waves washed back and forth on the beach. A few insects flew nearby.

Then I heard it, a very low rumble that the ocean's rhythms almost covered.

"Everybody up!" I shouted as I stood.

Han smiled and crawled over to Bob, who as usual was deep asleep. He could sleep through thunderstorms that left the rest of us wide-eyed and nervous.

Benny and Alex sputtered awake.

"What?" Benny said.

"Huh?" Alex added.

"I'm not positive," I said, "but Han might have heard the shuttle approaching."

"So why isn't it here?" Benny said, his eyes now clear. "That thing can move, really move. It could fly toward us faster than the sound of its approach."

"What did it do when it brought me?" I asked. I'd never really listened to the ships landing on Pinecone, and now I regretted not doing so.

"It circled a few times," Benny said, "probably to make sure the landing area was clear, and then it landed."

"So maybe it's doing that again," I said.

"No," Benny said, "because if it was that close, we'd hear it clearly." He paused for a few seconds and stared at the rock wall in front of him. "More likely, its pilot is being cautious and hovering offshore for a few minutes to see if anyone's going to appear at its destination." He fell silent again for a bit. We all listened and stayed quiet. The deep background noise didn't change. "No, that doesn't make sense, as I'd have realized if I were fully awake. If they were worried about this spot, they'd land somewhere else. No, this is probably just another approach route. No two shuttles have come in exactly the same way. It must be their standard protocol to vary their landing pattern each time." Benny stared at me before adding,

"Or maybe it's some other ship heading some other place, and it has nothing to do with us."

"When have we heard another shuttle?" I said. "Not once since I've been here."

Benny nodded. "Best to assume it's ours."

"So how long do we have?" I said.

"No way to tell," Benny said. "Maybe several minutes, maybe less—but not long."

I picked up my knife, two of the small bags we'd made of scraps of fabric and filled with sand, and two of the larger, thicker bags full of rocks. I stuffed the two with sand in the waistband of my pants, the tied parts hanging out, and the other pair in my pants pockets.

No one else moved.

"What are you waiting for?" I yelled. "Grab your weapons, and take your positions. This is it."

Han's head bobbed up and down in agreement. "This is it," he said. "This is it."

I grabbed his shoulders and shook him. "Look at me," I said. "Look into my eyes."

Han's head stopped moving, and he stared at me, but I couldn't tell if he was fully aware of me or looking somewhere else, someplace I couldn't see.

"If we go, we go full force, all of us, holding back nothing. If you're not ready, we can wait for another shuttle, but you have to decide now. Right now."

Han focused fully on me and nodded his head once. "Now," he said. "No more waiting."

"Bob?" I said. "Alex?"

They stepped next to Han, their knives in their hands, their hands shaking slightly, but their faces set.

"We go," Alex said.

"Yes, we do," Bob said.

I checked each of their eyes once more. They were scared, but they were as ready as they could be.

The low rumble we'd been barely able to detect washed over us in a loud roar.

They all stared at me, waiting.

I didn't know what to say. I didn't know if any or all of us would survive. I wanted to tell them something, give them some hope, thank them, come up with words that would somehow make it all a little better, but in all the times I'd imagined the attack, I'd never fully understood that of course it would come to this: Three other kids ready to risk their lives and looking to me to lead them.

I forced a smile. "Let's go get a ride off this dump!"

They smiled in return.

We crept to our positions.

The roaring grew louder. Dust blew down the path from the landing area.

The shadow of the shuttle darkened the ground. For the first time, we could see it hovering far overhead.

We flattened ourselves against the rock walls, hoping no one in it was looking at us.

It began its descent.

CHAPTER 44

In the former rebel complex, planet Tumani

BAD NEWS," Lobo said over the comm.

At almost the same time, I heard the shouting. I stood a hundred meters from the entrance Lim's ordnance disposal team used to leave and re-enter the complex as they slowly cleared the minefield outside. That door stood open; they were headed out to work today. The many devices buried in the cleared area that surrounded us varied so widely in technology that none of the gear Lim had been able to smuggle into the system could locate everything that lurked under the ground. Gustafson and I had suggested the ages-old method of letting a great many large animals wander the areas, but she'd immediately vetoed the notion. She was right to do so: Frequent, nearby explosions and animal deaths would not help the boys. For the same basic reason, she was committed to not triggering any of the mines, so the removal process unavoidably involved both people and machines. Those people also functioned as counselors, so they worked on the mines as time permitted, and progress was slow.

They'd cleared the full width of the complex on this side, but only outward for a total of twenty meters. Past that, to support ground transport they'd worked on just one road leading away to the forest.

"What is it?" I asked Lobo, "and does it have anything to do with all this shouting?"

"To answer your second question first," Lobo said, "yes. What you're hearing is an artifact of actions Wylak has taken."

"What actions?"

"In advance of his visit tomorrow, Wylak has forbidden anyone from exiting the complex on foot. Only supply ships are allowed in and out. His message to Lim claimed these rules were for the protection of all the boys, but he's really just buttoning up the place."

"He's stopping the clean-up crew?"

"Not only them," Lobo said. "He's given orders to the soldiers in the forest that they are to keep everyone inside, regardless of their reasons for leaving. So, the moment the external door opened, Tumani troops stormed up the ten-meter-wide cleared road. Now, Lim and four of her people are standing outside and arguing with the sergeant in charge of that squad."

"Why is Wylak bothering?"

"He's run a set of low-cost scenarios for keeping us all here. They figure that a single military fighter can destroy any of Lim's shuttles that tried to launch, the supply ships can't carry many people, and the troops already in place can blockade the only safe ground route out of here."

"So as long as we don't clear any more mines," I said, "they think they can control us cheaply and easily, because they have to guard just that road."

"That appears to be the case."

"Could their fighter stop you?"

"Please," Lobo said, "there's no need to be insulting. I'd obviously have to use my weapons and thus break cover, but assuming I did, no, of course not."

"So you and I and anyone we could carry could leave here easily enough."

"Yes," he said, "not that it matters. You know you won't go, not with hundreds of boys and all of Lim's team stuck here."

I stopped fifteen meters away from the open doorway and leaned against the external wall. The guards who policed the area had drifted outside, no doubt wanting to support Lim. The faces of boys crammed the windows of the nearest barracks, Bony's and Nagy's home. Our routine rarely changed, so I could imagine how exciting it must be to see a confrontation between adults—particularly adults who had steadfastly refused to fight. The kids had to be very curious to learn how Lim's people would deal with the soldiers in front of them. I scanned the line of windows and saw Bony, then Nagy, both of them staring intently at the action I could hear but not see.

I closed my eyes and considered the situation. Wylak's move was annoying, but it didn't pose any significant new threat, nor did it provide any new information; we'd known he was going to start squeezing us. How, though, was he explaining these changes to his people and to the troops?

"Can you hear the details of what's going on outside?"

"Are you just determined to annoy me today?" he said. "Of course. I've told you before: I have enough sensors in and around this place that I hear and see everything. It's a small enough area that it's no problem to cover."

"Sorry," I said. I didn't want to encourage a rant. "So what reason are these troops giving Lim for interfering with the mine-removal team?"

"One of the oldest and most annoying justifications of any government: They've told her that they're doing it for her protection. The sergeant in charge is claiming that the Tumani troops stationed in the surrounding forest have spotted rebel troops in the area and that a few of those troops have used secret paths through the mines to break into the complex and communicate with some of the boys. Consequently, the only way they can keep everyone safe is to make sure no one enters or leaves the compound."

"Because anyone going in could be a rebel spy, and anyone leaving could have been recruited by the rebels."

"Exactly."

"And they expect her to believe that?" I said. "That's a weak story."

"Yes, it is," Lobo said, "and I can't tell whether the sergeant thinks Lim will buy it, but I doubt he or Wylak cares. They know that what she believes simply doesn't matter. So far as they—and Lim—know, no one has sensors monitoring all of the external walls. The rebels didn't, and Lim didn't install any, either. She didn't think she needed them. So, she can't prove the rebels didn't enter here. Without proof, she's an off-worlder, they're the government, and so she loses."

"Lim has to accept their orders to stay in the complex," I said, "but that's only a small loss in the short term. The important work is what she's doing inside with the boys. Wylak's tightening his control on the area, but we knew that was coming."

"So we let it go?" Lobo said.

"Absolutely. The only way to fight it would be to expose what you're capable of doing, and that could create far greater problems for us."

"Nagy's on the run!" Lobo's voice boomed in my ear.

A second later, I saw Nagy round the corner of the barracks, a piece of a tree branch in his hand, screaming, "You killed my parents!"

I lost a second reacting before I took off to intercept him.

He raced closer to the exit, yelling as he ran, "I'll kill you!"

"Nagy, stop!" I yelled.

He ignored me.

I was a little bigger and probably faster if we'd both begun from a standing start, but we hadn't. He'd been running when I saw him, and he was still accelerating. He burst through the open doorway when I was still several meters away.

"No!"

I glanced to the right and saw the source of the scream: Bony, his much shorter legs stretching as he sprinted toward me.

I rounded the doorway in time to see Nagy push past Lim and rush toward the troops.

"No!" I screamed again.

"No!" Bony echoed from behind me.

The sound of the shots drowned out everything else. I couldn't tell how many, but it wasn't a large number, and they came in a quick burst. No more followed.

They'd fired enough, though, to do the job. I burst

past Lim in time to see Nagy hitting the ground and, a couple of meters behind him, a woman on the mine-disposal team spinning and falling.

"Stop!" I screamed. I forced myself to halt as I saw the soldiers take aim at me. I held up my hands. "I'm not armed. I just want to get the boy."

"No one move!" the sergeant said.

"You killed him!" Bony screamed. "You killed my brother!"

I stayed where I was. I glanced over my shoulder: Lim had her arms around Bony and was controlling him.

Bony screamed and sobbed, his words now unintelligible.

The woman who'd caught the other round moaned and held her shoulder.

I faced the soldiers again. I clenched my fists and tightened my jaw as I fought to control the rising anger. When I spoke, the words emerged short and clipped. "Let us take the boy and the woman inside."

The sergeant stared at Nagy, who still hadn't moved.

I studied the man's face. He wasn't more than a few years older than Nagy, barely an adult.

I still wanted to kill him. I wanted to kill all of them.

The sergeant looked at me again. "He shouldn't have attacked us," he said.

I stared at the ground and struggled to stay under control. Though the heat of the day was behind us, sweat ran down my arms and back. My eyes burned. I tasted copper and felt my body ready itself for violence. I held up my hands. I could pick up some dirt, spit in it, and instruct the nanomachines to replicate and consume everything human in front of them. I could kill the sergeant and his troops and the men in the surrounding woods. I could destroy them, erase them so it would be as if they'd never existed. They'd shot and killed a boy, and they were helping a man who planned to make the other boys into soldiers again. They deserved to die.

"Jon," Lobo said, "I assume you know this, but I could wipe out that entire platoon before they could reach the cover of the forest."

"It's not your fault," I heard Lim whisper to Bony. "It's not your fault."

I could do all that, I could kill the soldiers, or I could say the word and let Lobo do it, but what would that teach Bony? These men shouldn't have shot Nagy, but did they all deserve to die for doing it? They saw a threat and reacted the way they were trained: They fired. At least part of Nagy knew he should never have charged at armed men in a tense situation. Maybe another part of Nagy had learned what so many veterans, young and old, have burned into their subconscious: The only final relief comes with death. But did he want to die? I'd never be able to ask him.

What was certain was that the soldiers were wrong. They'd responded entirely out of proportion to what Nagy had done, but did that give me the right do to the same to them?

No. I wouldn't kill them.

I looked back up at the sergeant. "He was just an angry kid with a stick," I said. "You didn't need to shoot him."

"He shouldn't have attacked us," the sergeant repeated.

I nodded. "You're right: He shouldn't have done that. But you shouldn't have shot him."

The sergeant stared at me for several seconds. He tilted his head forward momentarily, an instant of acknowledgment, one I knew he wanted me to see and his men to miss.

It was all he would give me.

"Let us go back inside," I said.

"No more attacks," the sergeant said, his voice stronger and his focus clearer. He stared at me and past me at Lim.

"No more," I said. I turned my head to confirm my statement with Lim. "No more."

Her eyes were moist, and she shook with the effort of controlling herself. When she spoke, her voice was low and angry and hard. "Agreed," she said.

"Take him, take all of them," the sergeant said. "Go back inside, and stay there." He looked one last time at Nagy and shook his head. He motioned to his men. They backed up slowly, their weapons at the ready.

I faced Lim and the others. A man and a woman helped the wounded woman to her feet. Lim stared after the soldiers.

"Take them inside and tend to them," I said.

She glared at me, her expression furious.

"Please," I said. "They all need you." I tilted my head toward Nagy. "I'll get him."

She hugged Bony closer to her and wrapped her arm around his head, covering his ears. "This isn't over," she said.

"I know." After a few seconds, I added, more to myself than to her, "It never is."

She nodded and turned to take Bony inside.

He held his ground, wiped his eyes, and said to me, "You will take care of my brother, make sure he gets his honor?"

"I will," I said. "It is *my* honor."

Bony nodded once and let Lim lead him away.

I walked over to Nagy as the soldiers marched away and Lim and the others retreated to the complex, the two groups separating from us, from the dead boy and me, as if whatever afflicted us might infect them, too.

Nagy's lifeless eyes stared unseeing into the sky as his blood continued to drain into the ground. I crouched, put my arms under his shoulders and upper legs, and stood easily; for all his height, he weighed very little, his arms and legs no more than gristle and bone in a thin bag. His blood, still warm, soaked quickly into my left sleeve and onto my arm.

For a moment, I couldn't move. I stood there, alone on the one stretch of ground cleared of deadly mines, holding a dead boy. I'd known he was in a bad way, and I'd told Schmidt, but had I done enough? If I'd helped him more, might he have stayed inside with the others and remained alive?

Standing there, Nagy in my arms, I couldn't stop from thinking of all the boys and young men, themselves barely past boyhood, that I'd seen die over the decades and decades and decades since my time on Dump, since my own childhood ended.

I headed toward the complex. I walked slowly, pausing after each step, not wanting to see anyone else, not yet. Once I stepped inside, all the watching boys would see another of their friends dead; not long after that, all the boys would know of Nagy's death. To Wylak, those boys were disposable, tainted assets that would cost a great deal to integrate into society but very little to return to combat. The economic equations spoke clearly and loudly. Because of them, he wanted to send those same kids back into battle, where they would kill and be killed. Those who survived would be even less fit than they were now for life in a world that no longer needed their services.

I couldn't let that happen.

"Lobo," I said over the comm.

"Yes," he said. Before I could say anything else, he added, "I'm sorry."

I stared at the dead boy. I had nothing useful to say in response. The best I could do now was to try to stop this from happening to the others.

To do that, I needed help.

"Any word from Maggie?" I said.

CHAPTER 45

In the former rebel complex, planet Tumani

NOTHING," LOBO SAID, "but that's not surprising. According to the protocol she gave me, the response window opened less than an hour ago."

Schmidt met me the moment I stepped inside the complex and the door whisked shut behind me. Two medtechs stood beside her.

"We'll take him now," the nearer one said, his voice barely loud enough for me to hear.

I held on to the dead boy. "I promised Nagy would get the honor due him." The medtech stepped closer to me and reached for the body. I said, "*I* promised."

The medtech retreated.

Schmidt put her left hand on mine where it gripped the dead boy's shoulder. "We'll honor that promise, Jon," she said, "we all will, with a burial and a ceremony tomorrow afternoon. Right now, though, they need to look after him." She tilted her head toward the barracks where boys stood in clusters and stared at us. She lowered her voice to a whisper as she said, "We don't want to parade a dead body in front of them."

I scanned the boys and spotted Bony. He and Long were watching from the side, ten meters to my right. The boy clenched and unclenched his fists. The man kept his hand on the boy's shoulder.

"I'll take Nagy wherever they want him to go," I said.

Schmidt stared at me for a second. "Follow them to the med facility. Do it quickly. And clean up before you let anyone see you again."

I glanced at my blood-soaked left hand and nodded. "As soon as I have, I need to talk to Lim."

"She's a little busy right now."

"Tell her that I need to see her and continue our previous conversation. She'll understand, and she'll see me."

"Jon," Schmidt said.

Before she could continue, I said. *"Tell her."*

The medtechs turned and left. I followed them. I didn't wait for Schmidt to respond.

I ignored Schmidt's order to clean up, so my left arm was still soaked with Nagy's blood when I approached the command cabin. I didn't recognize the guard standing outside, but he clearly knew me, because he stepped out of my way and motioned me inside.

Lim held up her hand as I entered and continued the conversation she was having over the comm. "… an accident, I agree, but a preventable one and a terrible, terrible waste. If your soldiers—"

I couldn't hear the other party, but the person cut off Lim.

"I understand they aren't your soldiers *per se*, Senator," she continued, "but surely as a ranking member of the Tumani government you share my concern for the death of one of your citizens, a minor."

Another pause, this one longer.

"Yes, I appreciate that you do, sir," she said, "and I am sorry if I in any way implied that you did not. I look forward to our meeting tomorrow."

She slammed her fist into the wall beside her. Dust rose and marked the impact.

"That pompous, lying jerk!" she said. "There's no way those soldiers braced us on their own."

"You're right," I said. "He's behind it. His people are implementing a new strategy."

Lim turned her head and for the first time focused on me.

"What strategy?"

"They're pinning us in," I said, "initially by blocking the land exits. All for our own good, of course."

"Initially?"

I nodded. "If Wylak gets what he wants, they'll launch a fighter over us, escort all of us off-planet, and turn the boys over to the military. None of this is news or particularly surprising."

"How are you so certain?" she said.

"I just am," I said.

She stared at me for a few seconds. "How will he get away with this?"

"By letting us do the work for him, waiting for people not to notice us, and moving in."

"So this poor boy's death—"

"—only made his case stronger." I took a deep breath and fought to keep my voice under control. "Yes. When your weak security left a doorway open and Nagy took advantage of the error to charge those soldiers, he helped demonstrate that you can't control these ex-killers and that someone else should be in charge."

"That's crap!" she said. "In all the time we've been here, that's the only incident to occur outside these walls."

I held up my hands to placate her. "I understand. I really do. In this kind of game, though, you know that perception is vital, and a wrong single incident can do a great deal of damage."

Lim twisted her head a few times and rubbed her eyes. "Of course," she said. "We've been making such good progress with the boys that I hate that he'll be able to make anyone judge us by this one event."

"So do I," I said, "but I hate even more that this boy is dead. You do remember that part, don't you?" I stepped around the edge of the table and put my left arm on it, right in front of her. The drying blood read as black in the dim light. "Don't become like Wylak. Don't forget this blood, this boy's blood."

Lim shoved the table away and stood faster than I would have thought possible. "Don't you lecture me, Jon Moore, on remembering blood. I remember all of it, all the young dead bodies we've seen. You should know better."

I shook my head. "I do. I do. I'm just so damned frustrated, and for a moment there you sounded like him."

"It comes with this job," she said. "If I don't think about all the other boys, the hundreds and hundreds who are still alive, I'll screw up, and Wylak will send them back to fight."

"Of course."

"Speaking of them," she said, "you told me before you were working on a plan to help combat Wylak and his tactics—and, I assume, to stop him from taking control of the boys."

"I am," I said.

"So are you going to tell me about it now?" she said. "My team and I can't help if we don't know what's going on."

But you can't hurt, either, I thought but did not say. I had only the vague outline of an idea, but even with only that little bit clear to me, I knew that I couldn't afford for Lim or anyone else to behave differently.

"No," I said. "Not now."

Lim smacked the wall again. "Why not?"

"I'll explain later, if need be, but not now. Not now."

We stared at each other for a few seconds. Lim was furious, but she knew better than to believe she could push me into telling her something I wanted to keep private. She had to be searching for a way to persuade me.

"Maggie is in this system," Lobo said over the comm, "and ready to talk. She's brought Jack."

Unless someone had intercepted the transmissions and was trying to trick us, Maggie had moved fast, faster than I would have expected possible. Good, because right now we needed speed.

Perhaps, though, her security wasn't as good as she'd said. Perhaps someone had intercepted the message and was setting a trap.

"I have to go," I said to Lim. "I need some time to clear my head, so I'm heading into Ventura. I'll be back for the service tomorrow afternoon."

"What?" she said. "You can't leave. Wylak said only supply ships—"

I was out the door before she finished and never heard the end of her sentence.

"Lobo," I subvocalized as I headed to him, "do you have a safe house set up?"

"Of course," he said.

"Good," I said. "Put on your best supply transport camo. It's time to find out if Maggie is really here or if her protocols weren't as solid as she thought and someone is out to capture us."

CHAPTER 46

Ventura city, planet Tumani

LOBO'S CAMO MADE him look so much like one of Lim's supply ships that no one even contacted us as we lifted off and flew toward Ventura. Lobo stayed in character the entire flight, moving slowly and staying low.

I used the time to study the available data on the safe house Lobo had rented.

"These are standard advertising specs," I said. "I can't count on their accuracy."

"Not completely," Lobo said, "but I didn't have a lot of research options. It's not like I could have inspected the inside of the place for you, at least not without completely destroying it."

Great, he was in a mood.

"If you were so worried," he continued, "you should have checked it out earlier yourself."

"You're right, of course," I said. "I'm sorry."

"It's four minutes on foot from the landing site that Lim's supply ships use," Lobo said. "It's the tallest building in a very low area. It's one of the larger in the neighborhood—big enough that it has a flat roof for small air shuttles—but not the widest, so its height doesn't make it stand out too much. I can reach you in under a minute, hover over the roof, and take you out of there in no time. All the windows and doors are currently sealed. The interior floor plan is complicated, with four different external access points on the first floor. If Wylak or anyone else has hacked our transmissions to Maggie—which I seriously doubt—you'll have many options for escaping safely."

"And if everything is fine and Maggie shows up with Jack?"

"They'll think you're overly paranoid," Lobo said, "and shake their heads at the unnecessary time, caution, and cost that went into the meeting." After a couple of seconds, he added, "Not that there's anything newsworthy in such a realization."

Yeah, he was in a mood, and I saw no point in encouraging it. "Thank you for the thorough preparations. Please drop me at the landing site. I'll call you when I'm in position."

The building Lobo had rented stood a story taller than either of its neighbors but was, as he'd noted, otherwise unremarkable. A rectangular box with dark brown wood siding over permacrete and regularly spaced activeglass windows, it seemed to be aiming for frontier rustic, but it couldn't pull off the look. Instead, it, like all the buildings on this block, emitted an institutional vibe, as if a government designer were trying to convince neighborhood owners that prisons masquerading as shops wouldn't hurt their resale value.

Six structures lined each side of this street. A full third of the dozen sat dark, lifeless, and unoccupied, like headstones for the dying commercial zone.

I used the rental code to let myself in via a back door after both Lobo and I checked the area and spotted no one. Whoever owned the place had left the counters, tables, chairs, and kitchen of the restaurant that had previously been the first floor's sole tenant. Dust coated everything. I put a microcam high in the corner opposite the door and verified it was transmitting to Lobo.

The other three floors were far sadder, largely empty spaces with here and there a chair, a coat rack, scraps of electronics, and bits of fabric the only signs that anyone had ever worked there. I swept the entire space slowly and carefully, checking everything in both IR and visible light. Lobo ran a detailed scan with data from sensors in my shirt.

The building was, as he'd promised, entirely empty.

"Satisfied?" he said.

"Yes. Contact them and tell them to meet me in two hours." As good as being early to a meeting is, arriving at the meeting location before anyone else knows about it is even better. "Get them to give you a comm for contact along the way. Give them the address of the bar three buildings over, The Wooden Dream."

"In progress," Lobo said. "And if any additional people show up?"

"I don't believe that will happen," I said. "Do you think anyone's going to be able to crack the encryption you're using?"

"No," he said, "unless they have Maggie in custody,

in which case they only have to crack her, not the transmissions."

"I doubt either is happening," I said, "but to answer your question, if someone else does appear, I'll deal with the situation then. If it's a large group, I'll head back to you. If it's only a person or two, I'll try to snatch one for interrogation."

"Finally," Lobo said, "a task with which I could get personally involved. Let's hope for someone with information we need."

"Let's not," I said. "Let's hope for Maggie and Jack on their own. Time is short. Out."

I left the building and walked down to The Wooden Dream. I made a quick pass through the place, bought a take-out glass of a tasty golden fruit juice, left a big enough tip to wipe the disgust off the bartender's face, and headed outside again. I scanned the other side of the street until I found a good spot in an alley midway between the bar and my building, a stretch of paved nothingness a couple dozen meters long that had a decent view of both locations, and slipped into it. The glow of the merchant lights penetrated only a few meters into the alley, so I could remain in darkness and still watch the front of the bar.

If Maggie and Jack arrived alone and on schedule, I had a boring couple of hours ahead of me.

If anyone came to secure the area, my time would be far more exciting.

I sipped the juice slowly, making it last. I systematically and carefully scanned the bar and the surrounding buildings from top to bottom, checked both directions of the alleyway in which I stood, and hoped for continued boredom.

➤   ➤   ➤

Five minutes before they were due, Maggie and Jack strolled down the street to The Wooden Dream. When they reached its front walkway, Maggie turned to go inside, but Jack put his hand on her shoulder and shook his head. They looked like just another couple out for an evening drink. Maggie, her long red hair in a single thick braid hanging down her back, wore a fashionably tight one-piece suit whose fabric shimmered in different colors as light washed over it. Jack had clearly planned for the possibility of more action, because he was in matching pants and shirt that were almost exactly the same color as his night-black skin. The bar's signs and windows painted them in yellows and reds and blues that turned almost white as three couples burst out of the front door and the light from inside flooded the night.

Those six had been in the bar when I'd taken up my watch, but I still focused on them and looked for signs they might be either with Jack and Maggie or monitoring them.

They weren't: Without saying a word, the six veered away quickly.

Jack faced away from the bar, scanned the area for a moment, and spoke, his voice loud enough to carry all the way to me. "We won't need to go inside. He's not there. He's watching us, to be sure we're alone." He held out his arms and smiled. "We are, Jon. It's just the two of us."

I smiled despite myself. Jack and I had worked together too much for me to be able to fool him on something this simple. "Send them to the meeting house," I said to Lobo. "Tell them to go in the front and stay in the first room until I arrive."

"Done," Lobo said a few seconds later.

Jack took Maggie's elbow and guided her toward our building. As they walked, Jack said, "He won't be there, either, not yet, but we'll see him soon enough."

Maggie's reply was quieter, but I could just make out her words. "Must you two make everything so difficult?"

Jack laughed. His gentle humor reminded me of why he was such a superb con man: You couldn't help but trust and like him. Each person he met wanted to know him and, unless Jack was in a hurry, came away from even a brief encounter convinced that he truly was Jack's new friend.

"This is entirely Jon's show," Jack said, "so don't lump me with him. His choices, however, are simply prudent. You've seen firsthand how badly some seemingly innocent meetings can go, so let's play along with Jon's obsessive security measures—measures that are," Jack raised his voice, "completely unnecessary in this case, because we are alone." He stopped Maggie, surveyed the area once, smiled, shook his head, and continued walking. "Have it your way, Jon," he said more quietly. "We'll be seeing you."

Lobo monitored the data from my sensors while I spent ten minutes circling from my post in the alley to the rear of the house. I spotted nothing unusual.

"Either you're clear," Lobo said, "or the people following Maggie and Jack are so good that I also can't spot any sign of them. That's possible, of course, but it's unlikely. The two of them are sitting in the front room, waiting for you as I told them to do. Jack is still and calm. Maggie is pacing and annoyed. In other words, both are behaving consistently with their past patterns. I thus have to conclude that Maggie contacted Jack, that they both came of their own free wills, and that all is well."

"I agree," I said, "but he's called Slanted Jack for a reason, so I never want to assume that anything he does is straight."

"This time, though, Maggie is involved," he said, "so you might be able to trust her."

"Her group's agenda will always trump our relationship, so trusting her completely is not an option. I wouldn't even have asked for her help if I'd seen another way out of this."

"But you didn't, so stop stalling, go inside the house, and ask them."

I hate that Lobo is right so often, but I *was* stalling. Involving Maggie was bad enough, but having to rely on Jack was downright dangerous. Still, if all went well, I could make this profitable for him, and nothing garnered Jack's loyalty like money.

"I'm on it," I said. I dropped short-term, degradable sensor dust as I walked; if anyone came this way, we'd know. "Yell if you spot anything."

"As if I wouldn't," Lobo said, "though if you're wrong and someone did follow them, I could save you the interruption—and both of us a great deal of hassle—by blowing them apart before they reached the house."

"No, thank you, but no," I said. "In addition to being completely unnecessary killing, it would draw attention to us and thus make the mission harder."

"Fine," Lobo said. "I was just offering to help."

"Now *you're* stalling *me*," I said, "so let me get inside and talk to them."

"Out," Lobo said. The annoyance was still clear in his voice, but I ignored it.

I slipped in the back door as quietly as I could, but from the front Jack's words were clear.

"About time, Jon," he said.

I walked to the front room.

Maggie glared at me from the corner to the right of the door.

Jack sat on a chair one meter away from the front wall. He smiled slightly as I entered the room but otherwise did not move. He'd always possessed an uncanny ability to be completely calm and still, a very useful gift for a con man working long-term angles. "I wanted you to have a clear view of me," he said. He tilted his head slightly toward the microcam. "That's where I'd have put it," he said, "and we're not so very different."

"Yes, we are," I said. Jack also had a talent for quickly finding the best ways to tweak anyone.

"And yet you sent your pet messenger to summon me," he said, "so clearly you need me."

"Pet messenger?" Maggie said. For a moment, she looked like she couldn't decide which of us to hit first. She shook her head, smiled, and walked toward Jack.

"I'd rather you didn't," he said.

She ignored him and put her hand on his shoulder. A few seconds later, she said, "He's trying to split us in the hope that doing so will increase his profit."

"You don't have to be a mind-reader to know that," I said. "You just have to listen, or know Jack, or both." Maggie's smile vanished, so I added, "But, thank you for confirming it."

Jack stared at Maggie. Though his smile never

changed, his eyes hardened. "I hate when you do that. It's an invasion, a rape."

She looked at him for a few seconds before responding. "You're right. It is, and I'm sorry for reading you. Though you may not believe it, I hate hearing what others are thinking. I did it, though, not because you provoked me, but because I trust that Jon wouldn't have asked me to bring you if it weren't important, and I had to know what you were planning."

"Maggie," I said. I needed her to back off and let me run this, because the more we annoyed Jack, the more we'd have to squeeze him to make him help us—and the more we did that, the less we could trust him.

Before I could say anything else, Jack broke the tension for me.

"You could simply ask me," he said, "and we could have an open and honest dialog."

Maggie looked at me.

I glanced at Jack and back at her.

She and I both started laughing.

Jack joined us a moment later. For a short time, none of us could stop.

"Okay, okay," Jack said, gasping for air, "I guess that was a bit of a stretch." He calmed himself and said, "So what do you want?"

"Your help, obviously," I said, "at the kind of work you do best."

"You're running another con?" Jack said. "Why didn't you say so? I'd have come along without complaint."

"No, you wouldn't," I said, "and it's not a normal con. For one thing, there's no money in it."

Jack's smile vanished. "So we're back to doing good

for good's sake, is that it, Jon?"

I shrugged.

"Sorry, old friend, but you know that's not what I do. If you need to sting some bad guy, sign me up—but make sure a big payday is waiting."

"I didn't say there was no payday. I said there was no money in the con."

Jack leaned ever so slightly forward. "So how do we get paid?"

"*We* don't," I said. "You do." I faced Maggie. "You said your people had a great deal of money, and you'd do anything you could to help me and the boys if it came to that. It has. How much money do you have available, and how serious were you when you said that?"

A sad expression washed over her face. I wished I could have briefed her first so she'd understand the way I had to play this for Jack, but there was no time, so once again I'd hurt her. "More money than you could need," she said, "and yes, I believe I can explain the situation to them. I wouldn't have offered otherwise."

"My needs are many, vast, and expensive," Jack said, "so please never assume you have too much money."

Maggie's sadness turned to anger as she faced him. "Surely even you, a man who would sell a child, must have limits on your greed."

Jack's expression didn't change; Maggie didn't understand how important self-control was to a con man. "As I explained to you then," he said, "I never planned to sell or endanger the boy in any way. As for limits," he shrugged, "perhaps, but I've yet to encounter them."

Maggie shot him a dirty look. She opened her mouth to reply, but before she could, I stepped between them. I put my hand on her shoulder. "Maggie, I'm sorry for sounding like I doubted you. I did not. I know, though, that you're representing a larger organization, so I didn't want to take anything for granted. I appreciate your offer, and I feel bad for having to take you up on it." I stared into her eyes and hoped she could tell how much I needed her to follow my lead. "Are we good to go?"

She smiled slightly and nodded. "Of course." The smile disappeared as quickly as it had appeared. "There is one new development, though."

"What's that?" I said.

"My people have given me complete freedom to provide you with whatever you need, but you have to agree to one condition."

When she didn't continue, I said, "Which is?"

"You will owe them a job."

Jack leaned back and smiled. He knew how much I hated owing anything to anyone, and he was enjoying watching me suffer.

"What kind of job, and when?"

"I have no idea," she said, "though I do know they don't have anything currently in mind, so it probably won't be soon. Based on past experience, I'd expect it could even be years from now. I'm supposed to reassure you by telling you that they won't ask you to do anything that I don't first approve."

"That's my only option?"

"Yes," she said. If you want their help, you have to trust that they won't ask you to do anything I don't vet." Her expression softened. "I'm sorry, Jon. If I'd known about this, I would have warned you."

"So one day they'll find me and cash in this favor?" I said.

She nodded. "That's it."

"We could try to do this on our own," Lobo said privately over the comm. "If you make this deal, you know you're obligating both of us."

He was right, and I knew it, but I wasn't going to let down those boys. "Okay," I said. "Deal."

"Fine," Lobo said, "don't ask me. For what it's worth, I would have agreed."

I ignored him and focused on Maggie.

She nodded and said, "Again, I am sorry."

Anything the Children of Pinkelponker might ask of me would be a problem for another day. I had to focus on the challenge in front of me. I faced Jack. "I need you to run a gig for me. I have the outline, but you have to make it happen. Maggie will provide the resources you need, and when it succeeds—and only when it succeeds—she'll pay you a fee we'll negotiate."

"Perhaps she and I—" Jack said.

I cut him off. "No. You and I both know how much different games bring, so we'll settle the amount."

"And your cut?" he said.

"Nothing. I'm not going to make any money on this one."

"That's not like you," he said. "Even with the boy, you turned a profit—a healthy one, as I recall."

"Yes, I did, but not this time."

"Why not?"

I pulled over two of the dusty chairs and motioned to Maggie to take one. I sat in the other.

"Let me fill you in on what's happening," I said.

"That man Wylak is disgusting!" Maggie said. "He can't believe he'll get away with putting those boys back into combat."

"Of course he can," Jack said, "and he almost certainly will. People have an amazing capacity to ignore unpleasant facts. He needs more soldiers, and he's short on volunteers. As long as no one rubs their faces in what's happening, his constituency will happily ignore any little rumors they might hear."

Maggie shook her head. "Your view of people is so cynical." She faced me. "Jon, I'm sure if you inform the Tumani newstainment groups, they'll—"

"Do what?" Jack said. He looked at me and shrugged. "Are they going to believe their own Senator Wylak, whom they've almost certainly followed for years, or us?"

"I can't believe they wouldn't want to cover the story," Maggie said.

"It doesn't matter whether Jack is right or wrong," I said. "What we know for certain is that even if we found sympathizers in the Tumani media, Wylak would get us deported before their coverage could do any good. He'd then be in charge of the boys." I took a deep breath. "I wish there was another answer, but I can't see one. If I don't deal with this situation, there's every chance that those boys will be fighting in the jungle before anyone even knows it's happening."

Jack smiled. "So it's a perfect highlight reel"—he paused—"except it's not, because he has too much control."

"Would one of you—" Maggie said.

I nodded and interrupted her. "He does indeed. Nothing on this world is safe for us." I waited a few seconds.

Jack got it. He stood and for the first time showed signs of excitement. "How long do we have?"

"That's the problem," I said. "I don't know, but

no more than a month, maybe less." I thought about how Wylak could take advantage of Nagy's death, as I'd warned Lim he would. "Probably less."

"I'm glad you two are having so much fun," Maggie said, "but—"

Jack cut her off. "You're going to have to help me," he said to her, "because on this timetable I can't do everything alone. And, of course, you're going to have to pay me. A lot."

"Is money all you think about?" Maggie said.

"No," Jack said. "It should be clear that I'm already considering a great deal more, including how to make this plan work. But, you said you had money, and Jon expected you to pay me, so I see no reason you shouldn't do so."

"Yes," Maggie said, "I can pay you."

"And can you cover a great many rather steep expenses?" Jack said. Facing me, he added, "You know that rushing this will be tough."

"Yes," I said, "but not as tough as the timing. That's going to be even trickier."

"I'll do all I can to be ready," Jack said, "but I'll need at least some notice. You know that an instant turn isn't possible."

"I do," I said. I realized I was smiling. Despite everything, working with Jack was always a rush—at least in the early going, before anything could go seriously wrong. "I have some ideas."

"That's it!" Maggie said.

Her shout startled us.

We both turned to her.

"If I'm going to fund this," she said, "I am damn well going to understand what's going on."

"I'm sorry," I said. "Of course. We were just caught up in the planning."

"It is fun, isn't it, Jon?" Jack said. "You know you miss it. Come on, admit it."

"No," Maggie said, "don't. Before you two do anything else, explain to me just what you're talking about and exactly what it is that you want to do."

Jack and I sat.

After a few seconds, Maggie returned to her chair. We told her.

CHAPTER 47

Dump Island, planet Pinkelponker—139 years earlier

I MOTIONED TO THE others while the dust was still thin enough that we could see each other. I went through the ritual Benny had taught us: I tied a thick piece of cloth over my face, shut my eyes, and put my index fingers in my ears. I'd expressed concern that I wouldn't be able to tell when the shuttle was down, but Benny had, of course, been right that I wouldn't need to worry about that; the noise rattled my skull so hard that knowing when it had stopped would be easy.

As soon as the sound diminished, my heart started beating harder. The urge to charge ahead was strong, but I resisted it. When the guards had dropped me here, the world outside the shuttle had been quiet and dust-free. Benny said that's the way it had been for him, too, so we knew the guards liked to wait a while before opening the doors. Benny figured it was probably because they were making sure they were safe, but they might also have wanted to avoid all the noise and dust. The reason didn't matter as long as they did it again this time.

When I could hear nothing, I pulled out first my left finger, then my right. The only sounds were metallic ticks and, after a few seconds, the swish of the wind through the branches over us.

I wiped my hands on my shirt and pulled the cloth off my face. I carefully checked my eyelids: no dust. I opened my eyes and saw only a bright blur. I held that position for a few seconds to let my vision stabilize; Benny had made us practice this part so much I did it automatically. When the intensity of the light seemed normal, I opened them the rest of the way.

I held up my hand to the others, edged forward, and dropped to the ground when I was half a meter away from the edge. I crawled forward and peeked around the corner.

The shuttle was sitting side-on to us, the same position it had occupied when they'd dropped me here. The guard would be bringing our newest resident out of the opposite side.

As far as we knew, no one on Dump had ever attacked a shuttle. We were counting on the guards to be at ease and not expecting any trouble.

I heard the sound of a door sliding open. I rose to my knees and launched myself forward, motioning to the others as I ran. Han, the next strongest of us, was to follow me around the rear of the shuttle. Alex and Bob were to sprint to the front to distract the guard. I didn't check to see if they were all doing as they should; there was no time for that. I had to hope they held to the plan and no one panicked.

In a few seconds, I was at the far corner of the

shuttle's rear. I pulled up. Someone bumped into me. I ignored the urge to verify it was Han and instead took a deep breath. I pulled a cloth full of rocks and one of sand out of my pockets, rocks in the right, my strong side, and sand in the left. I tensed my legs and braced myself to go.

A low, wordless scream punched the air.

Right on time.

I pushed off and rounded the corner of the shuttle.

Everything moved so quickly that only later was I able to reconstruct what happened.

A guard turned to face Bob, who was desperately trying to stop, his momentum carrying him forward and making him an easy target.

Bob skidded to a halt and reversed direction, his face wide with fear, a low cry bursting out of him.

I yelled for the guard's attention.

He ignored me and pulled the trigger on his weapon. It boomed repeatedly as rounds slammed into the sand in a line heading for Bob.

I threw the cloth full of rocks at the guard's head. It sailed wide of him. I kept moving and crashed into his back with my shoulder. I stayed on him as he sprawled forward.

His gun fired a short burst as we tumbled to the ground.

I heard Bob cry out in pain but couldn't look because I had to focus on the guard.

As he hit the sand, he tried to roll to his right away from me.

I dropped the other cloth, grabbed his body with both hands, and went with him, his weight slamming into me at first and then pulling me up beside him.

He slashed an elbow backward toward my face.

I raised my right forearm in time to block it. My arm shook from the blow, and pain screamed through it into my shoulder.

He scrambled to his knees.

I reached for his foot with my left arm but missed.

Alex, his one arm twirling another piece of cloth full of rocks, ran at the guard.

The man pushed away from me but not far enough, as Alex let go of the cloth and followed the flying rocks toward the guard. Most of the rocks missed, but a couple hit him in the face.

Alex jumped on him.

The guard fell backward, more surprised and off balance than hurt.

Alex rode him to the ground and punched him in the face.

I shook my right arm and pulled my knife as I scrabbled to get to the guard.

Alex's blow hurt the man but not badly.

The man yelled and punched Alex in the neck hard enough that Alex choked, grabbed for his throat, and fell to the side. The guard pulled a handgun from his right hip and turned toward Alex.

I screamed, loudly but not with any conscious thought, and leapt onto the guard, slashing down with my knife as I did. The blade caught in the sand for an instant before I pulled it up and along the guard's neck.

He fired the handgun once into the sky as his throat split open and blood burbled out.

My left ear hurt from the sound but I didn't care. The anger took over and pain vanished and all I wanted to do was lash out. I plunged the knife into his throat again, this time in the center. A spray of blood hit me as I twisted the blade and moved it from side to side.

The guard shook once, then stopped moving. Blood streamed out of him. It was everywhere, coating my knife, soaking me.

I pulled out the knife, my grip on the bone blade as tight as if it had grown out of my arm. The blade was shaking. I wondered why.

Between the ringing in my left ear and the pounding of my own pulse I could barely hear anything, so the next scream was little louder than a whisper. I turned toward it with the dim knowledge that I had to get moving, that we weren't done.

The second guard stood in the open doorway of the shuttle, his face red with rage as he raised his rifle and aimed it at me.

Han, the source of the sound, reached the guard and pushed the end of the rifle so it no longer pointed at me.

A shot boomed and at what seemed like the same time bits of stone flew into the air on my right.

The guard pulled Han toward him and twisted his rifle.

I pushed off the ground with my left hand and launched myself toward the shuttle.

Han lost his grip on the weapon and fell backward.

The guard aimed the rifle at Han.

I screamed and tried to move faster.

The guard stayed focused on Han and pulled the trigger.

I ignored everything but the man, the target in front of me. I roared at him, my teeth pulling back, the world reducing to him and only him.

He swung the rifle toward me.

He was too late. I crashed into him, chopping forward with my knife as I did. The blade hit some type of armor and glanced off it as my momentum carried the guard and me backward into the shuttle and all the way to its far wall.

He dropped the weapon as we hit.

I raised my right knee into his crotch as hard as I could and connected firmly. He croaked in pain and surprise but managed to push me off him.

I stumbled backward and lost my grip on my knife.

The guard reached for his handgun.

He didn't make it as Alex ran into him, my friend's entire weight connecting at speed with the man's shoulder.

Alex bounced off the man and stumbled backward.

I pushed myself up.

The guard kicked Alex in the crotch.

Alex fell and the guard kicked him in the head.

I hit the guard in the face with my left hand and then my right.

He screamed and raised his arms to cover himself.

I grabbed the back of his head with my left hand and pulled it down while at the same time I kicked up with my knee as hard as I could. My knee smashed into his face.

He screamed again, but this time he fell to his knees, his legs buckling.

I spun behind him and kicked his spine.

He fell face forward.

I leapt onto him and punched the side of his head a couple of times with both hands.

At first his hands blocked me, but then they fell and were still.

I grabbed his head with both hands and slammed it onto the floor again and again and again. I screamed, no words, just howls. My hands turned slick and blood poured out of him and still I smashed his face up and down.

"Jon!"

The word sounded as if it had come from a very great distance. I couldn't see anything.

"Jon!"

I heard it a little more clearly.

Something grabbed my right arm and pulled it off the guard's head.

I let go with my left hand, balled my fist, and swiveled to my right, ready to smash whatever was attacking me.

"Jon!"

My vision cleared enough that I could see it was Alex, his one arm on my right, his body leaning against my shoulder, his mouth and ear bleeding.

I stopped the punch short of his face and stared at him. I wondered what he was doing.

"Jon, stop. He's dead. Stop." He paused and sucked in air. "They're both dead. It's over."

I stared at my blood-soaked hands. I had to concentrate to make my fingers release their grip.

Alex stumbled out of the shuttle, coughing and crying as he went.

I took a deep breath to try to calm myself. As my senses returned, the stench hit me, and my stomach churned. I ran for the open doorway and made it a few steps outside before I doubled over and threw up. My eyes watered and my gut hurt and still I kept heaving.

When my body relaxed enough that I could stand up, I looked around.

Alex sat on the ground a few meters away, bleeding and sobbing and staring at the shuttle.

I followed the line of his gaze and saw Han stretched out on the sand. I stepped toward him but stopped short when I saw the huge hole in his chest. His eyes were open and fixed on the sky, but he wasn't ever going to see anything again.

Alex hurt and Han dead and Bob—where was Bob?

I spotted his legs sticking out from the end of the shuttle. "Bob!" I said as I walked over to him. "Bob!"

He didn't answer. He didn't move.

When I could see the rest of him, I learned why: Blood seeped from a hole in his neck that he'd tried to cover with his left hand, back when that hand worked. Back when Bob was alive. He had launched himself for cover and, from the smooth patches in the sand behind him, even managed to crawl a bit before the wound overcame him and he bled to death.

Bob dead. Han dead. Alex crying behind me. We'd won, but Bob and Han were dead.

My body shook. I hugged myself but couldn't stop.

I heard the sound of Benny's cart coming around the corner at the same time that he said, "Jon?"

He emerged into the clearing a few seconds later.

I stared at him. I felt cold. My body screamed in pain in too many places for me to count. I shook my head, all the explanation I could muster.

"Jon?" he said. "Are you injured?"

"Injured?" I said, my voice rising to a scream in one word. Before I could stop myself, more words raced out of me. "You ask if I'm injured? Bob is dead and

Han is dead and Alex is sitting on the ground crying and useless and I've killed two guards and I can't stop shaking—and you ask if I'm injured?"

Benny quit rolling. He looked at me. He stared at Bob for a long time. When he faced me again, his eyes were wet. After a few seconds, he said, "I'm sorry. I've known them all longer than you have. I'm so very, very sorry. We knew the risks."

"Did we?" I said. "You and I have talked about it, sure, many times, but did we really understand? You were the one who said we didn't."

"No," he said, so softly I had trouble hearing him, "of course we didn't." He cleared his throat. When he spoke again, his voice was clear and strong. "We have to go. We don't have long. They may have sent a distress signal, but even if they didn't, the shuttle will be due back. We have to get out of here and hide. We'll come back later for the others."

"That's it?" I said. "Our friends are dead on the ground, and we leave?"

"Yes," Benny said, "because if we don't, they will have died for absolutely nothing. I can't fly the shuttle without you. You know that. We have to go together."

I glanced back at Han and Alex. I shook my head as if I could somehow force out all the bad things that had happened.

Benny rolled forward, past Bob's corpse and all the way to me.

"Jon, we leave now, or we may never get the chance again. I obviously can't force you, so the choice is yours."

He waited until I finally looked down at him. "Decide."

CHAPTER 48

In the former rebel complex, planet Tumani

"IM IS FURIOUS with you," Lobo said.

After talking with Jack and Maggie and running a counter-surveillance route on my way back to Lobo, I'd been exhausted. I'd fallen asleep in my quarters inside Lobo as soon as we'd touched down in the complex. The sun was rising as we hit the ground, so I hadn't slept a lot, but thanks to the nanomachines my body was completely rested. My mind, though, was another story; I'd awakened as jangled as when I'd stretched out on the cot.

"That's not surprising," I said, "but it also doesn't change anything."

"I thought you should know," he said. "You should also be aware that the service for Nagy starts in ten minutes."

"Ten minutes?" I said. "Why didn't you wake me earlier?"

"Because I know your sleeping patterns, and your vitals suggested that you were on track to be ready in time. As you indeed are."

Lobo's smug tone may be his most annoying attribute, but there was no point in calling him on it. I walked out of the side hatch he opened for me. "Any update on Wylak's visit?" I said over the comm.

"He'll arrive after the service," Lobo said, his voice back to all business. "Lim suggested that would be best, and he agreed. No other activity."

"Thanks," I said.

Lobo guided me to the gathering. By the time I reached it, most of the boys were already there. They stood in a huge arc that formed two-thirds of a circle around the cloth-covered body. In accord with Tumani custom, Nagy's corpse and shroud lay on a simple wooden platform. Lim and most of the rest of the staff, all but those on duty elsewhere, stood in a clump in the opening in the semicircle. A few meters separated them from the edges of the groups of boys on either side of them.

Lim glared at me as I entered the area. I ignored her and went to Nagy. I stayed well back from him, but for reasons I couldn't explain, it wasn't enough for me to stand with only the living. For a moment, I wanted to be with the dead. The sight of Nagy's long, thin, lifeless body transported me back to Dump, to the moment when I realized Bob was dead. I'd screamed then, and I wanted to scream now, but I didn't. I shook my head at all of it, the fighting and the dying and the loss of childhood, Nagy's and Bob's and even my own. No. I had no right to that, not then, not in front of a dead boy. Nagy and Bob and Han and so many others that I had seen die—all of them were gone. They had paid everything. I was alive.

I walked to a spot between the boys and Lim's people. I didn't belong with either group.

Lim had arranged for two local priests to come and offer prayers. I didn't hear anything they said. Their voices blended into the background like the wind and the calls of the birds in the trees above us. The sun beat down and I sweated heavily, but I didn't mind. I didn't care at all. I didn't even feel it.

My attention returned as Long was talking.

"Though we'd known Nagy for far less time than many of you, we'd come to care very much for him," he said. "We can't know how you feel, but we can tell you how sorry we are at this senseless loss, at the way he died for nothing."

"No," I said, "that's not quite right."

Long and Lim and Schmidt stared at me, their expressions and their postures telling me to shut up and back off.

I couldn't.

"He died trying to be the soldier that was all he knew how to be," I said. "It was all that was left inside him. Fighting had kept him alive when he had nothing else, and fighting killed him."

"I think we can all agree—" Lim said.

I waved my hand and cut her off. "He didn't die for nothing!" Murmurs spread through the boys. "He died being the only thing he knew how to be. If he'd been in the jungle fighting, he'd have done the same thing, and his death would have been honored."

"That's enough!" Lim said.

"No," I said, "it's not. These boys, these former soldiers, they understand. No matter what you say, they understand. They've felt the same urges Nagy did. They know."

The whispers of the boys grew louder.

I walked a few meters forward, closer to Nagy's corpse and farther from Lim. I spoke now to the boys.

"What *was* senseless here, what *was* for nothing, was not Nagy's death. It was his *life*, the life the rebels made him live. What was so utterly wrong was the fact that Nagy was ever a soldier."

The boys fell quiet.

"What *is* so wrong—" I said. I paused and scanned the semicircle of boys. "—is that any of you were ever soldiers. It should never have happened."

A few angry shouts from the boys. "We were good fighters!" one said.

"I'm not saying you weren't. I'm sure you fought as well and as hard as you could—but you should never have had to fight! We shouldn't be here now, standing around this boy's dead body. We shouldn't be together. You should be playing or going to school or eating with your parents and brothers and sisters. None of this should ever have happened!"

I closed my eyes and took a deep breath. The boys were quieter now.

"But it did." I opened my eyes. "It did. The rebels captured you and turned you into soldiers. It was senseless and wrong, but it happened. I wish it hadn't, but it did."

I wanted to stop myself, but I couldn't. The words kept coming.

"I understand it. You may not believe me, but I do. I've been fighting my whole life, since I was a kid, and I lost my family and I had to fight to get anywhere. Sometimes, I think it's all I know. Sometimes, late at night, when I can't fall asleep or I wake up sweaty and shaking, I wish it all hadn't happened.

But it did." I paused for a few seconds and looked at the ground. "I've seen my friends die, many, many before Nagy, and I've done bad things."

My voice wavered. I tried to control it, but I couldn't. I kept talking anyway.

"These people"—I gestured toward Lim and her team—"they tell you over and over that it's not your fault, and I see in your eyes that you don't believe them, not most of the time. But you should. It isn't your fault." I paused. "It's not your fault." I pointed at Nagy's body. "It's not Nagy's fault. Yes, he ran where he shouldn't have. He did a stupid thing, and he got himself killed. But if you aim a gun at a target and pull the trigger, the round will hit the target. When the rebels turned you into soldiers, they aimed you and pulled the trigger. They aimed Nagy, and he hit the place his path was always going to take him: Death. He died."

I stared at the corpse for a bit and looked back at the now quiet boys.

"You don't have to join him there. You don't have to die. The rebels trained you and aimed you, but you are not weapons! Not if you choose not to be. You can stop it now. You can try what the counselors tell you or find your own way or do whatever it takes, but however you do it, you *can* stop. You can learn again what it's like to be a kid, and you can live again. Just live."

I turned around and headed back to where I'd initially stood. A step away, I stopped and faced the boys once more. "I won't lie to you. You'll have many bad nights and some bad days. Sometimes, the awful past will wrap so tightly around you that you'll barely be able to breathe. Sometimes, the ghosts of Nagy and your other dead friends will invade your dreams. But you'll be *alive*. You'll be alive."

The circle was silent.

"And you'll have *won*. Every day you stay alive, every day you refuse to be that weapon, every day you live a normal life, you'll be beating the rebels, winning against the people who tried to ruin you, who did stupid and senseless and wrong things to you. You'll be alive." I took a deep breath. "You'll be winning."

I wondered at myself, at how I'd lost so much control, at the sudden need I'd felt to speak, at my inability to stop.

I had to go. I left the circle, the boys, the counselors, the death. I couldn't stay there any longer. My pulse drummed in my ears. My fists clenched and unclenched. My body shook.

Lim began speaking again, but I couldn't focus on her words.

I picked up my pace. I wanted to get back inside Lobo.

I heard the footsteps closing on me and whirled around to face the attacker.

Bony ran to me.

I put my arms behind my back to hide my fists.

The kid studied my face for a few seconds. He nodded his head. "You gave Nagy respect," he said. "My brother would have liked that." He moved his foot back and forth on the ground and stared at it before he looked again at me. "I don't know about all that other stuff you said, but I'll think on it. I'll think on it."

We stood in silence for a bit, both of us out of

words. I knew I should do something, but I had no clue what.

Finally, Bony nodded his head again, turned, and jogged back to the other boys.

I watched until he disappeared into the crowd and no one was looking at me any longer. I started for Lobo. I walked a few steps, but it wasn't enough. I picked up the pace until I was jogging, but that wasn't right, either. I pumped my legs harder, forcing myself to move faster, slamming into the ground with each footfall, my breaths coming harder and harder, my body hurtling ever faster forward, my eyes blurring, my heart pounding with effort and fear and anger, and still I could not escape. Though I ran alone and nothing was chasing me, I could not escape.

CHAPTER 49

In the former rebel complex, planet Tumani

LOBO'S SIDE HATCH slid open when I was fifty meters out. It shut as soon as I crashed into the wall opposite it. I leaned against the cool metal and struggled to breathe.

"I'm not sure I've ever heard you reveal so much about yourself at one stretch," Lobo said over the speakers, his voice lower than usual.

I pushed off the wall and walked to the front. I paced back and forth in the pilot area. Moving was good. My breathing slowly returned to normal.

"For whatever my opinion is worth to you," Lobo said, "what you said to the boys was right."

My heart stopped pounding.

"Damn it!" I said.

"Everyone loses control sometime," Lobo said. "All you did was talk. It could have been much, much worse—and you know it."

"That's no excuse," I said. "And, *you* never do."

After a very long pause, Lobo said, "So far, that's

been true. There are things, though, that could make me. You have to know that." He paused again. "Stay around so we don't have to find out."

I smiled briefly. "That's my plan."

"Lim is approaching," he said, his voice back to the usual volume and all business.

I leaned against the wall farthest from the entrance. "Let her in. We might as well get this over with. She has every right to be furious."

"Okay," he said.

I stood in silence, not even trying to understand my loss of control. All I wanted was to be sure I was over it and had regained command of myself.

Lim entered the small area a few minutes later. She leaned against the wall opposite me. Her face was tight with tension, her body as taut as if she were already in a fight.

We faced each other across the empty space.

I'd said all I had to say, so I stayed quiet.

After a bit, she nodded her head and said, "Thank you."

I hadn't expected that reaction. I tilted my head in question.

"You were right. Long made a small error in expression, but still, you were right, and your correction"—she chuckled—"your tirade, it helped us reach a lot of the boys." Her face and stance softened. "Jon, I know what it cost me to listen to you and think about what I've seen, about some of what we've seen together, so I have a sense of what it must have cost you to say."

I nodded. She did. I could never forget standing with her among the corpses of murdered children in a village on Nana's Curse. We were both in the same Saw unit. We'd seen a lot, enough that we foolishly believed we'd seen it all, but not enough to know better, to know that you can never see, never even imagine all the bad things that people can do to one another.

I still had nothing to say to her, though, so I kept listening.

Lim nodded in return, as if we'd agreed on something. Maybe we had.

"The timing sucks, but Wylak will be here soon. You were gone a big chunk of the night, so I have to ask: Did your trip go well?"

"I think so," I said, "but I won't know for sure for a while."

"What does that mean?"

I'd contemplated explaining it all to her, but there was too great a chance that knowing what I was planning would affect the way she behaved. We couldn't afford that. We needed her to do what she was doing: everything she could to buy time with Wylak.

"It's still too early and too risky to be worth discussing," I said.

"Have you considered the possibility that I might be able to help?" she said.

"Yes, and you can't."

She rolled her shoulders. "You're asking me to trust you with a lot," she said, "and without explaining why."

"Yes."

"Okay," she said, "okay. So what do we do now?"

"Meet with Wylak as planned. Do what I'm sure you were planning to do: yield on as many points as you can to buy more time to reintegrate the boys."

"Do you really believe that strategy can get us the kind of time we need?"

"No," I said, "I don't. I do believe you have a small shot at persuading him to give us more time, and right now we can use every day we can get."

"I'll do my best."

"I know you will." She turned as if to leave, and I said, "One more thing: Take me to the meeting with you."

"Why?"

"Because the more I can learn about this guy, the better. It shouldn't be hard; he already thinks I'm your aide."

We stood again in silence.

"This isn't easy or natural for me," she said. "Yielding to your demands while you give nothing in return, spending time prostrating myself before this asshole—none of it sits well with me."

"I know."

She took a long, deep breath. "I'll do it because this effort—these boys—matter that much to me."

I nodded and smiled. "I know that, too."

She smiled, too, a full-on grin that lit her face. "Okay. Enough of this talking with each other crap; let's get ready for the meeting with Wylak."

Wylak's shuttle was larger and more clearly a military vehicle than the one that had flown him here last time. More guards surrounded this one, and they acted much more serious than their predecessors. Even from thirty meters out, they looked like they knew what they were doing. They kept moving, and their weapons were always at the ready.

I put my hand on Lim's arm to stop her. "Call your people," I said. "Tell them not to let any boy come within sight of this shuttle."

"You don't really think—"

"Yes, I do. Compare this crew to the help he brought last time. These guys are with him because they'll follow any order he gives. All we need is for some boy to approach them while carrying just about anything, and they'll have all the excuse they need to shoot—and more proof of our failure to reintegrate the boys."

"I can't believe he'd kill an innocent kid."

"He wouldn't," I said. "He'd have these guys do it. That's how people like Wylak always work—and you know it."

She made the call.

When she finished, we resumed walking. I held my arms out to my side, palms facing forward.

"I could solve this problem for you," Lobo said. "I could be in position to trank them in less than a minute."

"No," I subvocalized. I wanted to avoid letting Wylak have any data about Lobo's capabilities in case we needed to fight seriously. I had to hope it never came to that.

"Your choice," Lobo said, "unless they shoot you. If they do, I'm coming for you."

"Good," I subvocalized.

Lim stared at me. "What?"

"Nothing worth discussing," I said.

The guards stopped us and scanned us for weapons. They were thorough, very thorough, particularly with Lim, who showed no reaction to their groping. Wylak had definitely opted for a rougher group this time around.

When they couldn't find any excuses to detain us any longer, the one nearest the door whispered into a comm.

The door opened. They motioned us inside.

It shut as soon as we were clear of it.

Another guard stood in front of us and blocked our way.

We waited. Government officials and corporate bigwigs often feel the need to flaunt their power. It's always struck me as stupid, because those with real power don't need to prove it, and those with none aren't going to convince anyone with a senseless display of their own importance. I'm good at waiting, though, so I just stood there.

Lim glanced at me in annoyance.

Behind her, the guard smiled slightly.

Wylak wasn't showing off his power. He was hoping to annoy us into acting foolishly and giving him an excuse for taking over earlier than he already planned. That was also not a good bet, but from his perspective it was a tactic worth exploring: It was cheap to try, and if it worked, the payoff was huge.

I responded to Lim by closing my eyes for a second, opening them, and shaking my head slightly.

She faced forward.

The guard caught our interchange and shrugged a question: Why not? He lowered his rifle in invitation.

I smiled at him and turned my palms outward: Not today.

He shrugged again.

We waited some more.

After half an hour, another guard emerged from the door behind the man in front of us. "The Senator will see you now," she said.

We followed her into a spare, functional space with rows of seats along the external walls and a row of back-to-back seats running down the center. Wylak sat in one of the seats nearest the rear right corner. The guard led us down the narrow walkway and pointed to two seats opposite the Senator. She took up a position beside him. Her eyes never left us.

Wylak stared at a display in his lap and occasionally mumbled a few words.

We waited some more. I counted the seats; just this chamber, if fully packed, could bring in two dozen soldiers.

After a few minutes, the man finished what he was doing and stared at Lim. "My apologies, Ms. Lim," he said. "The work of a servant of the people is never done, particularly during wartime."

He ignored me completely. Fine by me; the more arrogant he was, the better for us.

"The Tumani people are fortunate to have such a devoted Senator," Lim said. "How may we serve you today?" Her posture and her tone didn't match her words, but at least she was trying.

He leaned forward and smiled. "Let me begin by apologizing for bothering you in the middle of such important work. We share a deep respect for the sanctity of childhood. Nothing matters more to me than the youth of our country."

He was focusing to the right of Lim; he was recording this entire exchange, with the video aimed solely at him. The guard was his witness. When he pulled the plug on us, he'd leave no doubt with the public that he had done so for the sake of the boys.

"Of course," Lim said. "The welfare of these boys is my top—my only—concern."

He nodded as if both agreeing and thinking. "So

I'm sure," he said, "that you must share my deep sorrow at the senseless loss of that poor child's life yesterday." He sat straighter. When he continued, his voice had hardened. "A loss for which I trust you assume full responsibility."

"Excuse me?" Lim said.

Wylak clasped his hands. "I appreciate your reluctance, but you had agreed to control these poor children, which is why our troops were so caught off-guard by the sight of one of the boys—a very tall, adult-looking boy, it must be noted—charging them and waving a weapon."

"A weapon?" Lim said. "He was carrying—"

"Now, now, Ms. Lim," Wylak said as he cut her off and stood, "this is not the time to try to avoid—"

She interrupted him. "If you think you can—"

"What I can do," he said, "is whatever the Tumani people need me to do, including kicking out of this system any off-worlder who puts the lives of our citizens at risk."

Lim stood. Her eyes blazed. Her fists were clenched at her sides. "All we have tried to do is take care of these boys—"

"And you have done all you could with your meager resources," Wylak said, his voice now smooth as oil, "but trying is not the same as doing."

"Why, you—" Lim said.

I stood and put my hand on her shoulder as I interrupted her. "What I believe Ms. Lim is trying to say, Senator, is that the tragic loss of this boy is, as you've said, one for which someone must assume responsibility. We look forward to the full investigation that will surely be necessary to identify that responsible

party. Would you be willing to divulge at this stage
the timing of the government's inquiry?"

Wylak stared at me. For the first time, he really
saw me. He remained quiet for several seconds as
he assessed me.

I did my best to look like a bureaucrat who'd spotted an opportunity for career advancement.

He didn't buy it, but it was also clear that he didn't
care much about who I was. Lim had already given
him the emotional reaction he needed to support his
case. He could afford to be gracious and move on.

He focused again on her as he continued. "Of
course we all want to understand what in your process
failed and allowed this poor, troubled boy to leave the
compound while armed, but that can wait. Our focus
now must be on the future, on the fate of the rest of
the young men currently under your care."

Lim stepped forward.

Wylak didn't move. He smiled.

The guard stepped toward Lim.

I squeezed Lim's shoulder hard enough that she
turned toward me for a second. I smiled at her and
took a gamble that she'd understood me: I released
her shoulder and sat.

She forced a smile and sat.

Wylak worked hard not to show his disappointment,
but enough was evident in the expression that swept
across his face that I knew Lim had seen it.

"The future of these boys should of course be your
primary concern now," Lim said, "as it has been ours
all along. As we've discussed before, the reintegration
process requires a great deal of time. So far, you've
given us very little. We are making great progress,

quite frankly doing better than I had ever expected, but much work remains."

Wylak nodded as if he were seriously contemplating Lim's words. "Though Tumani is still a small and poor planet, we are, of course, sophisticated enough to understand the difficulties you face. At the same time, I trust that you appreciate the fact that we have all invested a great deal of time already, more time than any of us had expected would be necessary."

"That's not—" Lim said.

Wylak held up his hands and interrupted her. "Please, Ms. Lim, I realize how difficult it can be to hear criticism of your work, but sometimes course adjustments are necessary in even the best of programs—which I'm sure you would admit yours is not. In this case, we in the government have an obligation to our people that should—no, that *must*—supersede any arrangement with any private organization such as yours." His voice rose in volume as it lowered in tone. He'd stopped talking and was now campaigning, though whether by habit or for some real goal I could not tell. "Given the terrible incident of yesterday and how far you still have to go after so long a time with these boys, I'm sure you'll agree that a schedule review is in order."

"How long?" Lim said. "We've had so little time. We're nowhere near—"

"The end?" he said. "I feared as much, which is why I am here."

Lim opened her mouth to continue.

I touched her shoulder again.

She whipped around to face me. Her expression was so full of rage that she could barely speak. Wylak had manipulated her perfectly.

I shook my head slightly, faced him, and said, "What do you propose, Senator?"

He spread his hands wide, magnanimous in victory. He ignored me and continued to speak to Lim. "We do not expect miracles, of course, but as we've made clear from the start, we cannot support this endeavor forever. We've also received some information—confidential, of course; I'm sure you'll understand—that leaves us concerned about the motives of some of your staff."

"What?" Lim said.

Before she could say another word, he continued. "We've thus informed both the Expansion Coalition and Frontier Coalition representatives at our jump station of the possibility that those same people whose motives worry us might try to kidnap some of the boys. We must protect the children."

"I cannot believe you would dare accuse—" Lim paused, so angry she could barely speak.

I took advantage of her momentary silence and said, "Senator, I believe you were going to tell us your proposal."

He continued to ignore me and address only Lim. "I suggest we return in two weeks," he said. "If the boys are through the reintegration program and ready to go home at that time, wonderful. If not, then I'm sure we can all agree that some changes in the program are in order."

"I cannot speak for Ms. Lim," I said, "but I am positive that she would *not* agree with that statement. I believe, however, that you have already decided you'll be back in two weeks, so there is no point in further discussion. Is that correct?"

He didn't like me being that direct. He had to

struggle to maintain a smile as he stared at Lim and said, "Only because of our strong working relationship, Ms. Lim, am I able to overlook your aide's implication that we approached this discussion with anything other than an open mind. If you'd like to suggest an alternative timetable, please do."

Lim forced a smile and leaned against the wall behind her. "I think three months would be more reasonable, as you and I have discussed in the past, Senator."

She was back in the game, and he was getting angrier by the second. Either he'd lost control, or he had all the recordings he thought he needed, because when he next spoke, the politician was gone. In his place stood the fighter who had earned all those thick scars and chosen to keep them. "Two weeks. If you're not done by then, we take over." He turned his back on us. "Escort them out."

Lim shook her head and glared at me, but when I stayed quiet, she did the same.

The guard led us out of the room, through the shuttle hatch that was open when we reached it, and into the afternoon sunlight.

Lim stopped, turned, and stared at the shuttle.

The guards spread around us.

"We're leaving," I said to them, "and we're still unarmed."

Lim glanced at me, turned, and stomped off.

I followed her, my back tingling until we reached the closest dorm and turned its corner.

The moment we did and were safely out of sight of the guards, Lim wheeled on me.

"What was that all about, Moore?"

I backed away from her. "He came to annoy you and manipulate you into saying things he could use later when he showed the meeting to others. He got what he wanted."

"So what do you think I should have done?" she said. "Should I have sat there like you did and accept everything he said?"

"I think we both should have fought more intelligently with our words," I said, "but only so we'd feel better later. We entered the meeting knowing what he wanted. We left it with him getting exactly that. It was always going to proceed that way. Nothing we could have done would have changed the outcome."

"You're saying we've already lost?" she said. "You're giving up? I thought I knew you better than that."

Playing the calm one in a tense situation is not something that comes naturally to me. I'd far rather fight, but I've learned that sometimes the most effective combat strategy is to speak very carefully. I'd tried, but today had been hard, brutally hard, and I was almost out of what little control I'd regained.

I stepped forward until I was inches from her face. "You do," I said, "and you'd do well to remember it. You do *not* want to screw with me right now. I did everything I could to save your ass in there, and if you'd calm down and admit you screwed up, you'd see that I did. Even so, none of it mattered, because as I told you yesterday, he'd already decided to come back in two weeks. He was simply working us, and he did a very good job of it."

She looked into my eyes, and for a bit we stood like that, friends and former squad mates teetering on the edge. "I did screw up," she said, "and I'm sorry.

I'm frustrated by what Wylak is doing, the way he's setting us up to fail all these boys, and I'm angry at myself for not seeing it coming all along. I expected him to push on the timeframe, but never this much." She shook her head and stared at the ground. "He knows there's no way we can succeed in only two more weeks."

"Of course he does," I said. "He's counting on it. If he gave you enough time to reintegrate the boys, they'd be of less use to him as soldiers."

"So what now?" she said. "Even if we had the resources, we couldn't get them off the planet; the coalitions would never let us."

"No," I said, "they wouldn't. We could never do it." I took a deep breath and stepped backward a meter. "What you need to do now is get your team to help the boys as much as possible in the next two weeks, and hope that's enough time."

"Enough for what?" she said. "I already told you—"

I held up my hand. "For my backup plan to work."

"Are you finally going to explain this plan of yours?" she said.

I looked at her and thought about the meeting with Wylak. I pictured what might happen if Maggie and Jack couldn't pull off what I'd asked, imagined what Lobo and I might have to do, and I knew there was no way I could tell her. I couldn't trust her to keep it all secret, not when she was as emotionally involved as she was, not when there were so many ways this could go wrong. My outburst to the boys scared me enough. We couldn't take any more chances.

"No," I said, "I'm not. You concentrate on the boys. Let me take care of this."

"We're already focusing on the boys. We can't do anything different or faster; it doesn't work like that. They need time, a lot of time, to deal with what they've experienced."

I stared at the sky and the trees and the birds—anywhere but at Lim. When she'd stayed silent for a few seconds, I looked at her again and said, "I understand that. I do. I'm not the enemy. I know you're doing the best you can. From everything I've seen, you and your team are doing a great job. I realize you can't make the process go any faster. All I'm saying is that over the next two weeks, the best you can do is to keep on helping the boys."

"And you?" she said. "What are you going to be doing?"

"Most of the time, I'll be walking the perimeter and cleaning the dorms—whatever Schmidt tells me to do. I'll also be coordinating and working on certain aspects of my plan."

"And I'm supposed to leave you alone and hope you'll rescue us?"

I wanted to explain it to her. I wanted to tell her I wasn't doing it alone. I couldn't, though, take the risk that she might tell someone, not with what I was asking Jack and Maggie to do.

"Yes," I said. "As hard as that will be for you, yes. You can't even tell anyone else there might be a plan. Everyone has to stay the course you've charted."

Lim stared at me for a long time. Finally, she said, "I hope you know what you're asking, and what you're taking on. You have to decide if you want to do this by yourself. If you do, it's all on you, Jon. The fate of these boys, of all of our work, of everything: It will all depend on you. Are you really ready to make that decision, to accept that responsibility?"

I thought about how many times I'd put myself in that situation and about all the deaths and pain that had resulted from my past failures. One by one, the decisions pile up, and in the blink of an eye, a lifetime of them tower over you, blocking the light and leaving you in darkness. I flashed again on Nagy's body and all the way back to when I was sixteen, to the first time I let my teammates down, to Bob and Han dead on the ground around me, their blood soaking into the soil, and Benny asking one more decision of me.

All I could do was nod my head and walk away.

CHAPTER 50

Dump Island, planet Pinkelponker—139 years earlier

I HEARD BENNY'S VOICE, but I couldn't make any sense of what he was saying. Bob and Han dead on the ground, Alex sobbing, his head bleeding—it was all too much. I was afraid to open my mouth lest the screams inside my head escape into the air, but trying to contain them left me shaking and unable to hear anything outside me.

Benny rolled backward for almost a meter.

I barely noticed him.

He pushed forward as fast as he could until the front edge of his cart smacked into my leg.

"Ow," I said, startled by the pain in my shin. "What are you doing?"

"Trying to get you to focus on me," Benny said, "and apparently succeeding. We have to go now, Jon, or soon a backup ship will arrive, and we'll be stuck here. It's time for you to decide."

"We can't leave them here," I said. "We have to do something for them."

"They're dead, Jon. There's nothing we can do."

"We should bury them, or at least get them out of the way, put them somewhere safe. Something."

"Jon!" Benny screamed at me, louder than he ever had in training. "We don't have the time. When the others hear the shuttle take off and we don't return, they'll come here. They'll take care of...the bodies. If we want to help all those people, our friends, the ones still alive, we have to go. *Now*."

He was right. I knew he was right, but running away and leaving Bob and Han where they lay, where the shuttle's take-off would cover them with dust, seemed an insult to them. They were dead, so I knew it couldn't matter to them, but the idea of abandoning them gnawed at me.

I glanced at Alex, who had not moved or even acknowledged us. "Alex?" He didn't answer, so I ran to him, knelt so my face was level with his, and said again, "Alex?"

He looked at me for several seconds as if I was a stranger. "Jon?"

I nodded. "Alex, we have to go now. We have to get the shuttle out of here, or we could end up losing it."

He tilted his head toward Han's body but wouldn't look at it, wouldn't look anywhere except down or straight at me. "And them?" he said. "What about them?"

"We have to leave them. The others will come for them as soon as we're gone."

"I don't know, Jon."

Behind Alex, Benny rolled along the side of the shuttle and toward its entrance.

"We're out of time," I said.

Alex shook his head and rocked back and forth. "I can't. I just can't. I can't do it anymore."

Benny rolled into the shuttle. "Jon," he said, "it's time."

"If we take off," I said, "we could hurt Alex."

"If we don't," Benny said, "we'll be condemning everyone, including him, to staying here until they die."

I grabbed Alex's shoulders. "You heard Benny, Alex. You know he's right. You have to go with us. We'll come back for the others later, when it's safe, like we planned."

"I can't," he said. "I can't I can't I can't."

I stared at him for a few seconds and nodded my agreement. He couldn't. He'd be of no use to us.

I moved close enough to him that I could get my left arm under his legs and my right around his back. I pulled him close and stood. He was heavier than I expected but not a problem to lift.

"No!" he screamed. He pounded against my leg with his one arm. "I don't want to."

"Stop," I said, keeping my voice as calm as I could. "I'm not going to make you. I'm moving you back to the path, where you'll be safe when we take off."

He turned his head so he could see my eyes. "Really?"

"Yes."

He nodded and fell quiet. He huddled against my body the way I'd seen sleeping babies resting on their mothers.

I walked around the shuttle's front, to the path, and down it to our sleeping area. I put Alex on the ground carefully, so he was under the cover of the branches. I leaned him against the rock. "You rest. The others will be along soon enough."

"Jon!" Benny's cry sounded far away; the shuttle must have muffled his voice.

"I'm going now," I said to Alex, "but I'll be back for you. I'll be back for all of you. You tell the others. Okay?"

Alex said nothing. His eyes focused nowhere at all.

I grabbed his chin. "Okay?"

He finally saw me and said, "Yes. I'll tell them."

"Good."

I jogged to the shuttle.

Benny waited inside the door. "We're way past time, Jon. You have to get me up front, lift me so I can see the controls, and operate them as I tell you. Just like we rehearsed."

"I have to move Han and Bob first," I said.

"No!" Benny looked frantic. "I'm telling you: We are out of time. We're past out of time. We must take off. Now!"

I was exhausted and yet trembling with rage. I wanted to punch something, but our enemies were dead. Our only way to help our remaining friends was to leave two of them behind. If Benny had said another word, I might well have started hitting him—and if I had, I'm not sure I'd have been able to stop.

Instead, he stayed silent.

I took a deep breath. We'd done too much, lost too much, to let this opportunity go.

"Tell me what to do," I said.

CHAPTER 51

In the former rebel complex, planet Tumani

TWO WEEKS. That's all you have, Jack. I'm sorry I didn't guess more accurately. Once Wylak's people take over this place, the boys are doomed. He'll have them back in combat as soon as the last of Lim's team have jumped from the system. I won't let that happen, so if you don't want to come back to a bloodbath, make it work. Two weeks." I paused. "Cut it there, and send it everywhere you can."

"Maggie gave me multiple protocols and destinations," Lobo said. "The last transmission reached her quickly, so it's likely this one will, too. Before I send it, though, I have to ask: Will we really fight if necessary?"

I hadn't decided until the end of the recording, but the moment I said the words, I started wondering if they were true. Still, I could not think of any other viable option. "Yes."

"We'll win," he said, "but only at first. The troops around this place won't be any problem for me, and because they won't be expecting me, neither will the ships that bring Wylak. Our casualties should be minimal, because none of the opposition will be prepared. The second wave, though, will know what it's facing. The battle with them won't go as well."

"I know," I said. I didn't tell him that we could stay here safely for as long as I was willing to use my nanomachines to disassemble any attackers. Doing that would mean letting a lot of people know what I was, something I'd avoided for almost a hundred and forty years. Of course, if they bombed us, we'd lose, because I'd never made a nanocloud that could disassemble anything moving at the speed of a missile. "The alternative is to let him take the boys."

"Okay," Lobo said. "I've sent the transmission. Now, I have a great deal of work to do."

"What work?"

"The only logical thing: Prepare for battle. I'm going to try to inject triggers into every communications and power system on the planet, so that if it comes to war, we can disrupt every system I can reach."

I started to say that his response was extreme, but it wasn't. He was right. If we killed a senator of a planetary government and all the troops who were backing him, we were declaring war. "Good thinking."

"Of course," he said. "Thinking is what I do best." After a pause, he said, "Will Lim's people back us?"

"I don't know. I haven't discussed it with her."

"So you're willing to make this decision on your own?"

"I'm not doing that," I said. "I'm making it with you."

"No," Lobo said. "You're leading. I'm following. I'm with you. It's that simple."

"And what would you do?"

"Hand the complex over to Wylak and leave the planet," he said. "Sometimes, we lose."

"You'd abandon hundreds of boys who'd counted on us? You'd let Wylak throw them back into combat?"

"Yes," Lobo said, "when the alternative was a full-scale war with the two of us taking on an entire planet and thousands of people certain to die. Yes."

"I can't believe that."

"It's the truth," he said. "That is what I, left on my own, would do. It is what Lim would do. It is what any sane and rational person would do."

"So what does that make me?"

"On this topic," Lobo said, "insane and irrational. Obviously."

I opened my mouth to argue, but I couldn't; he was right. I should walk away. If Jack couldn't implement the plan on the new schedule, and I wasn't at all sure that he could, I should walk away.

No. Not this time. Insane, irrational, whatever; I was not leaving this time.

"You're right," I said, "but I won't go."

"So we'll fight," Lobo said.

"You could head out," I said.

"You know better," he said. "When I asked you to help find the man who created me, you did. Why?"

That incident had cost me a lot, including having to watch several people die. With the same information, though, I'd make the same choice again. "Because you asked," I said, "and we're a team."

"Exactly," Lobo said. "I'm with you."

"So let's hope Jack succeeds and we don't have to fight."

"Indeed," Lobo said, "but while we're hoping, let's also make the right preparations. If we go to war, I can promise you that before we go down, they will pay dearly."

CHAPTER 52

In the former rebel complex, planet Tumani

LONG AND A dozen of the boys stood in a large circle and kicked a ball around. The game seemed to involve stopping the ball and quickly redirecting it to another player. Most handled the task with ease, but every now and then one of them would let the ball slip by, and the others would poke fun at him. No one seemed to get angry, even those who missed.

The only games I'd ever played were with Jennie, and none of were physical. By the time my mind had developed enough that I could handle any kid game that interested her, I was already so much bigger than she was that we stuck to hide-and-seek, cloud shape naming, running, and building sandcastles. The idea of being a kid who had friends and played games with them was appealing but no more relevant to me than the flight of the birds that zipped from tree to tree overhead.

"Moore," Long called, "want to join us?"

I'd been walking patrol along the perimeter and hadn't even realized I'd stopped and was watching them. Guard duty had become dramatically more boring since Nagy's death, because everyone knew now what could happen if you tried to leave. Still, Lim insisted we keep at it, which was wise; Wylak would be on us in an instant if anything else were to go wrong right now, and we needed every bit of the two weeks he'd given us.

We actually needed more, but we couldn't have it, so I had to hope Jack was at the top of his game.

I also didn't mind the patrols. They kept me outdoors, in the world. When you know you might be fighting in less than a dozen days, the air tastes cleaner, the trees smell nicer, and even the food in the meal tents tastes better.

"What about it, Moore?" Long said.

I smiled and said, "No, thanks. I've never done anything like it, so I'd be terrible at it."

"Only one way to get better," he said. "Besides, it's good to do things in a group. Builds teamwork."

"Big Man afraid of a little ball," Bony said, shaking his head in mock disbelief. "Makes no sense."

The other boys laughed.

"You going to let that challenge stand?" Long said. "You're giving us grown-ups a bad reputation." His tone was joking, but his expression made it clear that he wanted me to join them.

I had no idea why, but I also couldn't see how it could hurt. "Okay," I said. "I'll try. You guys have to take it easy on me, though, and someone has to show me what to do."

Bony and the boy next to him, whose name I didn't know, made room for me between them.

A kid kicked the ball to Long, who stopped it with his foot.

"Do what I did," Long said. "As soon as you've stopped the ball, pass it to anyone you want except the guys on either side of you or the one who sent it to you."

He kicked the ball to Bony, who stopped it and sent it to a boy to his right.

"That's it," Long said.

"Seems easy enough," I said.

The kid with the ball fired it at me. I moved my foot a second after the ball shot past me.

Everyone laughed.

"Oh, yeah," Long said, "I forgot one other rule: You miss it, you run and fetch it. Better get moving."

Everyone laughed again.

By reflex, I began to get angry, but as I looked at the faces of the kids in the circle, it was obvious that though they were laughing at me, it was with no particular malice or meanness. So, I smiled and chased down the ball.

When Long called the end of the game forty-five minutes later, so we could all get ready for dinner, I was soaked with sweat. I was also more often than not stopping the shots that came my way. After watching me be everyone's target for the first ten minutes, Bony had taken pity on me and showed me how to move my foot slightly backward as the ball made contact, so I was absorbing the momentum rather than bouncing the ball off my rigid leg. The combination of exercise and the focus necessary to handle the kicks had let me escape for a time the problems we were facing. I was grateful for that and thanked the others as they left.

Bony and three other boys stayed behind, so I

waited with them. When the remainder of the group was out of earshot, he said, "How old were you?"

"Huh?" I said.

"How old were you when you first had to fight?"

"It's complicated," I said.

He shook his head and turned away. "I should have known," he said to the others. "Let's go."

I caught him in a few steps and knelt so I was face-to-face with him. "I'm not avoiding the answer. It's complicated because—" I stopped as I realized that Lobo was going to hear all of this. If I was going to tell Bony, I should have told Lobo first, but the boy was reaching out, and I didn't want to turn him away. The more I thought about it, the less I wanted to go into details. Finally, I said, "It's complicated because I don't like to talk about my past. That's all." I decided to go with my mental age, which was hard to nail down, because I had been learning so quickly after Jennie fixed me. "About ten," I said. "I don't remember exactly."

He nodded. "I'm eleven."

"Twelve."

"Ten."

"Eight," the smallest boy said, clearly proud.

Nothing I could say would make clear why this was nothing to be proud about, so I stayed quiet.

After a bit, Bony said, "How bad did it get?"

"Bad enough," I said. My mind flooded with images of Bob and Han dead on the sand on Dump and of Alex crying in my arms. "I lost friends." Benny next to me, both of us strapped into chairs in the Aggro labs—torture rooms, really, but they called them labs. All the pain, all the deaths, all the people I'd never see again—it all washed over me. "I lost a lot."

Bony nodded again. "You want us to stop fighting so no more of that happens to us."

"Yes," I said. "You've seen too much already."

"But you're still fighting," he said. "How long have you been doing it?"

"Most of my life," I said without even thinking. "Pretty much all of it."

"And you're okay," he said. "You're doing good. So fighting can work out."

I wanted to scream how wrong he was, how the cost grew and grew as the years wore on, but I knew from watching Schmidt and Long and all the other counselors that responding violently never helped. I took a deep breath and said, "You don't see it, but I pay every day. If you stop now, you'll have days, maybe even weeks, possibly whole months, when everything is good and your time as a soldier doesn't enter your mind. I don't have that."

"Maybe," Bony said.

It was my turn to nod. "Maybe. That's the best I can offer you, because I don't know for sure. These counselors tell me the pain will fade, and I believe them."

"Maybe is better than no chance at all," Bony said.

"It is," I said. "It most definitely is."

"So why are you still fighting?" he said. "The way you walk, the way you look around, everything about you says you're a soldier."

I started to answer but couldn't. I wasn't sure I knew. "That really is complicated," I said.

"The lines at dinner are always long," he said. "We have time."

I sat and considered his question.

He and the other three sat in front of me. They all stared at me. Two played with the grass. Bony and the other one remained still.

Finally, I said, "You may not believe me, but I'm honestly not completely sure. I'll tell you what I know, and it'll have to be enough, because it's all I have. Partly, I fight because people need help. Even when I'm trying to hide, people who need someone like me seem to find me."

"You must not be trying very hard," Bony said. "You're a grown-up. You can go anywhere. It's a big universe."

"You're probably right," I said, "though it always feels like I'm trying. That's why that answer is only part of it. Another part is that fighting has become what I do, like some people build things and others staff jump gates." I took a deep breath. "And part of it is probably because I need to—though I'm not sure why."

"Being like you doesn't sound so bad," he said. The other three nodded their agreement.

I wanted to grab them and shake them and tell them how wrong they were, but instead I hit the ground hard with my right fist.

"It's worse than you know," I said. I leaned toward them. "Listen, I'm no good at explaining this, but if there's any chance at all that you can have a normal life—and you can, all of you can, I really believe that—then you should jump at that chance. These people are here to prepare you for that kind of life. When you're ready, they'll find you families." I closed my eyes and saw Jennie on the day she'd left me, Benny as we were boarding the shuttle on Dump, all the people I'd cared about and lost over so very many years. When I looked at the boys again, my throat was full and talking was difficult. "You'll have that chance. You have to take it, you really do. Be glad every day for the new life you get."

"What if that man Wylak kicks out the counselors?" Bony said.

I leaned back in surprise.

"What, you don't think we hear things?" he said. He chuckled. "We all listen, and we all talk. Just because you're big doesn't mean you always remember to close a window or whisper or look around before you open your mouth."

I smiled. "You're right about that," I said.

"So what about that man?" Bony said.

I shook my head. "I won't let that happen."

"So to stop us from having to fight, you plan to fight?" He paused. "That doesn't seem like a great plan."

"You're right," I said. "It doesn't."

He nodded, tilted his head, and said, "Were you trying to hide before somebody got you involved in all this?"

"Yeah," I said. "I was."

"You're not very good at the hiding game, are you?" he said.

The others laughed.

I joined them. "No, I guess not."

"And now you'll end up fighting again," he said.

"I hope not. I don't want to fight. Sometimes, many times—most times—there are other options." I needed Jack and Maggie to succeed. "I think this is one of those times."

"But you're not sure," Bony said.

"No," I said, "not completely."

"Then we'll fight with you," he said.

"No!" I said, my voice louder than I'd intended. I held up my hands and quickly said, "I'm sorry. I didn't mean to yell. It's just that if you're ever going to have those normal lives, you have to stop being soldiers sometime. That time is now. You're kids. Fighting is not your job."

"We were good fighters," Bony said. "We could help."

I stood. "I'm sure you could, but no more. No more. With any luck at all, none of us will have to fight. No matter what, though, you won't."

Lobo's voice came over the comm. "As honest as you're trying to be, do you want to make that promise? I have news."

I did, so I didn't bother to answer him. I stared at the boys. "No more fighting for you."

"You say that now," Bony said, "but when you need soldiers, we'll be ready."

I wasn't going to change his mind, so I ignored him and forced a smile. "Let's get some dinner. I'll race you."

I took off at a slow jog so they'd have a chance of catching me.

While I was still in front of them, I said over the comm, "Please don't tell me the news is bad."

"I wish I could comply with that request," he said.

CHAPTER 53

In the former rebel complex, planet Tumani

I FOLLOWED THE BOYS to the dinner line but wandered away as soon as they joined the crowd of hungry kids. I didn't want to have this conversation anywhere that anyone might have even a small chance of hearing it, so I quick-walked to Lobo and stayed silent until I was inside his front pilot area.

"What's happening?" I said.

"Wylak's been showing the highlights from your meeting," Lobo said, "with an emphasis on the parts where Lim turns emotional. He's selling the idea that they can no longer trust her with the boys. He's getting a lot of buyers."

"Do we care?" I said. "We already know he's coming."

"I see that I should not have taken your question literally," Lobo said, "and instead jumped right to the most important point: Wylak and hundreds of soldiers will be here five days early."

"So we have only eight more days?"

"I'm glad to see your arithmetic skills are still in order."

"You can joke about this?" I screamed. "We may lose all these boys, and you're making jokes."

"Yes," Lobo said, "so that we can move quickly past the part where you get emotional and instead focus on dealing with the problem. You entered here with an elevated pulse, and this news was sure to upset you, so I simply hastened the process."

I sat on the couch. He was right. I'd spent this whole job fighting my emotions, letting them affect me more than I should allow. If we were going to save these kids from Wylak, I had to do better. He'd goaded Lim easily, and now we were paying for her mistakes. I couldn't add mine to our troubles.

"Sorry. I won't do that again. From now on until we're done, you can count on it." I took a deep breath. "So, where are you on the preparations?"

"Ahead of schedule, which is good," Lobo said, "but it's not clear if I'm ahead enough to cope with this acceleration. I'm penetrating the key Tumani networks, but I'm nowhere near where I want to be. I can't go any faster, though, without leaving traces they might detect."

"Will you finish before Wylak arrives?"

"Maybe, but I can't be sure. There's no way from the outside to tell how many layers of protections I'm going to have to pierce. My best estimation is that I will be into some but not all of the defensive, power, and communication systems."

"So if we have to fight?"

"We disable what we can, hope the resulting chaos affects the networks that are still operational, and battle whatever forces reach us."

I wanted to push him harder, but that was another dumb, emotional urge; he was doing the best he could. I twisted my neck to work out some tension. "We have to figure out how to draw the troops away from here as quickly as possible. We need them focusing on us, not the complex, or we'll endanger the boys too much."

"If we leave, they'll also be vulnerable to a secondary attack while we're occupied."

"Lim and her people can defend the narrow entrance path for a while," I said, "as long as we can stop any of Wylak's troops from entering this airspace and landing."

"I can do that," Lobo said, "but you know I can't stop a full-fledged airborne assault—missiles or bombs—on this place."

"Wylak wants the boys alive," I said. "He won't kill them. He won't even be expecting any resistance, at least not initially."

"And when he encounters us?"

"I don't know," I said. "The more I think about it, the less I like fighting. It exposes us and the boys to a host of potential dangers. That's why it's only an alternative if Jack doesn't come through."

"We have other options," Lobo said. "We could leave."

"I already told you—"

"I remember, of course," Lobo said, cutting me off, "but I need to raise a vital point: If we stay and fight, we will be risking the lives of all the people here, including the boys. Once we take on the Tumani armed forces, we'll be in a war. Politicians who make wartime decisions are often willing to sacrifice civilians for victory."

"If it comes to that, we could contact the coalitions—"

"And give them what evidence?" Lobo said. "Wylak has primed them to see us as the problem. All the data would be easy for us to fabricate—and even easier for Wylak to deny."

I stood and paced back and forth in the small space. Endangering the boys would be a self-defeating choice for Wylak, because the whole point of his maneuvering was to get more soldiers. On the other hand, he was a man who fought to win. If we challenged the entire government on its own turf, he would easily gain the support he needed to wipe us out. He might even get the EC and the FC to help him, because no coalition looked kindly on an attack on a sovereign government. Once either coalition had troops on the ground, he would also be a big step closer to getting them to fight the rebels for him. Going to war with him and his troops could ultimately prove to be the biggest favor we could do for him.

Damn.

"I said I wouldn't let him take these boys. I said I'd fight. If it comes down to fighting or leaving, though, I can either risk their lives or abandon them to being soldiers again."

"Yes. At least as soldiers, some might survive."

"To live what kinds of lives?" I said.

"Maybe the kind you live," Lobo said.

I didn't know what to say to that. I couldn't save myself from the hard nights and the dark dreams and the visions of past losses that were always at the edge of my mind. I'd thought I could help save the boys. I still wanted to believe that.

"I need to think," I said. "We have some time. Besides, maybe we won't have to fight. Anything from Jack or Maggie?"

"Yes," Lobo said, "to my surprise. That's the one bit

of good news: As we were talking, an encrypted but verifiable burst from Jack arrived. He said he could handle the new, shorter schedule you sent."

"Good," I said, "because now we have to tell him that he just lost five more days."

I was too tense to eat, but I wasn't yet sufficiently in control of myself that I was willing to risk talking to Lim or any of her people. One of the lessons I'd learned early in my time with the Saw is that when a mission gives you a chance to sleep, take it. I stretched out on my cot and tried to calm myself.

In eight days, I might have to choose what to do about the boys, but I didn't have to make that choice now. In eight days, I might fail them, might send Bony and his friends and all the rest back to war for Tumani. In eight days, I might fail them a different way, turn them into soldiers fighting alongside me by dragging them into a conflict they had no clue was brewing. I might soon do those horrible things.

But not today.

Today, I could hope that Jack would come through.

Today, I wasn't failing anyone.

Today, they were boys safe in a complex with people who cared about them and who were trying to help them return to normal lives.

Today, everything was okay.

I fell asleep wishing foolishly that it could stay that way and fighting to stave off the memories of my own past failures, those many days when the best plan I had simply wasn't good enough.

CHAPTER 54

Dump Island, planet Pinkelponker—139 years earlier

GET INSIDE," Benny said, "and push that top button."

I did. The door shut.

Benny's eyes were half closed.

"Are you falling asleep?"

He blinked a few times and said, "Are you crazy? No, I'm not sleeping. I'm reviewing everything I learned so I don't crash us into the side of the mountain." He shook his head. "Pick me up and take me up to the front of the shuttle."

Benny was heavier than I expected, and my muscles were sore, but I lifted him and slung him over my left shoulder.

"No," he said. "Turn me around. Carry me facing forward. I need to see everything clearly."

I put my right arm between his legs and pulled him across my body to the position he wanted. My arms shook with the effort of holding him, and I had to fight to maintain my balance with all of his weight in front of me. I took small steps to avoid falling as I made my way toward the front. After three paces, the walls opened into what looked like people-size cages, three to a side, each one a barred area barely big enough for a person my size to sit. They'd changed the shuttles since they'd brought me here; I'd ridden in a plain room, not a cage.

Benny started shaking. "Oh, no!" he said. "Move faster!"

I picked up the pace. "What?" We reached the front in a few seconds.

"Put me in that chair," Benny said, his left flipper pointing to a very large, padded seat on our left. "Help me sit up."

I did.

"What's wrong?" I said.

He studied the controls on a panel in front of us, his eyes frantically scanning back and forth. "Where was the person the guard was bringing here?" he said.

I shook my arms to loosen the muscles as I recalled my initial sighting of the first guard. He'd been alone. The only people I'd seen emerge from this shuttle were that man and the other one who'd followed him, the one whose head I'd pounded into the floor.

"I didn't see anyone," I said. "Maybe that person is somewhere else on board."

"No," Benny said. "No, no, no." He hit his thighs in frustration. "They weren't coming to drop off anyone, Jon."

"What do you mean? That's the only thing they come here for."

"They were coming to collect," he said. "Maybe they were monitoring us and wanted to stop what we were doing. Maybe they wanted one or more of us for some other purpose. I don't know. But they were coming to kidnap some of us."

"So?" I said. "We stopped them. We have the shuttle. Nothing changes."

"Maybe," Benny said, "but I read that hunter teams are usually more careful than the transport teams."

"So let's get the others before they can send anyone else. We can cram them into here—there's enough room—and then leave. Once we're somewhere safe, we can figure out what to do with everyone."

"No," Benny said, his voice calmer now, his words slow and distinct. "We can't take that chance. We have to leave. I'll tell you what to do. You'll be my hands—just like we planned." He pointed at a button in front of him. "Push this."

I did.

A display snapped to life along the opaque window in front of us. It showed a lot of words and numbers. None of it made sense to me.

"Do you hear the engines?" Benny said.

"No. What's wrong?"

"They should have started," he said.

"Maybe all that stuff—" I pointed at the display "—is telling you what to do next."

He shook his head. "No. Everything there says the engines are working, but they're not. We have to get out of here. Pick me up!" His face turned red. "Now!"

I'd never seen Benny scared before. I threw him over my shoulder and ran for the front.

As we approached the door, Benny said, "Hit the same button."

His voice sounded far away. I felt like I was maintaining my pace, but when I looked at my feet, they seemed to be a great distance below me and made of rock.

I pushed the button.

Nothing happened.

"No," Benny said. "No." Tears ran down his face. "I'm sorry. I couldn't even save you. I'm sorry."

My legs wouldn't hold me. I sank to my knees.

I was still too high. I managed to lower Benny onto the floor. It looked so nice that I joined him there, on my side. Everything spun in tight circles.

Darkness inked along the walls and the ceiling and covered the lights.

The world fell away into a perfect black pit.

"Up!"

I heard the word at the same time that I registered the pain in my belly. Light blinded me as I opened my eyes. I blinked to clear my vision.

A man in a dark blue jumpsuit stood over me. He kicked me again in the stomach, stepped back, and pointed his rifle at me. "You're obviously awake. I know you heard me. They pay us the same even if you're a little banged up. Save us both a lot of trouble, and get up."

I didn't want him to hurt me again, so I rolled onto my stomach and got to my hands and knees. My arms and thighs shook, the floor spun, and I vomited. I fell onto my side on the cold, white floor and barely missed hitting the mess I'd made.

"It's the gas," he said. "Does it to all the new subjects. One of the reasons we have the hoses and the drains." He stepped backward. "Second try will go better. Up."

I repeated the process of getting to my hands and knees. He was right; I was steadier.

Benny.

I glanced around the room.

He was on the floor to my right and behind me, unmoving.

I turned to him. "Benny?"

"Stop!" the man said. "He's not your problem. Stand."

"Is he—"

"No," the man said. "He's not dead. He's just not conscious yet. You came around faster."

"Jon," Benny said. His voice wavered. His eyelids fluttered but he couldn't keep them open. "I thought I could save you all."

The man laughed. "A freak like you saving anyone? Yeah, right."

"Let me help him," I said.

The man kicked Benny in the head.

Benny's head snapped backward. His mouth dripped blood.

The man turned back to me and stomped on my stomach so hard that I rolled onto my back. I gasped and choked and struggled to breathe. "You better worry about yourself," he said. "Now, get up. The doctors need new subjects, and they don't like to wait."

I rolled as if I couldn't control the pain and managed to get closer to him. I curled into a ball on my knees and elbows. I pushed my toes against the ground and tensed my legs. Benny had trained me well. I had taken out the other guards. I could do it again and save Benny. "Where are we?" I said.

Before the guard could answer, I launched myself at him, springing as hard as I could for his knees.

I hit the opposite wall instead. I never even saw him move out of the way.

I glanced back in time to see him turn his rifle so the butt was facing me.

"The last place you'll ever be," he said. "Aggro."

The rifle smashing into my face turned the room a fiery red, and I was gone.

CHAPTER 55

In the former rebel complex, planet Tumani

I WOKE UP SCREAMING soundlessly, my throat tight with the effort of choking off the sound. I'd learned long ago that no matter how bad the dream, I had to wake silently. All too often, any sound would make my real-world situation much worse.

For the first few years after I escaped from Aggro, the memory of those initial minutes on that hellish space station visited me every night. They would come first, lights strobing in my unconscious mind. A rapid-fire succession of other awful moments on Aggro would then smash into me until I wrenched myself from sleep.

Listening to the screams of other prisoners and knowing my turn was coming.

Seeing a new face in a cell down the row and realizing I hadn't yet learned the name of the previous occupant.

Watching them drag Benny to the lockdown and drop him on the floor, unwilling to do him even the small kindess of aiming for the cot.

Waking in my cell after a session in the chair and seeing my skin shifting and my muscles cramping and wondering if this was the dose that would kill me, if whatever miracle of resistance that had kept me alive so far had finally proven inadequate.

Most of all, the hours I was strapped in the chair, my entire body immobilized, my eyelids held open, as they talked about me as if I was a weed they were going to pull. They cut me and injected me and stuck electrodes in me and kept at it until I passed out.

When Benny and I escaped, he'd sacrificed himself to destroy the station, so that there would be no trace of what had happened there and nothing to connect me to it, so I could lead a normal life.

I shook my head at the naïveté of my younger self. I'd never known a normal life, and after Dump and Aggro, I certainly wasn't suited for one.

I stood and stretched. I couldn't let that happen to these boys. Lim and Schmidt and Gustafson and Long and all the others had given them a chance, and now all that work might prove to have been for nothing. I wished I could fix it myself, not have to depend on anyone except Lobo, just get him moving and somehow make it all better, but I couldn't.

I hated it. I hated the powerlessness, the lack of good options.

I could fight, take on a planet's army, and put the boys at risk, or I could trust Jack to come through. He was the best con man I'd ever known. He could do the job, but when I'd needed him before, I'd always been there to help him, to make sure he got it right, to catch and correct any errors.

The more I thought about it, the more I realized

I'd always depended on others. I'd always needed help, from Jennie and Benny on Pinkelponker, through Jack and the others on our crew, to Lim and the rest of my unit in the Saw, all the way to the present. I'd never done it entirely alone. No one does.

My head spun with frustration that was morphing into anger. I needed to burn off some energy.

"I'm going for a run," I said to Lobo.

"I have new information," he said. "We need to talk."

"Over the comm," I said as I stepped to the side hatch, "unless my leaving will somehow increase our risk."

Lobo answered by opening the door.

I sprang out as if the guards on Aggro were chasing me. I pushed the pace hard for the first ten minutes, wanting my lungs and legs to hurt so much that I could feel no other pain. I ignored the boys and counselors I passed, barely noted the morning cool or the fresh wet smell, and ran. I headed for the rear of the complex, the area with the fewest people. Whenever I could, I cut off the cleared paths and through openings among the trees. As my mind focused entirely on running despite the throbbing in my legs and the lack of oxygen, I slowed my pace and worked to bring my breathing under control.

When I could finally speak clearly, I was alone and winding in and out of stands of trees at the far back of the complex. "What's up?" I said.

"I have a secured a great deal more data," Lobo said, "which is good. I have also received a very brief transmission from Maggie. It said only, 'On it.'"

"Why so short?" I said. "Can you tell when she sent it and what messages of mine she had received?"

"I don't know," he said, "and no. My guess—and it is only a guess, though of course I'm rather good at such speculations—is that she and Jack received your second message but are very busy. Of course, they're probably in another system, which would mean they'd have to use one or more couriers to relay their response to us. Perhaps for reasons we cannot know she did not trust the encryption—a poor choice on her part, but a possible one—and so rather than risk someone decrypting what she said, she kept it vague. That way, anyone who might crack the message would learn nothing from it." He paused. "Or maybe they don't feel the need to report to you. One cannot be sure; that's the interesting part of guessing."

"I'm glad *you're* having fun."

"Both of us are doing all that we can usefully do," Lobo said. "Even as you and I talk, most of me is working on security systems all over this planet. Small bits of me are also monitoring everything in the complex and, to the degree that my sensors let me, the troops outside it. What is wrong with enjoying the work I'm doing?"

I stopped jogging in a small clearing and walked back and forth across it. "Nothing. I'm sorry. Being here has stirred up a lot of memories. Few of them are good."

"Talking about them might help. If you can't tell me, who can you tell?"

I shook my head. "Maybe someday, but not now. I need to focus on the work."

"Okay," Lobo said. "I'll be around—unless, of course, we go to war with the entire planet and lose. In that case, there won't be enough of either us left to worry about what the mysterious Jon Moore never chose to share."

I laughed. A few seconds later, I stopped walking and said, "You did that intentionally. You were trying to cheer me up."

"Of course," he said. "And I succeeded."

"For an AI," I said, "you're amazingly sensitive."

"Technically speaking, and with all the data available to me, I can say with a high degree of certainty that no qualification is necessary. I am amazing."

I laughed again. "And now you manage to continue to cheer me while being completely honest and highly egotistical. Well done."

"Is it egotistical if it's true?" Lobo said.

"It can be," I said, "but you've distracted me enough. It's time to get back to business. You told me about Maggie's brief response. What other information do you have?"

"Wylak has been recruiting support both among his colleagues and in the military. He plans to show up an hour after sunrise. He's told the supporting troop leaders to expect armed resistance and to fire at the first sign they might be in danger."

"Damn. He wants everyone awake. He wants a conflict. He's preparing for a massacre."

"That's the logical inference."

There would be no halfway in any conflict with Wylak. If I decided we would fight, we would have to enter the battle completely, without reservation. It would be a massacre, but at least initially, his troops, not Lim's, would die.

None of that was news, though, not really. If we were to take on a planet, holding back would not be a viable option. Surprise and, at least initially, superior firepower from Lobo would be the only advantages we'd have.

"So we make sure we're ready," I said.

"Yes," Lobo said. "All that's changed is that we know the hour of his arrival."

"Is there any chance we could smuggle out the kids beforehand?"

"As Wylak said he would, he's alerted the jump station staff to that possibility, and they're searching all departing ships. He's also monitoring all flights in and out of the complex. We might get some of the boys into town on the pretense of supply runs, but unusual traffic would cause him to shut us down. We might well end up accelerating his timetable."

"Not worth it," I said. Any way I looked at it, either Jack and Maggie came through, or we would have to fight or surrender the boys.

"Incoming armed adults!" Lobo said. "Four of Lim's team, approaching in a spread formation, weapons in hand. ETA two minutes. Should I come to you?"

Lim must have tired of waiting for me to explain what I was doing. I was surprised that she was willing to use weapons, but I'd played right into that strategy by going so deep into the complex. The worst they would do initially, though, was try to hurt me; killing me wouldn't accomplish anything. If they shot me anywhere but the head, my nanomachines should be able to repair the damage. More than likely, they were here to make sure I went to Lim. She wouldn't want anyone else to hear the plan first.

"Is Lim among them?"

"No," he said.

"Don't come yet," I said. "If they shoot me, trank them if you can, and pick me up before they can haul me to Lim."

"I may have to clear a landing space," Lobo said, "which would make quite a mess."

"If you have to, do it," I said, "but I don't think it will come to that. Monitor our progress. When we go into a building, scan all around it and tell me the locations of the nearest boys."

"Why?" Lobo said. "It makes no sense for you to need them or use them for assistance when your goal is to stop them from fighting."

"I'm not planning on asking them to help. I have a feeling some will be listening."

"As you wish," he said. "ETA forty-five seconds."

I sat with my back against a rough black tree, spread my arms, turned my palms face up, and waited for my interrogators to arrive.

CHAPTER 56

In the former rebel complex, planet Tumani

LONG'S LAUGH PRECEDED him. He stopped three meters short of me and stood beside a tree. He held the pistol in his right hand and pointed it not at me but definitely in my direction. I had no doubt that he could shoot me before I could reach him. From the look on his face, neither did he.

"She said you'd know we were coming."

Long and I had become casual friends during our time here, but when a friend comes for you with a gun, you have to treat him like an enemy. I stayed silent.

"Your choice," he said, still smiling. "You can walk there, or we can carry you."

"Maybe," I said.

"There are—"

"Four of you," I said. "I know. But you can't afford to significantly damage me, and I don't care at all how much I hurt you."

The smile vanished. "You're not that good," he said.

"Maybe."

He shook his head. "Not for four."

"Maybe, but do you want to explain to her why I can't answer her questions when you've beaten me unconscious? Because that's what you'll have to do to win. And, do you want to risk blowing your only hope for these kids by hurting me so badly I can't execute my plan?"

"We could subdue you."

I shook my head and smiled. "You're not that good."

"One male is five meters behind you," Lobo said over the comm, "and the other two, woman on your left and man on your right, are roughly six meters either side of him."

"If the guy behind me comes any closer," I said, "I'm going to take him down first."

"Everybody hold," Long said. "Why are you making this so hard?"

"The other three are stationary," Lobo said.

"Because you came with guns," I said. "The boys will notice, and it will undercut what you've been teaching them." I smiled. "And because Lim should know better."

"Four are around me," Lobo said.

I bent my head, coughed, and subvocalized, "Any onlookers?"

"No."

"Trank 'em," I said.

I looked back up at Long.

Three seconds later, Lobo said, "Done."

"The four near my ship are now asleep," I said. "Even considering attacking it is far stupider than coming after me. Nothing in this complex is a match for its automatic defense systems."

"Automatic defense systems indeed!" Lobo said.

I ignored him and stood.

Long visibly tensed and pointed the pistol at my legs.

"Here's what we're going to do," I said. "You're going to tell me what building she's in and head there. Hide your guns as you walk. After I've finished my run, I'll meet you there, and we can all chat."

Long shook his head. "Our orders are different."

I shrugged. "Check on the four near my ship. Talk to Lim. Decide." I crossed my arms behind my head and leaned against the tree.

Long backed behind the cover of the tree nearest him and whispered briefly.

I waited.

When he stepped back into view, he tucked his gun into his waistband and pulled his shirt over it. "Easier for everyone," he said. "I can't say I liked this plan in the first place."

"Neither did I."

We both laughed.

"Do me a favor?" he said.

"What?"

"Show up, so I don't end up being the ass in all this. You know how she can be."

I nodded. "I do, and I will. About half an hour should do it."

"Thanks," he said. He turned and left.

"All are withdrawing," Lobo said.

I stayed where I was until Lobo told me they had reached the center of the complex. I resumed jogging. As I ran, I thought about my responses to Lim's questions and how she would react.

One thing was for certain: There was no chance she would be happy.

➤   ➤   ➤

"Yes, you are going to tell us," Lim said. The air in the little room was hot and still from too many people sharing too small a space. Long stood beside me. Schmidt and Gustafson guarded the door behind me. Lim sat behind the small table in front of me. "This has gone on long enough."

I said nothing. Sweat ran down my arms and chest and back. My breathing was back to normal, but I still had the warm glow you get when you stop running.

"One boy on the roof," Lobo said, "at the left rear corner, left as you enter. Another under the small window opposite the entrance."

I motioned for Lim to continue talking and turned to face the door.

"What are—" Lim said.

I whipped around and gestured again for her to keep talking.

"—you going to do exactly?" she said, playing along.

I stepped to the door.

Gustafson and Schmidt blocked my exit. Long stepped next to me.

I mouthed, "Follow me" to him and waited.

They moved aside.

Long followed me out.

I crept around the corner of the building.

Inside, Lim kept talking. "You know that we have a right to participate in any planning that concerns this complex. As I'm sure you are aware—"

I tuned out her voice and focused on listening for movement overhead. I reached the rear corner. I stopped and motioned to Long to come closer. When he was next to me, I pointed down the side of the building. I leaned forward just far enough to spot the boy under the window. I pulled back immediately.

Long did the same.

I walked slowly backward until the edge of the roof was visible and tilted my head toward the boy waiting there.

Long saw him, too, and nodded.

We headed inside the building.

He whispered to Schmidt and Gustafson, and they all went outside.

A few seconds later, scuffling sounds crossed the roof, and I heard Long yell, "Eavesdropping on private conversations is rude and wrong!"

He returned, chuckling. "Two boys were listening to us," he said to Lim. "Moore knew about it."

Lim nodded. "So that's why you won't explain your plan?" she said to me.

"That's part of it," I said. "These boys know everything you guys say and do. They probably learned about Wylak's plan before you'd finished briefing all the adults. I heard about it from Bony, but the boys with him also knew. They all volunteered to help us fight." Before she could say anything, I added, "I told them, no."

"They're not listening now."

"No," I said, "they're not—not right this minute. Five minutes from now, they will be. If you keep them away from here, they'll eavesdrop on others on your staff. You can't expect all of these counselors to stay quiet all the time, so what they know, the boys will know. I can't have that."

"*You* can't have it?" she said. "Who put you in charge?"

I opened my mouth to answer but stopped as I understood for the first time how stupid I'd been. I'd never truly understood why she'd sent for me. Until now.

Part of me wanted to hate her for it, but I couldn't; I had too much invested in what happened here.

"Well?" she said.

"You did," I said, "though it took me a long time to realize it. You put me in charge of saving us, should we ever need saving, when you recruited me. You did it again when you took me to your meetings with Wylak. You didn't ask me to come just because you needed help in the assault on this place. You could have beaten those rebels without me, and we all know it. You brought me here because you knew that if things went nonlinear, I—no, my ship and I—could be very useful. You roped me into this mess as your insurance policy." I glanced at Schmidt and Gustafson. Schmidt wouldn't meet my gaze; Gustafson shrugged and mouthed, "Sorry." I put my hands on the desk and leaned closer to her. "You all used me—and you were right to do it, because I *am* going to do my damndest to save these boys—but I'm going to do it my way."

Lim gave me a hard stare.

I didn't turn away.

"And your way has to include keeping us in the dark?" she said.

"Yes." I straightened. My hands, still damp from the run, left prints on the wooden table. "Look, Alissa, you've worked with me before. We've served together. I've pulled you out of some bad situations, and you've saved my life." I nodded toward Schmidt and Gustafson. "They've worked with me, too. You all know that I didn't withhold information before. I'm asking you to trust that I'm doing so now for good reasons."

"And if I don't?" she said. "If I decide to make you tell me?"

I didn't stop looking into her eyes as I stepped backward until I was leaning against the wall opposite her. "You'll fail, and you'll jeopardize the only plan anyone has for saving these boys."

"We might succeed, and we might be able to execute your plan better than you can."

"You won't, and you can't." I crossed my arms. "I appreciate how hard this is for you. I understand it better than you'll believe. But we both know how this will turn out if you try to get information from me, so we both know you won't." Lim had seen Lobo in action, so even though she had no clue as to just how powerful he was, she understood enough to realize that he could take out her entire team way before I'd break.

She closed her eyes for a minute. "I hate this."

"That's a lot to ask, Gunny," Gustafson said.

I nodded. "It is, and I'm sorry, but it has to be this way."

"What *can* we usefully do?" Schmidt said.

"Exactly what we discussed before: Keep helping the boys. Prepare them to live normally. Teach them ways to cope with what's happened to them. Do the best you can with the time you have."

"And when Wylak comes?" she said. "When he shows up way before we can finish with the boys, long before they're ready for reintegration, then what do we do?"

"Hope my plan works, and follow my lead."

She shook her head and chuckled. "That's a lousy answer."

I smiled. "Yeah, but it's the only one I have."

"We don't have a better option," Gustafson said. "I say we let Moore do his job."

"Jon played by our rules," Schmidt said, "even when it meant cleaning barracks and walking useless patrols."

Lim looked over my shoulder at them and nodded. Her shoulders sagged. "It's going to be hard," she said, "going about our business as usual while the days fall away, knowing he's coming."

"The time will pass faster than you'd believe," I said. In that moment, with all of them finally agreeing to let me run my plan, I felt the cost to them and hated that I was making them pay it. I wanted to tell them about the accelerated timetable, to tell them all of it, but I didn't. My reasoning had been sound before. It still was. I had to do everything I could to increase our chances of success, so I stayed quiet as I walked out of the small building and back to Lobo.

"Look at the bright side," Lobo said over the comm. "You only have to lie to them for six and a half more days."

CHAPTER 57

In the former rebel complex, planet Tumani

BY MORNING, I was going stir-crazy. Lim and all the other adults were angry and frustrated with me. Bony and his friends wanted to fight alongside me, and I didn't know how to dissuade them. Leaving would only bring me trouble. Though most of the complex was wooded, the rebels had cleared it enough that people outside the trees could easily spot others moving around inside them.

Remaining in Lobo, however, would drive me insane, because all I could do there was exercise or sleep. I needed to stay busy, or the remaining five full days until Wylak's visit would pass painfully slowly.

Staying busy.

I wasn't the only one with that problem.

Standing alone in Lobo, staring at nothing and only moments before having felt trapped and frustrated, I now smiled broadly.

"I'm going to see Lim," I said. "She's going to love this."

393

> ➤ ➤ ➤

"You want to do what?" she said.

"Lead a bunch of the counselors and as many boys as will join in a work project," I said.

"That's not what you said before. You said you wanted to cut down a huge square of trees near the gate where Wylak's troops will enter."

I shrugged. "Same place, different descriptions. We need space for the kids to play in groups. That's a great location." I recalled Long leading the boys in the kick-the-ball game. "And, it'll help build teamwork."

She took off walking toward the food tent nearest that gate and motioned me to follow.

I fell into place beside her.

"It'll also help pass the remaining time," she said.

I said nothing.

"If I ask you if this has anything to do with your plan, you either won't answer me or lie to me, right?"

I stayed quiet.

"Learning to work together in non-violent pursuits is a valid form of therapy for the boys," she said. "Did you know that, were you guessing, or don't you care?"

I hadn't known more than what Long had told me, but it had seemed only sensible that teaching new skills to the boys would be good.

"For those who return to farming," she said, "knowing how to clear land is a very useful skill on such a heavily forested planet."

"Yes," I said. I motioned to her to stop. "We'd clear from here all the way over to the barracks, and go back into the woods about a hundred and fifty meters. The physical labor would be good for all of us, boys and counselors alike. When we finished, we'd have a great clear space." I smiled. "Plus, using cutting tapes to drop the trees would be a lot of fun."

"I could shoot down some of them," Lobo said. "Put a twig on the ground, and I could drop a tree on it."

I ignored him.

"So, what do you think?" I said. "I need your approval and the help of the counselors to make it happen."

She chuckled. "When we're done on Tumani, you're going to explain all this to me."

"If any explanation is necessary," I said, "sure, I'll provide it. What do you say?"

"You can do it," she said. "I'll call a meeting of the team leads for right after breakfast. When do you want to start?"

"As soon as you've told them," I said. I pointed at the trees in front of us. "We have a lot of work to do."

"It would be more efficient to measure and calculate the angles first," Gustafson said, "and then drop them in bunches."

"Since when do you know about clearing forests?" Schmidt said. Her smile was the biggest I'd seen on her in a long time.

"Since I was a boy about the age of these here," he said. "There's a lot about my past you don't know."

"Are we going to take down this tree," Bony said, "or try to talk it into falling?"

We all laughed.

Though most of the boys had ignored our invitation, Bony and five of his friends had wandered over to see what we were going to do.

"We're going to take it down," I said, "and I'm

even going to let you trigger the cutting tapes"—Bony reached for the remote, but I didn't give it to him—"on one condition."

He pulled back his hand. "What's that?" he said.

"You guys help us cut up and haul off the pieces."

"That sounds like hard work," he said.

"It is, but as soon we clear the first one, we're going to try out Top's idea and drop a bunch of them at once."

"I bet that'll make one big noise, maybe shake the ground," Bony said.

"I bet it will," I said.

He looked at his friends.

They all nodded.

"Okay," he said. "We'll help. Now, give me that thing. Let's drop that tree!"

His friends cheered.

Gustafson and Schmidt laughed.

Gustafson tilted his head slightly, absorbed for a second in whatever he was hearing on his comm. "Long says the entire path is clear. Are we going to stand here all day, or are you going to let that young man kick off the project?"

I smiled and handed Bony the remote.

He took it and stared intently ahead at the target tree. He lifted the remote over his head and, as his friends cheered, he pressed the button.

I could barely hear the pop of the cutting tape over the applause of his friends. When nothing happened, however, they fell silent.

"It didn't work," Bony said. He looked around at all his friends. "We should have known better."

"Wait for it," I said. The chemicals and the short-duration nanomachines the tape had released would be eating into the wood and creating a cutout area. The tree's weight and gravity would do the rest. "The goal was control, not a big noise."

"How can we make a big tree fall without an explosion?" Bony said. "Big things take big shots; that's what they taught us."

With a loud crack, the tree bent and crashed toward the earth. As it fell, it tore off branches of other trees but did not knock over any of them. It hit with a huge thud and bounced twice. Dirt and debris flew from the impact area.

"I guess they taught you wrong," I said.

"The trunk covered the target," Lobo said over the comm. "Considering Gustafson applied the tape without the aid of any visible computational devices, that's rather impressive. For a human, of course."

Bony and his friends turned away from the tree and faced me. They were all smiling.

"Let's do another one!" he said.

"Yeah!" they all cheered.

"Absolutely," I said, "as soon as we cut up and haul off this one. Ready to get to it?"

Bony nodded.

He and Gustafson and I headed for the top of the tree.

The others fell in behind us.

A group of half a dozen boys trotted up to us. "Did you guys do that?" the one in front said.

Bony smiled. "Yeah."

"Can we blow up the next one?" the other kid said.

Bony shook his head. "We didn't blow it up." He glanced at me. "We used special stuff to make it fall where we wanted it to go. The next one is ours, too—but if you help us with 'em both, you can do the third." He checked with me again. "Right?"

"Absolutely," I said.

"Deal," the other kid said.

Gustafson shook his head and smiled. "Not bad, Moore," he whispered. "Not bad."

"I hope the boys aren't discouraged," I said to Lobo as I walked to the clearing site the next morning. Our crew had stayed small, our tools were basic, and the trees were large, so we had to cut up and haul off about half of the second one before we could drop another. "We didn't get as far as I'd hoped yesterday."

"I don't think you need to worry about team morale," Lobo said.

A few seconds later, I heard boys shouting and laughing. When I passed the last of the buildings between me and the half-demolished tree, I saw the source of the sounds: Almost three dozen boys stood in two groups facing one another, pointing fingers and laughing and occasionally kicking balls back and forth.

Long stood behind one of the sets of boys; Gustafson paced beside the one that included Bony.

"About time you got here," Bony said. "These fools think they can take us."

I looked first at Gustafson and then at Long, but neither one offered any explanation.

"Huh?" I finally said.

Bony pointed at the group opposite him. "These guys sleep in the dorms two over from ours. They don't know anything about clearing trees—"

Boos and shouts of "Yeah we do!" from the other boys drowned out his voice for a moment.

"—but they think they do," Bony said, when the others were quiet again. "They've challenged us to see who could cut up and haul off the most wood today."

"We have enough of the autocarts for everyone to stay busy," Long said, "though our team may move so fast that we have to borrow some of yours."

"Not a chance," Gustafson said.

I smiled. "Only one way to settle this," I said. I walked along the downed tree and subvocalized, "Tell me when I'm halfway—by mass, not length."

After ten more steps, Lobo said over the comm, "Stop. You're there."

I drew a line in the sand and pointed at the meter-thick trunk. "Put a mark here, at the halfway line for what's left of this one." I pointed at Long. "You guys, head up tree to my right; that's your half. The rest of you, take the bottom."

"That's not fair," Bony said. "We have the thicker part."

"Yeah, but it's shorter," I said, "and besides, do you really think these guys can compete with you?"

He nodded. "No way. You're right: It doesn't matter what part we have."

The two groups of boys drifted into position.

"Ready?" I said.

Both Gustafson and Long nodded. The boys cheered.

"Let the cutting begin!" I said.

Over a hundred boys showed up to work the next morning. At least another hundred milled around the edges of the small deforested area and watched while pretending to be doing other things. We'd taken out quite a few trees, but the more I looked at the forest and thought about all those boys, the more I believed we needed a much, much bigger clearing.

"What do you say we drop a lot of them today?" I said to Gustafson.

"Definitely!" said Bony, who had taken to following me around in breaks and when we were rigging the trees to fall. "How many could we bring down at once?"

I shrugged and looked at Gustafson.

"We have dozens of cutting tapes," he said, "so we could create a huge pile of trunks. We might even get lucky and have some falling trees take out others."

"Could we set off all of them at once?" I said.

"Let's do that!" Bony said. "That would be amazing!"

Gustafson shook his head. "We could, but preparing them would be a lot of work."

"So let's do all we can," I said.

He shook his head again. "It could take me hours to get a large batch ready. This crowd"—he waved to take in all the boys—"doesn't look like it wants to wait."

"That stuff is safe without the trigger, right?" I said.

"You know it is," he said. "No trigger, no problem."

"Let's team each counselor with a group of boys and have those groups prep the trees. All you'll have to do is inspect the work and hold the trigger."

Gustafson smiled. "That many trees falling at once would be a beautiful thing to see."

"So you'll do it?" Bony said.

"Yes," he said. "I will." He scanned the area until he saw Long. "Get all the free counselors you can," he yelled, "and double-time it to me."

Long's back stiffened by reflex at the order. For a second, it looked as if he was going to salute, but he relaxed, smiled, and said, "Will do."

➤   ➤   ➤

"Cutting and hauling isn't as much fun as cutting down," Bony said. He wiped the sweat from his forehead and checked the darkening sky. "I am way past ready for dinner. I don't care what they make; I'm going to eat a lot of it."

All the boys near him murmured in agreement.

I loaded the last log the hauler in front of us could handle. It rolled off to the rear edge of the complex. We had so much wood stacked back there that some of the boys had said we could have rebuilt their villages with it.

I straightened and looked around. All but ninety or so of the boys had shown up this morning; the news of Gustafson's mass tree-dropping had attracted a lot of the kids. Today, though, had been only hard labor: chopping and stripping and hauling, working the power saws and every other tool we had until we all ached. I'd expected to lose most of the boys as the day wore on, but only a few dozen had given up. We grown-ups stayed, and the kids stayed with us. I was amazed to see how much work over four hundred people could accomplish even with the primitive tools we had. We'd be ready to take down another large batch of trees tomorrow.

Lim appeared at the edge of the clearing closest to the barracks.

A moment later, the dinner call sounded.

Kids and grown-ups alike cheered it.

"You guys are amazing!" Gustafson yelled. He pointed at the large, flat area we'd created. "Great work!"

I nodded and smiled. "He's right: You are amazing! Thank you! Thank you, all!"

About half of the boys cheered themselves. The rest were already walking toward the food tents. Most stretched as they walked. All of us were stiff and sore from a long day of work.

I headed for dinner. I was hungry enough to eat two meals.

Bony stayed beside me. "How you eat so much and not get fat is a mystery," he said.

"You've seen how hard I work," I said. "Nothing mysterious about it." Having a body laced with nano-machines that would never let me gain weight also didn't hurt, but I was confident that with this work regimen I was legitimately earning my calories.

"I ate like you," he said, "and my belly would look like it was hiding a ball."

I laughed. "I am about twice your size."

"Yeah," he said, "but you're old."

I laughed again. "I am that."

As we drew near to Lim, she said, "Moore, got a minute?"

"Sure," I said.

Bony stopped and stared at her. "You want me to stay, Big Man?" he said.

I touched his shoulder lightly. "No need. You go on. I'll catch up to you in a few minutes. You save me some of that food?"

He smiled. "You better move fast if you expect to eat! We have a powerfully hungry crew."

"I will."

Lim led me a few meters away from the stream of boys and waited until Bony was out of earshot. "You're making them so hungry we're going to run out of food earlier than we planned."

I shrugged. "We're fine for at least a couple of months, right?"

She nodded.

"So that's the least of our problems. What do you really want?"

She pointed at the clearing. "If Wylak decides to bring in his troops, they now have many more landing options than before."

"True," I said, "but do you honestly believe getting people into here has ever been his main concern? If he wants to send soldiers, he can march them up that road, let them shoot at us from hovering ships, or do pretty much anything else they want. If he wanted them to land inside here, they would just blast the trees first—which would be dangerous for all of us."

She sighed. "You're right. I just wish I understood what was going on."

"I know," I said, "and I'm sorry."

She stared at me in silence for a long time.

I didn't look away.

Finally, she said, "You better know what you're doing, Moore." She waved toward the boys still visible to us. "You're playing with precious lives."

I had nothing new to say. I was making the best decisions I could with the data I had. That was all I could do.

"Okay," she said. She forced a smile. "Let's go get some dinner before the rest of them eat it all."

Gusts of wind whipped leaves and branches and sawdust around and onto us constantly. Storm clouds had rolled over us at mid-day, but we'd kept working.

Now, though, the fog of swirling debris was so thick that I was beginning to think we'd have to stop.

Lightning arced somewhere outside the complex. Thunder followed a few seconds later. The sky darkened.

"Rain comes, we stop," Bony said. Though at least half of the boys had abandoned the job since the weather had turned wild, Bony had kept at it, yelling at those who left and never letting anyone near him stop. "Right?"

"We should power down and put away the tools and haulers now," Gustafson said. He was finishing loading some logs a few meters away. "These machines are old enough that we shouldn't trust their waterproofing."

Thunder rumbled again.

I scanned the sky. Clouds like nighttime camo cloth covered us as far in every direction as I could see. "Yeah," I said.

"Bring in all the gear and machines!" Gustafson yelled. "It's time to stop."

The boys cheered. Most of the noise they made vanished in a wave of thunder.

"You don't have much time, Jon," Lobo said over the comm. "If keeping those machines dry matters, you better get them under cover quickly."

"Let's move!" I said. "Send everything into the sheds."

We sent Gustafson's hauler, full load and all, back to its home at its quickest pace. The boys were now used to working with it, so they stepped out of its way before it was within its two-meter sensor range of them. Other haulers rolled after it. Boys and counselors jogged with cutters toward the equipment buildings.

I ran the perimeter of the clearing looking for tools we might have missed, but the clean-up teams had been thorough, and I found nothing.

I turned toward the center of the large area and jogged through it, doing one last check. I couldn't help but smile; the boys and the counselors had done a very good job and become a decent work team in a few short days.

All the people hauling gear came running back to the clearing.

"Anything else?" several of them called.

"Not that I can see," I said. "I think we just—"

I could barely hear my own words as another blast of thunder hit us at the same moment as the clouds pounded us with rain. It fell hard and fast and steady, pushing the airborne debris to the ground and soaking us in seconds. Dust and dirt ran down my arms and face. The rain obscured the features of anyone more than ten meters away.

A boy laughed.

Another joined him.

I spotted Bony and Gustafson off to my right. Bony had turned his face to the sky and was smiling and shaking his head and drinking and laughing.

Gustafson stared at the boy as if he were crazy, but then a smile came over the man's face, too, and he laughed and tilted his head upward. He held his arms out to his sides and let the rain pelt him and laughed and laughed and laughed.

I followed his lead and looked to the heavens. Drops hit my eyes and my mouth. After all the work, it felt so wonderfully good that I couldn't help but smile.

I glanced around. Everywhere counselors and boys

alike stood in the rain and let it wash away the dirt and the twigs and the leaves and the dust. Some laughed; some were silent. Some danced, spinning and jumping as if listening to music; others stood as still as if the water had turned them to stone. Some rolled on the ground and covered themselves in mud; others pointed at them and laughed—and then joined them.

More boys ran into the clearing.

A wave of adults and still more boys followed them.

Bony walked over to me and motioned me to bend closer.

I did.

He blew a mouthful of water into my face and ran away laughing.

I shook my head to clear my eyes and gave chase. In a few seconds, I pulled alongside him, but before I could grab him, he juked to the right. When I tried to make the same maneuver, I slipped and fell. I hit on my left shoulder and rolled and ended up on my back, staring at the sky, soaked and covered in mud.

Bony ran to me. "Are you okay?"

I cupped my hand to my ear.

When he bent closer and opened his mouth to speak, I grabbed his arm and pulled him to the ground.

"Got you!" I said.

He shook his head, rolled onto his back, and laughed.

I joined him. The storm poured on us. All around us, boys and men and women danced and stood and laughed and talked in the pounding rain. For a short time, there was nothing else in the world, no threats or danger or worries, just rain and laughter and a pure and silly happiness that filled me completely and washed away everything that was not right there with us right then.

➤   ➤   ➤

"Any updates?" I said to Lobo when I returned later. I tracked mud and water everywhere I went, Lobo's small cleaning bots following me like pets hoping I'd drop some food.

"Nothing," Lobo said. "Wylak is sticking to the new schedule. All of Maggie's data drops are empty."

"Two more days. That's all we have."

"Yes."

"And if we have to fight?" I said. "How long will we last?"

"I don't know," Lobo said, "but I can tell you this: Between how deeply I've infiltrated their defense systems and how much better armed I am than their first-line ships, even if we lose, we'll do a lot of damage before we fall."

"But we will lose," I said. "It's not an 'if;' it's a when."

"The odds are indeed greatly against us," Lobo said. "There's always a chance they'll back down long enough to buy us more time, maybe enough time to save some of the boys."

I shook my head at the thought of having to pick which boys to take away and which to leave. I didn't have a clue how to make that choice. I didn't know how anyone could.

"Let's hope Jack pulls it off," I said.

"The haulers can't handle this much mud," Gustafson said. The rain had continued throughout the night and had stopped only half an hour earlier. We stood at the edge of the giant flat space and watched as the first full haulers tried with little success to make their way across it. "They've already done better than I'd expected from such cheap gear. If we keep pushing them, though, they're going to burn out their drive trains."

Cut logs lined the left side of the clearing. Branches and twigs and leaves coated the center, each green bit vibrant against the dark, almost black mud.

I studied the rough dirt rectangle we'd created. The borders were far from perfectly smooth, but they definitely looked man-made and as if someone had planned them. We could do better, though.

"Send them back," I said. "We don't need to take down any more trees. We don't even need to move any more of the logs to the back of the complex."

"We're going to leave them there?" Gustafson said. "That's good wood. If we don't stack it, it'll rot."

"No, we're not going to let them sit. We're going to use them."

"For what?" he said.

"To outline the clearing, so it has a nice, straight border."

Gustafson stepped closer to me, studied my face for a few seconds, and said, "Are you feeling okay?"

"I am," I said. "I really am."

"And why are we going to build this border?"

I smiled. "Because it'll be pretty." I closed my eyes for a few seconds and pictured it, opened them, and looked around once more. I nodded to myself. "It'll look very nice indeed."

"And why do we care about how it looks?" he said.

"Nice idea," Lobo said over the comm. "As an old Earth artist once said, 'Beauty is truth, truth beauty.' A very nice touch indeed."

Rather than try to respond to Lobo, I focused on Gustafson and said, "Because beauty is truth."

He shook his head, chuckled, and whispered, "It's your show, Gunny—but you *are* going to explain this to me one day."

I nodded. "If need be," I said, "I certainly will."

He headed off toward a team of boys loading a hauler. "Let's stop with those machines! Gather around, everybody. We're going to do something a little different today."

Heralds of gold and white light were announcing the dawn when I hit the clearing the next morning. The jungle soil had soaked up the rain and dried completely. The lines of logs that separated the trees from the large open space ran straight and true and transformed the area from a bald spot in the forest into a construct that people had intentionally created. I walked the perimeter and occasionally smiled and nodded in satisfaction; we'd done far better than I'd had any right to expect.

"The boys did good work," Gustafson said from the corner ten meters ahead, where he stood watching me.

"Everyone did."

"Mostly them, though," he said.

"Mostly them."

"It gives you hope, doesn't it? If they can work this well together, with no fights, then they can do other things without fighting."

"Yes, it does," I said. "I'm not competent to assess their progress, but they sure seem to me to have come a long way."

Schmidt strolled into view behind Gustafson. "They

have," she said. "They're not done, though; they need more time before we can put them into new homes."

"Let's hope they get it," I said.

"Now that we've congratulated ourselves on completing this project," Gustafson said, "would you mind telling us exactly what we've built and why?"

I smiled. "There's one little problem with that request, Top."

"What's that?" he said.

"We're not done."

He shook his head and chuckled. "I should have known. So now what do we have to do? Rake the dirt? Plant some flowers."

"No," I said, "nothing as pedestrian as that." I clapped him on the back. "We're going to persuade Lim to let us throw a really big party."

CHAPTER 58

In the former rebel complex, planet Tumani

YOU'RE KIDDING ME, right?" Lim said. "You decided my life wasn't stressful enough, so you thought you'd start off my day with a little joke."

"No," I said, "I'm not kidding. I want us to prepare for a party, a huge one, and I need your help to make it happen."

"Exactly what do we have to party about?" Lim said. She stepped from behind her desk and walked so close to me that I could smell the sour residue of sleep on her breath. "You know what's going to happen in a couple of weeks when Wylak shows up. You know we're not ready. We have nothing to celebrate."

"This has gone far enough, Gunny," Gustafson said from behind me. "It's time for you to leave."

I ignored him and focused on Lim. "We have plenty of cause for celebration. You, all of you, have made great progress with the boys. They've spent most of the past week showing they can work together and

411

not fight. Everyone here is on edge, which is another good reason to do something fun."

"You're not going to tell me what this is really about, are you?" she said.

"I am telling you: I want the boys to spend today getting the new field ready for a big party. I need your approval to make it happen."

She stared at me for a long time. "That's it? That's all you're going to say."

I nodded. "I want them to spend today preparing for a party tomorrow. In fact, I want us all doing that. We should thank them for all their work, and they should thank you. I know we have educational supplies and paints and paper and spare fabric; let's put some of that stuff to a fun use. I'm picturing one side of the clearing lined with thank-you signs from the boys, and the other with similar banners from the counselors. You get the cooks to prepare a lot of extra food for lunch tomorrow, and we'll be set."

"Why now?" she said. "Why tomorrow for the party?"

"We finished clearing and bordering the field yesterday," I said, "so that activity is over. I don't want to lose the energy and teamwork we have, so a party seemed like a perfect way to keep it going a little longer. It'll take a day to make all the party preparations, but we can make that day be fun in its own right. That's it."

"Is something else happening today?" she said. "Tomorrow?

I'd known she would ask this question, so I'd rehearsed mentally so many times that the lie came out as smoothly as everything else I'd told her. "Party prep is today. The party is tomorrow—if you allow it. That's it."

"So do I need to put the whole staff on alert for the next two days?" Lim said.

I kept my tone the same as I said, "No." That was the worst thing she could do. Her surprise at Wylak's visit had to be genuine, or he would know something was going on. "No, you do not." I shrugged and said, "Look, if you don't want to do this, say so, and we won't. I don't, though, see any harm in keeping the boys busy for another day or in having a big party."

"Most of them have enjoyed clearing the field," Schmidt said from behind me, "and they've worked really hard at it. It's been decent therapy for them. A party would be a nice way to thank them for all that work."

"Work on taking down perfectly good trees to create a big flat stretch of ground we don't need," Gustafson said.

"All of this is beside the point," Lim said. She pointed at me. "He's misdirecting us every chance he gets. We all know he's planning something, and somehow everything he's doing is tied to it. We also know he's not going to tell us. We've agreed that torturing him to get the answer isn't a viable option—though sometimes I regret that decision." She turned and went back to her desk. "At least this would keep the boys focused on non-destructive tasks."

She sat and faced us. "Moore, we'll give you what you want."

She waved us all to go.

As I stepped through the doorway, she said, "Moore." I turned around.

"I know I keep repeating this," she said, "but I can't tell if you really understand me. You better know what you're doing. These boys are amazing, and unless your mystery plan works, soon Wylak is going to take them away."

"I know," I said. "I do understand."

"Make signs?" Bony said. "You want us to paint signs?"

"Yes," I said. "Thank-you signs. Little ones and big ones, some like giant banners. Lots of them, hundreds of them, one from each of you if we can manage it, maybe even more."

"Hundreds of them?" another boy said. "Why?"

"To thank the counselors for all they've done for you."

Bony faced Gustafson and Schmidt and Long and all the others standing off to the side. "Do you guys want those signs?"

"Not really," Gustafson said. "It's his idea; don't blame us."

"The whole point is to decorate for the party," I said. I stepped back to get a broader view of the growing crowd of boys. "We're going to have a huge party tomorrow, right here in the clearing that you guys created. I thought it would look amazing to tack thank-you signs to all the trees around the perimeter."

Bony shook his head.

A lot of the boys stared at me as if I were insane.

"There's something you're not telling us," Bony said. "What would it cost you to make the signs and put them up? How could it hurt?"

"You want us to spend a whole day on it," another boy said. "That's a lot of time, a lot of work."

"Yeah, but it's a day you wouldn't have to listen to

the grown-ups talk to you, a day without any classes, a day doing easy stuff."

A murmur of agreement swept through a lot of the boys.

"And what will they be doing?" Bony said.

"Making signs to thank you," Schmidt said.

"For what?" a boy off to my left called out.

"No one thing," Schmidt said. "For trying, for working so hard, for everything."

Bony walked up to me. "I'm trusting you, big man," he whispered. He turned and faced all the other boys. "So let's make thank-you signs," he shouted. "It's not like we have anything better to do." He pointed to the adults. "If that's all it takes to get them to give us a party, it's a pretty good deal."

A lot of boys nodded and stepped forward.

After a few seconds, more followed.

Bony walked over to Schmidt. "Show me how to do this," he said.

She smiled and said, "My pleasure."

Counselors spread among the boys.

As Gustafson passed me, he paused and said, "I feel like a damn fool idiot. You know that, right?"

I nodded. "So do I."

He headed to his group.

"They're all trusting you," Lobo said over the comm. "Amazing."

"I'm doing my best," I subvocalized.

"I know," he said. "Before you ask, no, there's no word from Jack and no sign of him or Maggie."

"But there wouldn't be," I said, "not yet, would there?"

"Probably not," Lobo said, "not if he was able to make it all work out."

"So there's still hope," I said.

"Yes."

I glanced at the sky and hoped that Jack had been able to execute our plan, that he and Maggie would show up on time, that I wasn't making these boys spend their last safe day doing something that might never make sense to them, that they wouldn't ever be soldiers again—either for Wylak or with me in a battle against him.

Tomorrow morning, I'd find out if my hopes would come true.

CHAPTER 59

In the former rebel complex, planet Tumani

As EVERYONE ELSE headed to dinner and the sun dropped behind the horizon, I surveyed the clearing for the last time. All around its perimeter, trees hosted signs shouting "Thank you!" in words big and small, on single sheets and multi-page assemblages, in red and black and green and blue and purple and gold and many other colors.

We were done.

Long and a few of the counselors called to me to join them for dinner, but I waved them off. I'd kept myself cheerful in front of everyone for the entire day. I couldn't do it any longer.

I headed to Lobo. I'd eat a little and get as much rest as I could.

One way or another, in the morning I'd need it.

That night, I dreamed.

At first, I was aware I was dreaming, but that awareness faded as the vision grew increasingly vivid and the dreamscape coalesced around me. I stood outside the complex, the morning sun bright and the air still chilled from the night. I was on the road, but this one ran downhill straight to the sea, which tossed and churned as if in the grip of a storm. The sky directly overhead was clear, but dark gray clouds blanketed the ocean. I glanced behind me at the complex, and it now rose in terraces on the side of the mountain at the center of Dump. Gone were the trees of Tumani; in their place jutted sharp outcroppings of polished stone only a shade darker than the sand.

I closed my eyes, confused at what I saw.

When I opened them again, soldiers standing ten abreast filled the road in front of me. Only twenty meters separated us. All of them pointed rifles at me. Hovering on either side of them was a line of shuttles like the one that had brought me to Dump.

I heard movement behind me and checked there again.

To my right, two lines of boys stretched as far up the mountain as I could see. At the heads of the lines, Bony and Nagy pulled rifles and pistols and spears and sticks and knives from open wooden boxes and handed them as fast as they could to the front boys, who passed the weapons up the line. Lim and Schmidt and Gustafson and Long and all the other counselors stood farther to the side, shaking their heads and checking their own weapons.

To my left, Bob and Alex and Han fought with a huge guard, a man wearing an Aggro uniform and standing easily eight feet tall. They struggled to stop him from pointing his rifle at them. Benny, his discarded cart behind him, clung with his front flippers to the guard's left boot and kept biting the man's leg. Jennie held the other leg and tried to stop the man from walking, but he moved with ease, attacking my three friends as if neither she nor Benny were there at all.

"You're done, Moore," a voice said.

When I faced front again, Wylak stood only two meters away. The first rank of soldiers was only a meter behind him. On either side of him stood two more of the giant Aggro guards. They smiled and shook their heads as if laughing at the weak anger of a child.

"You let them down," Wylak said. "They counted on you, they bet everything on you, and you let them down."

"No," I said.

"Oh, yes," Wylak said.

The guards nodded their agreement.

"You always do," he said.

The guards nodded again.

Behind me, Benny screamed, "I'm sorry!"

A shot pierced the day.

I turned in time to see Bob fall.

Alex and Han pushed upward on the rifle, trying to save themselves.

Wylak stepped closer and slapped me. "What made you think one stupid boy could help them? If it weren't for you, we might have been able to let them live, to give them at least a chance at survival as they fought the rebels. Now, though"—he paused and shrugged—"we're going to have to kill them all."

"No," I said. "You don't have to do that. Leave them alone. Leave them all alone."

He slapped me again. "Or what? *You'll* stop us. One scared pathetic boy?"

I glanced at my body and saw my sixteen-year-old self, lean from my time on Dump and lacking the muscle I later gained.

Another shot rang out.

A scream followed it.

I looked over my shoulder and saw Alex go down, blood geysering out of his neck.

"Please," I said. Tears poured down my cheeks. "Please stop. Let them alone."

Wylak laughed. "It's too late for that, Moore. If they'd never involved you, maybe they could have lived, but not now, not what with all that you've done." He put his hand on my neck and pulled me so close I could see the hairs in his nose as he grew a meter taller and towered over me. "This is on you."

I fell to my knees. "No!" I screamed.

"Jon!"

The cry came from behind me. Benny and Han and Jennie were screaming my name. The guard had swatted away Han and was pointing his rifle at Benny.

"Big man!" Bony called.

A line of soldiers marched past me and aimed their weapons at the boys.

Nagy charged them with a spear.

The soldiers opened fire. Even after Nagy fell, they kept shooting. The bullets ripped through his body and drove into the sand.

I stared at Wylak, hoping I could find a way to get him to stop, but he wasn't even looking at me. He stepped to the side and motioned the troops to proceed.

I pounded the sand in front of me with my fists.

"No!" I said.

More shots sounded.

The soldiers marched on.

"No!" I said again. I hit the sand once more, grabbed some with each hand, and rubbed it on my face. I mixed it with my tears and willed my nanomachines to use the sand to make more of themselves. I instructed them to target the guards and the soldiers and Wylak. Small gray clouds formed in front of me, grew rapidly, and spread like whirlwinds sweeping upward from my eyes, upward and outward, racing from me in all directions.

They made contact with the soldiers.

The men swatted and screamed and fired but could do nothing as the nanomachines converted their bodies into more nanomachines and moved on, each person transforming ever more rapidly into a part of the cloud that swept over the land, a mist of charging death darker than the sky over the ocean.

In seconds, the soldiers were gone, but the nano-machine swarm kept moving, consuming everyone and everything in its path. Benny and Jennie vanished. The corpses of my dead friends disappeared, as did Bony and Nagy, Lim and Gustafson. Everyone and everything turned into part of the ever-growing dull gray cloud as the darkness from within me fanned across the island.

When all that remained was the sand and the rocky husk of Dump and the buildings and walls of the complex, the nanoclouds dissolved and fell to the sand like black rain.

"No!" I screamed. "I didn't mean—" I spun around and around, hoping to see someone, anyone, still alive, but everywhere the world was still and dead. "No! I thought I could—"

➤   ➤   ➤

I sat upright in my cot, soaked in sweat, my mouth open in a silent scream, my training too good to let me make a sound, though my neck was so taut with the effort of containment that it ached.

"You better get over whatever you were dreaming," Lobo said, "because it's time. Wylak is on the move and two hours away."

The lights came up.

I swiveled my legs to the floor and gripped the edge of my cot. I willed my heart to beat less frantically and breathed slowly and deeply through my nose.

I wouldn't fight. I knew it now. No matter how much I might posture, the risk to the boys was too great. Lobo and I would probably win for a while, but in the end we'd lose, and the casualties along the way would be enormous.

I also couldn't bear to let them down.

I needed Jack and Maggie.

"We have another problem," Lobo said, "one we hadn't anticipated."

CHAPTER 60

In the former rebel complex, planet Tumani

WHAT?" I SAID. We'd always faced the risk that Jack and Maggie might not be able to execute the plan, but I'd been confident that the plan itself was sound, that as long as there was enough time it would work.

"Wylak has jammed all transmissions. Nothing electronic is getting in or out of here."

"How?"

"Two ships hovering a few klicks off the north and south sides of the complex have thrown an electronic net over us."

If Jack and Maggie were successful, this wouldn't matter, though it would make coordination with them difficult. "What about ground-to-ground comms?"

"They'll work," Lobo said. "All my sensors in the area are still transmitting. The ships threw the blanket on us a little over two hours ago, but they're flying high enough that as long as we don't need to bounce off a sat, we can talk."

"Two hours ago?" I stood. "Why didn't you wake me?"

"To what end?" Lobo said. "So you could lose sleep while we argued pointlessly?"

"You're right," I said. "Sorry. It just means that coordination with Jack will be tougher."

"We'll hear him once he's under five hundred feet and our comm link takes over," Lobo said.

"I assume no word from him prior to the blackout."

"You assume correctly," Lobo said. "You know I would have told you."

I nodded. "I do. I'm just thorough by habit."

"I know," Lobo said. "This isn't our first mission. In the same spirit, let me point out that I could easily shoot down those ships."

"And give away your capabilities and provoke Wylak into stronger actions and almost certainly push us into a fight with him." Images of the dead from the dream lingered vividly in my mind. "No. I know you could, but no."

"As I said, like you, I was simply being thorough."

"So we proceed as planned," I said. "We're functioning with less data, but the situation is the same: we meet with Wylak, hope that Jack and Maggie make it and that they're ready, and if they're not, we surrender the boys or start a war."

"Correct," Lobo said, "but since when has reason stopped you from fretting?"

"When it's go time," I said, "and you know it." I stretched and started getting ready. I wanted to look right when we greeted Wylak.

"Your first morning meeting will be starting early," Lobo said.

"What? Wylak is arriving earlier than he said?"

"Not that meeting," Lobo said. "Wylak wouldn't come at night because it would make his visit appear too aggressive. I'm talking about the meeting you're about to have with Lim. Her team's comms are buzzing. One of her communication monitors noticed the blackout and woke her. She'll be here soon."

"This isn't going to be fun," I said.

"Come in," I said as Lobo slid a side hatch open, "and stop banging on my ship. All you'll do is hurt your hand."

Lim glared at me and stormed inside Lobo.

He closed the hatch behind her, stranding Long and another counselor outside.

"What do you know—" she said.

"—about the communications blackout?" I smiled. "Everything that matters. I think—"

"I don't care what you think!" she said. She stepped closer to me. "Tell me what's going on!"

"What I was about to say is that I think it's time for me to explain a few things."

"If you brief her on the entire situation now," Lobo said privately, "you risk all the same problems as before. There's too much that could still go wrong."

I turned and walked toward the pilot area. As I did, I subvocalized to Lobo, "I know."

Lim followed me without saying anything else. When we reached Lobo's front, she leaned against the near wall, crossed her arms, and said, "I'm waiting."

"Two small Tumani government ships are hovering about five hundred feet above the ground a few klicks away from our north and south perimeters. They're jamming all transmissions in and out of this place."

"How do you have this information?"

Lim already knew more about Lobo's capabilities than I found comfortable, so I said, "Intel sources transmitted it right before the ships cut us off from the world."

She pushed off the wall. "And you decided to keep this to yourself instead of telling us?"

I held up my hands and said, "No. I didn't actually see the data until a few minutes ago. By the time I was ready to go outside, you were already here."

"What else?"

I shrugged. "That's it." *For now*, I thought but did not say.

She was silent for a few seconds. "Tell me if I'm missing something. You got out of bed more than two hours earlier than any of us have ever seen you out and around. Intelligence sources you won't name sent you a warning about a communications blackout, but Lobo chose not to wake you with the news. Is that about right?"

I nodded. "That covers it."

"How stupid does that tale sound to you?" Lim said. "I can't decide whether to be angrier about your lies or about your belief that I'm dumb enough to buy that weak crap."

I smiled despite myself. "Fair enough," I said. "It's not the whole story."

"Obviously." Lim stared at me, waiting for me to continue.

"You know you have to stall her long enough that her team can't make any serious preparations," Lobo said. "Wylak has to believe we're surprised. We have a hundred minutes left, more than enough time for her to ruin that illusion."

I bent my head and subvocalized, "No. He has to know we'd twig to the blackout."

"Well?" Lim said.

"It's still too risky," Lobo said.

I nodded, hoping Lobo would take it as a response to him, and looked at Lim again. "You're right," I said. "We need to talk, but not just us, not here, and not on an empty stomach. Can you call Gustafson and Schmidt to your HQ, have someone bring us some food, and have people you completely trust—maybe Long?—keep the boys away from that place long enough that we can have a truly private conversation?"

Her face tightened. "You don't command me or my staff, Moore. You tell me, and I'll decide what to do with the information."

I shook my head. "This is not a contest. I don't want to command anyone. You said you'd trust me, and you've done so. All I'm doing is asking you to trust me a little longer. That's it."

We stared at each other for a bit.

She shook her head and smiled slightly. "Why do I put up with you?"

I smiled in return. "Because you know I'll do everything in my power to come through for you."

"Breakfast? You want to eat now?"

"Yes," I said, "I do. Please."

She shook her head and headed toward the hatch. I heard it open at her approach and followed her.

As she was about to step outside, she faced me and said, "Be there in fifteen, and after we eat, we talk. One way or another, we *will* talk."

CHAPTER 61

In the former rebel complex, planet Tumani

THE FOOD WAS already on Lim's desk when I arrived. The meal wasn't much—chunks of bread, a hunk of cheese, some cured meat, and a pitcher of water—but I piled a plate and started eating as if it were the best food I'd ever tasted. I chewed each bite slowly, taking my time, letting Wylak draw ever closer, hoping Jack and Maggie were doing the same.

At first, the other three stared at me as if I had been kidding and couldn't have been planning to eat, but after half a dozen slow bites, Gustafson shrugged, filled a plate, and ate a bit of bread. Schmidt followed a few seconds later. Finally, Lim gave in and got her own food.

After a few minutes, I set my plate on Lim's desk. Before she could yell at me, I said, "For Long." I assembled a little of everything and took it outside where Long was leaning against the wall to the right of the doorway.

"We'll be eating for a few minutes," I said, "so you

might as well do the same. Once we start talking, though, I'd appreciate it if you'd keep circling this building and make sure we continue to be alone."

He took the plate, nodded, and said, "You bet. Thanks."

Even eating slowly, I could kill only so much time. The others finished, pushed away their plates, leaned back, and stared at me.

"About seventy-five minutes until Wylak is due," Lobo said over the comm, "though from some movement I'm detecting in the troops down the road, he may be running a bit early."

I closed my eyes for a second and focused on staying calm. If Wylak was early, I'd have to stall until either Jack and Maggie arrived or it was clear they weren't coming. As long as the Senator didn't beat his schedule by too much, I should be fine.

I opened my eyes again, picked up the last piece of cheese from my plate, and ate it.

"Okay," I said, "let me tell you what I know." I turned to the door and said, "Long, time to earn that breakfast."

"Doing it," he said. "I'll yell if I anyone comes close."

As soon as I turned back to her, Lim said, "*All* of what you know?"

I smiled. "You know I've been around, so that would take a lot longer than we have. How about I just go over the parts that matter right now?"

Lim's expression didn't change. She didn't appreciate my humor, but at least she also didn't point out the potential lie in what I'd said. She sat and waited.

"I'll take that as a yes," I said. I took a deep breath and pushed back from the desk; if Lim lunged for me, I wanted room to maneuver. "The short form is this: Wylak is on his way here now."

"What?" Lim said. She rose. "Why? He's not due for five more days."

"He decided to make his move earlier."

"Why bother?" Lim said. "He knows we can't have completed the reintegration training. A few boys are close to ready, but not most of them. It's too soon, and he has to be aware that it is."

I nodded. "Yes, he is, but that's not the point, and you know it. Once he's gone through the motions of meeting with you, he'll have the proof he wants. He'll return to his colleagues, declare this exercise a failure, and demand custody of the boys."

"So he can turn them into soldiers again!" Lim smacked the desk with the flat of her hand, and all of our plates shook. "No, he can't do that."

"Yes, he can," I said, "and he's bringing a lot of the troops that are guarding the road to help make that point."

"How can you be sure about all this?" Lim said.

"The same sources that told me about the blackout before you learned about it."

"How long have you known about Wylak coming early?" Schmidt said. Her voice and expression were completely neutral, but fury showed in her eyes. "How long?"

I focused on her. "That doesn't matter," I said. She started to speak, but I held up my hand to stop her. "If we in any way let on that we were aware he was coming, he'll realize we have an intel source in his team and change his comm protocols. We have to act surprised and do what we can to show him some boys who are ready for reintegration."

"Is there any chance he'll throw us out today?" Gustafson said.

I took a deep breath and nodded. "Yes. He'll have the firepower, and he already has the desire. We have to consider it a possibility."

"So," Lim said, "you've known for some time—it doesn't matter how long, some time—that Wylak was coming and might take the boys, and you didn't think you should tell us." She leaned closer. "Do you realize what you've done?"

"Yes," I said. "I've stopped you from doing anything that might endanger either these boys or the only reliable information sources we have—or both."

"We could have been preparing," Schmidt said.

"To do what?" I said.

To Schmidt's credit, despite how upset she was, she considered the question. After a few seconds, she said, "We could have contacted local media or tried to get at least some of the boys off the planet."

"Lim and I have already been through this," I said, "and I expect she's reviewed the subject with you as well."

"I have," Lim said.

Schmidt banged her fist on the desk. "We could have tried to do something!"

"None of the options available to you would have helped," I said. "Most would have made matters much worse and played right into Wylak's plans."

"Okay," Lim said, "let's grant that we had no viable alternatives. You said you had a plan, and you said you were working on it. Isn't it about time to brief us on that?"

"No," I said. "There is absolutely nothing I could say that would help."

"With all the knowledge you had," Lim said, "why did you have us clear away those trees? Paint those signs and plan a party we'll never be able to hold?" She studied me closely. "Or is all of that part of your plan?"

I didn't look away as I answered. "The boys learned important lessons. Those activities seemed like a good idea at the time. I still hope for a positive outcome."

Schmidt looked like she wanted to shoot me.

Gustafson showed no reaction; he just watched everything.

Lim fought to control her anger. Her eyes widened slightly and she looked up and to her left; some new tactic was coming.

"Or am I giving you too much credit?" she said. "Did you even have a plan, or were you simply trying to keep me calm once you knew the situation was hopeless? Were you able to sacrifice all of the boys that coldly? Do none of them mean anything to you?"

Even though I could tell that she was trying to get to me, I couldn't stop the anger that flooded my body. I ground my teeth and forced myself to take a long, slow breath through my nose before I spoke. "You know me better than that. I appreciate how hard this is for you, but I promise you that continuing to push and attack me is not going to accomplish anything useful."

"What would you have us do?" Gustafson said. His face now looked as tight as mine felt, but his words came out flat.

"Keep trusting me," I said. "Carry on as normally as possible until we meet with Wylak. Lim, act surprised when he calls, but don't act stupid; he's too smart not to notice changes in your behavior. Be indignant about the comm blackout, and ask him what he knows about it." I stood. "In other words, act like we never had this talk, which is what I'd wanted in the first place."

"Where do you think you're going?" Lim said.

"Out. To clear my head and get ready for our meeting on the road outside the complex."

"'Our' meeting?" Lim said. "And on the road? Wylak will want to meet with me, not us, and I assume he'll fly in here as usual."

"You're going to bring me," I said. "He'll wait outside the complex. He'll have troops behind him, lots of them. He'll know what he's started. You've demonstrated enough anger in front of him that he won't want to take the chance that you'll try to hold him hostage, so he'll stay where he feels he's completely safe." I headed for the door.

Long appeared in the doorway and blocked my path.

"And if instead I have Long lock you up and meet with Wylak myself?" Lim said.

I stepped to the side so I was more than a meter from Long and had clear views of all of them.

"Say the word," Lobo said, "and I will blow the top off that shack and trank them all."

Gustafson stood and stepped closer to Long.

I glanced at the floor and subvocalized, "Get ready."

Long angled his body toward me.

I made eye contact with each of them, Lim last. I stared directly at her. "If you *try* to do that," I said, "then you'll have started something you cannot hope to finish, and I'll end up meeting with Wylak on my own. That is not my preference, but I will do whatever I can to save those boys. Letting you detain me and deal with Wylak on your own will hurt them, not help them."

"Hovering," Lobo said.

"Your call," I said to Lim. "What'll it be?"

CHAPTER 62

In the former rebel complex, planet Tumani

YOU'RE NOT THAT good," Long said.

"Son," Gustafson said, his eyes never leaving me, "you'd do well not to speak when you don't know what you're talking about."

"There are four of us," Long said. "If by some miracle he takes us all, dozens of reinforcements are one call away."

Lim shook her head slowly and faced Long. "Stand down, Chris. He doesn't need to do more than survive the couple of minutes it would take for his ship to reach us."

"Less than thirty seconds," Lobo said over my comm. "Would you like me to show them?"

"No," I subvocalized.

Long didn't like Lim's order, but he stayed put.

After a few seconds, she nodded and focused again on me. "You were right a while back," she said, "when you realized that I'd brought you along in case things went nonlinear. They have. You say you still have hope,

435

so I'm going to continue to trust you." She glanced briefly at Long. "We're *all* going to trust you. So, I'll do as you instructed when Wylak calls, and I'll bring you to the meeting."

"Thank you," I said. "Now, I need to get ready."

She tilted her head. Long stepped clear of the doorway.

"Just one more thing, Moore," Lim said.

"Yes?"

"If this ends badly and I find out you were lying, that you never had a real shot at saving these kids, then I'll get my own ships, a lot of them if I have to, more than yours can handle, and I'll find you. You understand?"

"Yeah," I said. "I'd do the same in your shoes, but it won't come to that."

I walked out the door. When I was ten meters away, I said to Lobo, "Tell me you have news from Jack and Maggie."

"Not yet," Lobo said, "but as I warned, with this blackout we won't know until either they're very close or the time passes and they don't show."

"Great," I said. "Just wonderful." I glanced backward. No one was anywhere near me. I picked up my pace. "I'm on my way in. Brief me on everything you have on Wylak's movements and the soldiers' activities." Lim had yielded mighty quickly. She was probably telling the truth, but she might have been playing me in some way I hadn't yet figured out. Being cautious at this stage of any operation was only prudent. "Monitor everything Lim and her people say. If anything starts to go off track, I want to know about it immediately."

"Already doing it," Lobo said. "As for Wylak, from

what I can pick up of the chatter of the nearby soldiers, he'll reach them about half an hour before the meeting, do a quick review of the goals with the leaders, and ceremoniously lead them up the road to us."

"Making a show of it suggests that he brought others; he wouldn't bother with the performance if the only observers were the soldiers. Can you tell if he did?"

"Yes. I haven't been able to hack into his ship, because it's not one he used before, but I had tapped into the systems at the government transport station where his staff filed his travel plans. According to the records I received from it before the blackout, he's traveling with three other senators, a general, a couple of media handlers, and two holo recording teams."

"So all the logs will appear clean and above board," I said, "especially after his people edit the recordings."

"Update: He contacted Lim and told her he'd arrive in less than an hour."

"How she'd do?"

"As well as the extremely brief call permitted," Lobo said. "She protested about the early visit and the blackout. He claimed both were for the safety of the boys. Before she could say anything else, he cut her off."

"Excellent," I said. "Short is good."

"Lim wants to talk to you."

I nodded.

Her voice filled the front of Lobo. "Wylak will be here within the hour," she said. "He just called. Before you ask, I played it right—not that I had much of a choice, because he disconnected almost immediately."

"Thank you," I said.

"So what now?" she said.

"Make it as much a normal morning as possible, but post a team you trust—preferably including Gustafson and Schmidt—on the exit to the road. I'll meet you there when Wylak is five minutes out."

"He'll want to come inside."

"I know, and we'll probably have to let him, but we'll start out stalling."

"How long do you expect to be able to do that?"

"Nothing from Jack and Maggie," Lobo said privately.

"I'm not sure," I said to Lim. "I figure we'll do our best."

"Lovely," Lim said. "Out."

Jack, I thought, *I sure hope you make it.*

CHAPTER 63

On the road outside the former rebel complex, planet Tumani

I'D BEEN CONCERNED that Wylak might bring only a few soldiers, try to play it conservative lest his force look overpowering.

I needn't have worried.

Lim and I watched from a meter outside the doorway to the road as row after row of soldiers marched toward us. Wylak and his entourage rode in an open hoversled in front of the troops, moving so slowly that the marching men and women had no trouble keeping up.

"Why so many?" Lim asked.

"It allows him to send three messages at once," I said. "First, to the Tumani citizens who will watch the holos, he is showing that the nation's army is strong enough to be able to spare forces even as the war with the rebels rages. Second, he's making the points that the sixty of us are nowhere near enough to handle five hundred boys, that he understands this fact, and that, unlike us, he is able to staff appropriately. And third, of course, he's showing us that fighting him would end badly."

"None of them are heavily armored," Lobo said over the comm, "and none of them are carrying any surface-to-air weapons. As long as you let me kill them, it doesn't need to end at all badly for us. I could shoot them all in minutes; the mines will take care of any that try to get away."

"I don't plan to let it get to that," I subvocalized.

One of the holo teams in Wylak's transport turned to face us, no doubt recording our every move. Their directional mics would be able to capture our words when the hoversled shut down, but for now they couldn't hear us.

I raised my hand as if covering a cough and said, "They're capturing video of us, though the hoversled's noise will stop them from hearing us. From here on, cover your mouth or look down if you need to speak to me. Otherwise, do exactly as I say."

Lim scanned the area as much as she could without moving her head. She looked down as she spoke. "They're in front of us. Our staff and the boys are behind us. Nothing is different. This is your plan?"

"Wait for it," I said.

"Before you can ask," Lobo said, "nothing yet from Jack and Maggie, but with the blackout that doesn't mean anything. I'll tell you the moment I hear from them."

"Yes, this is my plan," I said, also staring at the ground. "Trust me." I tried to sound a lot more confident than I felt. Maybe Maggie and Lobo had been right that I was foolish to trust Jack. Maybe he'd given her the slip already. Maybe he'd tried and failed. Or maybe her people had refused to fund this very expensive endeavor, in which case he would have vanished quickly.

I shook my head. I was destroying my calm uselessly. Either Jack would show up, or we'd lose the boys. I'd already resolved not to fight Wylak, but to maintain that resolve I had to stay focused and centered, not let him provoke me into doing something stupid.

Or if he did, I had to send in Lobo with everything firing and be prepared for all-out war.

No. I recalled the dream. I would not do that. I'd been over and over this issue. There was no way to fight Wylak's forces without starting a series of battles that would inevitably end with a lot of boys dying.

Lim stared at me for a moment before returning her gaze to the road. "I'd be a whole lot happier right now if you had a more substantial plan, say an armada to wipe out these fools and take the boys off planet."

"So you want our last act with the boys to be the killing of hundreds of Tumani soldiers?"

"No, but it'd be better than watching helplessly as Wylak turns them into jungle fighters again."

"Would it?" I said. "You think I haven't considered this option? What if we fight? Maybe we'll win at first, but they'll send more troops. We can't leave the planet with the boys without bucking the jump station authorities. If we do that, we'll be starting a war with both the Expansion Coalition and the Frontier Coalition. No, we can't fight them."

"So what do you think we should do?"

"Trust me," I said. "That's all the answer I have." *And I have that much only if Jack and Maggie show.*

I had to stop thinking about what could go wrong,

stop worrying about whether others would deliver, and instead concentrate on executing my part of the plan.

I looked again at the people in front of us.

Wylak's transport closed to thirty meters away, settled to the ground, and turned off.

The troops halted. A couple of seconds later, they snapped to parade rest.

Wylak addressed the party in his hoversled as one holo team took footage of the soldiers and the surroundings and the other documented the conversations of the senators and the generals.

I glanced over my shoulder. Gustafson and Schmidt were leaning halfway out the door, watching with blank expressions. I smiled at them and faced front again. The smile felt more like a grimace, but I had to work at it; I needed to do a lot of smiling.

"Walk with me," I said to Lim.

She shook her head slightly but followed my lead as we stepped ten meters forward and stopped.

"Why are we waiting?" she said, her hand covering her mouth. "Let's get this over with."

"Wave," I said through clenched teeth. I smiled and waved at Wylak and his party. Lim joined me a second later.

One of the holo team members noticed us and tapped Wylak on the shoulder. Others on her team recorded us.

Wylak turned and tilted his head in question.

"Welcome, Senator," I said in a very loud voice. "It's so great to see you again. Thank you for coming."

Lim glanced at me as if I were insane.

I coughed into my hand and said, "Do as I do. Look happy no matter what."

The smile she forced wouldn't have convinced anyone who knew her, but none of these people did, so maybe it would pass muster with them. "Senator Wylak," she said, "we're so pleased to see you again."

Anger replaced confusion on Wylak's face. He knew something was up, and though he had no idea what it was, he didn't like it. He turned to his party, spoke a few words, and motioned them to stay. One of the holo team argued, but Wylak cut her off. All six of the holo crew sat, their frustration and annoyance clear in their expressions.

Wylak walked slowly toward us, his movements doing a good job of showing a confidence and clarity of focus that his angry face belied.

"Still no word," Lobo said, "but we're five minutes early."

Wylak stopped less than a meter away.

"Lim," he said. "I must confess that your reaction rather surprises me."

"Why shouldn't we be pleased to see you, sir?" I said. "We share a common goal: to provide the best possible future for these boys." My face hurt from maintaining the forced smile, but I didn't let the expression waver.

He glanced at me but remained focused on Lim. "What are your thoughts?" he said to her.

Her neck and face were tight with tension, but her words came out calm. "They echo my aide's, of course." After a second, she added, "You may assume that whatever he says comes from both of us."

Wylak scowled at the implication that he would have to deal with me, but he composed himself quickly.

"No!"

The cry came from behind us. I turned in time to see Bony dart through a gap between Gustafson and Schmidt. Schmidt screamed again, "Get back here!"

I heard the soldiers moving but didn't turn around to check on them.

Gustafson lunged after the boy and caught him when he was still five meters away.

Bony held up his empty hands, the lesson from Nagy not lost on him.

"More proof you can't control these boys," Wylak said.

"I said I'd stand with you," Bony said, staring right at me. "I keep my promises."

Gustafson dragged the boy back toward the complex.

I didn't like putting Bony at risk, but now that he'd done that on his own, I saw a potential advantage in it. "Hold up!" I said. "Let him come here."

Gustafson didn't release Bony until Lim nodded her agreement.

As Bony ran to me, I said to Wylak, "Given that the future of the boys is what we're discussing, I'm sure you won't mind one of them taking part in our talks. Think of him as their representative."

Bony stood to my left. He put his right hand on me, as if leaning.

"This is most irregular and inappropriate," Wylak said. "I don't know what game you're playing, but I'm getting rather tired of it. It also certainly cannot help this young man's progress to have to participate in such adult discussions."

"Don't talk about me like I'm not here," Bony said. "I hear you."

I patted Bony on the back, glanced down, and shook my head.

"No game at all, Senator," I said as I faced him again. "We're here to meet you, as you requested."

He clenched his fists and tilted his head slightly. I don't know whether my story or my treatment of his orders as a request annoyed him more, but he was no longer trying to hide his anger.

He faced Lim again, as if by ignoring me he could make me disappear. "Are you ready for the inspection?" he said.

"No," I said. "More to the point, we see no need for any inspection. You know we haven't had enough time to complete our work. There's really nothing to see that you haven't already seen, so we should skip the formality entirely and save all of us some time."

He raised his hand as if he was going to hit me.

I shook my head and pointed at his hoversled.

He forced a smile, turned, and waved to the people waiting there. When he faced us again, his eyes were wide and his words clipped. "Do you see those soldiers behind me?"

"They're pretty hard to miss," I said.

"More than I've ever seen all at one time," Bony said.

Lim chuckled and said, "Of course, Senator."

He opened his mouth and leaned forward as if he was going to scream, but he didn't. He tilted his head slightly, blinked, and stopped. He settled back, crossed his arms, and nodded as if we'd all just agreed on a key point. "I don't understand your behavior," he said, "nor what you think it's going to accomplish. Other than wasting a few minutes and making me momentarily angry, however, I can assure you it will have no effect on what happens. So let's get to it, shall we?" He raised his right hand and ticked off points on his fingers. "I represent the government of Tumani. You are holding captive some young Tumani citizens. We authorized your work with them after trusting your promise that you would produce satisfactory results on a timetable acceptable to us. You have not delivered what you promised."

Lim stepped so close to him that their chests were almost touching. "That's a lie, and you know it."

He didn't move. Instead, he smiled and said, "It's not my fault that you cannot remember your commitments and are incompetent to fulfill them."

Before Lim could react, I put my hand on her left shoulder, squeezed hard enough that she wheeled on me, and hugged her as she turned. As I pulled her to me, I whispered, "Stop reacting. It's what he wants. Do as I do." I let her go and said to Wylak, "My apologies for our behavior. We're overcome with happiness and gratitude for all you've done." I leaned around him and yelled to the people on the hoversled, "Thank you all so much!"

"Are you crazy, Big Man?" Bony said.

Wylak smiled—a real, genuine smile—and said, "I was about to ask the same thing."

Lim glared at me.

"As I'm sure my colleague will agree," I said, "we have a great deal to thank you for."

Wylak stared at me for several seconds. "You want to ditch the boys? If so, perhaps I've misjudged the situation and our interests coincide more than I'd expected."

"Not at all, sir," I said, "not at all."

"What then?" he said.

"Maggie's made contact," Lobo said over the comm.

"She told me to tell you that Jack said, 'It will be quite something.' She and Jack are less than two minutes out. We'll hear them in ninety seconds."

I didn't have to force the smile this time; when I felt the huge grin coming, I went with it. I shook my head and chuckled.

All three of them looked at me as if I'd lost my mind.

"I'll need to explain quickly," I said, "so that we're all on the same page."

"What are you talking about?" Lim said.

Bony shook his head.

Wylak said, "Should you be foolish enough to consider some type of attack on me personally, you should know that I'm armed and quite confident I can take care of myself for the few seconds until my troops overrun you."

"Hurting you is the farthest thing from my mind, Senator," I said. "No, I don't want to harm you." I thought I heard a faint rumbling to my left, but I couldn't be positive. "No, sir, what I intend to do is honor you."

"What?" Lim said.

"Excuse me?" Wylak said.

Now I was sure: They were indeed approaching from my left. I turned forty-five degrees in that direction, stepped back a bit, and leaned out as if wanting a better view of the people on the hoversled.

"Explain yourself now," Wylak said, "or I will have my men remove you and proceed with the inspection."

"It's show time," Lobo said.

CHAPTER 64

On the road outside the former rebel complex, planet Tumani

THE RUMBLING ROSE into a roar. For a moment, everyone scanned the ground to my left. Almost as one, Wylak and Lim and Bony and the generals and the soldiers turned their gazes to the sky. Many of the troops pointed their weapons upward.

"Tell Jack to dampen the noise and announce himself," I subvocalized to Lobo, "or he'll get shot."

"Done," Lobo said.

Wylak glared at me. Sweat beaded on his temples. "If you think the presence of this boy will stop me from using my soldiers," he said, "or if what I hear is the beginning of an attack you think will buy you time, you have gravely misjudged your situation. I can assure you that I'm willing to use force." He clenched his fists. "If we end up in a battle, I will personally kill you first."

My body tensed involuntarily at the threat, but I didn't let myself move. Instead, I held up my hands.

"I promise you, Senator, that no one will attack you or anyone else today. As I said, I'm here to honor you."

"Ten seconds," Lobo said.

The rumbling stayed low. In the distance, lights danced crazily in the sky as the morning sun reflected off the oncoming metal.

"Senator," I said, "You and Lim should shake hands to seal the deal."

"What deal?" he said. "Are you agreeing to the inspection?"

A ship half the size of Lobo hurtled toward us, slowed abruptly, swung about, and settled to the ground twenty meters to our left. A commercial transport, it showed no signs of weapons. A hatch opened in its side. A giant holo of Wylak, Lim, Bony, and me popped into the air above it.

Half a dozen other ships zipped into view and swung about similarly, but they remained hovering. Logos I didn't recognize played on their sides as more hatches opened. A few people stuck their heads out of two of them.

The front ranks of the soldiers circled the hoversled and aimed their weapons at the ships.

"The deal in which you arranged to save these boys," I said. "Tell the soldiers to put down their weapons; you don't want an accidental shooting to mar your shining moment."

"What?" he said. "You're not making any sense."

I ignored him and said, "Lim!" I nodded toward Wylak.

She scowled at me but grabbed his hand and pumped it.

"Hug him," I said to Bony.

The boy shook his head but obeyed. He threw his arms as far around the large man's waist as he could reach.

Wylak started to push them away but stared again at all the ships and let his arms hang at his sides.

Jack appeared in the open hatch of the landed ship. A three-person holo team crowded around him. Multiple recorders captured him and everything in front of him. "Sorry I'm late, Senator!" he said. He leaned back for a second, said, "Bring in the others!" and faced us again. "Senator, Ms. Lim, young man: Hold that pose for a few more seconds, please."

"Let go of me," Wylak said quietly, his lips barely moving.

I turned my back to Jack and said, "You don't want them to do that, Senator."

Jack and the holo team stepped out of his ship. The other vessels jockeyed for landing areas as they settled to the ground in the cleared area behind him.

"Just a minute, folks!" Jack said. His amplified voice filled the air as he smiled and waved at all the ships.

He ran to us, clapped Wylak on the back, and leaned in so only we could hear him. "Go with it, Senator, and you'll end up a hero. Fight it, and you'll only look bad—and I'll still keep praising you. It's what you hired me to do."

Wylak opened his mouth to speak, but Jack turned and walked away from us. Jack positioned himself three meters in front of Wylak. He motioned two of his recording team to his left, where there was more free space, and one to his right.

Hatches in the other ships opened. Men and women streamed out of them and ran toward us. Logo-based credentials scrolled and blinked and flashed and danced on activefiber shirts and hats. Several people wore old-fashioned badges and carried faux notepads with pens I doubted they had any clue how to use. I recognized the logos of three major newstainment megacorps that served the Expansion Coalition and two that worked the Frontier Coalition planets. Both fed off-planet news to many Tumani outlets, so the story should hit the local media before Wylak or any of his people could try to spin it; Jack had done an excellent job. Other familiar logos included those of several green activist groups no doubt seeking the "save the planet" angle to the story, a couple of EC financial management firms figuring that every new foundation brought with it a new money-management opportunity, and three different religious conglomerates that actually might be trying to help. Woven through the crowd like dull support threads in a light-emitting jacket were at least half a dozen men and women with unfamiliar logos that all featured children in various poses of distress; either Jack had tapped into a set of related cause-groups that were new to me, or they were shills he'd paid to bulk out the crowd and get us more off-planet media coverage. Either would work for me. A tall thin woman with brown hair that fell in a straight line to her waist sported a rotating holo badge with "Pets 4 Life" wrapped over a small globe across which cats and dogs and ducks and creatures I didn't recognize ran rapidly. She had a pair of Basset Hounds on a bifurcated leash; each dog wore brown leather goggles with large black BassetCam trademark symbols.

I had to give Jack credit: He'd delivered the size

crowd we'd needed, and as best I could tell, he'd done it without ever alerting the Tumani media. I hoped that Wylak wasn't studying the individual reporters and newstainment personalities as closely as I was. I checked him: He was whispering and glancing back at his hoversled.

Standing next to the Basset woman was a tall woman who looked like Maggie but with short, black hair. She made eye contact with me, tilted her head toward the hounds, rolled her eyes, winked, and faded backward until I couldn't see her face again. It was definitely Maggie.

"The Senator's willing to have me answer a few questions right now," Jack said to the people in front of him, "but only a few before we move inside."

When the first people had closed to within two meters of him, Jack held up his hands and said, "Please, give us some room. After all, we don't want to force the Senator to have all these soldiers protect him from us." He smiled. All the shills laughed on cue. Others in the crowd chuckled a moment later.

At least two dozen people signaled they had questions, but one voice rang out. "Senator, why so many soldiers?" It was Maggie; I could no longer see her in the crowd, but it was definitely her voice.

Holo crews leaned closer and held recorders above their heads.

Jack nodded, his expression thoughtful. "That's an excellent question," he said, the ship amplifying his voice so everyone in the area could hear it. "Senator Wylak could have sent the transport craft on their own"—Jack paused and pointed above and behind the other ships, where two huge vessels floated toward us—"but they would have been at risk of attack from the rebels, who have recently been quite active in this area. By bringing all these troops, he insured the safety of those ships and, more importantly, of the boys who are and were his primary concern." He smiled broadly. "Next?"

"Why the comm blackout over the area?" a woman on the far left asked.

Jack faced her. "Though I was obviously able to persuade the Senator to let us see the evacuation of the boys, he wisely insisted that we keep the news under wraps until the last minute, so that the rebels could not learn of the move. That's also why no Tumani media outlets are here; the rebels have contacts everywhere."

A man's voice I didn't recognize said, "Why won't Senator Wylak answer us himself?"

"He will," Jack said, "but as you can probably tell from my earlier comment and from the look on his face, the Senator didn't call this conference. He didn't want it at all. Isn't that right, Senator?" Jack glanced at Wylak, who glowered for a moment, forced a smile, and nodded. "No, I was the one who insisted on it. When his foundation, ChildSave, hired me to document the sad story of these boys, I agreed on the condition that we publicize its great work so that others could learn from it and, we all hope, one day emulate it. What the Senator and his team are doing here is simply too important to stay private. That said, when we move inside, the Senator will answer your questions personally."

"Then let's go!" another voice said.

"We certainly will," Jack said, "but I wanted us to begin here so you would all have a full appreciation of the obstacles this project faced. Look around." Jack spun slowly, his arms out, his face concerned and a bit sad. "This compound sits in the middle of a huge clearing teeming with mines, each of them a danger to current and future generations. Only in these small, cleaned areas are we safe. In the forest beyond this clearing, armed rebels prowl—the same rebels who forced these hundreds of young men to become soldiers. Tumani is not a rich planet. With the drain of the war on its citizens, its government, and its economic resources, the massive investment necessary to retrain and reintegrate these children would have been a huge burden." He shook his head for a moment. His eyes filled with tears.

I found myself feeling the sadness. I'd forgotten how good he was. His posture was relaxed, his expression adapting to the questions. It was a natural role for him; the line between con man and media spokesperson was very thin indeed.

"That's why Senator Wylak took it upon himself to create ChildSave using both his own funds and additional money he helped raise. ChildSafe recruited Ms. Lim and her team of noble volunteers. Together, they orchestrated the rescue and initial retraining of the boys. They had hoped to complete the process here, but with the current high rebel threat level and with the safety of these children always his primary concern, the Senator made the tough call that they should finish on another planet."

Wylak stared at the ground, shook his head, and chuckled.

"Will the back story hold?" I subvocalized to Lobo.

"As they were settling," he said, "Jack and Maggie

sent me a long comm with the enhancements Jack's made while we were apart. I've altered the records accordingly and will upload them the moment Wylak lifts the comm blackout. It should hold long enough."

Time to find out if Wylak was ready to play.

I bumped Lim's shoulder, pointed to Wylak's hand, and with my right palm made a small lifting motion.

After a second, she nodded, smiled, and lifted Wylak's hand into the air.

"Let's hear it for the Senator!" I yelled.

Jack applauded. Several of the reporters joined him immediately. The others began clapping as well.

Wylak shot me a sideways dirty look before he faced the crowd. He nodded shyly, as if embarrassed. As the cheers continued, he let a smile blossom on his face and waved his thanks.

Jack and I hadn't had time to work out comm protocols, so I had no easy way to tell him about the signs inside. He should recognize that they could help solidify the story and distract the newstainment crowd, but I didn't want to take any chances. "If you can communicate with Jack and Maggie," I subvocalized to Lobo, "tell them about the clearing for the transport ships and the thank-you signs. Also, get the first transport on the ground in the complex."

"I already did the background work," Lobo said. "Of course. Note Jack's mention of going inside. Communicating with the transports, Jack, and Maggie now."

Jack studied Wylak for a moment, walked to the Senator, put his arm around the man's shoulders, and led him forward to face the crowd.

I leaned closer to Lim. "Those two large transports will take you and the boys off Tumani. One will land now. Head inside and start loading the boys and your staff. We won't be coming back."

"What about their possessions?" she said. "And, they're not ready. You know that."

"Take what they can carry," I said. "Leave the rest. To make this work, we have to move now."

"Who's paying and—" she said.

I cut her off. "We don't have time for this. You need to get the boys out of here. I'll fill you in later. Okay?"

She didn't like my answer, but she nodded and headed into the complex.

"Go with her," I said to Bony.

"I stand with you," the boy said.

"I'll find you later," I said. "You have to go. Please."

He nodded, turned, and ran after Lim.

I focused again on Jack and Wylak.

"...you can see, Senator Wylak is a bit bashful about all that he's done here," Jack said, "because like any true public servant, he knows that the greatest reward of service is the chance to continue to serve."

Wylak nodded thoughtfully.

"Still, before he answers your questions, he needs a few minutes to set up." Jack used his hand to turn Wylak toward me. I stepped forward, touched the man's elbow, and pointed to the complex.

"Come with me, please, Senator," I whispered. "Wave, and smile."

He did.

We headed off.

"Plus, the staff on the big ships behind you"—Jack said, pausing to let the crowd take some footage of the two transports, one hovering in the distance, the other already over the complex—"need time to help the adults on the ground load the boys. That process will go fastest without our interference."

The newstainment crowd moaned as one.

"No way we're not capturing that!" a voice said. One of the shills was talking, but all around him the others nodded their heads in agreement. "A bunch of poor boy soldiers on their way to salvation; come on, that's—"

Jack finished his sentence, saving the guy. "—a process that can provide vital information to other organizations. I completely agree. Still, as I'm sure you appreciate, none of us wants to be in the way or stand and watch such a long process, so I thought we'd take a few more questions out here, and when the Senator is ready and the loading is well along, we'll move inside, where he'll personally answer anything you want to ask."

As Wylak and I reached the open doorway to the complex, Jack said, "Now, who's next?"

CHAPTER 65

In the former rebel complex, planet Tumani

THE FIRST TRANSPORT was settling to the ground as we passed through the doorway. Though I couldn't see all of the area we'd cleared, it looked like the ship would occupy two-thirds of it. That was okay; we'd still have room for Wylak's part of the Q&A. We turned right at the far edge of the nearest dorm and walked toward the clearing.

As soon as we were out of sight of the people outside, Wylak pivoted away from me, shoved me into the side of the building with his left hand, and in one smooth motion pulled a pistol from under his coat and pressed it against my chest. His strength wasn't surprising, but his speed was.

"You move," he said, "and I'll shoot."

I stayed still. Though theoretically my nanomachines would repair even a hole in my heart, I'd never tested that theory. I didn't want to start now.

"What's your game?" he said. He changed his angle slightly so the path from the outside to our position was visible to my left, over my shoulder; that way, he didn't have to look away from me to watch for visitors. His left hand maintained a tight grip on my shoulder.

Talking was preferable to fighting and possibly hurting the man I'd turned into the celebrity of the hour. There was also always the chance that I might lose, which would be worse, so I answered him. "Exactly what it looks like. You become the hero who saved the child soldiers of Tumani. The kids leave the planet and ultimately get new homes."

"What's in it for you?"

"Helping the boys. That's it."

"How much of my money did you steal to fund this so-called Foundation?"

"None," I said, "and it's very much a real foundation. The financial history will stand up for more than long enough for all those newstainment groups to lose interest."

He tilted his head and stared intently at me as if I were something bumpy and troubling he'd found growing on his arm. "You expect me to believe that you arranged and paid for all of this to save a bunch of boys you don't know on a planet where you're not even a citizen?"

"I don't care what you believe," I said, maintaining eye contact with him, "but that's the truth." No way was I giving up Maggie or her group's involvement.

"And the smooth talker out there?"

"Jack," I said. "He's a documentarian and PR agent I hired." I smiled and added, "I told him I worked for you, so he believes you engaged him."

"I've been recording this conversation and will feed it to Jack when he heads inside," Lobo said.

"Speaking of which," I said, "I've contracted him and paid him only through the end of the day. If you want to keep him longer for the media follow-on pieces, you'll need to negotiate a new contract."

Wylak smiled and shook his head. "Amazing. I suppose that's when you and he blackmail me."

I didn't shake my head. I didn't want to give him any excuse to shoot or, worse, cause him to do it accidentally. "No," I said. "He's expensive, so you might have sticker shock, but I won't know about it or have any further contact with you. I'm leaving Tumani right behind these boys."

"What about Lim?" Wylak said. "What was her role in this plan?"

"She didn't have one. I didn't tell her. You saw the way she behaved; did she look to you like she knew what was going on?"

He considered the question. "No, but that doesn't mean a thing. Why would you keep your plans from her?"

"Precisely because of the way she behaves. You saw how quickly she lost her composure when you prodded her on your shuttle. I couldn't trust her to sell the story, and I also couldn't trust her team to keep it quiet."

"So you did all this on your own?" he said. "Exactly who are you?"

"No one who will ever matter to you again," I said.

"But you're mine right now," he said, "and you have caused me a great deal of trouble." Most of what I'd told him was true, and none of it had to be bad for him, but that didn't mean he had to like my answers. He clearly didn't. All they'd done was make him angrier. His hand shook slightly with the rage he was barely controlling. "I could shoot you," he continued, "and claim you attacked me. No one would question me."

"But then all those people would make my murder the story of the hour," I said, "instead of telling the tale of the heroic Senator who almost singlehandedly gave hundreds of boys new lives. The first headline can't help you, and it might hurt you. The second can make you the hero of Tumani and raise your profile in both of the coalitions that will eventually want your planet to join them."

Though Wylak's hand still trembled, his words came out calm. "You make a good case."

"Problem!" Lobo said. "Bony running toward you."

I must have glanced left, because Wylak also looked that way in time to see Bony dart around the corner, spot us, and stop a couple of meters away.

The boy stood as tall as he could, balled his fists, and said to Wylak, "You hurt him, and I will kill you."

Wylak chuckled.

"Go get ready to leave, Bony," I said. I tried to make my voice sound as normal as possible. "This isn't a problem. I'm fine."

He shook his head. "Let Jon go." He took two steps forward, so he was little more than a meter from us. "You think I don't remember killing your soldiers, government man? Many died screaming under my knife."

For a moment, I couldn't feel the gun on my chest or the hand gripping my shoulder, the morning sun's heat or the slight breeze. My world reduced to Bony, once again having to fight, despite everything Lim and her people had done, despite the plan working, within an hour of heading to a new, safe life. I'd failed him.

In an instant, he'd gone back to the jungle, back to the darkness inside him.

Wylak brought the gun up and into my chin, smacking me hard enough that for a few seconds I couldn't see straight.

When my vision cleared, his left hand was pressing the weapon into me and his right was around Bony's neck, choking the boy enough that he had stopped resisting.

"Jack and all the others are heading inside," Lobo said. "They'll be on you soon. I'm coming to get you."

From behind us the sound of a lot of people moving and talking grew closer.

My heart raced and my breathing sped up. I wouldn't let Wylak do this. Not to this boy. Not now. "Put the gun away," I said through gritted teeth, "and prepare to answer questions. Enjoy your fame." Without looking away from him, I raised my right hand and put it on the barrel of the gun. This time, my hand was the one that shook. "Or shoot me."

I pulled the gun into my chest.

Tears ran down Bony's cheeks.

"If you hurt that boy," I said, "you will die. If you kill me, the men in my ship—the one in the air behind you—will kill you before my body hits the ground."

"You're lying about the ship," Wylak said. "I can shoot you, choke the boy, put the gun in his hand, and use this sad case as an example of why it's best these killers leave our planet and seek help elsewhere."

"No, I'm not," I said. "Let us go, and you can be the star of the morning. We'll leave, and you'll never see us again. Hurt either of us, though, and you *will* die. I promise you."

Behind him and to the right, far into the middle of the compound, Lobo hovered above the huts. "I can take him out now," Lobo said, "though it's likely a round will go through him and into you, so I don't recommend it. Moving to a better angle."

I shook my head and hoped Lobo would understand I was responding to him. To save the boys, I needed Wylak alive. I couldn't afford a government investigation into his death, because the first step in that process would be to keep everyone here. I leaned hard into the gun, hoping to distract Wylak from Bony.

"They're almost here," I said. "Decide."

CHAPTER 66

In the former rebel complex, planet Tumani

THE SOUND OF the crowd drew close enough that we could make out individual words. I didn't look away from Wylak, but I was aware of Lobo's motion behind him.

"I have the shot," Lobo said.

Wylak glanced to his right, toward the oncoming newspeople. He released his grip on Bony, nodded once, backed up two steps, and tucked his gun under his coat. He kept his weight distributed well and brought up his hands, ready for a fight just in case I'd been lying.

Bony grabbed my arm and held on. He faced the barracks, embarrassed of the tears I'd glimpsed.

"Nod if I should return to ground," Lobo said, "assuming you still don't want me to kill him."

I nodded very slightly and quickly.

"Fine," Lobo said, "but I'm keeping him in my sights until you're clear."

"We're not done," Wylak said, "and I still don't

believe you. No one goes to this much expense and effort without getting anything for it."

"Yes, we are," I said. I pulled Bony closer. "And I get a very great deal from it."

Jack rounded the corner. "Ah, Senator!" he said. "How very nice of you to wait for us. Shall we show these good people the charming signs the boys made for you?"

Wylak smiled and said, "Definitely, Jack. Please take the lead so I can greet some of these fine folks." He waded into the group, shaking hands and saying hellos.

Jack glanced at me, smiled, and tilted his head to the left. His message was clear: I've got this. Get out of here.

I kept a hold on Bony and left.

I didn't relax my grip on the boy until we were three buildings away and none of the visitors were in sight.

As soon as I did, he stepped in front of me and said, "We could have taken him."

I shook my head. "Not without one of us getting hurt, maybe dying. It wasn't worth it."

"I saw your ship. You could have told the people in it to shoot him."

"Yes, but it would have been the wrong choice."

"Why? Man pulls a gun on you, you shoot him before he shoots you." Bony crossed his arms. "It's simple."

Ten meters north of us, counselors were hustling boys to the transport. Some of the kids had nothing with them; others carried a single bag or a shirt folded to hold a few pieces of clothing or some small personal treasures. Leaving with nothing was awful, but not leaving would have been far worse.

Gustafson and Schmidt led a group of a dozen kids

at a trot to the ship. He spotted me, told Schmidt to keep moving, and yelled for Bony.

I held up a finger and kneeled in front of the boy. "I'm not going to lie to you, Bony. Sometimes it is that simple—but not this time. That man needs to be alive for all of you to be able to get off this planet safely and find new homes."

"This is my home."

"Not any more. If you stay here, they'll make you into soldiers again. I can't accept that. You don't have to fight any more."

"So I have to go?"

"Yes, you do. In fact"—I pointed to Gustafson, and Bony glanced over his shoulder at the man—"you have to leave right now."

"Where are we going?"

I shook my head. "I'm not going with you."

"Why not?"

A lot of answers ran through my head. Because I can't stay anywhere for long or people will figure out that I don't age. Because I'm no kind of parent. Because I don't know how to live in a group. Because I can never let anyone know all about me. Because people around me always seem to get hurt. So many reasons, all of them true, none of them complete. I went with the last one, an incomplete response but at least a true one. "Because none of you would be safe if I was there."

"Then I'll stay," he said. Tears filled his eyes. "I'm with you. I stood with you. I earned the right to be with you."

Bony's lips trembled, but he stood strong and loyal and just wanting somewhere to belong, someone he could count on. I knew exactly how he felt. My heart beat harder and my breaths came faster. My chest tightened. For a few seconds, I was sixteen again, on Dump, with Benny and Alex and Bob and Han and all the rest, a family I'd worked to join, all I had after the government had taken away Jennie—and they were all now dead.

I put my hands on Bony's shoulders and stared into his eyes. "You can't. It wouldn't be safe. I can't let anything happen to you." He opened his mouth to speak, but I shook my head, and he stayed silent. "I fought when I was a boy, like you, and like you, I watched my friends die."

"And you grew up fine."

"No," I said, "I didn't. I grew up, but not fine, not fine at all. But you can—as long as you go with them." I cradled his cheek in my right hand. He leaned into it. "Bony, your fights stop now."

He crashed forward into me and wrapped his arms around my neck and sobbed. His tears dampened my throat and hair. I put my right arm around his body, still so thin despite all the meals, and with my left hand I held his head. "It'll be better," I said, "after a while. It really will."

"I don't believe you," he said.

Gustafson walked toward us. "The first transport is almost full," he said, "and Bony should get on it."

I nodded without releasing the boy. I whispered into his ear, "It will. I promise." I pulled his head away from me so we could see one another. "I've been straight with you before. I'm being straight now: You will get better." I let go of him and stood. "You have to go."

His arms fell away, but he didn't back up. "I won't forget you," he said.

I wanted to tell him the truth, that with any luck at all he would, that we had to hope that all of the time here and the months fighting in the jungle would fade away, like etchings in sand washing out to sea in the rolling currents of time until just the faintest of impressions remained, impressions visible only in the light of moons and stars on the darkest nights, but I didn't. Instead, I told him a different truth, one I knew with utter certainty. "Nor I, you."

Gustafson took Bony's shoulder, turned him, and led him off. As he steered the boy, the man glanced at me, smiled, and nodded his head. He focused again on Bony. The two of them merged into the ongoing rush.

I watched until they disappeared into the streaming crowd of boys and counselors, long past when I could track either of their heads, until I was sure they were gone, and for a bit after that. I thought about following them, about going with them, even if for just a little while, but I was only trying to fool myself.

It didn't work.

I headed to Lobo.

CHAPTER 67

In the former rebel complex, planet Tumani

"IM'S WAITING OUTSIDE," Lobo said over the comm when I was less than half a minute away from him. "It's time to go; want me to trank her?"

I sighed. "No. She has every reason to yell at me. Maybe she'll feel better after she does."

I turned the corner of the nearest building and saw her. She was leaning against Lobo and staring straight ahead. I don't know where her mind was, but she didn't notice me until I was only a few meters away.

"Inside?" I said.

She nodded.

Lobo opened a side hatch. As soon as we'd entered him, he closed it.

"Look," I said, "I know you're mad, and I'm sorry I had to play it this way, but—"

She held up her hands. "Stop. I'm not angry at you." She twisted her head a bit as if trying to work out a kink in her neck. "Well, I'm not as mad as you'd expect. I'm more upset with myself."

"What?"

"I've been thinking about it ever since I left Wylak. I have to admit that you made the right call—though not, I suspect, for the right reasons. You didn't tell me because you thought I'd give away the plan or let others learn about it, right?"

I nodded. "Both."

"Well," she said, "those were the wrong reasons. I could have played my part in your little drama more than well enough, and I know how to control the flow of information to a team when necessary. The reason you were right not to tell me, though, is simple: I wouldn't have gone along with it."

I suspect the expression on my face matched my internal confusion. "Why? It worked, the boys are heading safely out of this system, and so we achieved our objective."

"Because of what we're leaving behind," she said, her anger evident for the first time. "You've turned that evil bastard into a hero—and almost certainly given him more power in the government."

"Yes," I said. "It was the only answer I could find. It was far from ideal: I also forced the boys to move to a new planet." I closed my eyes and took a deep breath. "If I could have thought of a better solution, I would have gone with it." I didn't tell her what would happen eventually, that Jack wouldn't stop until he'd taken everything from Wylak, because as far as anyone except Maggie knew, Jack was just a mouthpiece—and I had promised Jack I'd keep it that way.

"I know," she said, "and that's my point. I didn't have a plan. You came up with one. If you would have told me about it, I would have vetoed it immediately. You were right to keep it to yourself. I still can't help but hate what you've done for Wylak. You understand that as soon as this dies down—and that won't take long—he'll be free to press more kids into service, turn more children into soldiers, send more of them to their deaths."

"Of course," I said, "but that was a possibility no matter what we did."

"How do you live with that?" Sadness more than anger filled her face.

"Live with what?" I said. "Live with the fact that a single bad politician on a single backwater planet can persuade a tired and over-taxed population to use children as soldiers? Is that what you're talking about?" The pounding of my pulse in my ears made it hard for me to hear anything else, but that didn't matter, because I wasn't waiting for her to respond. "We all live with that every single day. It was true before we came here, though it happened to be the rebel leadership, not the government, that was using the boys. It may well happen again, maybe this time with Wylak ruining the lives of more children. Are you out policing every planet? I know I'm not." I forced myself to take a slow, deep breath, unclench my fists, and lower my voice. "We saved *these* kids. *These* boys get new homes and don't have to go back to being soldiers. We fought the battle in front of us, and we won it. Maybe it's not much when you think about all the worlds and all the people, but it's everything to these kids."

Lim stared at me for several seconds, her eyes hard. She looked away, and when she faced me again, her expression was softer. "You're right. I don't have a better answer, but at least we accomplished what we set out to do. I won't be able to see it all the way to completion, but the boys will get the lives they deserve. That's enough." She turned to leave.

Lobo opened the side hatch.

She stepped out. "I wouldn't have supported you, though. I wouldn't have been able to stomach helping that man. You were right: I brought you here to do things I didn't want to do, maybe even things I couldn't do. You stay safe—but don't be surprised if it's a long time before we talk again."

"I won't be," I said as the hatch snicked shut. I kept talking, though she could no longer hear me. "No one calls me unless they need me."

"Are we going swimming in the sea of self-pity?" Lobo said, his voice booming all around me.

I chuckled.

"If so," he said, "I suggest we do it on another planet, many jumps away, someplace where you're not quite so attractive a target. The news of Wylak's rescue of the kids is all over Tumani. No one's stopping jump gate traffic any longer, but I don't know how long our passage will be safe."

"You're right, of course," I said. "Let's head to the gate. I want to beat the transports there so I can make sure the boys get safely out of this system. I want to see it end."

"Doing it," Lobo said. "As you contemplate your own painful condition, please do keep one crucial fact in mind."

"What's that?" I said.

"I can trank you anywhere inside me and keep you unconscious for as long as I want."

I laughed as we rose into the sky.

CHAPTER 68

At the Tumani jump gate station

I WATCHED IN A front display in Lobo as the first
transport slid through the jump gate, the ship moving
slowly into the perfect blackness of the aperture and
leaving this part of the universe, to appear elsewhere
instantly. When the last of it had disappeared, Lobo
closed the display.

"How long until the next transport jumps?"

"Only a few minutes," Lobo said. "We have two
incoming comms: Maggie and Jack. Jack's in a hurry,
and it's audio only."

"Him first," I said.

Jack's smooth voice filled the air. "Heading out, Jon?"

"Yes."

"Excellent choice. My man is not your biggest fan, but
fortunately he's rather too busy right now to send many
people after you and instead delegated the task to me.
I jumped on it and instructed his staff to hold a set of
investigative meetings and prepare a presentation on a
broad range of options for keeping you in this system."

"Thanks," I said. "Don't help him too much, though, or you might get me killed."

"Jon, Jon, Jon," Jack said. "You know me better than that. We're friends."

"And Maggie won't transfer the remainder of the funds to you until the boys, she, and I are all safely out of the system."

"That's certainly true," he said, "but even without that incentive, I wouldn't let him harm you."

Jack was such a good con man that you could never tell when he was lying; many times, I doubt he knew. He lived each story he told. This time, though, I believed him.

"Thanks, Jack. A word of warning: Be careful with the Senator. He can be very dangerous when he's angry."

"He won't trust me for a while," Jack said, "but at least for as long as he's paying me, he feels he has some control over me."

"And does he?"

Jack laughed. "No more than any other mark."

"Good," I said, "because on your way out the door, please be sure to empty the house. I don't want him left with anything."

"After even this short amount of time with him," Jack said, "I can assure you that doing so will be my great—and, I suspect, lucrative—pleasure."

Jack and I had spent several years working cons on bad people, so I was confident he'd succeed. He knew this game well. "Thanks."

"My master summons," Jack said, "and I must convince him he controls me, so to work I go. I wanted to say, though, that it felt good to help these boys. Thanks for bringing me into it."

"I'm glad," I said. "Let me know when you go full-time into volunteer work."

"Have you seen my wardrobe?" Jack said, chuckling again. "Not likely. I could never bear to dress as conservatively as those folks do." He lowered his voice. "Leave soon, Jon, and be safe."

The holo vanished. The air went still and quiet.

"The second transport is nearing the front of the queue," Lobo said. "Maggie is calling from it."

"Accept."

She appeared in a holo in the air in front of the pilot couch where I sat, turned until she was facing me, and said, "We'll be gone soon, Jon."

I nodded. I didn't know what else to do.

"You could follow us," she said.

"It wouldn't be safe for the boys, at least not for a while." I shook my head. "No, it's best I vanish for a time."

"Maybe," she said, "but I'm not staying with them, either. As soon as they're set up, I'm heading back to my people. You could follow me, join us."

"No," I said, "I couldn't. It wouldn't be safe for you or them, and you know it." Or for me. If I stayed too long, they'd notice I didn't age, or I'd slip up and they'd spot me using my nanomachines, or someone else would be able to read my thoughts even though Maggie could not. No, I couldn't stay with them.

I couldn't stay with anyone.

"You know that's not the truth," Maggie said, "and I know it, too. We can take care of ourselves. Maybe someday you'll tell me the real reason you're letting me go again."

I didn't move. I didn't speak. I did everything I

could to remain completely still and show absolutely nothing even as my heart felt like it was exploding and I knew that once more I was losing her.

She nodded her head. "I won't wait forever for you to do that, you know."

"Yes. Yes, I do." To my ears, my voice sounded choked, tight, on the edge of breaking. I hoped it came across better to her.

"We're set to jump," she said. "Goodbye, Jon."

"Goodbye, Maggie."

The holo disappeared.

I stared at the empty air.

Lobo stayed quiet, for which I was grateful.

Floating there in space, already missing Maggie, waiting for the shuttle to take her and the rest of the boys to safety, I could not help but think of the last time I saw Benny.

CHAPTER 69

*Aggro space station, in orbit around planet
Pinkelponker—139 years earlier*

SHOTS SLAMMED INTO the airlock door as it clanged
shut. I wheeled around and smashed the control
mechanism with the piece of metal bar I'd taken from
my cell. Horns and alarms blared. Warning lights
flashed bursts of red.

I put Benny on the floor and ran to the escape pod
entrances. I punched open the closest one. "They'll
break through soon," I said. "We have to go."

"No, Jon," Benny said. "*You* have to go. I'm staying."

"No!" I said. "We can both make it. There's plenty
of room in the pod. Like you told me, it'll take us
straight to the jump gate and out of this system."

"Long before we get there," Benny said, "they'll
blow us up. One missile, and we're dead. Or worse,
they'll chase us, capture us, and bring us back here.
I can't go back in the chair, Jon. I can't."

"So we disarm the missiles before we leave and
hide once we're away."

He shook his head. "You don't understand those machines well enough to do that, and neither do I. And we don't know anything about hiding."

The door shook.

"We can figure it out," I said. "I'm not leaving you."

"No," Benny said, "we can't. There's only one way you can be safe. I'm going to use the nanomachines to destroy this place, turn it into dust, so there's no trace we were ever here."

"No!" I said. "I've lost everyone else. I'm not going to lose you. We'll get away together, or we'll die together."

The door shook again. A fist-size section in its center buckled inward a couple of centimeters.

"I was in charge," Benny said. "I was supposed to get everyone off Dump."

I wouldn't abandon him. I bent to pick him up.

"Leave me!" he screamed. "Go! If you don't get out of here, it's all been for nothing. Let me save you! *Let me at least save one person!*" He put his right arm flipper in his mouth and bit so hard that tears came to his eyes. When he pulled it back, drops of blood appeared on his skin. "Go now!"

He stared at the blood. The drops dissolved into bits of gray mist that merged into a small gray cloud. It flew to the wall beside the door and spread along a metal conduit. Seconds later, the metal vanished, and the cloud grew.

"You've started it," I said. "We can both leave now."

I reached for him.

He slapped me. "No, we can't. If we go before the nanomachines destroy the electrical systems, they'll still be able to come for us. Get in the pod. Put me on the counter by the controls. When it's safe, I'll signal you."

A section of the wall as wide as my hand and as high as my knees was now part of the gray cloud.

"The more the nanomachines consume," Benny said, "the more of themselves they make. You have to go now!"

"You leave," I said. "I can take care of this. You can explain what they did here better than I can. You can make sure nothing like it ever happens again."

"No!" he screamed again. He rubbed a drop of blood from his arm on the door and focused on it. Another small cloud appeared. "By the time they break through," he said, "the nanomachines will be ready." He stared at me again. Tears washed down his cheeks. "I told everyone I'd save them, and I failed them all. Let me have this one victory. Please, Jon. Put me on the counter, and go."

I picked him up. After our time on Aggro, he weighed nothing, his body little more than skin over bones. I set him gently on the counter.

He smiled. "This one time, we win." He focused on the controls in front of him. "Get out of here."

Benny was right. He usually was. If we both stayed, we both died. If we both stayed, I ripped from him the one last good thing he could do.

I entered the escape pod.

He pushed a button and shut its door before I could.

I stared into the room through the small viewport in the pod's door. The nanocloud had grown so big it covered the entire wall next to the door. Lights flickered.

Benny's voice came over the pod's speakers. "The station's systems are dying, Jon. Time to go."

I dove into the couch. Its arms extended and held me in place a few seconds before a cover slid over the viewport and the pod shot into space.

"At least I saved one of you, Jon," Benny said. "At least—"

The speakers cut off, and I was alone.

CHAPTER 70

At the Tumani jump gate station

L OBO RESTORED THE front display. The second transport, its nose only meters from the aperture, slid forward, its progress slow but inevitable. One instant, it was still here; the next, part of it was here, part elsewhere, like a moment you wish could live forever, perfect but becoming a memory no matter how hard you tried to hold onto it. With each second that passed, more of the ship left Tumani and carried Bony and the other boys to a new world, to new homes, new lives, a chance to stop fighting and for a while become children once more.

I'd never had that chance. Neither had Benny, or Alex, or Bob, or Han, all now gone, all dead from failed attempts to secure their own better futures. Benny had given up his life so that I could have mine. From the day he died, I've known I would never be able to repay him.

Maybe, though, by helping these boys I was passing on the smallest bit of that sacrifice, paying forward a tiny portion of the debt I would forever owe him. By saving me, he had also helped save these children, saved more of us than he'd ever imagined.

"We did it, Benny," I whispered. "We did it."

AFTERWORD

MY FIRST GOAL in any book is to tell a good story. In the course of doing so, themes naturally arise. Sometimes, those themes are clear only in hindsight, when the work is complete.

Other times, as in *Children No More*, they appear the moment the idea for the book pops into my brain.

The use of children as soldiers is one of those topics that few people like to discuss. Depending on what you read and watch, you can go a very long time without bumping into it. Do a Web search on the subject, however, and you'll find that children are fighting and dying every day. Hard numbers are, as you might expect, difficult to come by, but groups such as The International Rescue Committee (www. theirc.org) estimate about 300,000 boys and girls are involved today in this horrific practice.

I find this deeply disturbing. I think everyone should.

I understand that in the catalog of the world's woes, a cause with only a few hundred thousand sufferers may seem like a small thing. Numerically, it certainly falls way below hunger, disease, poverty, and many other vital issues humanity must address. But these are children, children whom adults are turning into soldiers, and that is simply wrong.

I must confess to a special connection to this cause because of personal experience—not, I hasten to note, as a child soldier. I have never experienced anything as bad as what these boys and girls undergo.

I did, however, spend three years in a youth group that trained young boys to be soldiers. The group's intentions were good: To use military conventions and structures to teach discipline, fitness, teamwork, and many other valuable lessons. It certainly accomplished many of those goals with me.

The year I joined, however, was 1965, and war was ramping up in Viet Nam. I was ten years old. On my first day, an active soldier on leave showed up and acted as our drill sergeant. That afternoon, I saw my first—but not my last—necklace of human ears and learned the ethics of collecting them. That day, I stood at attention in the hot Florida sun while this grown man screamed at me and, when I cried, punched me in the stomach so hard that I fell to the ground and threw up. He put his boot on my head and ground the side of my face into my vomit.

That was not the worst day I had in those three years. It wasn't even close.

My worst days with that group were nothing compared to what the child soldiers endure. Nothing.

The basics of this novel sprang into my mind a few years ago while I was driving with my family back from lunch. I knew it would involve child soldiers, the story of how Jon changed from the gentle boy he had been into the hard man he became, and the challenges of reintegrating child soldiers. I also knew in that same flash of insight that the book would let me depart from the classic outsider hero story structure and instead force Jon to do the one thing outsider heroes never do: Stay after the fighting is done. All of this was secondary, of course, to the story, but it all arrived at once.

I grew up believing in a number of virtues that my mother taught me were essential American beliefs. One of the most important and powerful of them was something that seemed—and still seems—so obvious to me that I have always held it close: Each generation owes the next one a better world. We owe our children a better life than the one we enjoyed.

When any group makes its children into soldiers, it is abandoning that responsibility. That group is wrong. This practice must stop, and we owe it to the former child soldiers to help reintegrate them into their societies.

I hope we pay that debt.

ACKNOWLEDGMENTS

A S WITH MY earlier novels, David Drake reviewed and offered insightful comments on the second draft of this book. This time, though, I did not show him the outline, partly because I had not told him I was dedicating the book to him, and partly because I wanted to construct the plot and outline with no help from anyone. Despite entering later in the process, however, he still gave me vital advice that greatly improved the book. All of the problems herein are my fault, of course, but Dave again deserves credit for making the novel better than it would have been without his input.

Toni Weisskopf, my Publisher, has my gratitude for believing in the series and helping give it the success it has enjoyed. Her editorial comments on the draft I sent her were few but pitch-perfect; each one made the book better.

To everyone who purchased the earlier Jon and Lobo novels (*One Jump Ahead*, *Slanted Jack*, and *Overthrowing Heaven*), I offer my deep and sincere gratitude. You've made it possible for me to get paid to live and write a while longer in the universe I share with Jon and Lobo.

My business partner, Bill Catchings, has as always both done all he could to encourage and support my writing and been a great colleague for going on twenty-five years.

Elizabeth Barnes fought (and continues to fight) to tame the library portions of my home office, an effort that helps me calm myself for the work.

As I've done in the course of my previous novels, I've traveled a fair amount while working on this one, and each of the places I've visited has affected me and thus the work. I want to tip my virtual hat to the people and sites of (in rough order of my first visits there during the writing of this novel) Cambridge and Boston, Massachusetts; Austin, Texas; Las Vegas, Nevada; Portland, Oregon; Seattle, Redmond, and Kirkland, Washington; Baltimore and the surrounding suburbs, Maryland; Washington, Virginia; Holden Beach, North Carolina; San Francisco, California; Indianapolis, Indiana; San Jose and Yountville, California; and, of course, my home in North Carolina.

As always, I am grateful to my children, Sarah and Scott, who continue to be amazing teenagers and wonderful people despite having The Weird Dad and needing to put up with me regularly disappearing into my office for long periods of time. Thanks, kids.

Several extraordinary women—my wife, Rana Van Name; Jennie Faries; Gina Massel-Castater; and Allyn Vogel—grace my life with their intelligence and support, for which I'm incredibly grateful.

Thank you, all.

ABOUT THE AUTHOR

MARK L. VAN Name is a writer and technologist. As a science fiction author, he has published three previous novels, edited or co-edited two anthologies, and written many short stories. Those stories have appeared in a wide variety of books and magazines, including *Asimov's Science Fiction Magazine*, many original anthologies, and *The Year's Best Science Fiction*. As a technologist, he is the CEO of a fact-based marketing and technology assessment firm, Principled Technologies, Inc., that is based in the Research Triangle area of North Carolina. He has worked with computer technology for his entire professional career and has published over a thousand articles in the computer trade press, as well as a broad assortment of essays and reviews.

For more information, visit his Web site, www. marklvanname.com, or follow his blog, markvanname. blogspot.com.

The following is an excerpt from:

THE WILD SIDE

EDITED BY
MARK L. VAN NAME

As the editor of *The Wild Side*, Mark L. Van Name has joined with best-selling authors Tanya Huff, Caitlin Kittredge and Toni L.P. Kelner as well as Dana Cameron, Sarah Hoyt, John Lambshead, and Diana Rowland to bring you a collection of contemporary urban fantasy stories ranging from light-spirited romps to black-hearted noir, from steampunk London to the bleeding edge of the present, with tales of love, eros, betrayal and seduction in a beguiling vein.

Mark's own contribution to this anthology, excerpted here, introduces us to Diego Chan, described by Mark as "a character with whom I hope to spend a lot of time over the next several years."

Available from Baen Books
August 2011
trade paperback

Take a Walk on the Wild Side

When Lou Reed exhorted us to do just that in his 1972 song, he was singing about a very particular urban landscape—New York City—teeming with many different types of people. Urban fantasy writers have for some time explored a far broader range of cityscapes—and inhabitants. When I invited the authors whose tales you're about to read, I told them only that we were looking for stories that mixed urban fantasy and an erotic edge. The way each combined the ingredients was up to her.

The resulting stories cover a wide range indeed. Vampires, shape shifters, witches, demons, fallen angels, and more. Toronto, Las Vegas, San Francisco, London, New England, and other locales. Positively chaste to a tad raunchy. What they share, though, is more important than their differences: all are good stories that will take you into another world.

As a reader, I'm always curious what writers have to say about their works, so I asked these authors to provide afterwords. I think you'll find them interesting.

Enjoy.

This story is the first in the Diego Chan saga.

THE LONG DARK NIGHT OF DIEGO CHAN

Mark L. Van Name

"Sam's gone over," the first line of the text message said.

"You said you'd help if it ever came to this," the second continued.

"It has."

"Barbara."

Diego Chan kept running but reversed direction and headed back to the Super 8 that was passing for home this week. His legs carried him easily, his heart beat a steady rhythm, and his muscles moved smoothly and with power. He brushed the sweat from his eyes and thumbed a response, "Okay." He sent it on its way through the three redirectors that would mask its origins before it reached her.

He pulled up the tracking display on his phone: five miles out, a hair over seven minutes a mile so far, over thirty-five minutes to make it back. Not good enough. He pushed harder but not so hard that anyone would notice. That wouldn't buy him much time, but if she was right, the clock had started ticking a while ago.

The morning sun was still coming into its own when he reached the motel thirty-one minutes later.

✧   ✧   ✧

"I can't believe he chose this," Barbara said. "He was sick, real sick—pancreatic cancer—and he knew he was probably going to die, but he had decided to fight it. He'd been at it for two months."

Chan froze. Sam hadn't contacted him. Once, Sam would have told him anything that mattered. That was a long time ago, though. A long time.

"Did you hear me?" she said.

"Yes." Chan moved the phone to his right hand and resumed toweling himself dry. "Did he file new paperwork?"

"No," she said. "What you have is all there is. That's part of why I'm sure. The rest is—" she paused "—you know, he's just too strong. Even sick." She paused again as her voice caught. "If he did decide he wanted to change, he'd talk to me first. I know he would."

"Yes," Chan said. "He would." He put the phone back in his left hand as he began to dress. "Why do you think this happened, that one of them took him?"

"He'd mentioned approaches from some guy, Matt something, somebody he said you both knew from a long time ago. Said the guy had heard about his cancer and wouldn't give up. Asked him to come to a club he owned."

Yeah, a long time, as far back as Chan had memories, all the way to the first foster home. When Matt had decided to make the move, Chan hadn't liked it, but Matt had done it straight, filed the paperwork, gone over, what, maybe six years ago now.

"When?" Chan said.

"I can't be sure," she said, "but they usually leave the restaurant about one, sometimes two, so after that."

Her voice trailed off. "He's never come home later than three. Never."

From anyone else, Chan would have considered this an over-reaction, encouraged them to wait a day for the missing person to show up, but not Barbara. Sam was never late and kept every appointment.

Chan checked the time: 7:00 a.m. here in Raleigh, 4:00 in San Francisco. Sam leaves no earlier than one, no later than two, so roughly a two- to three-hour window from when he left work to now. Matt would play it smart, ask to talk to Sam, lure him over, maybe spend an hour doing all of that. One to two hours already ticked off. Twenty-two he could reasonably count on, twenty-three if he was lucky.

"What's the name of Matt's club?" he said.

"Changes." she said. "It's, uh, a sex club. Serves everybody. He runs it, makes the *Chronicle* now and then, keeps it clean and on the level. They say."

Chan nodded. That was good: He had somewhere to start.

"I'll catch the first flight I can," he said.

"Will that be soon enough? We only have—" she choked back a sob "—before..."

"Yeah," she said, "I do, but this is what he would have wanted. He always said that."

"Yes," Chan said, "he did." He terminated the call.

He opened a browser on his laptop to search for flights.

"I'm coming," he said to the still, empty room.

The American Airlines terminal at Raleigh-Durham International airport sported the same chrome and wood and glass design of every major airport with a redesign within the last five years. Chan liked it well enough when he bothered to look at it, but mostly he didn't notice it. He wasn't on a job, but he might as well have been, so he focused on the people and watched for signs of trouble. He had to assume that Matt would know Barbara would call him, but he had no reason to believe Matt would know where he was. Still, it always paid to be careful.

He needed to be rested when he arrived, so he blew almost two grand on a one-way first-class ticket on the 10:15 via Chicago, then forked over the day fee for the Admiral's Club. He crammed himself into a corner chair where he could watch the door. No way had they designed these things for people his size; at six-four and two-forty, he rarely found comfortable seats.

Decision time.

He could try it on his own, but that would cost time, maybe a lot of it, to acquire what he'd need to invade a club that he had to assume would be full of them. If he asked for help, though, he'd owe them.

Chan hated owing anything to anyone.

He was wasting time. He already knew the answer. He'd promised Sam, so he had to do everything in his power to keep that promise.

He booted his laptop, brought up a clock, sent the message with the number of the mobile he was about to destroy, and waited.

The phone rang two minutes later.

He pressed the connect button but said nothing.

Silence.

After thirty seconds, he said, "I need a package and some data."

"We have no current contract," a scrambled voice replied.

Chan waited. They both knew how this would go, so there was no point in playing.

After a few seconds, the voice laughed, a sound more like car fenders screeching on impact than human laughter. "It'll come out of the next job."

"Yes."

"How complete a package?"

Chan glanced at his nearly empty backpack. Between jobs, he never carried more than the pack could hold, and he rarely took that much. Aside from his documentation, the usual travel basics, a few wads of cash, and the slim, waterproof envelope of key papers—one of which was Sam's—he had nothing he'd need.

"Complete." He shrugged. The heavy leather jacket slid over him, so worn and smooth it moved liked water. "I have a jacket; that's it."

After a pause, the voice said, "Will this come back on us?"

"No. The paperwork is good."

"Where?"

"San Francisco."

"The data?"

"All filed paperwork for Sam Flynn, plus background on Matt Gresham."

The pause was longer this time. "Matt Gresham is involved in this?"

Chan sighed. "Is that a problem?"

The car fenders screeched again. "No, but if you end up canceling him, we might make a little profit on this."

"It's only him if he forces it to go that way. It's not my goal."

"Then we'll hope for the worst."

Chan said nothing. The easiest way to get in trouble

with these people was to talk. The less he said, the less likely he was to screw up.

"Intercontinental Hotel. A room will be waiting in your name. It'll be there."

After a pause, the voice added, "You know you owe us, right."

It wasn't a question.

The call ended.

Chan went into the men's restroom, closed the door of the rearmost stall, and smashed the phone. He broke the SIM card in half, then flushed those two pieces. Habit. Probably unnecessary now, but not harmful, either.

9:35 a.m.

6:35 there.

Twenty-plus hours.

He headed for the gate.

On the first plane, Chan bought Internet access with a credit card in an identity so thin it would rip easier than a wet sheet of notepaper.

Barbara was right: Nothing about the Changes club was secret. Its Web site offered an event listing, membership plans and costs, the disclaimer forms you'd have to sign to enter, customer testimonials, photos of all the rooms—play spaces, it called them—and even a floor plan. Formerly a theater, it sprawled across three levels: balcony, main, and basement. Every floor had at least one room with dirt for burial and rebirth play.

Great. Lots to search.

Matt's picture graced half a dozen pages that explained how very safe you could be there as you indulged your wildest dreams. Sex club. Kink club. All in private or in public, as you chose. Watch, play, or do both. Regularly inspected and licensed by city and state health authorities. Full bar, alcohol and blood. On-site security and medical staff. Humans and vampires playing together. Open from ten to sunrise.

Its neighbors—strip shows, cheap hotels, two diners open late—gave their own endorsements that included thin pitches for their own goods.

Chan enlarged his search to include articles about the club. News services attacked it in slow times but lost their energy for the fight faster than three-pack-a-day smokers sprinting up Lombard Street. No one had ever found any evidence of anyone being turned there without the proper paperwork. Members and even a couple of former beat cops gave testimonials when it won an online vote for being the safest of the late-night San Francisco clubs. Not a single news story mentioned a fight or an arrest inside it.

All of that information proved only that Matt was smart, which Chan already knew.

He also knew but had no way to prove that Matt had taken Sam. Since before he'd turned, Matt had been evangelical on the benefits and how good it was. He'd want to save Sam—and to have Sam join him.

No, Chan had no doubt that Matt had Sam. The question was, which risk was greater for Matt: leaving the club in the wee hours to go somewhere at the key time, or bringing Sam there.

Matt hated variables he couldn't control, so he'd prefer Sam be there, but then he'd be taking on other risks: finding a safe burial spot, minimizing the number of people who knew, and making sure no one checking the club found out. Meeting Sam elsewhere might be a simpler answer.

No way to know by staring at the screen.

Chan would have to ask Matt.

When they announced the descent into Chicago, Chan turned off the laptop. He knew all he could about the club without going there.

Chan dozed the second leg and left it feeling as rested as he reasonably could given that even the first-class seats weren't a good fit for him. He'd normally invest the first few days in a new place making sure no one was tracking him, but he didn't have the time. The plane landed slightly late, so he didn't make it to the cab line until 4:45, which put him smack in the middle of the worst of the rush-hour traffic.

He walked into the gleaming glass tower of the Intercontinental a few minutes before six.

Eight hours to go, give or take.

He fought the urge to rush everyone he encountered. It wouldn't help, and it could attract attention to him or even slow him.

At the check-in desk, he gave his name and asked if they'd bring the package from his room so he could keep waiting for his friends in the lobby.

Their smiles never wavered. An earthquake wouldn't change their expressions; it was that kind of hotel.

He tipped the bellman a twenty and grabbed the heavy, locked duffel bag from the guy's two hands with one of his. He headed for the bar and kept on going past it, through the restaurant and out the side door. The short time meant he had to ask for the package, but he didn't have to trust his occasional employer to give him a room. He could expect them to be watching him, because if they thought they might be able to

make money off him, they'd try to steer events their
way. With no definite engagement on the line, however,
the surveillance team wouldn't be large.

They stared at him.

He ignored them.

When the doors opened on the top floor, the mother
rushed them out of the elevator.

He rode it back down one level, stepped out, and
followed signs to a luggage store. They'd have a tracker
in the bag to help the follow team. It's what he would
have done. With a small team, they'd use it to know
when he left the mall. They might also have observers on the exits, but they wouldn't risk following him
in a five-story structure; too much turf to cover. He
bought a huge, red rolling suitcase composed of some
polycarbonate material so light it weighed less than his
reinforced jacket. It cost all the cash in his wallet, but
he had ten grand more in the backpack.

At a big-and-tall store a floor further down, he
picked up a tweed sport coat that billowed around his
waist but fit his shoulders and was tight but tolerable
on his arms.

He snagged a Giants cap and XXXL t-shirt from a
temple-like shop dedicated to the team.

An electronics store sold him a pre-paid mobile phone.

He bought clear spectacles at an eyewear kiosk.

He added his backpack, shirt, and leather jacket to
the big suitcase. He closed the suitcase and folded the
duffel. He tore the tags off his new clothing and donned
the t-shirt and sport coat. He tied his hair in a ponytail
and tucked it under the cap. He put on the glasses.

He checked himself in the restroom mirror. He was
too big to blend in easily, but with a bit of a slouch to

cut some height, he could pass for an overweight local fan, at least from a distance.

He stuffed the duffel in the first trashcan he passed.

He bought a giant red slushie in a transparent cup and sipped it very slowly as he rode the escalators to the bottom floor and ambled out of the mall. No one on the run drinks a slushie.

If they were looking for him, they'd now have trouble finding him. They'd know he'd end up at Changes, but at least he could establish a private base of operations.

If Matt was expecting him, and Chan had to assume he was, anyone Matt sent would be unlikely to recognize him. It was still daylight, though just barely, so Matt himself certainly wouldn't be out.

Both his employers and Matt would expect him to keep a low profile, so he did the opposite: walked to Union Square and checked into the Westin St. Francis with another paper-thin id. With a few sad comments about a rough divorce and a big cash deposit, he persuaded the guy at the desk to record but not charge the long-dead credit card he showed them.

He'd need more throwaway identities after this was over.

He chose a suite near the stairs and was finally settled in it at 8:15.

An hour and a half before he had to leave so he'd arrive at Changes just as it opened, then four hours to find Sam.

Not much time, but all he was going to have.

Maybe it did happen later, maybe closer to three or even four, and he'd have that extra hour or two.

He shook his head. He wanted the extra time so badly that he kept circling back to it, but wanting it didn't make it real. Stick with the worst case. Let the good news surprise you.

He stood under a long hot shower and pushed everything out of his mind except what he had to do.

At 9:15, he loaded his jacket with everything he could from the package. The slots and clasps in the sleeves held the stakes and baton firmly.

At 9:40, he walked out of the front of the hotel.

Night owned the city now. The streets fought back with neon and crowds and cars and trolleys, but before it surrendered to the morning sun the night would claim victory, first in the suburbs, then in the rougher areas, and eventually even here, in the heart of the urban resistance.

Chan turned left and left again at the corner. About a mile to walk, twenty minutes to do it, plenty of time to check out the area around Changes before he entered it.

One more street to cross, then a turn at the next one, and the club would come into view down the road on his left. Chan's constant stride had carried him a step into that street when he noticed an alley ahead on his left.

If he were Matt and thought he was coming, he'd consider an ambush. No point in letting potential trouble into the club if you could help it.

He backed out of the street and slid to his left until he was in the shadow of an awning over a dark doorway.

He slowed his breathing, closed his eyes, and listened. Cars rolling past. A light breeze channeling through the streets. Settling sounds he couldn't identify.

Nothing from across the street.

That didn't mean anything, though; he was too far away to hear them if they were trying to keep quiet.

He'd have to move closer.

A car rolled down the street in front of him, the woman driving it talking on her mobile and gesturing with her other hand, the car apparently steering itself.

He crossed as it passed, using its sonic wake to cover any sounds he might make.

He slowed as he touched the sidewalk and moved slowly ahead. He was wasting precious time if no one was there, but he'd lose far more if he walked into an ambush unprepared.

He edged carefully along the wall and stopped a few inches from the opening to the alley.

He listened again.

Nothing for a few seconds. A murmur. Swallowing. A mumbled, "Thanks."

It could be some guys enjoying the night, but then they'd be unlikely to be so quiet. They might not have anything to do with him, might be muggers waiting for traffic. He could engage them, or he could try to cross down a block. He didn't mind fighting, even expected to have to fight before the night was over, but he didn't care about thieves plying their trade.

He backed slowly along the wall until he reached the corner, then walked down a block. He kept his pace slow. If the people in the alley were waiting for him, how would they have known he was coming this way? Had he failed to spot a tail?

Unlikely, but possible.

Matt would have figured he would come and known it had to be tonight. He might have put teams on all four approach vectors. If the ambushes worked, Matt won. If they failed, as long as the attackers weren't important to him, Matt won that way, too, because Chan lost time.

The other alley entrance would tell the story.

At the end of the block, Chan again edged to the alley opening, stopped, and listened.

This group was far less professional than the first one. Whispered conversation. Intake on a cigarette. A chuckle.

Decision time.

He could slip by them, or he could confront them. If he dealt with them, they'd alert Matt, but there was no down side in that; Matt knew he was coming. Of course, they might hurt him, but he doubted it. He knew the worst he could be facing; they did not. Plus, odds were good that if he didn't take them out now, he'd see them later: When he reached the club, Matt could call them as reinforcements.

Of course, if he was entirely wrong, if this alley was a neighborhood hang-out area, then attacking them would be hurting innocents. If it was a target-rich zone for muggers, he'd be wasting time.

He'd give them a fair chance: Show himself, and let them move first.

He moved back around the corner of the building to prepare. He tied back his hair and rolled his neck and shoulders. He unclipped the holder on the baton in his right jacket sleeve, slid it into his hand, and slowly pulled it open. The lock engaged with a small metallic pop.

He crouched and waited. No way to know if anyone had heard the sound.

No one came.

He let down a purpleheart stake from his left sleeve. If they were human, it made a fine club.

He stood and zipped up his jacket for maximum protection. Its thin Kevlar lining would be little help against high-velocity bullets or direct thrusts with good blades, but every bit of protection was good.

He walked quietly to the edge of the alley, inhaled and focused himself, and stepped into a pool of shadows at its end. His boots hit the street loudly.

Three men swiveled as one to face him. All were tall, over six feet. The two on the sides were also big, guys who hit a gym regularly, while the middle one was weedy thin.

The one on the right was passing a butt to the one on the left but dropped it instantly when Chan appeared.

"Looking for me?" Chan said.

—end excerpt—

from *The Wild Side*
available in trade paperback,
August 2011, from Baen Books